LES CENT CINQUANTE PSEAUMES DE DAVID, MIS EN MUSIQUE A QUATRE [ET CINQ] PARTIES

RECENT RESEARCHES IN THE MUSIC OF THE RENAISSANCE

James Haar, general editor

A-R Editions, Inc., publishes seven series of musicological editions that present music brought to light in the course of current research:

Recent Researches in the Music of the Middle Ages and Early Renaissance
Charles M. Atkinson, general editor

Recent Researches in the Music of the Renaissance
James Haar, general editor

Recent Researches in the Music of the Baroque Era
Christoph Wolff, general editor

Recent Researches in the Music of the Classical Era
Eugene K. Wolf, general editor

Recent Researches in the Music of the Nineteenth and Early Twentieth Centuries
Rufus Hallmark, general editor

Recent Researches in American Music
H. Wiley Hitchcock, general editor

Recent Researches in the Oral Traditions of Music
Philip V. Bohlman, general editor

Each *Recent Researches* edition is devoted to works by a single composer or to a single genre of composition. The contents are chosen for their potential interest to scholars and performers, then prepared for publication according to the standards that govern the making of all reliable historical editions.

Subscribers to any of these series, as well as patrons of subscribing institutions, are invited to apply for information about the "Copyright-Sharing Policy" of A-R Editions, Inc., under which policy any part of an edition may be reproduced free of charge for study or performance.

Address correspondence to

A-R EDITIONS, INC.
801 Deming Way
Madison, Wisconsin 53717

(608) 836-9000

RECENT RESEARCHES IN THE MUSIC OF THE RENAISSANCE • VOLUME 98

Claude Le Jeune

LES CENT CINQUANTE PSEAUMES DE DAVID, MIS EN MUSIQUE A QUATRE [ET CINQ] PARTIES

Edited by Anne Harrington Heider

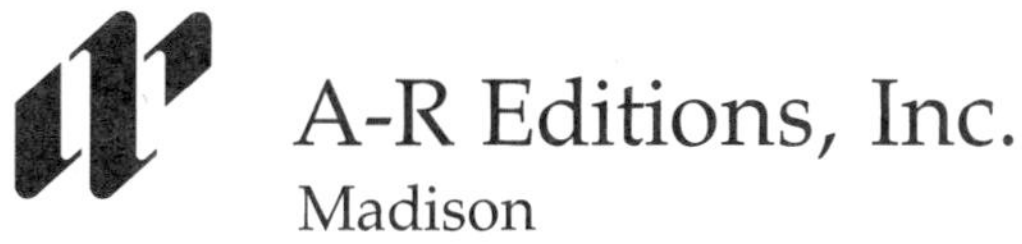

A-R Editions, Inc.
Madison

Printed in the United States of America

Library of Congress Cataloging-in-Publication Data

Le Jeune, Claude, d. 1600.
[Pseaumes de David (1601)]
Les cent cinquante Pseaumes de David : mis en musique à quatre (et cinq) parties / Claude Le Jeune ; edited by Anne Harrington Heider.
1 score. — (Recent researches in the music of the Renaissance ; v. 98)
Settings for 4–5 voices (dessus, haute-contre, taille, basse -contre, cinquiesme) of melodies from the Genevan Psalter.
Middle French words, also printed as text with English translation; pref. and notes in English.
Includes bibliographical references.
ISBN 0-89579-312-1
1. Choruses, Sacred (Mixed voices, 4 parts), Unaccompanied.
2. Choruses, Sacred (Mixed voices, 5 parts), Unaccompanied.
3. Psalms (Music) I. Heider, Anne. II. Psautier de Genève.
III. Title. IV. Series.
M2.R2384 vol. 98
[M2092] 94-45128
CIP
M

Epigrams

On the Psalms in Counterpoint of Monsieur Le Jeune:

These simple psalms composing,
He hides an admirable skill:
The more artful, in that they will
Not seem at all imposing.

Odet de la Noue,
Les cent cinquante pseaumes de David (1601)

Le Jeune . . . succeeded particularly in giving beautiful melodies to the texts he chose, and he used a variety of rhythms, which make his music lively.

Marin Mersenne,
Harmonie universelle (1636)

Claude Le Jeune was doubtless a great master of harmony, which no judge of musical composition, who takes the trouble to score his Metrical Psalms in plain counterpoint, will dispute. . . . Of his Psalms I have three editions, printed in different forms, and in different countries: . . . they went through more editions perhaps than any musical work since the invention of printing.

Charles Burney,
A General History of Music (1776)

Claude Le Jeune and Du Caurroy began the era of decadence in the French school.

François Joseph Fétis,
Biographie universelle des musiciens (1873)

It was on the Book of Psalms and on the melodies consecrated to those psalms that skillful masters and men of genius such as Bourgeois, Jambe-de-Fer, Goudimel, and Le Jeune worked their exquisite counterpoint and built their grand and powerful works.

Henry Expert,
Encyclopédie de la musique (1925)

His oeuvre is the most important of the French Renaissance. It is above all an oeuvre in which the strength of writing and the diversity make it the most worthy to remain in the choral repertory.

François Lesure,
Encyclopédie de la musique (1961)

Contents

Preface

Introduction

Claude Le Jeune (ca. 1530–1600) was one of the most innovative and important composers of the late Renaissance. To quote Gustave Reese's magisterial *Music in the Renaissance,* Le Jeune was "a brilliant artist" with "an extraordinary gift for graceful melodies and original harmonies."[1] His secular airs and chansons are available in modern editions and are well known to scholars and performers. Yet the same cannot be said of significant publications of his sacred music.

Among these is *Les cent cinquante pseaumes de David mis en musique à quatre parties* (first edition 1601). This psalter in simple hymn style was enormously popular in the first half of the seventeenth century: fifteen different editions subsequent to the first are recorded in various bibliographies (e.g., Bovet, Fétis, and Douen); eight are verified in RISM; and an additional two have been verified more recently by Noailly.[2] For a collection of part-music this is an extraordinarily large number. These editions appeared at fairly regular intervals up to 1665. Two have German psalm translations substituted for the original French poetry of Clément Marot and Théodore de Bèze; two have Dutch translations similarly substituted; and the very last (1737) has Romansch translations. The unusual number of editions and the fact that some appeared in translation testify to the popularity of Le Jeune's psalter.

The music in the 1601 psalter is unlike anything else in Le Jeune's oeuvre. Most of his works, whether sacred or secular, were written for the elite audiences of the French court and the Académie de poésie et de musique and are learned, often elaborately contrapuntal, and rhythmically complex. Not so the psalm settings in the 1601 psalter. These pieces are simple, chordal, and tuneful. The entire collection is based on the original melodies of the Genevan Psalter (1562),[3] which usually appear in the tenor, though sometimes in the treble, depending on the voice range of the pre-existing tune. The harmonizations are masterful: far more colorful and imaginative than those of Goudimel (1564 and 1568)[4] yet achieved through logical voice leading, so that the individual parts are not beyond the capacities of the amateur singer. The chordal style never obscures the phrase structure of the borrowed melody, yet the texture is enlivened with melodic and rhythmic embellishment.

An unusual feature of *Les cent cinquante pseaumes* is the use of what are now called slurs to clarify text underlay (see Plate 2). This feature tends to confirm that the collection was intended for inexperienced singers, for at this period in the history of part-music, text underlay was typically indicated solely by vertical alignment—which might or might not be carefully done—and left to the discretion of the performer. The slurs in *Les cent cinquante pseaumes* are an exceptionally early example of what was to become a common practice in later compilations of psalmody and hymnody destined for amateur use.

Notwithstanding the original title of Le Jeune's collection, there are twelve psalms that have five-part harmonizations. Three of these actually have a spacious six-part texture because the fifth part—the Genevan melody—includes an instruction to double it an octave higher or lower.

The Genevan Psalter

The Genevan Psalter contains rhymed, metrical French translations of the entire Book of Psalms and two additional canticles, the Old Testament Decalogue (Exodus 20:2–17) and the New Testament Song of Simeon (Luke 2:29–32). The poems are strophic and each one is set to a monophonic melody that is sufficient for one strophe and is repeated as many times as necessary. The music and poetry of this psalter inspired some of the finest polyphonic works of French late-Renaissance composers, Catholic as well as Protestant, though the man primarily responsible for the existence of the Genevan Psalter, John Calvin, never permitted polyphonic music in public worship.

Calvin recognized the affective power of music and attributed to it "a mysterious and almost unbelievable strength to move the hearts."[5] Therefore, he maintained that music for worship services should have "weight and majesty." He forbade absolutely the use of any musical instruments in public worship, as well as the use of polyphony; unaccompanied unison singing, which does indeed have weight and majesty, was the music he believed best served the purpose of public worship.[6] Trained in philosophy and classical languages as well as in law, he was aware of the humanistic trends which at that time were sweeping through European intellectual life, and his view that music must be the servant of the text was perfectly in keeping not only with the goals of religious reform but also with one of the shaping forces in Renaissance secular musical composition. Calvin's humanism also appears in his attitude towards language. To attend services conducted in a foreign language was, he believed, not worship but superstition. He made the creation of a vernacular liturgy an important part of his life's work.[7] Calvin, like the other reformers Zwingli and Luther, accepted only the Bible as the authority for God's will. But unlike Zwingli, who banned all music whatsoever from worship, or Luther, who embraced a wide variety of liturgical music, Calvin relied mainly on the Book of Psalms as the source of proper music for worship, since it comes from the Bible itself.[8]

Four elements, then, converged to foster the compilation of the Genevan Psalter: Calvin's recognition of the benefits of music in worship, his humanistic attitude towards music as the servant of the text, his insistence on the vernacular as the proper language of worship, and his acceptance of the Book of Psalms as poetry inspired by God.

Compiling the psalter took over twenty years. Partial psalters, prepared under Calvin's supervision, were published in Strasbourg in 1539 and in Geneva in 1542, 1551, and 1555. The first complete edition, entitled *Les Pseaumes mis en rime françoise par Clément Marot & Théodore de Bèze,* appeared in 1562. It rapidly achieved acceptance as the musical canon of the Reformed Church. Protestant publishers and printers, notably Antoine Vincent, mounted a campaign to provide every Huguenot with his or her own psalter; in a few months the presses of Geneva and Lyon produced over 27,000 copies.[9] It was translated into many languages, published in hundreds of later editions with only minor revisions of orthography, and widely distributed in Europe and the New World.[10]

The rhymed, metrical French translations of the psalms in the 1562 psalter are the work of two men. Clément Marot (1497–1544) had been a protegé of the French royal court, but his conversion to the Reform caused his eventual exile. The metrical translations of forty-nine of the psalms and the two canticles are his work. The remaining 101 psalm translations are the work of Théodore de Bèze (1519–1605). Trained as a classical scholar, de Bèze became Calvin's friend, chief administrator, and occasional ambassador to the French court. At Calvin's urging he completed the enormous task begun by Marot of translating the psalms.

The poetry in the Genevan Psalter offers a rich variety of rhyme schemes and metrical patterns. Rhymed couplets (*aabbcc*) are the most common rhyme scheme, but more elaborate schemes, such as that of Psalm 138 (*aabccbddeffe*), abound. Metrical plans (expressed in number of syllables per line in each strophe) range from the simple (8.8.8.8. as in Psalm 131) to the elaborate (9.8.9.8.6.6.5.6.6.5. in Psalm 67).

Though the author of each psalter text is identified as either "CL.MA." or "TH. DE BE," no composer is named for any of the melodies that accompany the texts. In all, 125 different tunes were written for the 152 psalter texts by a series of musicians active in Geneva.

Guillaume Franc, a Parisian musician, arrived in Geneva in 1541 and obtained a licence to hold a school of music. Since he is the only singer mentioned in the Genevan records of this time as instructing the children "to sing the psalms of David in the temple," new melodies appearing in the 1542 edition of the Genevan Psalter are probably his work. The next musician to take on the responsibilities of music master was Loys Bourgeois (ca. 1500–ca. 1565). Bourgeois was employed by the city of Geneva to teach choristers to lead psalm singing for about seven years (1545–ca. 1552). During the course of this employment, Bourgeois revised twelve of the tunes and composed thirty-four new ones, which appear in the 1551 edition. The tunes that appear for the first time only in the 1562 edition are the work of one Maître Pierre, who could have been Pierre Dubuisson, Pierre Dagues, Pierre Vallette, or Pierre Davantès—all musicians mentioned in the Genevan records of the time.[11]

Orentin Douen championed the notion that many of the psalter tunes were borrowed or paraphrased from pre-existing secular melodies.[12] Walter Blankenburg and Pierre Pidoux both point out instances where the psalter tunes bear some resemblance to well-known melodies from the Catholic liturgy.[13] The majority of the psalter melodies, though, were newly created expressly for Marot's and de Bèze's poetic psalm translations along lines laid down by Calvin: the music was to be the servant of the text, reflecting its message and assisting in worship by opening the hearts of the faithful to the word of God.

The melodies in the Genevan Psalter are conjunct and lie within the range of an octave, nearly always descending to the final. They make use of only two rhythmic values: short (minim) and long (semibreve). The verses of poetry are clearly delineated by rests at the end of each line. The melodies are, in short, just right for large gatherings of people with scant musical literacy. The tunes were written to support and strengthen the poetry; and the poetry is wonderfully varied, not only in its metric schemes but also in the subtler matter of internal rhythms. "It is to that element," wrote Blankenburg of the settings, "that they mainly owe their extraordinary effectiveness and widespread acceptance."

> Never again, at any time or place in the history of Protestant hymnals based on Calvin's principles, would there be a treasury of poems and songs, of sheer ecumenical significance, equal to the Genevan Psalter in unity, durability, and, eventually, wide dissemination.[14]

See Plate 3 for the most durable and widely disseminated melody from the Genevan Psalter as it appeared in the Taille book of *Les cent cinquante pseaumes*.

Polyphonic Settings of the Complete Genevan Psalter through Le Jeune

Catholic as well as Reformed composers were inspired by the Genevan Psalter as a rich new source of poetry and melody. Harmonized settings and contrapuntal, motet-like treatments of the poems and their melodies began to appear in published collections of music even before the psalter was complete. Since Calvin never authorized the use of polyphonic music in public worship, one must assume that the numerous extant polyphonic settings of Genevan psalm tunes were all created for private use in Huguenot homes of the educated classes. There were even settings of Genevan psalm tunes for the lute[15]—surely the antithesis of Calvin's intent in creating the Genevan Psalter.

Harmonized settings of the complete psalter are understandably rarer. Claude Goudimel (ca. 1505–72) completed two psalters in four-part music, one in strict note-against-note style with the Genevan tunes in the tenor (1564), one in polyphonically animated homophony with the tunes in the treble (1568). Each contains all 150 psalms, providing music and text for the first strophe only.

Le Jeune's immediate predecessor was Paschal de l'Estocart, who in 1583 published a complete psalter in four and five parts. Only the first stanza of each psalm is set, with the unaltered Genevan tunes in the tenor, the other parts moving in generally faster note values.[16] The texture of l'Estocart's psalm settings is not unlike the texture of Le Jeune's through-composed cantus-firmus settings in the *Dodecacorde*, and it is quite possible that Le Jeune and l'Estocart knew each other, or knew each other's work, for both were under the protection of the Protestant house of Bouillon.

Le Jeune created two complete psalters in polyphonic music in his lifetime; both were published posthumously. *Les cent cinquante pseaumes* appeared in 1601, immediately after his death. In 1602 the first volume of a three-volume set of *Pseaumes à 3* appeared (the second volume came out in 1608, the third in 1610). These three together make a complete psalter. They are dedicated to Princess Louise of Nassau, to whom, with her sister Elizabeth, Le Jeune taught "the principles of music." Some are in cantus firmus style; most use a freely expanded, imitative treatment of the pre-existing melodies.[17]

Les cent cinquante pseaumes contains the simplest, most accessible music Le Jeune ever wrote. This collection alone employs the utterly simple, note-against-note style that suggests a serious attempt to reconcile Calvin's demand for sacred music of weight and majesty, suitable for large numbers of lay people to sing in public worship, with the demand among the educated classes for part-music. It most closely resembles Goudimel's 1564 collection in texture, but Le Jeune's harmonic language is much more adventuresome. To indulge briefly in anachronistic terminology, Le Jeune made far more frequent use of inverted triads, diminished chords, secondary dominants, Picardy thirds at cadences, and ornamental passing tones than Goudimel did.

Claude Le Jeune: Biography

Very little information about the details of Claude Le Jeune's life survives today. An examination of his large and varied musical output makes it clear that he was not only versatile and innovative but also learned and devout.

He was a native of Valenciennes, probably born between 1525 and 1530. Nothing is known about his youthful years nor about his education, though there were in Valenciennes several choir-schools where he might have received his training.[18] Kenneth Levy makes a plausible case, on admittedly slight evidence, for Le Jeune's having visited Italy as a young man and having made the acquaintance of Willaert at Venice.[19]

Le Jeune's first publication, *Dix pseaumes de David* (1564), is dedicated to François de la Noue and Charles de Téligny, two noblemen who actively supported the Protestant leader Gaspard de Coligny in the civil war of 1562–63. Thus Le Jeune's public identification as a Huguenot was early and explicit.

Nevertheless, throughout his career he was also closely identified with events and undertakings that had royal (which meant, of course, Catholic) support. He provided music for at least two important weddings,[20] and he was invited to participate in the Académie de poésie et de musique established in Paris in 1570 by Jean-Antoine de Baïf. This select group of scholars, poets, and musicians dedicated itself to the application of classical Greek poetics to the French language and to the creation of *musique mesurée à l'antique*.

Some time before 1582 Le Jeune entered the household of the youngest Valois prince, François duc d'Alençon, with whom he may have traveled to England (when Alençon tried unsuccessfully to win Elizabeth I in marriage) and almost certainly traveled to the Low Countries (when Alençon headed a costly and disastrous military campaign there).[21]

For the rest of the 1580s and most of the 1590s, Le Jeune's whereabouts and means of livelihood are uncertain. Alençon died in 1584 and his household was disbanded. From then until 1598, when Le Jeune appears as *compositeur de la musique de la chambre du Roy*[22] (the *roy* in question being Henri IV), he was evidently under the protection of the duc de Bouillon, one of the powerful Huguenot nobles who spent most of his life in covert or open rebellion against the house of Valois. This is the period in which Le Jeune probably composed most of his polyphonic settings of psalms from the Genevan Psalter. We know that he was in Paris during the seige of 1590 and narrowly escaped being arrested for sedition.[23] He evidently went to La Rochelle, a Protestant stronghold, after his escape from Paris, for the *privilège* of the *Dodecacorde*, which is dated 1596, states that he was a resident there. His appointment as *compositeur de la musique de la chambre du Roy* may have occurred as early as 1594, the year that Henri IV was finally received in Paris as the king of France, or as late as 1598, the date of the publication of the *Dodecacorde*. The aging composer remained in the royal service until his death in September 1600. His oeuvre numbers over 650 works, most published posthumously. While Le Jeune's most striking contributions to the development of musical style were his secular works in the genre *musique mesurée à l'antique*, which have been quite thoroughly studied and anthologized, these constitute perhaps one-fourth of his life's work. At least half of Le Jeune's extant compositions are settings of the tunes and texts of the Genevan Psalter.[24]

Les cent cinquante pseaumes, the first of Le Jeune's posthumous publications, appeared so soon after the composer's death that it is entirely likely that Le Jeune himself had begun to prepare it for publication, a task finished by his sister Cécile Le Jeune with commendable dispatch. In writing the dedication to the duc de Bouillon, she tells us that the collection was "conceived . . . and nourished" under the aegis of the duke, and that the composer, knowing that his death was near, made her promise to see to completion the printing of his musical works, most especially the Psalms of David.[25] Cécile Le Jeune kept her word: in 1602 the first volume of the *Pseaumes à 3* was published; only then did she—later succeeded by her niece Judith Mardo—begin to bring out Le Jeune's hitherto unpublished airs, chansons, psalms in *musique mesurée* (which use neither tunes nor texts from the Genevan Psalter), fantasies for viols, chansons spirituelles, and even a mass setting and a few other short works of liturgical music for the Latin rite.

The Music of the 1601 Psalter

Of the 152 pieces in *Les cent cinquante pseaumes*, 140 are harmonized in four parts, nine in five parts, and three in six parts. The voices range from the Dessus, always the highest, to the Basse-Contre, the lowest printed part. The Haute-Contre and Taille parts lie between the two extremes; they are less distinct in range from each other than from the Dessus and Basse-Contre and they not infrequently cross. All of the parts, however, vary in tessitura from setting to setting, so that the original clefs of the parts provide better indications of ranges than do the names "Dessus," "Haute-Contre," and so on. For example, the Basse-Contre in Psalm 140 has a part that falls in the octave a–a' (embracing middle C), while in the very next psalm, the Basse-Contre has a range of E–g. In other words, the lowest Basse-Contre note in Psalm 140 is higher than the highest Basse-Contre note in Psalm 141. Thus specifying the original clef is the surest way to know the range of any voice part. Table 1 gives the clefs for the four-voice settings in the order Dessus, Haute-Contre, Taille, and Basse-Contre; the clefs are abbreviated as Tr (for treble), S (soprano), Mz (mezzo-soprano), A (alto), T (tenor), Bar (baritone), B (bass), and SubB (sub-bass).

TABLE 1
Tessitura of Settings in Four Parts
(listed in order from highest to lowest)

Clefs	Psalm numbers
Tr Mz A T	19, 27, 42, 46, 49, 57, 60, 66, 74, 79, 116, 124, 126, 136, 140
Tr Mz A Bar	4, 6, 11, 12, 21, 22, 29, 32, 38, 41, 45, 59, 65, 73, 75, 80, 84, 85, 89, 92, 94, 96, 97, 105, 107, 122, 128, 130, 133, 135, 138, 144, 145, 150
S Mz A Bar	5, 24, 50
S A A Bar	1, 2, 3, 13, 14, 15, 20, 36, 52
S A A B	47
S A T B	7, 8, 9, 16, 17, 18, 23, 28, 30, 33, 35, 37, 39, 40, 43, 44, 48, 53, 54, 55, 56, 58, 61, 62, 63, 64, 68, 71, 76, 77, 78, 81, 83, 87, 88, 91, 93, 100, 101, 102, 103, 104, 106, 108, 109, 110, 112, 113, 114, 115, 117, 119, 120, 121, 123, 125, 129, 131, 132, 137, 143, 146, 148, 149, Les Commandemens de Dieu, Le Cantique de Simeon
S T T B	10, 34, 127, 134
Mz A T B	25, 98, 99
Mz T T B	26, 31, 147
Mz T T SubB	51, 141

The five- and six-voice harmonizations also vary in tessitura. Moreover, the holder of the Cinquiesme book is instructed either to sing an octave higher than printed (in Psalms 67, 69, 72, and 82) or to sing the part as printed (in Psalms 70, 95, 118, 139, and 142). The three six-part pieces are created without need for a sixth partbook simply by stating in the Cinquiesme partbook that it should be doubled an octave lower (in Psalms 86 and 111) or an octave higher (in Psalm 90). Table 2 gives the clefs for the five- and six-voice settings in the order Dessus, Haute-Contre, Taille, Basse-Contre, Cinquiesme, and sixth part.

TABLE 2
Tessitura of Settings in Five or Six Parts
(listed in order of appearance)

Psalm number	Clefs					
67	Tr	A	T	B	T-8ve up	
69	Tr	A	T	SubB	T-8ve up	
70	S	A	T	SubB	T	
72	S	Mz	A	Bar	A-8ve up	
82	S	Mz	A	Bar	A-8ve up	
86	S	Mz	T	B	S	[S-8ve down]
90	Tr	Mz	A	Bar	T	[T-8ve up]
95	S	A	T	B	A	
111	S	A	T	Bar	A	[A-8ve down]
118	Tr	Mz	A	Bar	A	
139	Tr	S	A	Bar	S	
142	S	A	T	SubB	T	

Though the three six-part settings are marked *a cinq*, Psalm 111 in particular has evidence that six-part performance was expected: in the Basse-Contre book, Psalm 111 is labeled "Basse-Taille"—a clue to the performer that his part would not in fact be the lowest sounding part, since that role would be taken by the doubling, an octave lower, of the Genevan melody.

The Genevan melody is placed either in the Taille or the Dessus in the four-part settings; in the five- and six-part settings it is always placed in the Cinquiesme. Table 3 identifies the partbook in which each Genevan tune appears in *Les cent cinquante pseaumes*.

TABLE 3
Location of Genevan Melody

Partbook	Psalms/Canticles
Taille	1–27, 29, 31–33, 36–39, 41, 42, 44–52, 54–60, 65, 66, 73–76, 78–80, 83–85, 87–89, 91–94, 96, 97, 99–107, 109, 110, 112–15, 119–28, 130, 132–38, 140, 141, 143, 145, 147–50, Le Cantique de Simeon
Dessus	28, 30, 34, 35, 40, 43, 53, 61–64, 68, 71, 77, 81, 98, 108, 116, 117, 129, 131, 144, 146, Les Commandemens de Dieu
Cinquiesme	67, 69, 70, 72, 82, 86, 90, 95, 111, 118, 139, 142

In most of the settings, the Genevan melody has the same clef and key as in the 1562 psalter. This is always the case for the initial setting of a tune as well as for any third or even fourth setting. The exceptions, then, are to be found in second settings of tunes, all of which are transposed by a fourth, a fifth, or an octave from their original pitch levels. For example, the melody of Psalm 5 is found in the Taille part, but in Psalm 64, which uses the same melody, Le Jeune transposed it up a fifth and placed it in the Dessus part (see Table 4). This alteration leads to other differences between the two settings as well. While the harmonic progressions approaching cadences are essentially unchanged, the two settings differ in harmonic progressions at the beginnings of phrases, in chord spacings, and in the melodic embellishments used to enliven and rhythmically propel the voices not carrying the Genevan tune. A comparison of other pairs or groups of settings of the same tune yields the same observations: that the goals of cadential progressions, especially in opening and closing phrases, are retained; that variations in the harmonization occur at the beginnings of phrases; and that chord spacings and melodic embellishments are the chief sources of variety from one setting of the same tune to another.

TABLE 4
Settings with the same Genevan Melody
(but different texts and different harmonizations)

5, 64	31, 71	66, 98, 118
14, 53	33, 67	74, 116
17, 63, 70	36, 68	77, 86
18, 144	46, 82	78, 90
24, 62, 95, 111	51, 69	100, 131, 142
28, 109	60, 108	117, 127
30, 76, 139	65, 72	140, Commandemens

The melody for Psalms 24, 62, 95, and 111—the only melody that occurs four times in the Genevan Psalter—offers a capsule view of Le Jeune's method. In Psalm 24 (*à 4*), the Genevan melody appears in the Taille, in its original clef and key. In Psalm 62 (also *à 4*), the same melody is transposed up a fifth and placed in the Dessus. Psalm 95 (*à 5*) finds the melody back in its original clef and key, in the Cinquiesme partbook, with the instruction, "This fifth part is the melody of this psalm and is sung just as it is" [Cette cinquiesme partie, est le subjet de ce pseaume, et se chante ainsi qu'il est]. The holders of the Dessus, Haute-Contre, Taille, and Basse-Contre books, meanwhile, are informed that the fifth part, and melody of this psalm, "is sung on the 24th [that is, sung to the tune of the 24th Psalm], just as it is" [sur le XXIIII, ainsi qu'il est]. (For a similar instruction found in the Basse-Contre of Psalm 69, see Plate 4.) Lastly, in Psalm 111 (*à 6*), Le Jeune again placed the melody in the Cinquiesme book, in its original clef and key, but with the instruction to double it an octave lower ("Cette cinquiesme partie, est le subjet de ce pseaume, et se chante a la double en bas"). The headings in Dessus, Haute-Contre, Taille, and Basse-Contre books provide the same information for those performers ("The fifth part and melody of this psalm is sung on the 24th, doubled in the bass"). The harmonizations of Psalms 24, 62, and 95 differ in detail but the goals of cadential movement and many of the progressions are essentially the same. The fourth treatment, that in Psalm 111, is truly a re-harmonization, occasioned by the placement of the melody in the lowest sounding voice.

All of the tunes harmonized in five or six parts are also present in the psalter in one or more four-part harmonizations, though the converse is not true: not all melodies that occur more than once in the Genevan Psalter are given five- or six-part settings in second appearances. As for tunes making third appearances, this happens four times, all of which involve transposition in the second occurrence and a return to the original key and tessitura but with a more complex texture in the third (see Psalms 70, 139, 118, and 142).

Le Jeune's compositional technique in these psalm settings is a delight to behold. Odet de la Noue's quatrain, part of the prefatory matter of the first edition, praises Le Jeune's admirable art "hidden" in simple counterpoint, and indeed the settings are deceptively simple in appearance; yet they are as expressive as they are well-constructed.

The Basse-Contre and the Genevan melody can together make a contrapuntally correct and self-sufficient duet in any of the 140 four-part settings in *Les cent cinquante pseaumes*. Adding the Dessus, or, in pieces where the pre-existing tune is in the Dessus, adding the Taille, creates a trio which is similarly sufficient. This countermelody is usually an attractive tune in its own right, similar to the style of the Genevan melodies (see, for example, the Dessus in Psalm 16). The Haute-Contre is the part that evidently was composed last. Because its role is simply to enrich the sonority, covering whatever notes are left over after the bass line and the countermelody have been created, it sometimes hangs tediously on one note for two or three syllables in a row (an extreme example of this, with seven repeated notes, occurs in Psalm 144, phrase 1). The Haute-Contre also sometimes makes surprising and downright difficult skips. Augmented fourths, diminished octaves, ninths, sevenths—nothing is off limits for this part. These startling leaps, however, always occur between phrases (see, for example, Psalm 27, between phrases 4 and 5; Psalm 71, between phrases 5 and 6; and Psalm 52, between phrases 4 and 5). Within a phrase, nothing more taxing than an octave leap occurs.

The five- and six-part pieces are less markedly layered. The voice parts other than the Genevan melody and the Basse-Contre tend to be similar in character to one another rather than falling into the distinct categories of "countermelody" and "harmonic filler."

Le Jeune's observance of the basic rules of counterpoint is impeccable within phrases, but between phrases one can find numerous instances of parallel fifths and parallel octaves. In Psalm 17, for example, all four voices move up a third in exact parallel motion between phrases 7 and 8. Since Le Jeune was a master of part-writing in homophonic texture, as his *Pseaumes en vers mesurés* can attest, clearly these "incorrect" parallels occur not because the composer was careless or incompetent but because he viewed *Les cent cinquante pseaumes* differently from anything else in his oeuvre. The prohibition of parallel perfect intervals had evolved to control a polyphonic web of equal voices, whereas in *Les cent cinquante pseaumes* the voices are patently unequal. The need to avoid parallel perfect intervals is superseded by the need to support the melody with full sonorities.

Le Jeune was well known not only for his melodic and harmonic skills, but also for his skill in the use of rhythm. Mersenne, writing several decades after Le Jeune's death, mentions him in *Harmonie universelle* with respect and admiration:

> Le Jeune . . . succeeded particularly in giving beautiful melodies to the texts he chose, and he used a variety of rhythms, which make his music lively.[26]

And further:

> The excellence of music lies not only in harmonies well set but also in the beauty and variety of rhythms, which are the reason why Claudin Le Jeune is better received by many than du Caurroy.[27]

D. P. Walker, writing on Le Jeune's *Airs* (1608), praised the "great rhythmic variety achieved within the very narrow limits imposed by *musique mesurée*."[28]

The narrow limits imposed by homophonic settings of the Genevan Psalter tunes, similarly, did not prevent Le Jeune from enlivening the texture with rhythmic embellishments. The stanza form of the cantus firmus is never obscured; each line of poetry begins and ends together in all parts. Within lines, however, Le Jeune's rhythmic genius appears over and over, in syncopations, in ornamental passing tones that add forward momentum, and—more rarely—in passages of triple rhythms reminiscent of *musique mesurée*. The second phrase of Psalm 22 exemplifies all three: (1) a syncope in the Haute-Contre part to create a 7-6 suspension on the word *oppressé*; (2) semiminims in Basse-Contre and Haute-Contre to fill in a leap (Basse-Contre) and to call attention to an important note with an anticipation (Haute-Contre); and (3) Basse-Contre and Dessus moving together in the 3 + 3 + 2 + 2 rhythms so common in Le Jeune's airs (— ⏑ — ⏑ — —).

The closing phrase of Psalm 124 shows both syncopation in the Dessus and a very typical dotted pattern in the Basse-Contre that propels the phrase towards the cadence. The ornamental use of fast notes can have the function not only of highlighting an important note or of adding momentum, however, but also of simply adding activity to what would otherwise be a dull phrase (as in Psalm 73, phrase 6, Haute-Contre).

The Genevan melodies for the most part proceed in duple patterns, regardless of what the text may be. That is their strength and part of their charm. Sometimes Le Jeune overrode the rhythm of his cantus firmus, writing harmonizing parts in triple patterns that better express the text. Psalm 88, phrase 5, offers an example of such a passage, as does the aforementioned Psalm 22, phrase 2.

The rests between phrases are nearly all of a semibreve's duration. Occasionally, however, phrases are separated by minim rests and the following phrase begins with a minim in all voices (as in Psalm 1, phrases 2 and 5). There are also numerous instances where no rest intervenes between phrases, for example in Psalm 23, where phrase 3 flows into phrase 4 without a break. In every case Le Jeune simply followed the rhythm dictated by the Genevan melody.

While the basic technique of construction in *Les cent cinquante pseaumes* shows an admirable unity and coherence of style, the harmonic vocabulary and the quantity of rhythmic embellishment vary enough to indicate either that the pieces in this collection were not all written at the same time or that they were not all written for the same patron (or performers, or audience). Some are similar in style to Goudimel's 1564 collection, with a preponderance of root-position chords and a close adherence in all voice parts to the rhythms of the original melody (see, for example, Psalm 125), while some make more frequent use of first and second inversions, diminished chords and seventh chords, which not only enrich the harmonic vocabulary but also create smoother, more melodic bass lines (see Psalm 128, phrases 4 and 6; Psalm 46, phrase 3; Psalm 87, phrase 3; and Psalm 88, phrase 4). One might at first think that the former would predate the latter, but the degree of harmonic variety is probably not a reliable indicator of chronology of composition. After 1584, when the household of the duc d'Alençon was disbanded, Le Jeune would have been called upon to write new harmonizations of Genevan tunes favored by members of whatever household was currently employing him; and the musical tastes and capabilities of those for whom Le Jeune composed would necessarily have affected the harmonic and rhythmic vocabularies he deployed. Not every Huguenot noble was a musical sophisticate.

The unexpected chromatic alteration, added simply for color, is a noteworthy characteristic of Le Jeune's harmonic language. Two B-flats in Psalm 16 (phrases 4 and 5) temporarily take us far from the Mode XII of the psalm tune and its setting. Raised thirds in the resolutions of internal cadences (the cause of some of the infamous leaps in the Haute-Contre part, as in Psalm 71, between phrases 5 and 6), while they eventually cease to be unexpected, always add color and richness.

The mode of the Genevan melody determines the mode of the setting in *Les cent cinquante pseaumes* in all but two cases (see Table 5). The numbering system for the modes is that proposed by Zarlino and followed by Le Jeune in his *Dodecacorde*: the C modes—Ionian, Hypoionian—are numbered I and II, the D modes are numbered III and IV, and so forth to the A modes, numbered XI and XII.

Observations on Performance Practices

What do we know and what can we deduce about the people who performed *Les cent cinquante pseaumes* in Le Jeune's four- and five-part settings? In the last few years of his life, Le Jeune held the position of Master of Chamber Music at Henri IV's court. This meant that he was living in Paris; and because he was Protestant, he was undoubtedly connected with the Reformed congregation that met to worship in the large temple at Charenton, outside the city. Félix Bovet writes:

> Every Sunday morning the road from Paris to Charenton was covered with a great crowd of men, women, and children, some on foot, some on horseback or in a car-

TABLE 5
Psalm Tunes Classified by Mode

Mode	Psalms/Canticles
I.	68, 81
I. on F	1, 3, 21, 29, 32, 36, 47, 52, 73, 75, 84, 97, 105, 122, 133, 135, 138, 150
II.	42, 49, 60, 66, 79, 89, 118, 124, 140
II. on F	25, 35, 43, 54, 56, 98, 99, 101, 108, 119, 123, 134, Les Commandemens de Dieu, Le Cantique de Simeon
III.	8–10, 33, 34, 37, 48, 53, 62, 64, 67, 78, 88, 90, 91, 104, 112, 114, 115, 125, 137, 143, 148, 149
III. on G	2, 5, 11–14, 20, 24, 41, 45, 50, 59, 80, 92, 95, 96, 107, 111, 128, 130
IV.	none
IV. on G	7, 23, 28, 40, 61, 77, 86, 109, 120, 129, 146
V.	17, 26, 31, 63,* 70, 71, 100, 102, 131, 142
V. on A	94†
VI.	51, 69, 83, 132, 141, 147
VII.	none
VIII.	none
IX.	15, 19, 27, 46, 57, 74, 82, 85, 87, 116, 126, 136, 145
X.	30, 44, 58, 76, 93, 103, 113, 117, 121, 127, 139
XI.	4, 6, 22, 38, 65, 72
XII.	16, 18, 39, 55, 106, 110, 144

*The psalm tune is in Mode V, but the setting is in Mode XII.
†The psalm tune is in Mode V on A, but the setting is in Mode XI on D.

> riage, who sang psalms as they progressed towards the temple. . . . A good number of people went to Charenton by the Seine, and the songs which were raised all at once from various boats responded to those heard from the banks.[29]

These Huguenots were members of the educated classes. The congregation included artists and architects[30] as well as government ministers, functionaries (especially in finance), counselors, secretaries, lawyers, doctors, and engineers.[31] Though they did not sing the psalms in harmony during public worship services—not early in the seventeenth century, at any rate—these were musically literate people for whom home music-making was a popular pastime. Collections of part-music that included harmonizations of the Genevan Psalter tunes had been available since the mid-sixteenth century and Goudimel's complete psalter in four parts had been widely disseminated. Le Jeune's psalter was surely welcomed as an up-to-date substitute for the old, very plain settings by Goudimel.

Pidoux lists sixty-seven publications of part-music based on texts, music, or both from the Genevan Psalter between 1545 and 1598, with the greatest activity from 1555 to 1565.[32] Pannier describes the Parisian Huguenots singing or reading psalms as part of daily devotions.[33] Every church or temple had its school, directed by a *régent* who was a *chantre* and *lecteur* in the temple.[34]

But the flood of new part-music inspired by the Genevan Psalter slowed to a trickle and then dried up completely. To begin with, a goodly number of the publications listed by Pidoux came from the pens of Catholic composers who held secure appointments such as Lassus, Arcadelt, Certon, and Janequin. They could play with the new musical repertory coming out of Geneva, seeing in it as much a manifestation of humanism as of religious reform. In the seventeenth century, though, composers in similar circumstances ignored the Genevan repertory. The language of the poetry by then was outdated and few of the melodies possessed a structure or a melodic language adaptable to the revolutionary style of the early Baroque spreading north from Italy. Then, with the assassination of Henri IV in 1610, toleration of the Huguenots dwindled; their Protestantism became viewed as a rejection of the monarchy as much as of the Catholic church. As Huguenots became hedged about with restrictive and repressive laws during the course of the seventeenth century, their energies were more and more tied up with simply holding on and conserving the remnants of their heritage from the turbulent but expansive years of the Reformation.[35]

Many gave up the struggle against the strong nationalist current of the day and converted back to Catholicism. In their households, only a few of the best-loved psalms and psalm tunes might have remained a living—albeit a clandestine—musical tradition. Others made the painful decision to emigrate in order to keep their faith. They took their music with them, but their children learned the languages of their new homelands—Dutch, German, English—and soon were singing the Genevan tunes with texts in those languages. In time most of the tunes disappeared as well. Jon Butler's summation of the Huguenot diaspora both within Europe and to America is eloquent: "Everywhere they fled, everywhere they vanished."[36]

During this cultural twilight the only Huguenot music that seems to have been gaining in popularity was Le Jeune's *Cent cinquante pseaumes*, with its numerous editions and translations into other languages. The music can be sung or played in only two or three parts as well as the stated four or five (and the unstated six), which allows great flexibility in performance. Jean Le Grand's 1624 publication of additional fifth parts provides hard evidence that, in

Geneva at least, not only were Le Jeune's harmonizations widely known, but also that there was still a market for fresh harmonizations of the psalter melodies.[37] We can plausibly imagine family groups, or groups of friends, handing around the partbooks of an evening and enjoying Le Jeune's music with whatever resources were present: singing, doubling on soft chamber instruments such as the viol or flute, or even trying entirely instrumental renditions.[38] Calvin's prohibition of polyphonic sacred music, after all, applied only to music for public worship.

But was Le Jeune's psalter ever used in public worship? Most editions were in partbook format, which bespeaks home performance, but four (1635, 1646, 1659, and 1737) came out in miniature choirbook format (about 8.5 × 15 cm) and were probably intended to be carried to worship services. It is important to note that all four of these originated outside France, in Leyden, Amsterdam, Basel, and Straeda respectively.

In choirbook format, all four voice parts appear on facing pages, with the complete psalm text below and continued on following pages as necessary. These choirbooks are tiny, however: the staves are no more than six millimeters wide, and the notes themselves as well as the words are minute. It is impossible to imagine any way in which four singers could have read from a single book. What seems most likely is that each singer had a copy, which he or she carried to the temple in place of the traditional monophonic psalter. One could sing from the melody line, in orthodox manner, or, if circumstances invited, sing a harmonizing line. That Calvin's proscription of part-singing in public worship had lost its force is shown not only indirectly by the choirbook format of these editions but is directly corroborated by the title of an edition of Goudimel's four-part psalms published in Geneva in 1667: *The Psalms of David . . . now conveniently arranged for the use of those who wish to sing in parts in church.*[39] Since one may safely assume that performance practices pre-date their first description in print, it seems likely that the Le Jeune psalters of 1635, 1646, 1659, and 1737 were indeed used in public worship as well as in the home, and that these simple yet eloquent pieces were genuinely congregational music.

Much comparative and analytical work needs to be done before Le Jeune's psalm settings and their place in the history of musical style and of Reformed psalmody are fully understood. It is my hope that this complete edition of *Les cent cinquante pseaumes* will make it possible for others to undertake such projects, which are beyond the scope of the present edition. Present-day performers as well as scholars will also, I hope, find in this collection a rich source of inspiration and new possibilities.

The Sources: Publication History of the 1601 Psalter

Les cent cinquante pseaumes de David mis en musique à quatre parties first appeared in 1601, within a year of Le Jeune's death. The dedication to the duc de Bouillon refers to the collection as "this orphan, which the father wished to present to you before his death."[40] This does not necessarily indicate that the psalm settings were composed in the last years of Le Jeune's life, but it does seem to indicate that he was working on them immediately before his death and indeed may already have begun preparing them for publication. In any case, once published, the collection was very well received, as confirmed by the extraordinary number of subsequent editions. The following list outlines the publication history of *Les cent cinquante pseaumes*:

1601 Paris, Ballard & son filz Pierre Ballard.
1613 Paris, Pierre Ballard.
1617 Geneva, François le Febvre.
1627 Geneva, Jean de Tournes/François le Febvre.*
1635 Leyden, Justus Livius.*
1646 Ambr. Lobwassers Psalmen Davids . . . Amsterdam, Ludovich Elzeviern.*
1650 Paris, Robert Ballard.
1659 Ambr. Lobwassers Psalmen Davids . . . Basel, Joh. Jacob Genaths.*
1664 De CL psalmen Davids . . . nu eerst met den Hollendsen text [trans. Petrus Dathenus] . . . Schiedam, Laurens van der Wiel'.*
1665 Schiedam, Laurens van der Wiel'.*
1737 Ils Psalms da David, Suainter la melodia francesa, schartaeda eir in tudaisch . . . Traes Iohanem Iacobum et Bartholomeum Gonzenbach . . . Straeda, Johan Janet.

(In the editions marked by an asterisk, the title was changed to read "in four and five parts" rather than simply "in four parts.")

There are two distinct "family groups" in the editions that have survived. The first is the French family, beginning with the prints put out by Ballard in 1601 and 1613 (also 1650) and continuing with editions showing typographical evidence of having been copied from them (the editions of 1635, 1664, and 1665). The second group, the Swiss family, consists of the editions of 1617, 1627, and 1646. I have not had the opportunity to examine the 1659 and 1737 editions.

The head of the French family is of course the 1601 edition (see Plate 1 for the title page of the Taille book). The beautifully printed partbooks measure 10 × 13.5 cm. Originally there were five partbooks in a set; examples of only the Taille and Basse-Contre books are still extant. The dedication is followed by four poetic *encomia* to the beauty and spiritual power of Le Jeune's music (Odet de la Noue's is translated as the first epigram to this edition) and a short canon *à 5* (transcribed on page 3). Each psalm has a Latin incipit as its title. The initial capitals are large (about one square inch) and varied (see Plates 2, 3, and 4). Slurs are used to indicate some melismas. A choice of two alternative pitches is occasionally provided to the performer, one being a note of normal size and shape, the alternative being of a smaller size and of indeterminate time value. Plate 2 shows Psalm 1 from the Basse-Contre partbook, with examples both of slurs and of pairs of alternative notes. Each psalm is provided with only the first stanza of the French poetry.

The editions of 1613 and 1650 are straightforward reissues of the first edition. The 1635 edition, while it keeps the slurs and alternative notes, has no Latin incipits. It is printed in choirbook format and includes additional stanzas of the poetry, so that it can serve as a complete psalter. The copy I examined in the Library of Congress also contains prayers, the proper forms for baptism, marriage, and the celebration of the Lord's Supper, as well as the Catechism and Confession of Faith. The edition of 1664 and 1665, in partbook format with Dutch texts by Petrus Dathenus, shows its relation to the French family by the inclusion of slurs and alternative notes. Like its cousin of 1635, this volume too contained additional liturgical items, including a Magnificat and a Lord's Prayer.

The editions of the Swiss family are characterized by more frequent printing errors and by the absence of slurs and alternative notes. The 1617 and 1627 editions are in partbook format with additional stanzas of the French poetry provided, as many as will fill each page, but no more. The music is printed out for these additional stanzas. There are no Latin incipits. The 1646 edition is in choirbook format, with German texts by Ambrosius Lobwasser, and likewise has no slurs, no alternative notes, and the same errors that appear in the Genevan editions.

A Genevan publication of 1624 by Jean Le Grand, as mentioned above, contains additional fifth parts, composed to complement Le Jeune's harmonizations, so that the number of psalms that can be performed in five parts is increased from twelve to thirty-eight.

I have prepared the present edition from the earliest extant edition of each partbook:

Dessus	1613	Duke University Library, A6.12mo M355 C
Haute-Contre	1613	Bibliothèque Nationale, Paris, Réserve Vm[1] 46
Taille	1601	Société de l'Histoire du Protestantisme français, A8
Basse-Contre	1601	Société de l'Histoire du Protestantisme français, R 8° 27 167 (Another copy, at Rouen, Bibliothèque Municipale, was not consulted for this edition.)
Cinquiesme	1613	Bibliothèque Nationale, Paris, in the collection of the Paris Conservatoire, Réserve 645

Copies of the 1613 Taille and Basse-Contre books (examined at the Bibliothèque Nationale and the Société de l'Histoire du Protestantisme français, respectively) proved to be musically identical to the 1601 Taille and Basse-Contre books. In light of this, the 1613 Dessus, Haute-Contre, and Cinquiesme books are here taken as accurate stand-ins for the now lost 1601 prints of those three parts.

This edition thus presents, in modern notation and with critical apparatus, the version of *Les cent cinquante pseaumes* closest to Le Jeune's actual artistic control.

Editorial Procedures

The music of *Les cent cinquante pseaumes* is presented in this edition in open score. Each voice part is provided with an incipit giving the original clef, key signature, mensuration sign, and first note. Voice parts originally in treble, soprano, or mezzo-soprano clef are transcribed in treble clef. Parts originally in alto or tenor clef are transcribed in treble clef with octave-down transposition. Parts originally in baritone, bass, or sub-bass clef are transcribed in bass clef. In the twelve psalms with five- or six-voice settings, the fifth and sixth voices are treated as follows. In the case of the Cinquiesme, when it bears an instruction such as "This fifth part is the melody of this psalm and is sung just as it is [or an octave higher]," the gist of the instruction as well as the normal elements of an incipit are given. When the Cinquiesme has the instruction that it is to be "doubled an octave higher [or lower]," the gist of the instruction is placed in the sixth part that is thereby created. These sixth parts, of course, have no incipits. For both the fifth and sixth voice parts, modern clefs have been chosen using the time-honored Ledger Line Avoidance Rule. The ranges of all the voice parts are indicated in the modern clefs.

No modern equivalent is given for the original mensuration sign. Rather, a "bar" line appears in the staff at the end of each phrase, as a visual guide for the singer's eye. Within the phrase, the music will be found to move in irregular groupings of two and three semibreves; to add barlines and frequently changing modern time signatures seemed an unnecessary encumbrance to the user. Phrases are numbered for ease in referring to specific locations when discussing or rehearsing the music (e.g., Psalm 72, phrase 3—or rehearsal number 3). There are a few instances (Psalm 61, phrase 1, for example) where a phrase does not end simultaneously in all parts, so that the phrase lines are staggered accordingly.

The slurs printed in the original partbooks to clarify text underlay (see Plate 2) are retained in the present edition. Sometimes, however, there is no slur in the source, yet one syllable must cover more than one note. The present edition relies—as the original did—on careful placement of text beneath the notes to indicate such melismas. Ligatures, another means of controlling text underlay, are indicated by a solid horizontal bracket above the staff. Plate 4 contains an example of a ligature.

With respect to the treatment of accidentals, a policy more in line with Le Jeune's time than with our own has been adopted. This has been made necessary because of the decision not to bar the music according to modern convention. The phrase is therefore the basic unit of division, not the bar, and a phrase is often too long to make practical the convention that accidentals remain in effect for an entire bar unless cancelled. In the case of Psalm 1, phrase 4, for instance, the initial sharp on f′ in the Dessus is repeated in the source at the very end of the phrase, too far away from the first sharp to make it feasible to tacitly remove the second. For this reason, all of the source accidentals have been retained and all of them apply only to the note they precede. This leads to many instances in which an inflected note is immediately repeated, again with the accidental (as in Psalm 1, phrase 1, Haute-Contre), but to allow this is only to retain a common practice of Le Jeune and his editors.

Editorial accidentals added to the present edition have been bracketed on the staff and, like source accidentals, apply to only one note. Many of these editorial accidentals are added in situations like that just mentioned, where an inflected note is immediately repeated and should remain inflected but is not so marked in the source.

Cautionary accidentals, placed in parentheses on the staff, have been added to aid the modern performer but have been added only to notes that were previously inflected within the same phrase and in the same voice. The phrase lines are not wholly unrelated to the application of accidentals, then, but provide a useful means of setting limits on the number of cautionaries used. Psalm 48, phrase 1, provides a clear example of the use of both editorial and cautionary accidentals.

Accidentals placed above the staff indicate what I believe are valid applications of musica ficta. Le Jeune —or his editors—took care to mark with accidentals most cases of necessary alterations of pitch. I have followed standard practice, described by Zarlino[41] and others, in suggesting raised leading tones in those instances where the source omitted the necessary accidental, unless the note to be altered is in the Genevan tune. Only Le Jeune's own chromatic alterations of Genevan melodies appear in the present edition. Compare Psalms 30 and 76: in Psalm 30 (melody in the Dessus) Le Jeune adds a sharp to the Genevan tune on the penultimate note to create a conventional cadence with raised leading tone, but in Psalm 76, where the same melody appears in the Taille, Le Jeune does not raise the penultimate note and this edition does not suggest raising it.

Sharp signs used to cancel flats in the source have been retained in the incipits but have been notated as natural signs in the transcriptions.

Alternative pitches, occasionally provided in the source without time value, are printed in the present edition as a small note with the time value of the main note. These notes are ignored in determining the range of each part. In a choral performance, or performance with stringed instruments, it is physically possible to sound both pitches, but care must be taken. In one instance (Psalm 3, last chord of phrase 8), sounding both the main note and its alternative produces a first-inversion chord as the final chord of a cadence—something so far beyond the fringe of Le Jeune's harmonic language as to be untenable.

In the partbooks, the final note of each psalm is printed as a longa with a *signe de concordance*, indicating that the note is to be held "until the other parts come together."[42] These are usually rendered in the transcriptions as breves. However, when one voice reaches its final note before the other voices, I have adjusted the length of its final note so that all voices end together at the conclusion of the psalm (see, for example, Psalm 17).

The first stanza of the French poetry is underlaid in all parts. This replicates exactly the practice of the 1601 edition. The spelling of the French has not been modernized, except that where *i* is pronounced [ʒ], it is replaced with *j*; where *u* is pronounced [v], it is replaced with *v*; and ſ is replaced with *s*. The space-saving ˜ (*chãps* for *champs*, *sõt* for *sont*) and & (for *et*) have been eliminated, and words are spelled out in full. Minor inconsistencies of spelling from part to part, and from edition to edition, are common in *Les cent cinquante pseaumes*; the present edition takes the Taille partbook of the 1601 edition as authoritative. Diacritical marks, especially the *accent grave* and *accent aigu*, appear infrequently in sixteenth-century French. Rather, an *s* or a *z* typically indicates lengthening of the *e*, as in, for example, *deuxiesme* rather than the modern *deuxième* or *affligez* rather than *affligé*. Words like *eschappez* will look peculiar to eyes accustomed to seeing *échappé*, but there is no difference in pronunciation.

The punctuation has not been modernized except in cases where it seriously misrepresents the grammatical structure of the text. In Psalm 18, for example, there is a period in the source at the end of phrase 10, but this has been tacitly changed to a comma to show that phrase 10 is a dependent clause which must be attached to the following subject and verb.

Psalm 124 presents a special case, since the entire first stanza is a dependent clause. I decided to underlay the second stanza of the French poetry for the sake of the grammatical structure, though in so doing I depart from the source.

Each psalm has been provided with a verse translation taken from *All the French psalm tunes with English words* (London: Thomas Harper, 1632).[43] The spelling and punctuation have not been modernized, except that where *u* is pronounced [v] it is replaced with *v*; where *v* is used as a vowel it is replaced with *u*; *vv* is replaced with *w*; ſ is replaced with *s*; and & is replaced with *and*.

The Harper translations follow the rhyme schemes and metrical patterns of the French originals faithfully, though often at the price of awkward word order and occasional mis-accentuation. I know of no historically documented connection between these translations and Le Jeune's harmonizations of the Genevan Psalter tunes. They are included solely in order to provide a singable translation of the French or, for those who find the seventeenth-century English too stilted to sing, to provide a starting point from which to create a singable translation. It is often possible to disentangle the syntax somewhat and update the diction without sacrificing the poetic structure of the original. For example, compare these two versions of the opening of Psalm 67:

Harper	Harper, adapted
Lord God to us be favourable,	May God be merciful unto us,
To us vouchsafe thou blessings thine,	And bless us all who him adore,
Thy gracious face most amiable,	And cause his face to shine upon us
Upon us make thou bright to shine.	With grace and love for- ever more.

The melodies of the Genevan Psalter adhere to the principle of one-syllable-one-note, which gives Reformation psalmody its wonderfully straightforward immediacy. However, one can sometimes achieve a better English version by slightly relaxing the rule and singing two notes to one syllable. For example, compare Harper's version of Psalm 9, where the singer is obliged to place a musical accent on the penultimate syllable of "incomparable" and "admirable," with my adaptation:

Harper	Harper, adapted
With all my heart O Lord most high,	With all my heart, O Lord most high,
I will extoll and magnifie	I will extol and magnify
All thy great works incomparable,	All thy great works beyond compare—
Which wondrous are, and admirable.	Thy wonders marvelous and rare—.

Users of this collection are encouraged to rewrite the Thomas Harper translations or to substitute other, more elegant ones that fit the Genevan tunes, if a singable English translation for use in contemporary performance is the goal. I believe that Le Jeune's harmonizations of these texts and tunes deserve to be revived and welcome any steps toward that end.

Critical Notes

Pitch designations are of the usual sort: middle C is c′.

Psalm 25, phrase 8, Dessus, note 5 is d′.

Psalm 32, phrase 8, Dessus, slur is from 1665 edition.

Psalm 36, phrase 4, Taille and Basse-Contre, *Car tant se paist.*

Psalm 52, phrase 2, Basse-Contre, notes 4–5 are slurred.

Psalm 55, phrase 2, Basse-Contre is as follows:

The text underlay selected for the present edition, which makes the Basse-Contre syllabication of *arriere* consistent with the other voice parts, is found in the 1627 edition: the only instance where one of the Swiss editions is preferable to any of the French editions.

Psalm 61, phrase 4, Basse-Contre, note 4 is E.

Psalm 82, phrase 4, Taille, note 1 is b.

Psalm 85, phrase 4, Taille, note 6 is b, note 7 is c′.

Psalm 87, Dessus, psalm number is 82.

Psalm 90, phrase 5, Cinquiesme, note 7 is b♮.

Psalm 91, phrase 8, Haute-Contre, note 5 is a.

Psalm 114, Dessus and Haute-Contre, psalm number is 113.

Psalm 137, phrase 1, Haute-Contre, note 11 is c′.

Psalm 139, phrase 3, Taille, note 11 is a.

Psalm 144, phrase 6, Basse-Contre, note 6 is c.

Acknowledgments

The Newberry Library (which holds a copy of the 1646 edition of *Les cent cinquante pseaumes*) provided an Unaffiliated Scholar grant in 1984–86 that enabled me to begin transcribing the music and to explore the social and historical context in which the collection appeared and became popular. The National Endowment for the Humanities provided partial support for travel to Paris in the summer of 1989 to compare various early editions; Roosevelt University provided a Faculty Research Grant to help support that trip and a Faculty Research Leave in 1993 for completion of the writing. Staff members of the Newberry Library, the Library of Congress, the Bibliothèque de la Société de l'Histoire du Protestantisme français, the Bibliothèque Sainte-Geneviève, the Bibliothèque Nationale, and Duke University Library were unfailingly gracious and helpful. Special thanks are due to M. Jean-Michel Noailly and M. Laurent Guillo for their assistance in clarifying for me the authenticity (or lack thereof) of certain editions of *Les cent cinquante pseaumes* listed by ninteenth-century scholars and for pointing out to me recent work in this field of which I would otherwise have been unaware. My gratitude goes also to Mme. I. Beauvais of the Société de l'Histoire du Protestantisme français for her assistance in obtaining microfilm copies of the 1601 Taille and Basse-Contre books and photographs for the plates in this edition. His Majestie's Clerkes, a Chicago-based professional chamber choir, has provided me with invaluable opportunities to rehearse and perform psalm settings from *Les cent cinquante pseaumes*; experience gained thereby has shaped certain editorial decisions. My neighbor Dr. Bernadette Fort has always been cheerfully willing to help me with problems of translation. Lila Aamodt, Kit Hill, and Steven LaRue of A-R Editions have guided this project faithfully to completion. David Birchler's editorial insights have helped enormously in clarifying the organization of the Preface and the editorial procedures best suited to *Les cent cinquante pseaumes*. Most of all I am grateful to my husband R. Stephen Warner and my daughter Sarah Dove Heider for their love and their loyalty throughout this lengthy project.

Notes

1. Gustave Reese, *Music in the Renaissance,* rev. ed. (New York: W. W. Norton, 1959), 383.

2. Félix Bovet, *Histoire du psautier des eglises reformées* (Neuchatel: Sandoz, 1872); François Joseph Fétis, *Biographie universelle des musiciens,* 1st ed. (Brussels: Leroux, 1835–44) and 2nd ed. (Paris: Firmin-Didot, 1873–80; reprint, Brussels: Culture et Civilisation, 1972); Orentin Douen, *Clément Marot et le psautier huguenot* (Paris: L'Imprimerie nationale, 1878–79; reprint, Amsterdam: P. Schippers, 1967); Répertoire international des sources musicales: *Einzeldrucke vor 1800* (Kassel: Bärenreiter, 1975); and Jean-Michel Noailly, "Les harmonisations des psaumes au XVIIe siècle: Claude Goudimel ou Claude Le Jeune?", *Psaume: Bulletin de la recherche sur le psautier huguenot,* no. 2 (fall 1988) (this article extracted from Noailly's dissertation, "Claude Goudimel, Adrian le Roy et les 150 Psaumes, Paris 1562–1567" [Ph.D. diss., University of St-Etienne, 1988]).

3. *Les Pseaumes mis en rime françoise par Clément Marot & Théodore de Bèze. . . .* (Geneva: Michel Blanchier pour Antoine Vincent, 1562; facs. ed. with introduction by Pierre Pidoux, Geneva: Librairie Droz, 1986), hereafter cited as Blanchier/Pidoux.

4. Claude Goudimel, *Oeuvres complètes,* ed. H. Gagnebin, R. Hausler, and E. Lawry, under the direction of Luther A. Dittmer and Pierre Pidoux (New York: Institute of Mediaeval Music, 1967–74).

5. John Calvin, letter of 10 June 1543, "A tous Chrestiens et amateurs de la parole de Dieu," in Pierre Pidoux, *Le Psautier huguenot du XVIe siècle* (Basel: Bärenreiter, 1962), 2:20.

6. John Calvin, *La Forme des prieres et chantz ecclesiastiques* (Geneva, 1542; facs. ed., Kassel: Barenreiter, 1959), 5.

7. Calvin, letter of 10 June 1543, "A tous Chrestiens et amateurs de la parole de Dieu," in Pidoux, *Le Psautier huguenot,* 2:16.

8. Ibid., 2:21.

9. Lucien Febvre and Henri-Jean Martin, *L'Apparition du livre* (Paris: Albin Michel, 1958), 165–69.

10. Waldo Seldon Pratt, *The Music of the French Psalter of 1562* (New York: Columbia University, 1939), 20–23.

11. Blanchier/Pidoux, 12–25.

12. Douen, *Clément Marot et le psautier huguenot,* 1:718–19.

13. Walter Blankenburg, "Church Music in Reformed Europe," in Friedrich Blume et al., *Protestant Church Music: A History* (New York: W. W. Norton, 1974), 522 and Pidoux, *Le Psautier huguenot,* 1:xvii.

14. Blankenburg, "Church Music," 523 and 530.

15. Ibid., 533–43.

16. Paschal de l'Estocart, *Cent cinquante pseaumes de David* (Geneva: Eustace Vignon, 1583; facs. ed., Kassel: Barenreiter, 1954 [five partbooks boxed]).

17. The first book of three-part psalms is available in a manuscript score in Donald Lee Breshears, "The Three-Part Psalms of Claude Le Jeune, Premier Livre: A Performance Edition and Commentary," 2 vols. (Ph.D. diss., University of Iowa, 1966).

18. D. P. Walker and François Lesure, "Claude Le Jeune and Musique Mesurée," *Musica Disciplina* 3 (1949): 151. This article is the most complete and accurate source of biographical information on Le Jeune.

19. Kenneth J. Levy, "The Chansons of Claude Le Jeune" (Ph.D. diss., Princeton University, 1955), 58–63.

20. The marriage of Henry of Navarre (the future Henri IV) and Marguerite de Valois in 1572 and the marriage of the duc de Joyeuse and Marguerite de Vaudemont in 1581; see Walker and Lesure, "Musique Mesurée," 158–59.

21. Le Jeune's next publication, the *Livre de mélanges* of 1585, was first published by Plantin in Antwerp, which argues strongly that the composer was there. This collection was subsequently published by LeRoy and Ballard as *Meslanges de la musique* (Paris, 1586 and 1587).

22. Title page of *Dodecacorde* (La Rochelle: Hierosme Haultin, 1598).

23. Marin Mersenne, *Harmonie universelle* (Paris: Cramoisy, 1636; facs. ed., Paris: Centre national de la recherche scientifique, 1975), Livre 7:64–65.

24. In addition to the two complete settings, three other collections make use of material drawn from the psalter. *Dix pseaumes de David* (1564) (edited by Nicole Labelle, *Les différents styles de la musique religieuse en France: Le Psaume de 1539 à 1572,* vol. 3 [Henryville, PA: Institute of Medieval Music, 1981]) used texts by de Bèze which had newly appeared in the 1562 edition of the Genevan Psalter but did not use the Genevan melodies. The texture is predominantly chordal, with a flexible and sensitive declamation of the text, occasional experiments with word-painting, and classical equal-voice polyphony only in sections *à 3*. The *Dodecacorde* (1598) (edited by Anne Harrington Heider, Recent Researches in the Music of the Renaissance, vols. 74, 75, and 76 [Madison: A-R Editions, 1989]), one of the most significant achievements of Le Jeune's career, uses Genevan texts and tunes as cantus firmi in a set of twelve multisectional, through-composed motets, one in each of the twelve modes (Zarlino's numbering system), each exemplifying not only the harmonic and melodic properties but also the affective properties of its mode. The texture shows a masterful integration of traditional polyphonic writing with the contrasting, homophonic style of *musique mesurée à l'antique.* There are two settings of Genevan psalms in the *Second livre des meslanges* (1612) (edited by Henry Expert, Monuments de la musique française au temps de la renaissance, vol. 8 [New York: Broude Brothers, 1924–30]), similar in style to those in the *Dodecacorde.* Finally, the *Pseaumes en vers mesurés* (1606) (edited by Henry Expert, Les maîtres musiciens de la renaissance française, vols. 20, 21, and 22 [Paris: Alphonse Leduc, 1894–1908]) should at least be mentioned to round out this brief survey of Le Jeune's psalmody, though they use neither the melodies nor the poetry of the Genevan Psalter. They represent a significant intersection between the humanism of the *Académie* and the humanism of the Reform movement.

25. The complete dedication is on page 1 of the present edition.

26. Mersenne, *Harmonie universelle,* Livre 7:61. "Claudin Le Ieune qui a vescu en mesme temps que du Caurroy, a particulierement reussi à donner de beaux chants à la lettre dont il s'est servy, & a usé de quantité de mouvemens, qui rendent sa Musique gaye, c'est pourquoy elle est en grand usage dans les Concerts ordinaires des Violes, & des voix."

27. Ibid., IV De la Composition, ii:205. "Mais il faut ajouter à la responce de ces deux dernieres objections, que la bonté & l'excellence de la Musique ne consiste pas seulement aux accords bien couchez, comme il sont dans la Musique du Caurroy, mais aussi dans la beauté & dans la diversité des mouvemens, qui sont cause que . . . Claudin Le Jeune est mieux receu de plusieurs que du Caurroy."

28. Walker and Lesure, "Musique Mesurée," 164.

29. Bovet, *Histoire du psautier des eglises reformées, 129–30.*

30. Jacques Pannier, *L'Eglise reformée de Paris sous Henri IV* (Paris: Honoré Champion, 1911), 178–87.

31. Emile G. Léonard, "Le Protestantisme français au XVIIe siècle," *Revue historique* 72 (1948), 154–79.

32. Pidoux, *Le Psautier huguenot,* vol. 2.

33. Pannier, *L'Eglise reformée,* 175.

34. Charles Bost, *Histoire des protestants de France,* 5th ed. (Carrières-sous-Poissy: La Cause, 1957), 135.

35. David Parker, "The Huguenots in seventeenth-century France," in A. C. Hepburn, ed., *Minorities in History* (London: Edward Arnold, 1978), 11–30.

36. Jon Butler, *The Huguenots in America: A Refugee People in New World Society* (Cambridge, MA: Harvard University Press, 1983), 199–215.

37. Jean Le Grand, *Suite des Pseaumes à cinq et six partis, jusques au nombre de trente huict, nouvelement adjoustez aux douze de Claude le Jeune . . .* (Genève: François le Fevre, 1624).

38. As early as 1554 Loys Bourgeois had published a collection of psalms of which, unfortunately, only the Bassus partbook survives; the title describes the contents as "set to music in familiar style, well suited to musical instruments" [mis en musique familiere bien consonante aux instrumentz musicaulx].

39. *Les Pseaumes de David, Mis en Rime Françoise par Cl. Marot & Th. De Beze. Et en musique à IV Parties, Par Claude Goudimel. Reveus de nouveau sur le Texte des derniers Exemplaires imprimez à Paris, & accommodez maintenant pour l'usage de ceux qui veulent chanter en Parties dans l'Eglise.* (Geneva: Ant. & Samuel De Tournes, 1667).

40. See below, page 1.

41. Gioseffo Zarlino, *Istitutioni armoniche,* rev. ed. (Venice: Senese, 1573; facs. ed., Ridgewood, NJ: Gregg Press, 1966), Terza parte, 222–23; translated by Guy A. Marco and Claude V. Palisca in *The Art of Counterpoint* (New York: W. W. Norton, 1976), 145–47.

42. Jean Yssandon, *Traite de la musique pratique* (Paris: Le Roy & Ballard, 1582; reprint, Geneva: Minkoff, 1972), 51.

43. I worked from a microfilm copy from the library of the University of Iowa. There are examples of the original publication both at Harvard University and at the New York Public Library.

Texts and Translations

These prose translations are literal to a fault; their intent is to provide a word-for-word understanding of the poetry of Marot and de Bèze, whose syntax and diction were already old-fashioned in Le Jeune's day.

Fugue

O que c'est chose belle
De te louër Seigneur,
Et du treshaut l'honneur
Chanter d'un coeur fidelle.
Chanter.

O how beautiful a thing it is
to praise thee, Lord,
and of the most high, the honor
to sing with a faithful heart,
to sing.

Psalm 1

Qui au conseil des malins n'a esté,
Qui n'est au trac des pecheurs arresté,
Qui des moqueurs au banc place n'a prise,
Mais nuict et jour la Loy contemple et prise
De l'Eternel et en est desireux,
Certainement cestui-là est heureux.

Clément Marot

Whoever does not remain in the confidence of evil ones,
whoever is not fixed in the path of sinners,
whoever does not take a place on the bench of mockers,
but night and day contemplates and holds to the Law
of the Eternal and longs for it,
certainly that one is happy.

Psalm 2

Pourquoy font bruit et s'assemblent les gens?
Quelle folie à murmurer les meine?
Pourquoy sont tant les peuples diligens
A mettre sus une entreprise vaine?
Bandez se sont les grans Roys de la terre,
Et les Primats ont bien tant presumé
De conspirer et vouloir faire guerre,
Tous contre Dieu, et son Roy bien-aimé.

Clément Marot

Why do the nations make noise and gather together?
What madness does the crowd mutter?
Why are so many tribes quick
to join a vain endeavor?
Banded together are the great Kings of the earth,
and the Potentates have willingly presumed
to conspire and willfully make war,
all against God, and his well-loved King.

Psalm 3

O Seigneur, que de gens,
A nuyre diligens,
Qui me troublent et grevent!
Mon Dieu que d'ennemis,
Qui aux champs se sont mis,
Et contre moy s'eslevent!
Certes plusieurs j'en voy,
Qui vont disans de moy,
Sa force est abolie,
Plus ne treuve en son Dieu,
Secours en aucun lieu:
Mais c'est à eux folie.

Clément Marot

O Lord, how many are the nations,
ready to do injury,
who trouble and burden me!
My God, how many are the enemies,
who are in the field,
and rise up against me!
Indeed I see many of them,
who go about saying of me,
his strength is vanquished,
he finds in his God,
no help anywhere:
But they are foolish.

Psalm 4

Quand je t'invoque, helas, escoute,
O Dieu, de ma cause et raison:
Mon coeur serré au large boute,
De ta pitié ne me reboute:
Mais exauce mon oraison.
Jusques à quand, gens inhumaines,
Ma gloire abatre tascherez;
Jusques à quand emprises vaines,
Sans fruict, et d'abusions pleines,
Aimerez vous et chercherez?

Clément Marot

When I invoke thee, alas, listen,
O God, to my cause and right:
My stricken heart seeks release,
do not deprive me of thy pity:
But hearken to my prayer.
How long, inhuman nations,
will you seek to abase my glory;
how long vain undertakings,
fruitless and full of delusions,
will you love and seek out?

Psalm 5

Aux paroles que je veux dire,
Plaise toy l'oreille prester,
Et à cognoistre t'arrester,
Pourquoy mon coeur pense et soupire,
Souverain Sire.

Clément Marot

To the words I wish to say,
may it please thee to lend an ear,
and to pause so as to recognize,
why my heart yearns and sighs,
Sovereign Lord.

Psalm 6

Ne vueilles pas ô Sire,
Me reprendre en ton ire,
Moy qui t'ay irrité:
N'en ta fureur terrible,
Me punir de l'horrible
Tourment qu'ay merité.

Clément Marot

Please do not wish, O Lord,
to reprove me in thy wrath,
I who have angered thee:
In thy terrible fury,
do not punish me with the horrible
torment that I have deserved.

Psalm 7

Mon Dieu, j'ay en toy esperance,
Donne moy donc sauve asseurance,
De tant d'ennemis inhumains,
Et fay que ne tombe en leurs mains,
A fin que leur chef ne me grippe,
Et ne me derompe et dissipe,
Ainsi qu'un lion devorant,
Sans que nul me soit secourant.

Clément Marot

My God, my hope is in thee,
give me therefore safe assurance,
against such inhuman enemies,
and keep me from falling into their hands,
so that their leader can not seize me,
and rend and scatter me,
like a devouring lion,
from whom there is no rescue.

Psalm 8

O nostre Dieu, et Seigneur amiable,
Combien ton nom est grand et admirable
Par tout ce val terrestre spacieux,
Qui ta puissance esleve sur les cieux.

Clément Marot

O our God, and kindly Lord,
how great and marvelous is thy name
throughout the wide earthly valley,
that exalts thy power in the heavens.

Psalm 9

De tout mon coeur t'exalteray,
Seigneur, et si raconteray,
Toutes tes oeuvres nompareilles
Qui sont dignes de grans merveilles.

Clément Marot

With all my heart I shall exalt thee,
Lord, and thus shall retell,
all thine unparalleled works
which are worthy of great marvels.

Psalm 10

D'où vient cela, Seigneur, je te suppli,
Que loin de nous te tiens les yeux couvers?
Te caches tu pour nous mettre en oubli,
Mesmes au temps qui est dur et divers?
Par leur orgeuil sont ardens les pervers,
A tormenter l'humble qui peu se prise:
Fay que sur eux tomble leur entreprise.

Clément Marot

From whence does this come, Lord, I entreat you,
that thou keepest far from us with covered eyes?
Dost thou hide thyself in order to forget us,
even in a hard and changeful time?
In their arrogance the wicked are inflamed,
to torment the humble one who has so little:
Let their own endeavors fall upon them.

Psalm 11

Veu que du tout en Dieu mon coeur s'appuie,
Je mesbahi comment de vostre mont,
Plustot qu'oiseau, dites que je m'enfuye.
Vray est que l'arc les malins tendu m'ont,
Et sur la corde ont assis leurs sagettes,
Pour contre ceux qui de coeur justes sont,
Les descocher jusques en leur cachettes.

Clément Marot

Given that my heart rests entirely in God,
I am astounded how from your mountain,
sooner than a bird, you say that I flee.
It is true that the wicked have aimed their bow at me,
and on the string have readied their arrows,
against those who are upright in heart,
to let them fly from their ambush.

Psalm 12

Donne secours, Seigneur, il en est heure:
Car d'hommes droits sommes tous desnuez:
Entre les fils des hommes ne demeure
Un qui ait foy, tant sont diminuez.

Clément Marot

Give help, Lord, it is time:
For we are stripped of upright men:
Among the sons of men dwells not
a single one who has faith, they are so diminished.

Psalm 13

Jusques a quand as establi,
Seigneur, de me mettre en oubli?
Est-ce à jamais? Par combien d'aage
Destourneras tu ton visage,
De moy, las! d'angoisse rempli?

Clément Marot

Until when hast thou decreed,
Lord, to forget me?
Is it forever? Through how many ages
wilt thou turn away thy face,
from me, alas! filled with anguish?

Psalm 14

Le fol malin en son coeur dit et croit,
Que Dieu n'est point, et corrompt et renverse,
Ses meurs, sa vie, horibles faits exerce.
Pas un tout seul ne fait rien bon ne droit,
Ni ne voudroit.

Clément Marot

The wicked fool says and believes in his heart,
that there is no God, and corrupts and overturns,
his customs, his life, performing horrible deeds.
Not a single one does good or right,
nor wishes to.

Psalm 15

Qui est-ce qui conversera,
O Seigneur en ton tabernacle?
Et qui est celuy qui sera
Si heureux que par grace aura
Sur ton saint mont seur habitacle?

Clément Marot

Who shall remain,
O Lord in thy tabernacle?
And who is the one who shall be
so happy that through grace he will have
his dwelling in thy holy mountain?

Psalm 16

Sois moy, Seigneur, ma gard' et mon appuy:	Be unto me, Lord, my safeguard and my resting place:
Car en toy gist toute mon esperance.	For in thee lives all my hope.
Sus donc aussi, ô mon ame, dy luy	Arise then, O my soul, say to him
Seigneur, tu as sur moy toute puissance:	Lord, thou hast all power over me:
Et toutes fois point n'y a d'oeuvre mienne,	Yet there is no work of mine,
Dont jusqu'à toy quelque profit revienne.	from which any profit returns to thee.
Théodore de Bèze	

Psalm 17

Seigneur, enten à mon bon droit,	Lord, listen to my right,
Enten, helas! ce que je crie:	listen, alas! to what I cry:
Vueilles ouir ce que je prie,	Be pleased to hear what I pray,
Et de bouche et de coeur tout droit.	with both mouth and heart upright.
De toy, qui cognois toute chose,	From thee, who knowest everything,
Je veux jugement recevoir:	I want to receive judgment:
Je te pri' toy-mesme de voir	I pray thee to see for thyself
Le droit de ce que je propose.	the justice of what I propose.
Théodore de Bèze	

Psalm 18

Je t'aymeray en toute obeissance,	I shall love thee in complete obedience,
Tant que vivray, ô mon Dieu ma puissance,	as long as I shall live, O my God my strength,
Dieu est mon roc, mon rempart haut et seur,	God is my rock, my rampart high and secure,
C'est ma rançon c'est mon fort defenseur.	he is my ransom and my strong defender.
En luy seul gist ma fiance parfaite,	In him alone lives my perfect confidence,
C'est mon pavois, mes armes, ma retraite.	he is my shield, my armor, my retreat.
Quand je l'exalt' et prie en ferme foy,	When I exalt him and pray in firm faith,
Soudain recoux des ennemis me voy.	I find immediate rescue from enemies.
Dangers de mort un jour m'environnerent,	When perils of death surrounded me,
Et grans torrens de malins m'estonnerent,	and great floods of wicked ones staggered me,
J'estoy' bien pres du sepulcre venu,	I came close to the tomb indeed,
Et des filets de la mort prevenu.	and was saved from the snares of death.
Clément Marot	

Psalm 19

Les cieux en chacun lieu,	The heavens in each place,
La puissance de Dieu	the power of God
Racontent aux humains.	tell to human beings.
Ce grand entour espars,	This great wide expanse,
Publie en toutes pars	makes known everywhere
L'ouvrage de ses mains.	the work of his hands.
Jour apres jour coulant,	Day flowing after day,
Du Seigneur va parlant,	speaks of the Lord,
Par longue experience.	through long experience.
La nuict suivant la nuict,	Night following night,
Nous presche et nous instruit	preaches to us and instructs us
De sa grand sapience.	about his great wisdom.
Clément Marot	

Psalm 20

Le Seigneur ta priere entende
En ta necessité,
Le Dieu de Jacob te defende
En ton adversité.
De ton lieu sainct en ta complainte
A tes maux il subviene,
De Sion sa montaigne sainte
Il te gard' et soustienne.

Théodore de Bèze

May the Lord hear thy prayer
in thy necessity,
may the God of Jacob defend thee
in thine adversity.
From thy holy place in thy complaint
may he relieve thine ills,
from Zion his holy mountain
may he guard and sustain thee.

Psalm 21

Seigneur, le Roy s'esjouira
D'avoir eu delivrance
Par ta grande puissance.
O combien joyeux il sera,
D'ainsi soudain se voir
Recoux par ton pouvoir.

Théodore de Bèze

Lord, the King will rejoice
to have been delivered
by thy great power.
O how joyous he will be,
thus suddenly to find himself
rescued by thy might.

Psalm 22

Mon Dieu, mon Dieu pourquoy m'as tu laissé
Loin de secours, d'ennuy tant oppressé,
Et loin du cri que je t'ay addressé
En ma complainte?
De jour mon Dieu, je t'invoque sans feinte,
Et toutesfois ne respond ta voix saincte:
De nuict aussi, et n'ay dequoy esteinte
Soit ma clameur.

Clément Marot

My God, my God, why hast thou abandoned me
far from assistance, so oppressed by misery,
and far from the plaint which I made to thee
in my crying?
Daily, my God, I invoke thee honestly,
yet thy holy voice does not answer:
By night also, and without ceasing
let my crying be [heard].

Psalm 23

Mon Dieu me pait sous sa puissance haute:
C'est mon berger, de rien je n'auray faute,
En tect bien seur, joignant les beaux herbages
Coucher me fait, me mein' aux clairs rivages:
Traite ma vie en douceur tres-humaine,
Et pour son Nom par droits sentiers me meine.

Clément Marot

My God pastures me under his exalted power:
He is my shepherd, nothing shall I lack,
In a very safe stable near lovely meadows
he makes me lie down, he leads me to limpid shores:
He treats my life with very benevolent sweetness,
and for his Name leads me along righteous paths.

Psalm 24

La terre au Seigneur appartient,
Tout ce qu'en sa rondeur contient,
Et ceux qui habitent en elle:
Sur mer fondement luy donna,
L'enrichit et l'environna,
De mainte riviere tresbelle.

Clément Marot

The earth belongs to the Lord,
all that is contained in its round,
and those who live on it:
He founded it upon the sea,
adorned it and surrounded it,
with many a beautiful river.

Psalm 25

A toy mon Dieu, mon coeur monte,
En toy mon espoir ay mis:
Fay que je ne tombe à honte,
Au gré de mes ennemis.
Honte n'auront voirement
Ceux qui dessus toy s'appuyent:
Mais bien ceux qui durement,
Et sans cause les ennuyent.

Clément Marot

To thee my God, my heart climbs up,
I have placed my hope in thee:
Let me not fall into shame,
at the mercy of my enemies.
Verily they will never be ashamed
who rest in thee:
But [let] them [be put to shame] indeed who harshly,
and without cause trouble them.

Psalm 26

Seigneur, garde mon droict:
Car j'ay en cest endroit
Cheminé droit et rondement:
J'ay en Dieu esperance,
Qui me donne asseurance,
Que choir ne pourray nullement.

Théodore de Bèze

Lord, safeguard my right:
For I have in this place
walked straight and briskly:
I hope in God,
who gives me assurance,
that I can in no way fall.

Psalm 27

Le Seigneur est la clarté qui m'addresse,
Et mon salut, que doy-je redouter?
Le Seigneur est l'appuy qui me redresse,
Où est celuy qui peust m'espouvanter?
Quand les malins m'ont dressé leurs combats,
Pour me cuider manger à belles dents,
Tous ces haineux, ces ennemis mordens,
J'ay veu broncher, et trebuscher en bas.

Théodore de Bèze

The Lord is my light,
and my safety, what should I dread?
The Lord is the resting place that restores me,
where is the one who can frighten me?
When wicked ones attacked me,
to cook and devour me with their teeth,
all those hateful ones, those deadly enemies,
I saw stumble and stagger down.

Psalm 28

O Dieu qui es ma forteresse,
C'est à toy que mon cri s'addresse:
Ne vueilles au besoin te taire,
Autrement je ne sçay que faire,
Sinon à ceux me comparer,
Qu'on veut au sepulchre enterrer.

Théodore de Bèze

O God who art my fortress,
it is to thee that my cry is addressed:
Please do not be silent,
otherwise I know not what to do,
except to compare myself to those,
who want to be buried in the tomb.

Psalm 29

Vous tous Princes et Seigneurs,
Remplis de gloire et d'honneurs,
Rendez, rendez au Seigneur,
Toute force et tout honneur.
Faites luy recognoissance
Qui responde à sa puissance:
En sa demeure tressaincte
Ployés les genoux en crainte.

Théodore de Bèze

All you Princes and Lords,
filled with glory and honors,
render, render to the Lord,
all strength and all honor.
Acknowledge him
who responds in his power:
In his holy dwelling
bend your knees in fear.

Psalm 30

Seigneur, puis que m'as retiré,
Puis que n'as jamais enduré,
Que mes haineux eussent de quoy
Se rire et se moquer de moy,
La gloire qu'en as meritée,
Par mes vers te sera chantée.

Théodore de Bèze

Lord, since thou raised me up,
since thou hast never allowed,
those who hate me
to laugh and mock at me,
The glory which thou hast deserved,
will be sung to thee by my verses.

Psalm 31

J'ay mis en toy mon esperance,
Garde moy donc, Seigneur,
D'eternel deshonneur:
Octroye moy ma delivrance,
Par ta grand bonté haute,
Qui jamais ne fit faute.

Théodore de Bèze

I place in thee my hope,
save me therefore, Lord,
from unending dishonor:
Grant me my deliverance,
by thy great high goodness,
that can never err.

Psalm 32

O bien heureux celuy dont les commises
Transgressions sont par grace remises,
Duquel aussi les iniques pechés
Devant son Dieu sont couvers et cachez!
O combien plein de bonheur je repute
L'homm' a qui Dieu son peché point n'impute!
Et en l'esprit duquel n'habite point
D'hypocrisie et de fraude un seul poinct!

Clément Marot

O happy the one whose committed
transgressions are pardoned by grace,
whose iniquitous sins
are covered and hidden before his God!
O how full of happiness I deem
the man to whom God does not impute his sin!
And in whose spirit lives not the least
hypocrisy and deception!

Psalm 33

Resveillez vous chacun fidelle,
Menez au Dieu joye or' endroit.
Louange est tresseante et belle
En la bouche de l'homme droit.
Sur la douce harpe,
Pendue en escharpe,
Le Seigneur louez:
De luts, d'espinettes,
Sainctes chansonnettes
A son nom jouez.

Clément Marot

Arise, each faithful one,
now rejoice in God.
Praise is very fitting and beautiful
in the mouth of the upright man.
On the sweet harp,
hung slantwise across the chest,
praise the Lord:
On lutes, on spinnets,
holy canzonets
play to his name.

Psalm 34

Jamais ne cesseray
De magnifier le Seigneur,
En ma bouche auray son honneur,
Tant que vivant seray.
Mon coeur plaisir n'aura
Qu'à voir son Dieu glorifié.
Dont maint bon coeur humilié
L'oyant s'esjouira.

Théodore de Bèze

Never shall I cease
to magnify the Lord,
his honor will be in my mouth,
as long as I shall live.
My heart will take pleasure only
in seeing God glorified.
Many a good humble heart
hearing this will rejoice.

Psalm 35

Deba contre mes debateurs,
Comba, Seigneur, mes combateurs,
Empoigne moy bouclier et lance,
Et pour me secourir t'avance.
Charge les, et marche au devant,
Garde les d'aller plus avant.
Di à mon ame, Ame, je suis
Celuy qui garentir te puis.

Théodore de Bèze

Contend with my adversaries,
fight, Lord, those who fight me,
seize for me buckler and lance,
and come forward to help me.
Charge them and go ahead,
stop them from advancing.
Say to my soul, Soul, I am
he who can protect thee.

Psalm 36

Du malin le meschant vouloir
Parl' en mon coeur, et me fait voir,
Qu'il n'a de Dieu la crainte:
Car tant se plaist en son erreur,
Que l'avoir en haine et horreur,
C'est bien forc' et contrainte.
Son parler est nuisant et fin:
Doctrine va fuyant, à fin
De jamais bien ne faire:
Song' en son lit meschanceté:
Au chemin tors est arresté:
A nul mal n'est contraire.

Clément Marot

The malicious will of the wicked
speaks in my heart, and makes me see,
that he has no fear of God:
For he is so pleased with himself in his error,
that to hold him in hate and horror,
it is indeed forced and constrained.
His speech is harmful and sharp:
Teaching flees away, so that
he does no good ever:
He dreams of mischief in his bed:
He is fixed on a wrong path:
He is averse to no evil.

Psalm 37

Ne sois faché si durant ceste vie,
Souvent tu vois prosperer les meschans
Et des malins aux biens ne porte envie:
Car en ruine à la fin trebuchans,
Seront fauchez comme foin en peu d'heure,
Et secheront comme l'herbe des champs.

Clément Marot

Be not angered if during this life,
thou often seest malicious ones prosper
and envy not the advantages of wicked ones:
For finally, stumbling into ruin,
they will be mown down like hay in a little time,
and will wither like grass in the fields.

Psalm 38

Las! en ta fureur aigue,
Ne m'argue
De mon faict, Dieu tout puissant:
Ton ardeur un peu retire,
N'en ton ire
Ne me puni languissant.

Clément Marot

Alas! in thy sharp fury,
do not rebuke me
for my deed, God almighty:
Withdraw thy passion a little,
nor in thine ire
punish me, languishing.

Psalm 39

J'ay dit en moy, de pres je viseray
A tout cela que je feray,
Pour ne parler un seul mot de travers,
En voyant debout le pervers.
Voire deusse-je à fin de ne parler,
Ma propre bouche emmuseler.

Théodore de Bèze

I said to myself, I will closely watch
everything that I do,
so as not to speak a single word amiss,
when seeing evil ones standing by.
Verily in order not to speak, I ought
to muzzle my own mouth.

Psalm 40

Apres avoir constamment attendu	After having waited steadfastly
De l'Eternel la volonté,	on the will of the Eternal,
Il s'est tourné de mon costé,	he turned to my side,
Et à mon cri au besoin entendu.	and listened to my cry of need.
Hors de fange et d'ordure,	From the mire and the muck,
Et profondeur obscure,	and dark depth,
D'un gouffre m'a tiré:	he pulled me from the pit:
A mes pieds affermis,	Set me on my feet,
Et au chemin remis,	in the right path,
Sus un roc asseuré.	on a solid rock.

Théodore de Bèze

Psalm 41

O bien-heureux qui juge sagement	O happy the one who judges wisely
Du pauvre en son tourment!	the poor man in his torment!
Certainement Dieu le soulagera,	Surely God will comfort him,
Quand affligé sera:	when he is afflicted:
Dieu le rendra sain et sauf, et fera	God will restore him whole and unscathed, and will make
Qu'encore il florira:	him flourish again:
Point ne voudra l'exposer aux souhaits	He will not deliver him over to the wishes
Que ses haineux ont faits.	that hateful ones have made.

Théodore de Bèze

Psalm 42

Ainsi qu'on oit le cerf bruire	Just as one hears the hart make a noise
Pourchassant le frais des eaux,	hunting for fresh water,
Ainsi mon coeur qui soupire,	thus my heart which sighs,
Seigneur apres tes ruisseaux,	Lord for thy running streams,
Va tousjours criant, suyvant	goes crying always, following
Le grand, le grand Dieu vivant.	the great, the great living God.
Helas donques, quand sera-ce,	Alas then, when will it be,
Que verray de Dieu la face?	that I shall see the face of God?

Théodore de Bèze

Psalm 43

Revenge moy, pren la querelle	Avenge me, take up my quarrel
De moy, Seigneur par ta merci,	Lord, in thy mercy,
Contre la gent faulse et cruelle:	against the false and cruel nation:
De l'homme rempli de cautelle,	From the man full of cunning,
Et en sa malice endurci,	and hardened in malice,
Delivre moy aussi.	also deliver me.

Clément Marot

Psalm 44

Or avons nous de noz aureilles,	Now we have with our own ears,
Seigneur, entendu tes merveilles:	Lord, heard thy marvels:
Raconter à noz peres vieux,	Told to our ancient fathers,
Faites jadis et devant eux.	already done before them.
Ta main à les peuples chassez,	Thy hand pursued the peoples,
Plantant noz peres en leur place:	planting our fathers in their place:
Tu as les peuples oppressés,	Thou hast put down the peoples,
Y faisant germer nostre race.	making our race spring up there.

Théodore de Bèze

Psalm 45

Propos exquis faut que de mon coeur sorte:
Car du Roy veux dire chanson de sorte,
Qu'à ceste fois ma langue mieux dira,
Qu'un scribe prompt de plume n'escrira.
Le mieux formé tu es d'humaine race:
En ton parler gist merveilleuse grace.
Parquoy, Dieu fait que toute nation
Sans fin te louë en benediction.

Clément Marot

A lovely theme must come only from my heart:
For of the King I want to sing, so
that at this time my tongue will speak better,
than a scribe swift of pen will write.
Thou art the fairest of the human race:
In thy speech lies marvelous grace.
Hence God makes every nation
eternally praise thee with blessings.

Psalm 46

Des qu'adversité nous offense,
Dieu nous est appuy et deffense:
Au besoin l'avons esprouvé,
Et grand secours en luy trouvé:
Dont plus n'aurons crainte ne doute,
Et deust trembler la terre toute,
Et les montaignes abysmer
Au milieu de la haute mer.

Clément Marot

As soon as adversity injures us,
God is our support and defense:
We have tried him in [our] need
and found great help in him:
Of this we will have no more fear or doubt,
though the whole earth should tremble,
and the mountains plunge
into the middle of the deep sea.

Psalm 47

Or sus, tous humains,
Frappez en vos mains:
Qu'on oye sonner,
Qu'on oye entonner
Le nom solennel
De Dieu eternel.
C'est le Dieu treshaut
Que craindr' il nous faut.
Le grand Roy qui fait
Sentir en effect
Sa force au travers
De tout l'univers.

Théodore de Bèze

Now arise, all people,
clap your hands:
So that one may hear sound,
so that one may hear thunder
the solemn name
of God eternal.
It is the most high God
whom we should fear.
The great King who makes
[us] to feel
his power throughout
the whole universe.

Psalm 48

C'est en sa tressaincte cité,
Lieu choisi pour sa sainctetė,
Que Dieu desploye en excellence
Sa gloire et sa magnificence.
La montaigne de Sion,
Devers le Septentrion,
Ville au grand Roy consacrée,
Est en si belle contrée,
Que la terre universelle
Ne doit s'esjouir qu'en elle.

Théodore de Bèze

It is in his most holy city,
a place chosen for its sanctity,
that God displays in excellence
his glory and his magnificence.
The mountain of Zion,
towards the North,
city consecrated to the great King,
is in such a beautiful region,
that the universal earth
should rejoice only in her.

Psalm 49

Peuples oyez, et l'aureille prestez,
Hommes mortels qui le monde habitez,
Des plus petis jusques aux plus puissans,
Riches hautains, et pauvres languissans,
Sages propos ma bouche annoncera,
Graves discours mon coeur entamera.
A mes beaux mots l'aureille je veux tendre,
Et sur mon lut grand's choses vous apprendre.
Théodore de Bèze

Peoples hear, and lend an ear,
mortal men who inhabit the world,
from the most humble right to the most powerful,
rich and arrogant, weak and poor,
my mouth will proclaim wise sayings,
my heart will set forth a serious discourse.
I want to direct the ear to my lovely words,
and I will teach you great things on my lute.

Psalm 50

Le Dieu le fort, l'Eternel parlera,
Et hault et clair la terre appellera:
De l'Orient jusques à l'Occident,
Devers Sion, Dieu clair et evident
Apparoistra, orné de beauté toute,
Nostre grand Dieu viendra, n'en faictes doute.
Clément Marot

I shall speak of God the strong, the Eternal,
and loud and clear I shall call to the earth:
From the East to the West,
from Zion, God bright and unmistakable
will appear, adorned in all beauty,
our great God will come, do not doubt it.

Psalm 51

Misericorde au pauvre vicieux,
Dieu tout puissant, selon ta grand' clemence:

Use â ce coup de ta bonté immence,
Pour effacer mon fait pernicieux.
Lave moy, Sire, et relave bien fort
De ma commise iniquité mauvaise,
Et du peché qui ma rendu si ord,
Me nettoyer d'eau de grace te plaise.
Clément Marot

Have mercy on a poor villain,
almighty God, according to thy great loving-kindness:
In one stroke, extend thine immense goodness,
to wipe out my pernicious deed.
Wash me, Lord, and wash me thoroughly
of the evil deed I have committed,
and of sin which has made me so foul,
be pleased to cleanse me with the water of grace.

Psalm 52

Di moy, malheureux, qui te fies
En ton authorité,
D'ou vient que tu te glorifies
De ta meschanceté?
Quoy que soit, de Dieu le secours
A tous les jours son cours.
Théodore de Bèze

Tell me, unhappy one, whom thou trustest
in thine authority,
why thou pridest thyself
in thy mischief?
Whatever may be, the help of God
is present at all times.

Psalm 53

Le fol malin en son coeur dit et croit
Que Dieu n'est point, et corrompt et renverse
Ses meurs, sa vie, horibles faits exerce:
Pas un tout seul ne fait rien bon, ne droit,
Ni ne voudroit.
Théodore de Bèze

The wicked fool says and believes in his heart
that there is no God, and corrupts and overturns
his customs, his life, performing horrible deeds:
Not a single one does good or right,
nor wishes to.

Psalm 54

O Dieu tout puissant, sauve moy
Par ton Nom et force immortelle,
Et pour defendre ma querelle
Fay sortir la force de toy.
Oy l'oraison que je feray,
Plaise toy l'aureille me tendre,
O Eternel, à fin d'entendre
Tous les mots que je te diray.

Théodore de Bèze

O God almighty, save me
by thy Name and immortal strength,
and to defend my cause
send forth thy power.
Hear the prayer I shall make,
be pleased to direct thine ear to me,
O Eternal, so as to understand
every word I shall say to thee.

Psalm 55

Exauce, ô mon Dieu, ma priere,
Ne te recule point arriere
De l'oraison que te presente.
Entens à moy, exauce moy,
Tandis qu'en priant devant toy
Je me complains et me tourmente.

Théodore de Bèze

Hear my prayer, O my God,
do not draw back in the least
from the prayer I present.
Listen to me, hear me,
while praying before thee
I lament and torment myself.

Psalm 56

Misericorde à moy pauvre affligé,
O Seigneur Dieu! car me voyla mangé
De ce meschant qui me tient assiegé,
Et tout les jours m'oppresse.
Mes envieux me devorent sans cesse:
Car contre moy un grand nombre se dresse,
O Dieu treshaut! mais quand la peur me presse,
En toy mon espoir j'ay.

Théodore de Bèze

Have mercy on me, poor and afflicted,
O Lord God! for there thou seest me swallowed up
by the wicked one who beseiges me,
and oppresses me daily.
Those who envy me devour me ceaselessly:
For a great number are arrayed against me,
O God most high! but when fear weighs me down,
my hope is in thee.

Psalm 57

Ayes pitié, ayes pitié de moy:
Car, ô mon Dieu, mon ame espere en toy:
Et jusqu'à tant que ces meschans rebelles
Soyent tous passez, esperance ne foy
Jamais n'auray qu'en l'ombre de tes ailes.

Théodore de Bèze

Have pity, have pity on me:
For, O my God, my soul hopes in thee:
And until those wicked rebels
be all gone, neither hope nor faith
shall I ever have except in the shadow of thy wings.

Psalm 58

Entre vous conseilliers, qui estes
Liguez, et bandez contre moy,
Dites un peu, en bonne foy,
Est-ce justice que vous faites?
Enfans d'Adam, vous meslez vous
De faire la raison à tous?

Théodore de Bèze

Among you counsellors, who are
in league and banded together against me,
say briefly, in good faith,
is it justice that you make?
Children of Adam, do you intervene
to do rightly to all?

Psalm 59

Mon Dieu l'ennemy m'environne,
Ta bonté donc secours me donne,
Garde moy des gens irritez,
Qui dessus moy se sont jettez.
Delivre moy de l'adversaire
Qui ne demande qu'a mal-faire,
Sauve moy des sanglantes mains
De ces meurtriers tant inhumains.

Théodore de Bèze

My God the enemy surrounds me,
of thy goodness therefore give me help,
guard me from the angry nations,
who have thrown themselves upon me.
Deliver me from the adversary
who asks only to do evil,
save me from the bloody hands
of these so inhuman murderers.

Psalm 60

O Dieu qui nous as deboutez,
Qui nous as de toy escartez,
Jadis contre nous irrité,
Tourne toy de nostre costé.
Tu as nostre païs secoux,
Et cassé à force de coups:
Guari sa plaie qui le presse,
Car tu vois comment il s'abaisse.

Théodore de Bèze

O God who hast rejected us,
who hast scattered us from thee,
of old angered against us,
turn to our side.
Thou hast shaken our country,
and broken it by strong blows:
Heal its wound that afflicts it,
for thou seest how it is bowed down.

Psalm 61

Entens pourquoy je m'écrie,
Je te prie,
O mon Dieu! exauce moy.
Du bout du monde mon ame,
Qui se pasme,
Ne reclame autre que toy.

Théodore de Bèze

Listen to why I cry out,
I pray thee,
O my God, hear me.
From the end of the earth my soul,
fainting,
begs for none but thee.

Psalm 62

Mon ame en Dieu tant seulement
Trouve tout son contentement:
Car luy seul est ma sauve-garde.
Luy seul est mon roc eslevé,
Mon salut, mon fort esprouvé:
De tomber trop bas je n'ay garde.

Théodore de Bèze

My soul only in God
finds all its contentment:
For in him alone is my safety.
He alone is my high rock,
my health, my proven strength:
I have no other guard than he to keep me from falling too low.

Psalm 63

O Dieu! je n'ay Dieu fors que toy,
Dés le matin je te reclame,
Et de ta soif je sen mon ame
Toute pasmée dedans moy.
Les pauvres sens d'humeur tous vuides
De mon corps mat et alteré,
Tousjours, Seigneur, t'ont desiré
En ces lieux deserts et arides.

Théodore de Bèze

O God! I have no God but thee,
early in the morning I call to thee,
and from thirst for thee I feel my soul
all fainting within me.
The poor senses, empty of moisture,
of my dull, parched body,
have always longed for thee, Lord
in these arid desert places.

Psalm 64

Entens à ce que je veux dire,
Quand je te prie sauve moy:
Que de mes ennemis l'effroy,
Ne vienne ma vie destruire,
Souverain Sire.

Listen to what I want to say,
when I pray thee, save me:
May fear of my enemies
not come to destroy my life,
Sovereign Lord.

Théodore de Bèze

Psalm 65

O Dieu, la gloire qui t'est deuë
T'attends dedans Sion:
En ce lieu te sera renduë
De voeus oblation:
Et d'autant que la voix entendre
Des tiens il te plaira,
Tout droit à toy se venir rendre
Toutes gens on verra.

O God, the glory due to thee
awaits thee in Zion:
In that place will be rendered to thee
oblations and vows:
And all the more so to hear the voice
of thy people it will please thee,
to make their way straight to thee
all nations will be seen.

Théodore de Bèze

Psalm 66

Or sus louëz Dieu tout le monde,
Chantez le los de son renom:
Chantez si haut que tout redonde
De la loüange de son Nom.
Dites, ô que tu es terrible,
Seigneur, en tout ce que tu fais:
Tes haineux, tant es invincible,
Te flatent pour avoir la paix.

Arise now, praise God all the earth,
sing the praise of his renown:
Sing so loudly that everything echoes
with the praise of his Name.
Say, O how terrible thou art,
Lord, in everything thou dost:
Thou art so invincible that those who hate thee,
flatter thee in order to have peace.

Théodore de Bèze

Psalm 67

Dieu nous soit doux et favorable,
Nous benissant par sa bonté,
Et de son visage amiable
Nous face luire la clarté:
A fin que sa voye
En terre se voye,
Et que bien à poinct
Chacun puisse entendre
Où c'est qu'il faut tendre,
Pour ne perir point.

God be sweet and kindly to us,
blessing us by his goodness,
and his amiable face
shine on us with brightness:
So that his way
may be known on earth,
and indeed exactly
each one may understand
where one must turn,
in order not to perish.

Théodore de Bèze

Psalm 68

Que Dieu se monstre seulement,
Et on verra soudainement
Abandonner la place.
Le camp des ennemis espars,
Et ses haineux de toutes pars
Fuir devant sa face:
Dieu les fera tous s'enfuir,
Ainsi qu'on void s'esvanoüir
Un amas de fumée,
Comme la cire au pres du feu,
Ainsi des meschans devant Dieu,
La force est consumée.

Let God only show himself,
and suddenly one will see
the place abandoned.
[One will see] the camp of the enemies scattered,
and all those who hate him
flee before his face:
God will make them all flee,
as one sees disappear
a drift of smoke,
as wax near fire,
so before God the wicked ones'
strength is consumed.

Théodore de Bèze

Psalm 69

Helas! Seigneur je te pri' sauve moy
Car les eaux m'ont saisi jusques à l'ame:
Et au bourbier tres-profond et infame,
Sans fond ne rive enfondré je me voy.
Ainsi plongé l'eau m'emporte, tant las
De m'escrier, que j'en ay gorge seiche:
Et de mon Dieu attendant le soulas,
De mes deux yeux la vigeur se desseiche.
Théodore de Bèze

Alas! Lord I pray thee save me
for the floods have seized even my soul:
And in a slough deep and vile,
without bottom or banks I am mired.
Thus submerged the water sweeps me away, despite
my crying until my throat is dry:
And awaiting solace from my God,
my eyes are drained of life.

Psalm 70

O Dieu où mon espoir j'ay mis,
Vien soudain à ma delivrance:
Seigneur que ton aide s'avance
Encontre tous mes ennemis.
Quiconques pourchasse mon ame,
Soit remply de honte et d'esmoy.
Quiconques, di-je en veut à moy,
Tourne en ariere tout infame.
Théodore de Bèze

O God in whom I placed my trust,
come soon to deliver me:
Lord let thy help be advanced
against all my enemies.
Whoever pursues my soul,
let him be filled with shame and alarm.
Whoever, I say, wishes such against me,
[let him be] turned back, every infamous one.

Psalm 71

J'ay mis en toy mon esperance
Garde moy donc, Seigneur,
D'eternel deshonneur:
Ottroye moy ma delivrance
Par ta misericorde,
Et ton secours m'accorde.
Théodore de Bèze

I placed my hope in thee,
keep me therefore, Lord,
from eternal dishonor:
Grant me my deliverance
by thy mercy,
and accord me thy help.

Psalm 72

Tes jugemens, Dieu veritable
Baille au Roy pour regner:
Vueilles ta justice equitable
Au fils du Roy donner:
Il tiendra ton peuple en justice,
Chassant iniquité:
A tes pauvres sera propice,
Leur gardant equité.
Clément Marot

Thy judgments, true God,
give to the King that he may reign:
Be pleased, thy equitable justice
to give to the son of the King:
He will keep thy people in justice,
pursuing iniquity:
Toward thy poor he will act rightly,
preserving righteousness for them.

Psalm 73

Si est-ce que Dieu est tres doux
A son Israël, voire à tous,
Qui gardent en toute droicture
Leur conscience entiere et pure.
Mais j'ay esté tout prest à voir
Mes pieds le bon chemin laisser,
Et mes pas tellement glisser,
Que me suis veu tout prest de choir.
Théodore de Bèze

If God is very sweet
to his Israel, indeed [he is so] to all,
who keep in complete uprightness
their conscience whole and pure.
But I well nigh saw
my feet leave the good path,
and my steps slip in such a way,
that I almost fell.

Psalm 74

D'où vient, Seigneur, que tu nous as espars,
Et si long temps ta fureur enflamée
Vomit sur nous tant espesse fumée,
Voire sur nous les brebis de tes parcs?

Théodore de Bèze

Why, Lord, hast thou scattered us,
and for so long thy hot fury
belches forth upon us such smoke,
verily on us the sheep of thy pastures?

Psalm 75

O Seigneur, loué sera,
Loüé sera ton renom.
Car la gloire de ton Nom
Pres de nous s'approchera:
Et de nous seront chantez
Les hauts faits de tes bontez.

Théodore de Bèze

O Lord, be praised,
thy renown be praised.
For the glory of thy Name
approaches near us:
And by us shall be sung
the high deeds of thy goodness.

Psalm 76

C'est en Judée proprement,
Que Dieu s'est acquis un renom:
C'est en Israël voirement,
Qu'on void la force de son Nom:
En Salem est son tabernacle,
En Sion son sainct habitacle.

Théodore de Bèze

It is in Judea indeed
that God has acquired renown:
It is in Israel truly
that the power of his Name is seen:
In Salem is his tabernacle,
in Zion his holy dwelling.

Psalm 77

A Dieu ma voix j'ay haussée,
Et ma clameur addressée,
A Dieu ma voix a monté,
Et mon Dieu m'a escouté.
Au jour de ma grand' detresse,
Dieu a esté mon addresse:
Et du soir au lendemain
Je luy ay tendu la main.

Théodore de Bèze

To God I raised my voice,
and addressed my cry,
to God my voice rose up,
and my God heard me.
In the day of my great distress,
God was my goal:
And evening and morning
I stretched out my hand to him.

Psalm 78

Sois ententif mon peuple à ma doctrine,
Soit ton oreille entierement encline
A bien ouïr tous les mots de ma bouche:
Car maintenant il faudra que je touche
Graves propos, et que par moy soient dits
Les grands secrets des oeuvres de jadis.

Théodore de Bèze

Be attentive, my people, to my teaching,
let thine ear wholly incline
to hear well all the words of my mouth:
For now I must touch on
serious things, and by me may be spoken
the great secrets of the works of the past.

Psalm 79

Les gens entrez sont en ton heritage,
Ils ont pollu, Seigneur, par leur outrage,
Ton Temple sainct, Jerusalem destruite,
Si qu'en monceaux de pierres l'on reduite.
Ils ont baillé les corps
De tes serviteurs morts,
Aux corbeaux pour les paistre.
La chair des biens vivans,
Aux animaux suivans
Bois et plaine champestre.

Clément Marot

The nations have entered into thy heritage,
they have defiled, Lord, by their outrage,
thy holy Temple, Jerusalem destroyed,
even reduced it to heaps of stones.
They have thrown the bodies
of thy dead servants,
to the ravens to feed them.
The flesh of the living [they have thrown],
to beasts following
in woods and fields.

Psalm 80

O pasteur d'Israël escoute,
Toy qui conduis la troupe toute,
De Joseph ainsi qu'un troupeau:
Monstre nous ton visage beau,
Toy qui te sieds en Majesté
Entre les Cherubins monté.

Théodore de Bèze

O shepherd of Israel hear,
Thou who leadest the whole tribe
of Joseph like a flock:
Show us thy beautiful face,
thou who seatest thyself in Majesty
mounted among the cherubim.

Psalm 81

Chantez gayement
A Dieu nostre force,
Que tout hautement
Au Dieu d'Israël,
Chant perpetuel
Chanter on s'efforce.

Théodore de Bèze

Sing cheerfully
to God our strength,
may loudly
to the God of Israel,
perpetual song
be sung.

Psalm 82

Dieu est assis en l'assemblée
Des Princes qu'il a assemblée.
Et des plus grands est au milieu,
Pour y presider comme Dieu.
Jusques à quand, juges iniques,
Ferez vous jugemens obliques,
Et vers ces meschans deceveurs
Userez vous de vos faveurs?

Théodore de Bèze

God is seated in the congregation
of Princes whom he has called together.
And he is in the midst of the greatest,
presiding there as God.
How long, iniquitous judges,
will you render crooked judgments,
and to wicked deceivers
dispense favors?

Psalm 83

O Dieu ne sois plus à recoy,
O Dieu ne demeure plus coy,
Et plus longuement ne t'arreste.
Car de ces ennemis la bande,
S'esmouvant de furie grande
A contre toy levé la teste.

Théodore de Bèze

O God be no longer in repose,
O God do not remain any longer silent,
and delay no longer.
For the band of enemies,
aroused to great fury
have raised up their heads against thee.

Psalm 84

O Dieu des armées! combien
Le sacré tabernacle tien
Est sur toutes choses aimable!
Mon coeur languit, mes sens ravis
Defaillent apres tes parvis,
O Seigneur Dieu tresdesirable!
Bref coeur et corps vont s'eslevant
Jusques à toy grand Dieu vivant.

Théodore de Bèze

O God of hosts! how
thy sacred tabernacle
is above all things pleasing!
My heart pines, my ravished senses
faint for thy courts,
O Lord God most desirable!
In brief, heart and body go soaring
even unto thee, great living God.

Psalm 85

Avec les tiens, Seigneur, tu as fait paix,	Lord, thou hast made peace with thy people,
Et de Jacob les prisonniers laschez,	and released the prisoners of Jacob,
Tu as quitté à ta gent ses mesfaits,	thou hast absolved thy nation of its misdeeds,
Voire tu as couvert tous ses pechez.	verily thou hast covered all its sins.
Tu as loin d'eux ton despit retiré,	Thou hast withdrawn thine anger far from them,
Et ton couroux violent moderé.	and moderated thy violent rage.
O Dieu! en qui gist le salut de nous,	O God! in whom lives our salvation,
Restabli-nous, appaisant ton courroux.	reestablish us, placating thy rage.
Théodore de Bèze	

Psalm 86

Mon Dieu preste moy l'oreille,	My God, lend me thine ear,
Par ta bonté nompareille:	in thy unequaled goodness:
Respon moi car plus n'en puis,	Answer me, for I can do no more,
Tant pauvre et affligé suis:	I am so poor and afflicted:
Garde je te pri' ma vie,	Guard, I pray thee, my life,
Car de bien faire ai envie,	for I long to do good,
Mon Dieu garde ton servant	my God, guard thy servant
En l'espoir de toy vivant.	living in hope of thee.
Clément Marot	

Psalm 87

Dieu pour fonder son tresseur habitacle,	God, to establish his very sure dwelling,
Es mons sacrez a prins affection,	in the holy mountains has held in affection,
Et mieux aime les portes de Sion,	and better loves the gates of Zion,
Que de Jacob oncques nul tabernacle.	than any tabernacle of Jacob.
Théodore de Bèze	

Psalm 88

O Dieu Eternel mon Sauveur,	O eternal God my savior,
Jour et nuict devant toy je crie:	day and night before thee I cry:
Parvienne ce dont je te prie	May my prayer reach
Jusques à toy par ta faveur:	even unto thee by thy favor:
Vueilles, helas! l'oreille tendre	Be pleased, alas! to direct thine ear
A mes clameurs pour les entendre.	to my entreaties to hear them.
Théodore de Bèze	

Psalm 89

Du Seigneur les bontez sans fin je chanterai,	The benefits of the Lord endlessly I shall sing,
Et sa fidelité à jamais prescherai:	and his faithfulness forever I shall proclaim:
Car c'est un point conclu, que sa grace est bastie,	For it is agreed that his grace is built,
Pour durer à jamais, comme on voit establie	to last forever, as one sees established
Dans le pourpris des cieux leur course invariable,	in the empurpled [night sky] the unvarying course of the heavens,
Signe seur et certain de son dire immuable.	a sure and certain sign of his unchanging word.
Théodore de Bèze	

Psalm 90

Tu as esté, Seigneur, nostre retraite	Thou hast been, Lord, our retreat
Et seur recours de lignée en lignée:	and sure recourse from generation to generation:
Mesme devant nulle montagne née,	Even before any mountain was born,
Et que le monde et la terre fust faite,	and the world and the earth were made,
Tu estois Dieu desja comme tu es,	thou wert God already as thou art,
Et comme aussi tu seras à jamais.	and as thou also wilt be forever.
Théodore de Bèze	

Psalm 91

Qui en la garde du haut Dieu
Pour jamais se retire,
En ombre bonne et en fort lieu
Retiré se peut dire.
Conclu donc en l'entendement,
Dieu est ma garde seure,
Ma haute tour et fondement,
Sur lequel je m'asseure.

Clément Marot

Who into the safekeeping of the high God
withdraws forever,
into a good shadow and into a strong place
can say he is withdrawn.
It is thus understood,
God is my certain guard,
my high tower and foundation,
in which I trust.

Psalm 92

O que c'est chose belle
De te louer, Seigneur,
Et du Treshaut, l'honneur
Chanter d'un coeur fidelle!
Preschant à la venuë
Du matin ta bonté,
Et ta fidelité
Quand la nuict est venue.

Théodore de Bèze

O how beautiful a thing it is
to praise thee, Lord,
and of the Most High, the honor
to sing with a faithful heart!
Preaching at the light
of dawn thy goodness,
and thy faithfulness
when night comes.

Psalm 93

Dieu est regnant de grandeur tout vestu,
Ceint et paré de force et de vertu,
Ayant le monde appuyé tellement,
Qu'il ne peut estre esbranlé nullement.

Théodore de Bèze

God is reigning all clothed in grandeur,
belted and robed in strength and virtue,
having so reinforced the world,
that it can in no way be shaken.

Psalm 94

O eternel Dieu des vengeances,
O Dieu punisseur des offences!
Fay toy congnoistre clairement:
Toy gouverneur de l'univers,
Hausse toy pour rendr' aux pervers,
De leur orgeuil le payement.

Théodore de Bèze

O eternal God of vengeance,
O God punisher of offences!
Make thyself clearly known:
Thou governor of the universe,
rise up to render to the wicked,
the payment for their arrogance.

Psalm 95

Sus, esgayons-nous au Seigneur,
Et chantons hautement l'honneur
De nostre salut et deffence.
Hâtons-nous de nous presenter
Devant sa face, et de chanter
Le los de sa magnificence.

Théodore de Bèze

Arise, let us rejoice in the Lord,
and sing loudly the honor
of our salvation and defense.
Let us hasten to present ourselves
before his face, and to sing
the praise of his magnificence.

Psalm 96

Chantez à Dieu chanson nouvelle,
Chantez, ô terre universelle,
Chantez, et son nom benissez,
Et de jour en jour annoncez
Sa delivrance solemnelle.

Théodore de Bèze

Sing to God a new song,
sing, O universal earth,
sing and bless his name,
and proclaim from day to day
his solemn deliverance.

Psalm 97

L'Eternel est regnant,
La terre maintenant
En soit joyeuse et gaye,
Toute isle s'en esgaye:
Espaisse obscurité
Cache sa majesté:
Justice et jugement,
Sont le seur fondement
De son throne arresté.

Théodore de Bèze

The Eternal is reigning,
let the earth now
be joyous and gay,
every isle therein rejoice:
Thick darkness
hides his majesty:
Justice and judgment,
are the sure foundation
of his established throne.

Psalm 98

Chantez à Dieu nouveau cantique,
Car il a puissamment ouvré:
Et par sa force magnifique,
Par soy-mesme il s'est delivré.
Dieu a fait son salut congnoistre,
Par lequel sommes garentis,
Et sa justice fait paroistre
En la presence des Gentils.

Théodore de Bèze

Sing to God a new song,
for he has worked powerfully:
And through his magnificent strength,
he has delivered himself.
God has made known his salvation,
by which we are assured,
and revealed his justice
in the presence of the Gentiles.

Psalm 99

Or est maintenant
L'Eternel regnant,
Peuples obstinez
En soient estonnez,
Cherubins sous luy
Luy servent d'appuy,
Que la terre toute
Tremblant le redoute.

Théodore de Bèze

Now is
the Eternal reigning,
obstinate peoples
are astounded at this,
cherubim beneath him
are his resting-place,
let all the earth
trembling fear him.

Psalm 100

Vous tous qui la terre habitez,
Chantez tout haut à Dieu chantés,
Servez à Dieu joyeusement,
Venez devant luy gayement.

Théodore de Bèze

All you who dwell on earth,
sing loudly to God,
serve God joyously,
come before him cheerfully.

Psalm 101

Vouloir m'est pris de mettre en escriture
Pseaume parlant de bonté et droiture,
Et si le veux à toy mon Dieu chanter,
Et presenter.

Clément Marot

I am seized with a desire to put in writing
a psalm speaking of goodness and uprightness,
and I want to sing it to thee, my God,
and present [it].

Psalm 102

Seigneur, enten ma requeste,	Lord, hear my petition,
Rien n'empesche ny n'arreste	let nothing prevent or stop
Mon cri d'aller jusqu'à toy,	my cry from going to thee,
Ne te cache point de moy.	do not hide thyself from me.
En ma douleur nompareille,	In my unequaled sadness,
Tourne vers moi ton oreille:	turn toward me thine ear:
Et pour m'ouïr quand je crie,	And to hear me when I cry,
Avance toy je te prie.	come close, I pray thee.
Théodore de Bèze	

Psalm 103

Sus louez Dieu, mon ame, en toute chose,	Arise, praise God, my soul, in everything,
Et tout cela qui dedans moy repose,	and all that is within me,
Louez son nom tressainct et accomply.	praise his holy and perfect name.
Presente à Dieu loüanges et services,	Present to God praises and worship,
O toy mon ame, et tant de benefices	O thou my soul, and the many benefits
Qu'en as receu, ne les mets en oubli.	which thou hast received, do not forget.
Clément Marot	

Psalm 104

Sus, sus, mon ame, il te faut dire bien	Up, up, my soul, thou must willingly say
De l'Eternel: ô mon vray Dieu, combien	of the Eternal: O my true God, how
Ta grandeur est excellente et notoire:	thy grandeur is excellent and widely known:
Tu es vestu de splendeur et de gloire:	Thou art robed in splendor and glory:
Tu es vestu de splendeur proprement,	Thou art robed in splendor properly,
Ne plus ne moins que d'un accoutrement:	neither more nor less than as a garment:
Pour pavillon qui d'un tel Roy soit digne,	For a tent which is worthy of such a King,
Tu tens le ciel ainsi qu'une courtine.	thou takest the sky as a covering.
Clément Marot	

Psalm 105

Sus, qu'un chacun de nous sans cesse	Arise, let each one of us without ceasing
Loue du Seigneur la hautesse,	praise the loftiness of the Lord,
Que son sainct Nom soit reclamé,	that his holy Name may be proclaimed,
Soit entre les peuples semé	among the scattered peoples [may] be [proclaimed]
Le renom grand et precieux	the great and precious renown
De tous ses gestes glorieux.	of all his glorious deeds.
Théodore de Bèze	

Psalm 106

Louez Dieu car il est benin,	Praise God for he is kind,
Et sa bonté n'a point de fin.	and his goodness has no end.
Où est celuy qui la prouësse	Where is the one who the prowess
De l'Eternel recitera	of the Eternal will recite
Et tous les faicts de sa hautesse	and all the deeds of his loftiness
Entierement nous chantera?	will fully sing to us?
Théodore de Bèze	

Psalm 107

Donnez au Seigneur gloire,
Il est doux et clément,
Et sa bonté notoire
Dure eternellement.
Ceux qu'il a rachetez,
Qu'ils chantent sa hautesse:
Et ceux qu'il a jettez
Hors de la main d'oppresse.

Clément Marot

Give to the Lord glory,
he is sweet and merciful,
and his widely-known goodness
endures forever.
Those whom he has redeemed,
let them sing of his greatness:
And those whom he has rescued
from the hand of oppression.

Psalm 108

Mon coeur est dispos, ô mon Dieu,
Mon coeur est tout prest en ce lieu
De te chanter tout à la fois,
Cantiques de main et de voix.
Psalterion, reveille toy
Harpe, ne demeure à recoy:
Car je veux de bout comparoistre
Dés que le jour vient apparoistre.

Théodore de Bèze

My heart is inclined, O my God,
my heart is entirely ready in this place
to sing of thee all at once,
songs of hand and of voice.
Psaltery, awake thee,
harp, do not dwell in repose:
For I wish from the outset to appear
before the day begins to dawn.

Psalm 109

O Dieu mon honneur et ma gloire
Ne vueilles maintenant te taire.
Car c'est contre moy que s'addresse
La bouche meschante et traistresse,
Et la fausse langue qui ment
A parler de moy faussement.

Théodore de Bèze

O God my honor and my glory,
be pleased not to delay.
For against me are set
the wicked and traitorous mouth,
and the false tongue that lies,
speaking falsely of me.

Psalm 110

L'Omnipotent à mon Seigneur et Maistre
A dit ce mot, à ma dextre te sieds,
Tant que j'auray renversé et fait estre
Tes ennemis le scabeau de tes pieds.

Clément Marot

The Almighty to my Lord and Master
said this word: To my right seat thyself,
until I have overthrown and made
thine enemies to be your footstool.

Psalm 111

Du Seigneur Dieu en tous endrois,
En l'assembée des plus droits,
De chanter à Dieu coustumiere,
La gloire je confesseray,
Et sa louange annonceray,
D'une affection toute entiere.

Théodore de Bèze

Of the Lord God in every place,
in the assembly of the most righteous,
to sing to God daily,
the glory I shall avow,
and his praise I shall proclaim,
with complete love.

Psalm 112

O bien-heureuse la personne
Qui craint l'Eternel, et s'addonne
Du tout à sa Loy tres-entiere:
Sa race en terre sera forte:
Car Dieu benit en toute forte,
Des bons la race droituriere.

Théodore de Bèze

O happy indeed the one
who fears the Eternal, and is devoted
above all to his whole Law:
His descendants will be strong in the earth:
For God blesses in all strength,
with benefits the upright nation.

Psalm 113

Enfans qui le Seigneur servez,
Louez-le et son Nom eslevez,
Louez son Nom et sa hautesse:
Soit presché, soit fait solennel,
Le Nom du Seigneur eternel,
Par tout en ce temps et sans cesse.

Clément Marot

Children who serve the Lord,
praise him and exalt his Name,
praise his Name and his greatness:
Let it be preached, let it be solemnized,
the Name of the eternal Lord,
by everyone in this time and without ceasing.

Psalm 114

Quand Israël hors d'Egipte sortit,
Et la maison de Jacob se partit
D'entre le peuple estrange,
Juda fut fait la grand' gloire de Dieu:
Et Dieu se fit Prince du peuple Hebrieu,
Prince de grand' loüange.

Clément Marot

When Israel departed out of Egypt,
and the house of Jacob was divided
among the strange people,
Judah was made the great glory of God:
And God was made Prince of the Hebrew people,
Prince of great praise.

Psalm 115

Non point à nous, non point à nous, Seigneur,
Mais à ton Nom donne gloire et honneur,
Pour ta grace et foy seure:
Pourquoy diroyent les gens en se moquant,
Où est ce Dieu qu'ils vont tant invoquant,
Où est-il à ceste heure?

Clément Marot

Not to us, not at all to us, Lord,
but to thy Name be glory and honor given,
for thy grace and steady faith:
Why should the nations say mockingly,
where is this God to whom they go crying,
where is he at this time?

Psalm 116

J'ayme mon Dieu: car lors que j'ay crié,
Je sçay qu'il a ma clameur entendue:
Et puis qu'il m'a son aureille tendue
En mon dur temps, par moy sera prié.

Théodore de Bèze

I love my God: for as soon as I called,
I knew that he heard my crying:
And since he has inclined his ear
in my difficult times, I will pray to him.

Psalm 117

Toutes gens, louez le Seigneur,
Tous peuples, chantez son honneur.
Car son vouloir benin et doux
Est multiplié dessus nous,
Et sa tresferme verité
Demeure à perpetuité.

Théodore de Bèze

All nations, praise the Lord,
all peoples, sing of his honor.
For his sweet good will
is increased upon us,
and his steadfast truth
lives forever.

Psalm 118

Rendez à Dieu loüange et gloire
Car il est benin et clement:
Qui plus est sa bonté notoire
Dure perpetuellement.
Qu'Israël ores se recorde
De chanter solennellement,
Que sa grande misericorde
Dure perpetuellement.

Clément Marot

Render to God praise and glory,
for he is kind and merciful:
Moreover his great goodness
endures forever.
Let Israel now say,
and solemnly sing,
that his great mercy
endures forever.

Psalm 119

Bien-heureuse est la personne qui vit
Avec entiere et saine conscience,
Et qui de Dieu les sainctes loix ensuit.
Heureux qui met tout soin et diligence
A bien garder ses statuts precieux,
Et qui de luy pourchasse la science.

Théodore de Bèze

Happy is the person who lives
with perfect and pure conscience,
and who follows the holy laws of God.
Happy the one who places all care and diligence
in guarding well his precious laws,
and who pursues the study of him.

Psalm 120

Alors qu'affliction me presse,
Ma clameur au Seigneur j'addresse:
Car quand je viens à le semondre,
Jamais ne faut à me respondre.
Contre ces levres tant menteuses,
Contre ces langues tant flateuses,
Vueilles, Seigneur par ta bonté,
Mettre ma vie à sauveté.

Théodore de Bèze

Then when affliction weighs on me,
my crying to the Lord I address:
For when I come to petition him,
he never fails to respond to me.
Against such lying lips,
against such flattering tongues,
be pleased, Lord, in thy goodness,
to keep my life in safety.

Psalm 121

Vers les monts j'ay levé mes yeux
Cuidant avoir d'enhaut
Le secours qu'il me faut:
Mais en Dieu qui a fait les cieux,
Et ceste terre ronde,
Maintenant je me fonde.

Théodore de Bèze

Towards the mountains I lifted my eyes
believing to have from on high
the help I need:
But in God who made the heavens,
and the round earth,
I am now established.

Psalm 122

Incontinent que j'eus ouï,
Sus allons le lieu visiter,
Où le Seigneur veut habiter:
O que mon coeur s'est resjoüi!
Or en tes porches entreront
Nos pieds et sejour y feront,
Jerusalem la bien dressée:
Jerusalem qui t'entretiens
Unie avecques tous les tiens,
Comme cité bien policée.

Théodore de Bèze

Straightaway when I heard,
up, let us go to visit the place,
where the Lord wants to dwell:
O how my heart rejoiced!
Now into thy courts will enter
our feet and there stay,
Jerusalem the well-erected:
Jerusalem who maintains thee
united with all thine own,
like a well-civilized city.

Psalm 123

A toy, ô Dieu qui es là haut aux cieux,
Nous eslevons nos yeux:
Comm' un servant qui pressé se voit estre,
N'a recours qu'à son maistre,
Et la servante a l'oeil sur sa maistresse,
Aussi tost qu'on la blesse:
Vers nostre Dieu nous regardons ainsi,
Attendans sa merci.

Théodore de Bèze

To thee, O God who art high in the heavens,
we lift up our eyes:
As a servant who sees himself hard-pressed,
has no recourse save in his master,
and [as] the maidservant has her eye on her mistress,
as soon as she is hurt:
To our God we look also,
waiting for his mercy.

Psalm 124

Or peut bien dire Israël maintenant,	Now Israel can say indeed,
Si le Seigneur pour nous n'eust point esté,	if the Lord had not been for us,
Si le Seigneur nostre droit n'eust porté,	if the Lord had not supported our cause,
Quand tout le monde à grand fureur venant,	when everyone, rising up in a great rage,
Pour nous meurtrir dessus nous s'est jetté,	threw themselves upon us to massacre us,
Pieça fussions vifs devorés par eux,	we would long since have been eaten alive by them,
Veu la fureur ardente des pervers:	in view of the burning rage of the vicious:
Pieça fussions sous les eaux à l'envers,	We would long since have been upside down beneath the waters,
Et tout ainsi qu'un flot impetueux	and they, just like a headlong rushing flood,
Nous eussent tous abysmés et couverts.	would have engulfed and covered us all.
Théodore de Bèze	

Psalm 125

Tout homme qui son esperance	Every man who his hope
En Dieu asseurera,	in God will fix,
Jamais ne versera:	will never be overturned:
Ains aura si grande asseurance,	Thus he will have such great confidence,
Que Sion montaigne tres-ferme,	that Zion, enduring mountain,
N'est point plus ferme.	is not more firm.
Théodore de Bèze	

Psalm 126

Alors que de captivité	When from captivity
Dieu mit Sion en liberté,	God set Zion at liberty,
Advis nous estoit proprement	we absolutely believed
Que nous songions tant seulement,	that we were only dreaming,
Bouches et langues à suffire	mouths and tongues were filled
Avoient dequoy chanter et rire:	with singing and laughter:
Chacun disoit voyant ceci,	Each one said, seeing this,
Dieu fait merveilles à ceux-cy.	God does marvels for them.
Théodore de Bèze	

Psalm 127

On a beau sa maison bastir,	Build his house as one may,
Si le Seigneur n'y met la main,	if the Lord does not have a hand in it,
Cela n'est que bastir en vain.	it is simply built in vain.
Quand on veut villes garentir,	When one wants to safeguard cities,
On a beau veiller et guetter,	stay awake and watch as one may,
Sans Dieu rien ne peut proffiter.	without God nothing can succeed.
Théodore de Bèze	

Psalm 128

Bien heureux est quiconques	Happy is whoever
Sert à Dieu volontiers	serves God willingly
Et ne se lassa onques	and never fails
De suivre ses sentiers.	to follow his paths.
Du labeur que sçais faire	From the labor that thou knowest to do
Vivras commodement,	thou shalt live comfortably,
Et ira ton affaire	and thy work shall go
Bien et heureusement.	well and happily.
Clément Marot	

Psalm 129

Des ma jeunesse ils m'ont fait mille assauts:

Israël peut à ceste heure bien dire,
Dés ma jeunesse ils m'ont fait mille maux,

Mais ils n'ont peu me vaincre ne destruire.

Théodore de Bèze

Since my youth they have made a thousand assaults on me:
Israel can well say at this time,
since my youth they have done me a thousand wrongs,
but they have not been able to conquer or destroy me.

Psalm 130

Du fonds de ma pensée,
Au fonds de tous ennuis,
A toy s'est addressée
Ma clameur jours et nuicts:
Enten ma voix plaintive,
Seigneur, il est saison,
Ton oreille ententive
Soit à mon oraison.

Clément Marot

From the depths of my thoughts,
in the depths of all sorrows,
to thee is addressed
my crying day and night:
Hear my plaintive voice,
Lord, it is time,
may thine ear be attentive
to my prayer.

Psalm 131

Seigneur, je n'ay point le coeur fier,
Je n'ay point le regard trop haut,
Et rien plus grand qu'il ne me faut
Ne voulus onques manier.

Théodore de Bèze

Lord, my heart is not at all proud,
my gaze is not at all too high,
and to nothing grander than I ought
have I aspired.

Psalm 132

Veille Seigneur, estre recors
De David et de son torment:
Lui qui à Dieu a fait serment,
Dieu de Jacob, le Fort des forts,
Et fait voeu solennellement.

Théodore de Bèze

Be mindful, Lord
of David and his torment:
Him who to God made an oath,
God of Jacob, the Strength of strengths,
and solemnly vowed.

Psalm 133

O combien est plaisant et souhaitable
De voir ensemble en concorde amiable
Freres unis s'entretenir.
Cela me fait de l'onguent souvenir
Tant precieux dont parfumer je voy
Aaron le prestre de la loy.

Théodore de Bèze

O how pleasant it is and desirable
to see together in amiable harmony
brothers united amongst themselves.
That reminds me of ointment
so precious, with which I see scented
Aaron the priest of the law.

Psalm 134

Or sus serviteurs du Seigneur,
Vous qui de nuict en son honneur
Dedans sa maison le servez,
Louëz-le et son Nom eslevez.

Théodore de Bèze

Now arise, servants of the Lord,
you who by night in his honor
serve him in his house,
praise him and exalt his Name.

Psalm 135

Chanter de Dieu le renom
Vous serviteurs du Seigneur:
Venez pour luy faire honneur,
Vous qui avez eu ce don,
D'estre habitans au milieu
Des parvis de nostre Dieu.

Théodore de Bèze

Sing of the renown of God
you servants of the Lord:
Come to do him honor,
you who have received this gift,
to be dwelling in the midst
of the courts of our God.

Psalm 136

Louez Dieu tout hautement,
Car il est doux et clement,
Et sa grand' benignité
Dure à perpetuité.

Théodore de Bèze

Praise God in the highest,
for he is sweet and merciful,
and his great goodness
endures forever.

Psalm 137

Estans assis aux rives aquatiques
De Babylon, plorions melancholiques,
Nous souvenans du païs de Sion,
Et au milieu de l'habitation,
Où de regret tant de pleurs espandismes,
Aux saules verds nos harpes nous pendismes.

Clément Marot

Seated by the watery banks
of Babylon, we wept, despondent,
remembering the country of Zion,
and in the midst of the dwelling,
where we wept so many tears of regret,
on green willows we hung our harps.

Psalm 138

Il faut que de tous mes espris
Ton los et pris
J'exalte et prise:
Devant les grands me presenter
Pour te chanter
J'ay fait emprise:
En ton sainct Temple adoreray,
Celebreray
Ta renommée,
Pour l'amour de ta grand' bonté,
Et feauté
Tant estimée.

Clément Marot

It must only be with my whole soul
that thy praise and worth
I exalt and cherish:
To come before the great
to sing of thee
I have undertaken:
In thy holy Temple I will worship,
I will celebrate
thy renown,
for love of thy great goodness,
and faithfulness
so well regarded.

Psalm 139

O Dieu, tu cognois qui je suis,
Tu sçais tout cela que je puis,
Soit que soy' assis ou debout,
Tu me cognois de bout en bout:
Et n'ay nulle chose conceuë,
Que n'ayes de loin apperceuë.

Théodore de Bèze

O God, thou seest who I am,
Thou knowest all that I can do,
whether I be lying down or arisen,
thou seest me through and through:
And there is nothing I have conceived,
that thou hast not perceived from afar.

Psalm 140

O Dieu, donne moy delivrance
De cest homme pernicieux,
Preserve-moy de la nuisance
De cest homme malicieux.

Théodore de Bèze

O God, deliver me
from the wicked man,
preserve me from injury
by that malicious man.

Psalm 141

O Seigneur à toy je m'escrie,
Plaise toy donques te haster,
Et vueilles ma voix escouter,
Car c'est toy qu'en criant je prie.

Théodore de Bèze

O Lord to thee I cry,
be pleased therefore to hasten,
and kindly hear my voice,
for it is to thee I pray crying.

Psalm 142

J'ai de ma voix à Dieu crié,
J'ai de ma voix mon Dieu prié,
J'espan tout mon coeur devant luy,
Et luy declare mon ennui.

Théodore de Bèze

I cried to God with my voice,
I prayed to God with my voice,
I poured out my whole heart before him,
and told him of my misery.

Psalm 143

Seigneur Dieu, oy l'oraison mienne,
Jusqu'à tes oreilles parvienne
Mon humble supplication:
Selon la vraye mercy tienne
Respon moy en affliction.

Clément Marot

Lord God, hear my prayer,
let approach unto thine ears
my humble supplication:
According to thy true mercy
answer me in my affliction.

Psalm 144

Loüé soit Dieu ma force en tous alarmes,
Qui duit mes mains à manier les armes,
Et rend mes doigts habiles aux combats,
Sa grand' bonté est sur moy haut et bas.
C'est mon chasteau, mon roc, ma delivrance,
C'est mon bouclier, c'est mon seul esperance:
C'est luy qui a malgré tous ennemis
Ce peuple mien à mon pouvoir sousmis.

Théodore de Bèze

Praised be God my strength in all dangers,
who guides my hands to wield weapons,
and makes my fingers adapted to combat,
his great goodness rests on me high and low.
He is my castle, my rock, my deliverance,
he is my shield, he is my only hope:
It is he that despite all enemies
brought my people under my rule.

Psalm 145

Mon Dieu, mon Roy, haut je t'éleveray,
Et ton nom sainct sans fin je beniray:
Je veux ton los chacun jour publier,
Et pour jamais ton Nom glorifier.
Le Seigneur est tresgrand et admirable,
Et sa grandeur n'est à nous comprenable.
De pere en fils ses faits on magnifie,
Et sa puissance entre iceux se publie.

Théodore de Bèze

My God, my King, I shall exalt thee high,
and thy holy name without end I shall bless:
I want to make known thy praise each day,
and glorify thy Name for ever.
The Lord is very great and excellent,
and his greatness is beyond our knowing.
From father to son his deeds are magnified,
and his power among them is made known.

Psalm 146

Sus mon ame, qu'on benie
Le Souverain, car il faut,
Tant que durera ma vie,
Que je loüe le treshaut,
Et tant que je dureray,
Pseaumes, je luy chanteray.

Théodore de Bèze

Arise, my soul, to bless
the Sovereign, for it is necessary,
so long as my life shall last,
that I praise the most high,
and as long as I shall endure,
I shall sing psalms to him.

Psalm 147

Louez Dieu, car c'est chose bonne
Qu'à nostre Dieu louange on donne,
C'est di-je, une chose plaisante
De le louer, et bien seante.
Puis que c'est luy qui de sa grace
Sa Jerusalem à bastie,
Il convient aussi qu'il ramasse
Sa gent ça et là departie.

Théodore de Bèze

Praise God, for it is a good thing
to give praise to our God,
it is, I say, a pleasing thing
to praise him, and very fitting.
For it is he who of his grace
has built his Jerusalem,
it is good also that he gathers together
his nation dispersed here and there.

Psalm 148

Vous tous les habitans des cieux,
Louëz hautement le Seigneur,
Vous les habitans des hauts lieux,
Chantez hautement son honneur.
Anges chantez sa renommée,
Louëz-le toute son armée:
Lune et soleil louëz son Nom,
Estoiles chantez son renom.

Théodore de Bèze

All you dwellers in the skies,
loudly praise the Lord,
you dwellers in high places,
sing loudly his honor.
Angels sing his fame,
praise him all his host:
Moon and sun praise his Name,
stars sing his renown.

Psalm 149

Chantez à Dieu chanson nouvelle,
Et sa louange solennelle,
Des bons parmi la compagnie
Maintenant soit oüie.
Israël s'esgaye en son coeur
De l'Eternel son Createur:
Et d'un tel Roy soyent triomphans
De Sion les enfans.

Théodore de Bèze

Sing to God a new song,
and let the solemn praise,
of his benefits among the company
now be heard.
Let Israel rejoice in his heart
in the Eternal his Creator:
And let triumph in such a King
the children of Zion.

Psalm 150

Or soit loüé l'Eternel
De son sainct lieu supernel:
Soit di-je, tout hautement
Loué de ce firmament
Plein de sa magnificence.
Loüez-le tous ses grands faits:
Soit loüé de tant d'effets,
Tesmoins de son excellence.

Théodore de Bèze

Now may the Eternal be praised
in his holy heavenly place:
Let him be, I say, loudly
praised in the firmament
full of his majesty.
Praise him for his great deeds:
Let him be praised for such effects,
witnesses of his excellence.

Decalogue, Exodus 20

Leve le coeur, ouvre l'aureille,
Peuple endurcy pour escouter
De ton Dieu la voix nompareille,
Et ses commandemens gouster.

Clément Marot

Lift the heart, open the ear,
obdurate people, to hear
the unequaled voice of your God,
and to appreciate his commandments.

The Song of Simeon, Luke 2

Or laisse Createur
En paix ton serviteur,
En suyvant ta promesse:
Puisque mes yeux ont eu
Ce credit d'avoir veu
De ton salut l'addresse.

Now release, Creator,
thy servant in peace,
according to thy promise:
For my eyes have had
the honor to have seen
the sign of thy salvation.

Clément Marot

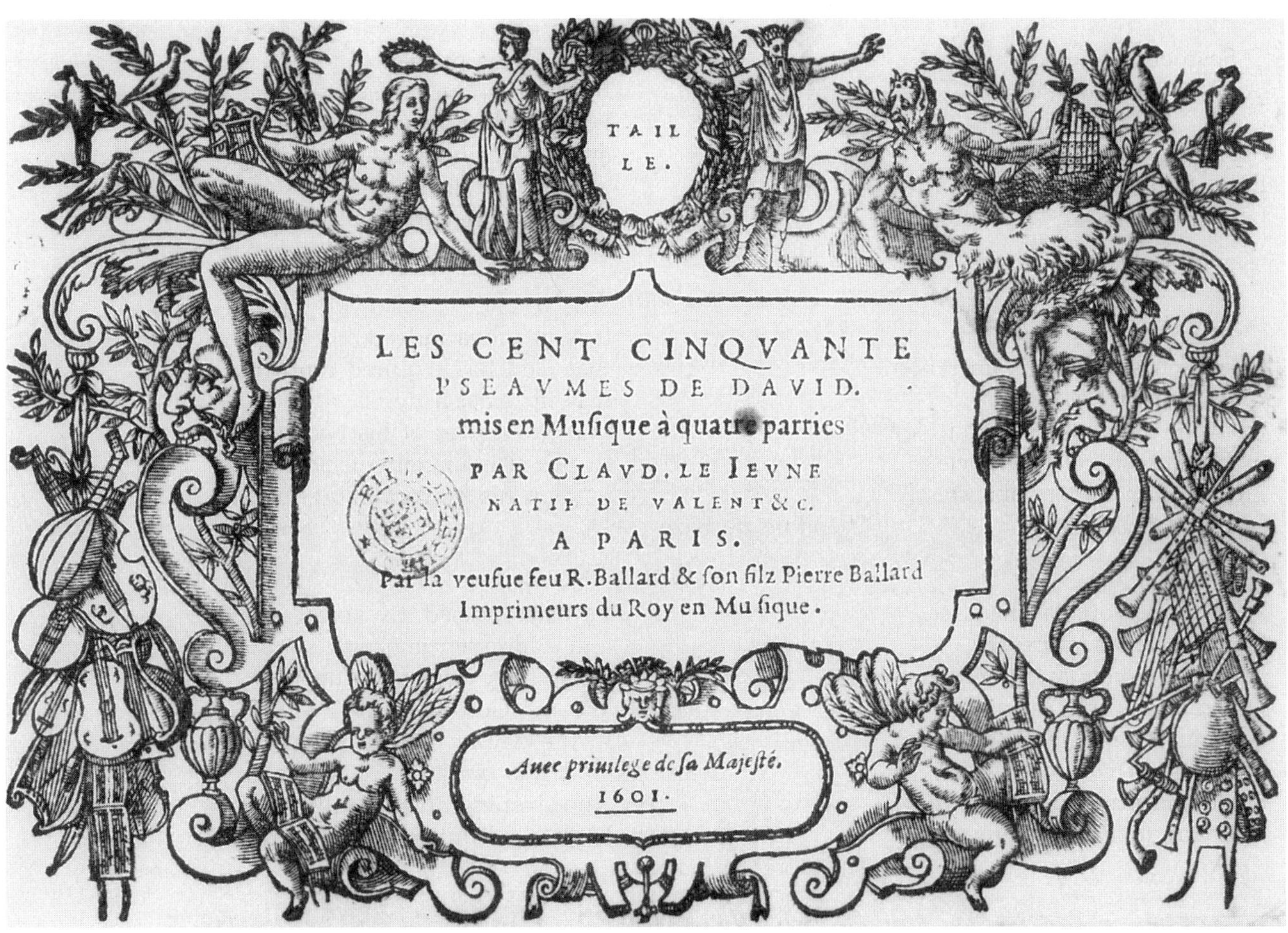

TAIL
LE.

LES CENT CINQVANTE
PSEAVMES DE DAVID.
mis en Muſique à quatre parries
PAR CLAVD. LE IEVNE
NATIF DE VALENT &c.
A PARIS.
Par la veufue feu R. Ballard & ſon filz Pierre Ballard
Imprimeurs du Roy en Muſique.

Auec priuilege de ſa Majeſté.
1601.

Plate 1. Claude Le Jeune, *Les cent cinquante pseaumes de David mis en musique à quatre parties* published in Paris by Robert & Pierre Ballard, 1601. Title page of Taille partbook (10 × 13.5 cm). (Reproduced by kind permission of the Société de l'Histoire du Protestantisme français)

Plate 2. *Les cent cinquante pseaumes* (1601), Basse-Contre partbook (10 × 13.5 cm), Psalm 1. (Reproduced by kind permission of the Société de l'Histoire du Protestantisme français)

TAILLE.
Ecce nunc benedicite.
PSAL. CXXXIIII.
72
R ſus ſeruiteurs du Seigneur, Vous qui de nuict en ſon hon-
neur
Dedans ſa maiſon le ſeruez, Louëz-le, & ſon Nom
eſleuez.

Plate 3. *Les cent cinquante pseaumes* (1601), Taille partbook, Psalm 134. (Reproduced by kind permission of the Société de l'Histoire du Protestantisme français)

Plate 4. *Les cent cinquante pseaumes* (1601), Basse-Contre partbook, Psalm 69. (Reproduced by kind permission of the Société de l'Histoire du Protestantisme français)

Dedication

A Monseigneur le Duc de Bouillon, Prince, Souverain de Sedan et Raucourt, Viconte de Turenne, Capitaine de cent hommes d'armes des ordonnances du Roy, Premier Gentilhomme de sa Chambre, Mareschal de France.

Monseigneur. Dieu vous avoit donné un serviteur entre plusieurs, et à moy un seul frere, qui sur la cognoissance qu'il eut de sa mort, de tout ce qu'il avoit resolu durant sa vie touchant l'Impression de ses oevres en Musique, et nommément des Pseaumes de David, desquels il vous en presenta douze, comme pour eschantillon, il y a quelques années, avec dessain quand il auroit ourdy tout l'oeuvre, de le vous offrir, affin qu'il eust cet honneur ayant à voiager par le monde, d'avoir tousjours pour saufconduit le titre de vost illustre nom, qui n'apporteroit moindre bon heur à l'ouvrage, que vos mains ont exercé de liberalité envers l'ouvrier. Or, Monseigneur, le sexe dont il a pleu à Dieu m'abbaisser, et les serieuses occupations qui vous detiennent estant ce que vous estes en son Eglise, et en cet estat, m'interdisent d'user de grand langage sur ce subjet. Car je croy de vostre pieté qu'elle aura pitié de cet orphelin que le pere desiroit vous presenter avant que luy defaillir: Ce que je vien faire à cette heure obeissant a sa derniere volonté. Et quoy que peut estre vous ne le cognoissiez par les mains qui le vous offrent, je m'asseure que s'il vous plaist seulement l'ouir, sa voix suffira pour vous le faire recognoistre, et que vous daignerez bien l'accueillir, affin que comme il a esté conceu en lieu de vostre authorité, et nourry sous l'ombre de vos faveurs, il puisse comparoistre plus hardiment en public, s'il a cette grace que vous estimiez qu'il en est digne. Car vostre jugement, grand es plus grandes choses, mais tresgrand en la musique (comme je l'ay souvent entendu du defunct, professeur de verité et non de flatterie;) vostre jugement, di-je, Monseigneur, luy servira de garand contre les atteintes de ceux qui pensent cacher leur ignorance par reprendre ce qu'ilz n'entendent pas, ou calomnier ce qui est preferable à ce qu'ilz peuvent. Si vous en recevez du plaisir le public y en cerchera à vostre exemple; et moy accomplissant en cecy le desir de l'autheur, lors que je le suivray ou il est, au moins j'emporteray ce contentement qu'en luy rendant cet office, vous, Monseigneur, aurez agrée le douceur ou s'en est mise

Vostre tres-humble et tres-obeissante servante,

Cecile Le Jeune

To my lord the Duke of Bouillon, Sovereign Prince of Sedan and Raucourt, Viscount of Turenne, Captain of one hundred of the King's men-at-arms, First Gentleman of his Chamber, Marshall of France.

My lord,

God gave you one servant among several, and me an only brother, who, in the knowledge of his impending death, of all that he left took particular care to make me promise to do that which he had resolved during his life, regarding the printing of his musical works, and namely the Psalms of David, of which he presented you twelve, as if for a token, some years ago, with the plan, when he had ordered the whole work, to offer it to you, so that it would have the honor, when launched in the world, to have always for safe-conduct the title of your illustrious name, which would bring no less happiness to the work than your hands have shown liberality to its creator.

But, my lord, the sex with which it pleased God to humble me and the momentous occupations which engage you, being that you are in his Church, and in this State, prevent me from using grand language on this topic. For I believe that your piety will have pity on this orphan, which the father wished to present to you before his death, a task I now do, obedient to his last wish. And though perhaps you do not recognize it by the hands that offer it to you, yet I am certain that if it pleased you to hear it, its voice will suffice to make you recognize it; and that you will deign to welcome it; since it was conceived in a place of your authority and nourished in the shadow of your favor, it might be able to make its appearance more strongly in public, if it has that grace of which you deem it to be worthy. For your judgment, great in great things, but very great in music (as I often heard from the deceased, who spoke truth and not flattery), your judgment, I say, my Lord, will serve to guard against the accusations of those who think to hide their ignorance by blaming that which they do not understand, or by calumniating that which is preferable to that which they are able to do. If you receive from this pleasure, the public will follow your example; and me accomplishing in this the wish of the author, for I will follow where he is, at least I will carry with me the contentment of having done him this favor, you, my Lord, having accepted the duty wherein is placed your very humble and obedient servant

Cecile Le Jeune

Fugue a l'unisson apres deux tens, a cinq. Canon.

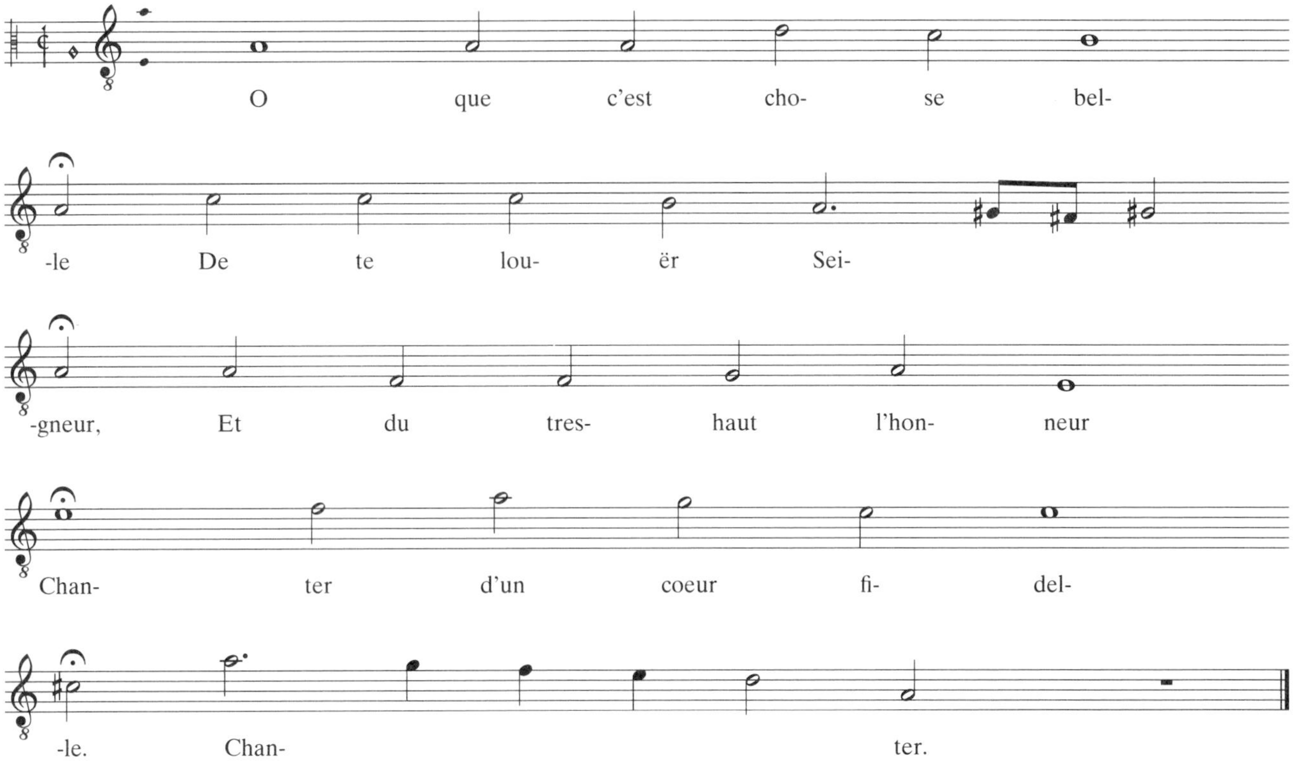

To God give thanks, confessing
It is a gracious thing,
Thy Name most high to sing:
In Psalms thy praise expressing[,
Singing].

[The text of the fugue is the first four verses of Psalm 92. The melody quotes the first eight notes of Psalm 92, transposed down a fourth, and then proceeds so as to make the canon work. *Apres deux tens* (*tens = temps*) indicates the time interval between successive voice entrances, two breves. The *signes de concordance* indicate not only where successive voices enter but also where to stop so that all voices can make a final cadence together.]

Psalm 1

Dessus
Haute-Contre
Taille
Basse-Contre
Genevan Tune
2
Qui au con- seil des ma- lins n'a es- té, Qui n'est au
Qui au con- seil des ma- lins n'a es- té, Qui n'est au
Qui au con- seil des ma- lins n'a es- té, Qui n'est au
Qui au con- seil des ma- lins n'a es- té, Qui n'est au
3
trac des pe- cheurs ar- res- té, Qui des mo- queurs au banc pla-
trac des pe- cheurs ar- res- té, Qui des mo- queurs au banc pla-
trac des pe- cheurs ar- res- té, Qui des mo- queurs au banc pla-
trac des pe- cheurs ar- res- té, Qui des mo- queurs au banc pla-
4
-ce n'a pri- se, Mais nuict et jour la Loy con-temple et pri- se
-ce n'a pri- se, Mais nuict et jour la Loy con-temple et pri- se
-ce n'a pri- se, Mais nuict et jour la Loy con-temple et pri- se
-ce n'a pri- se, Mais nuict et jour la Loy con-temple et pri- se

5
De l'E- ter- nel et en est de- si- reux,
De l'E- ter- nel et en est de- si- reux,
De l'E- ter- nel et en est de- si- reux,
De l'E- ter- nel et en est de- si- reux,
6
Cer- tai- ne- ment ces- tui- là est heu- reux.
Cer- tai- ne- ment ces- tui- là est heu- reux.
Cer- tai- ne- ment ces- tui- là est heu- reux.
Cer- tai- ne- ment ces- tui- là est heu- reux.

Who walketh not in counsell lewd astray,
Who standeth not in sinners wicked way,
Who sitteth not in scorners chaire deriding:
But day and night in Gods pure law abiding,
With true delight theron doth meditate,
That man is sure to live in blessed state.

Psalm 2

Dessus
Haute-Contre
Taille
Basse-Contre
Genevan tune
Pour- quoy font bruit et s'as- sem- blent les gens?
Quel- le fo- lie à mur- mu- rer les mei- ne?
Pour- quoy sont tant les peu- ples di- li- gens
A met- tre sus une en- tre- pri- se vai- ne?
2
3
4

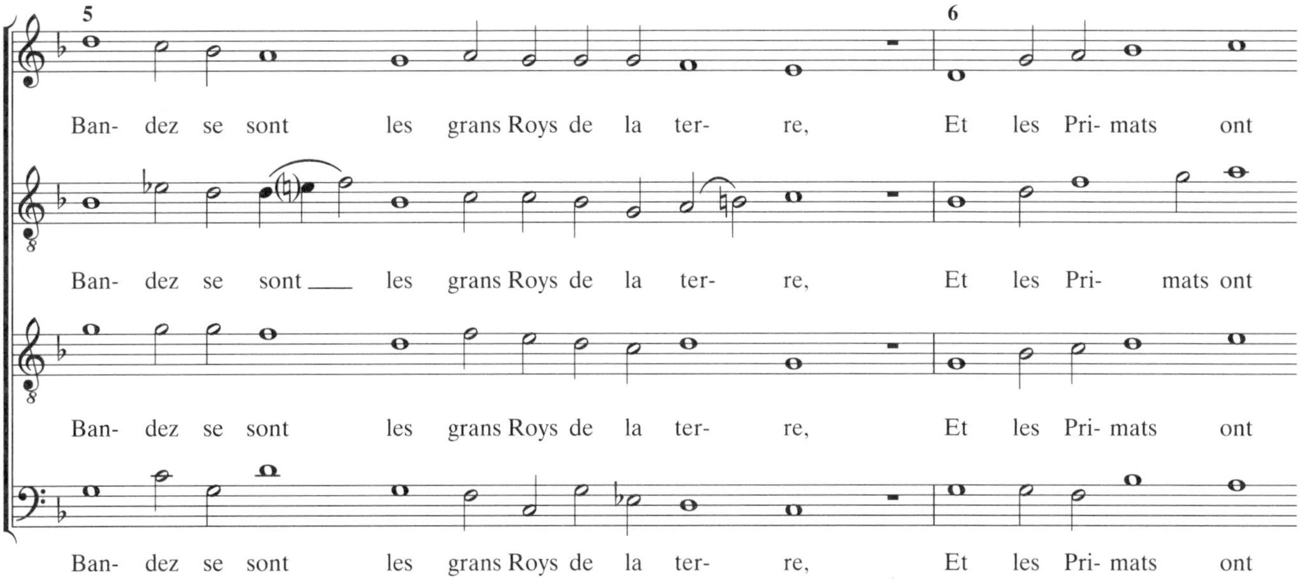

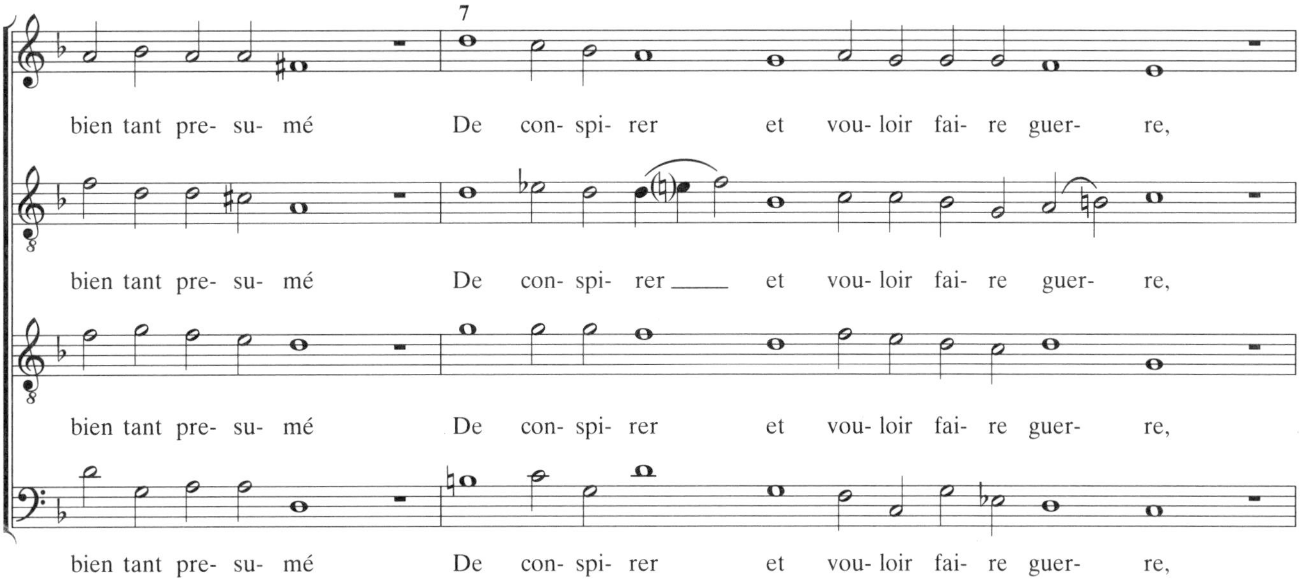

5
6
Ban- dez se sont les grans Roys de la ter- re, Et les Pri- mats ont
Ban- dez se sont les grans Roys de la ter- re, Et les Pri- mats ont
Ban- dez se sont les grans Roys de la ter- re, Et les Pri- mats ont
Ban- dez se sont les grans Roys de la ter- re, Et les Pri- mats ont

7
bien tant pre- su- mé De con- spi- rer et vou- loir fai- re guer- re,
bien tant pre- su- mé De con- spi- rer et vou- loir fai- re guer- re,
bien tant pre- su- mé De con- spi- rer et vou- loir fai- re guer- re,
bien tant pre- su- mé De con- spi- rer et vou- loir fai- re guer- re,

8
Tous con- tre Dieu, et son Roy bien- ai- mé.
Tous con- tre Dieu, et son Roy bien- ai- mé.
Tous con- tre Dieu, et son Roy bien- ai- mé.
Tous con- tre Dieu, et son Roy bien- ai- mé.

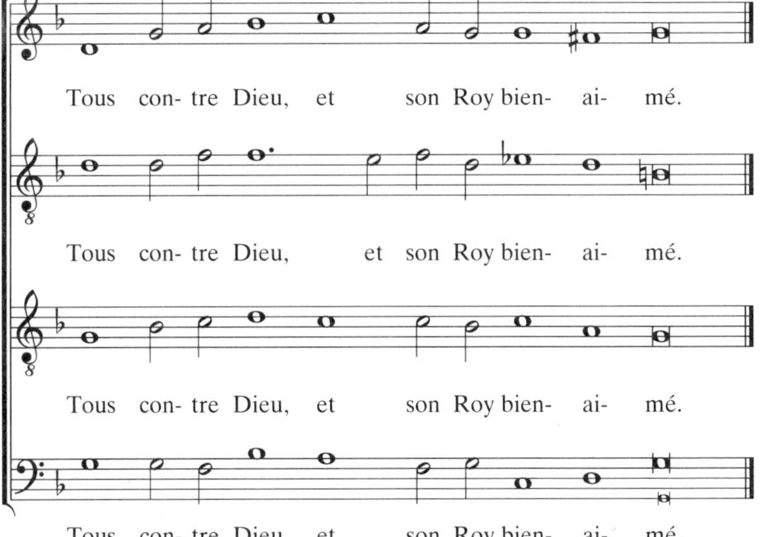

With brutish rage, why do the heathen rise,
Tumultuously assembling combinations?
What is the cause rude people enterprise
To execute their vain imaginations?
Kings of the earth, and Potentates aspiring,
Together all their armed forces bring,
They counsell take, rebelliously conspiring
Against the Lord and his anointed king.

Psalm 3

Dessus
O Sei- gneur, que de gens, A nuy- re di- li- gens,
Haute-Contre
O Sei- gneur, que de gens, A nuy- re di- li- gens,
Taille
Genevan tune
O Sei- gneur, que de gens, A nuy- re di- li- gens,
Basse-Contre
O Sei- gneur, que de gens, A nuy- re di- li- gens,
Qui me trou-blent et gre- vent! Mon Dieu que d'en- ne- mis, Qui aux champs
Qui me trou-blent et gre- vent! Mon Dieu que d'en- ne- mis, Qui aux champs
Qui me trou-blent et gre- vent! Mon Dieu que d'en- ne- mis, Qui aux champs
Qui me trou-blent et gre- vent! Mon Dieu que d'en- ne- mis, Qui aux champs
se sont mis, Et con- tre moy s'es- le- vent! Cer- tes plu-sieurs j'en voy,
se sont mis, Et con- tre moy s'es- le- vent! Cer- tes plu-sieurs j'en voy,
se sont mis, Et con- tre moy s'es- le- vent! Cer- tes plu-sieurs j'en voy,
se sont mis, Et con- tre moy s'es- le- vent! Cer- tes plu-sieurs j'en voy,

O Lord what numbers rise
Of spitefull enemies,
Even ready to assail me,
What multitudes, what swarmes,
Are ready up in armes,
To overcome and quail me.
How many is the roul
Of them that tell my soul,
It cannot be relieved,
It must be undertrod,
No help comes from his God,
But they are all deceived.

Psalm 4

Dessus
Haute-Contre
Taille
Basse-Contre
Genevan tune
2
3
4
5
Quand je t'in- voque, he- las, es- cou- te, O Dieu, de ma cause et rai- son: Mon coeur ser- ré au lar- ge bou- te, De ta pi- tié ne me re- bou- te: Mais ex- au- ce mon o- rai- son.

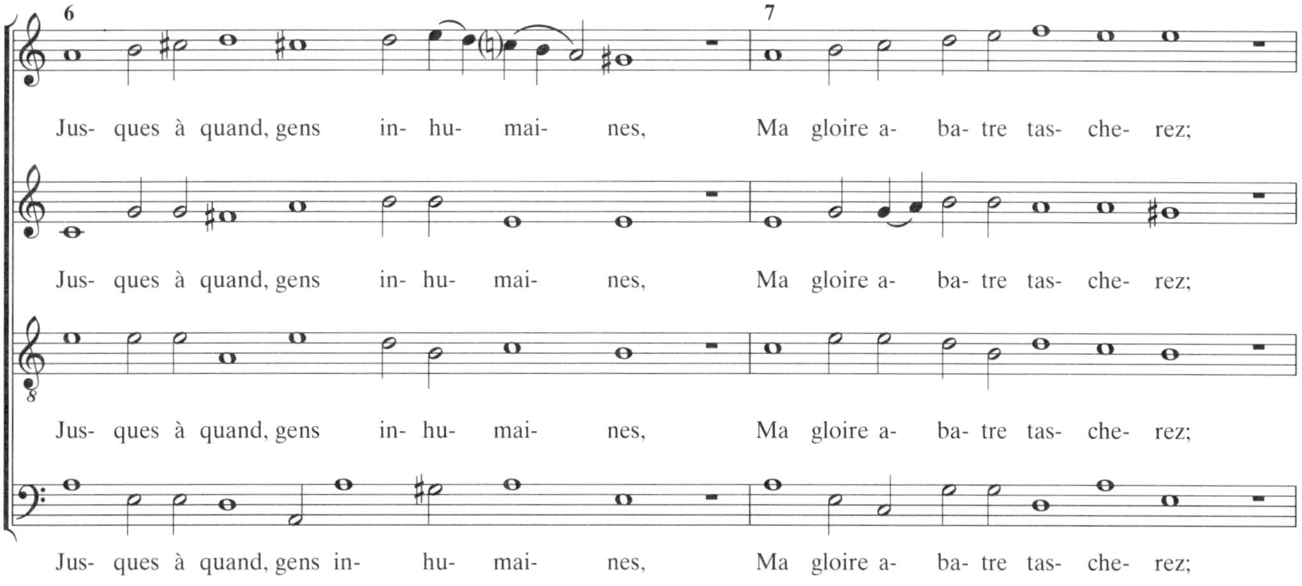

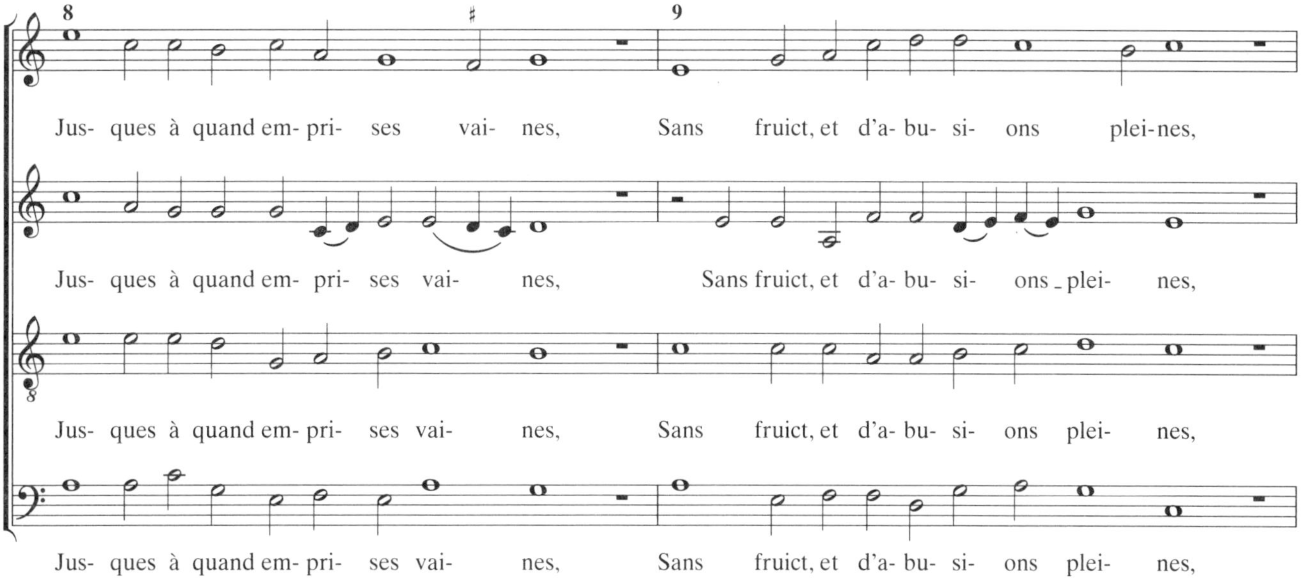

6
7
Jus- ques à quand, gens in- hu- mai- nes, Ma gloire a- ba- tre tas- che- rez;
Jus- ques à quand, gens in- hu- mai- nes, Ma gloire a- ba- tre tas- che- rez;
Jus- ques à quand, gens in- hu- mai- nes, Ma gloire a- ba- tre tas- che- rez;
Jus- ques à quand, gens in- hu- mai- nes, Ma gloire a- ba- tre tas- che- rez;

8
9
Jus- ques à quand em- pri- ses vai- nes, Sans fruict, et d'a- bu- si- ons plei- nes,
Jus- ques à quand em- pri- ses vai- nes, Sans fruict, et d'a- bu- si- ons _ plei- nes,
Jus- ques à quand em- pri- ses vai- nes, Sans fruict, et d'a- bu- si- ons plei- nes,
Jus- ques à quand em- pri- ses vai- nes, Sans fruict, et d'a- bu- si- ons plei- nes,

10
Ai- me- rez vous et _____ cher- che- rez?
Ai- me- rez vous et cher- che- rez?
Ai- me- rez vous et cher- che- rez?
Ai- me- rez vous et cher- che- rez?

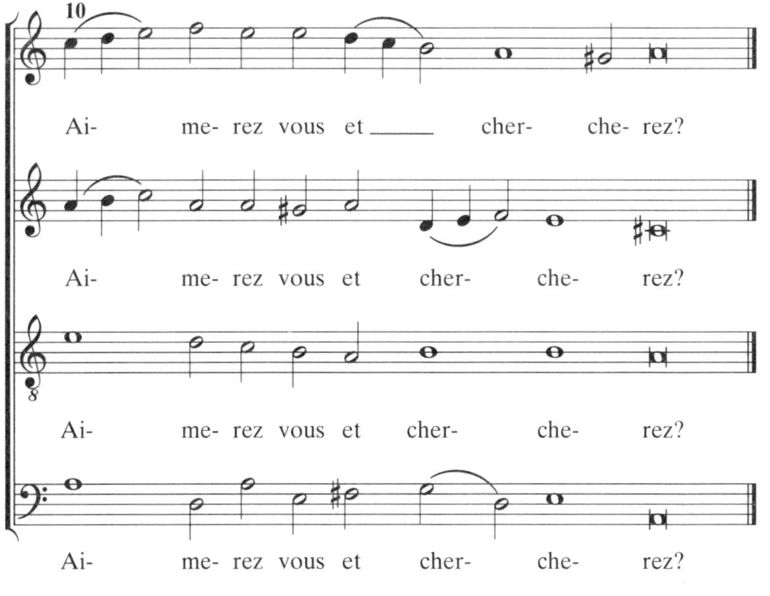

O Lord, my God, my rights defender,
Ah hearken to me when I call,
As thou my liberty didst render,
Deny me not, thy pitty tender,
But hear my earnest prayer withall.
How long O sonnes of mortals mighty,
My glory to disgrace, disguise,
And turn to shame, and scandal fight ye?
How long will ye in sinne delight ye,
In lewd designes, and seek for lyes?

Psalm 5

Unto the words of my complaining,
O Lord incline thy gratious ear,
Vouchsafe to understand and hear,
O thou that in the heav'ns art raigning,
My cause of plaining.

*Also set in Psalm 64

Psalm 6

Lord in thy furies terror,
Reprove thou not my error,
Though I thee high incense:
Nor in thy dread displeasure,
Correct me to the measure
Of my extreme offence.

Psalm 7

Dessus
Haute-Contre
Taille
Genevan tune
Basse-Contre
Mon Dieu, j'ay en toy es- pe- ran- ce, Don- ne moy
donc sauve as- seu- ran- ce, De tant d'en- ne- mis in- hu- mains,
Et fay que ne tombe en leurs mains, A fin que leur chef ne
Et fay que ne tombe en leurs mains, A fin que leur_ chef_ ne
Et fay que ne tombe en leurs mains, A fin_ que_ leur chef ne
2
3
4
5

In thee my God, my trust is ever,
Then save me Lord, and me deliver,
From all that me pursue with hate,
And from the cruell Potentate.
Lest like a Lyon in his power,
He tear my soul, and me devower:
While succorles I seem to be,
And ther is none to rescue me.

Psalm 8

4

Qui ta puis- sance es- le- ve sur les ____ cieux.

Qui ta puis- sance ___ es- le- ve ____ sur ___ les cieux.

Qui ta puis- sance es- le- ve sur les cieux.

Qui ta puis- sance ___ es- le- ve sur les cieux.

Eternall God, our Lord incomparable,
How excellent is thy Name, admirable
Ore all the world, thy glory manifold,
Is far above the highest heav'ns extold.

Psalm 9

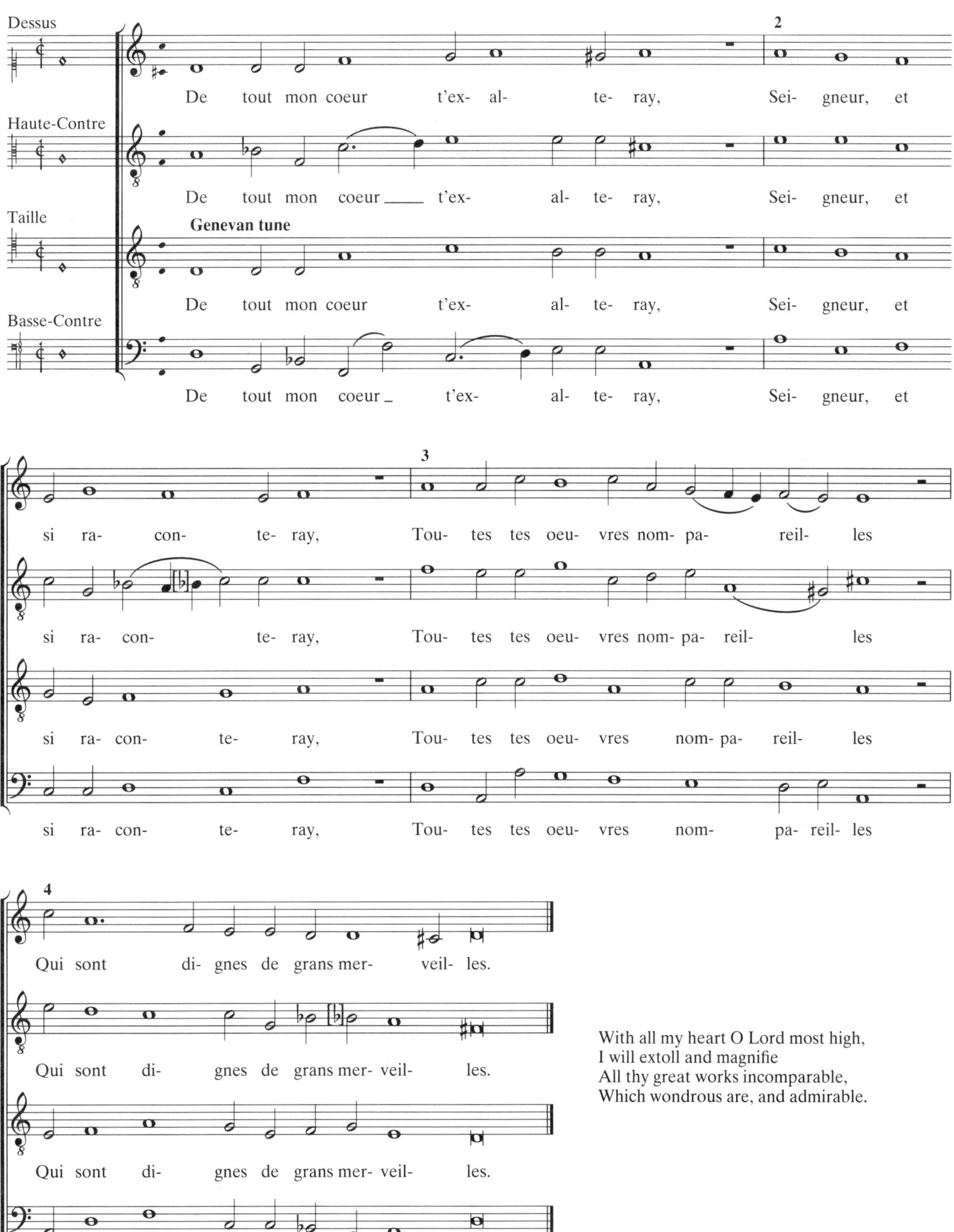

With all my heart O Lord most high,
I will extoll and magnifie
All thy great works incomparable,
Which wondrous are, and admirable.

Psalm 10

Dessus
Haute-Contre
Taille
Basse-Contre
Genevan tune
D'où vient ce- la, Sei- gneur, je te sup- pli,
D'où vient ce- la, Sei- gneur, je te sup- pli,
D'où vient ce- la, Sei- gneur, je te sup- pli,
D'où vient ce- la, Sei- gneur, je te sup- pli,
2
3
Que loin de nous te tiens les yeux cou-vers? Te ca- ches tu pour nous mettre
Que loin de nous te tiens les yeux cou- vers? Te ca- ches tu pour nous
Que loin de nous te tiens les yeux cou- vers? Te ca- ches tu pour nous mettre
Que loin de nous te tiens les yeux cou- vers? Te ca- ches tu pour nous mettre
4
en ou- bli, Mes- mes au temps qui est dur et di- vers?
mettre en ou- bli, Mes- mes au temps qui est dur et di- vers?
en ou- bli, Mes- mes au temps qui est dur et di- vers?
en ou- bli, Mes- mes au temps qui est dur et di- vers?

Why dost thou Lord withdraw from us thy grace?
Why standest thou from us departed far?
Why hidest thou the favor of thy face
In troublous times of need and grievous care?
Inflam'd with rage and pride the wicked are,
To vex the poor, but let them be surprised
In their own plots malitiously devised.

Psalm 11

Dessus
Haute-Contre
Taille
Basse-Contre
Genevan tune
2
Veu que du tout en Dieu mon coeur s'ap- pui- e, Je mes-
3
-ba- hi com- ment de vos- tre mont, Plus- tot qu'oi- seau, di- tes que je
4
5
m'en- fuy- e. Vray est que l'arc les ma- lins ten- du m'ont, Et sur la

6
corde ont as- sis leurs sa- get- tes, Pour con- tre ceux qui de coeur
corde ont as- sis leurs sa- get- tes, Pour con- tre ceux qui de coeur
corde ont as- sis leurs sa- get- tes, Pour con- tre ceux qui de coeur
corde ont as- sis leurs sa- get- tes, Pour con- tre ceux qui de coeur
7
jus- tes sont, Les des- co- cher jus- ques en leur ca- chet- tes.
jus- tes sont, Les des- co- cher jus- ques en leur ca- chet- tes.
jus- tes sont, Les des- co- cher jus- ques en leur ca- chet- tes.
jus- tes sont, Les des- co- cher jus- ques en leur ca- chet- tes.

In God, my hope of safety I have placed:
Why say ye then that I must take my flight
To mountains high, for refuge, as birds chased?
The wicked loe their bended bow have dight,
And on the string their arrows set, lye lurking
To shoot at them that be in heart upright,
Close out of sight their deadlie mischief working.

Psalm 12

Send help O Lord, thy speedy succor daigning,
For upright men departed are away:
Among the sons of men are none remaining,
Who speak the truth, the faithfull do decay.

Psalm 13

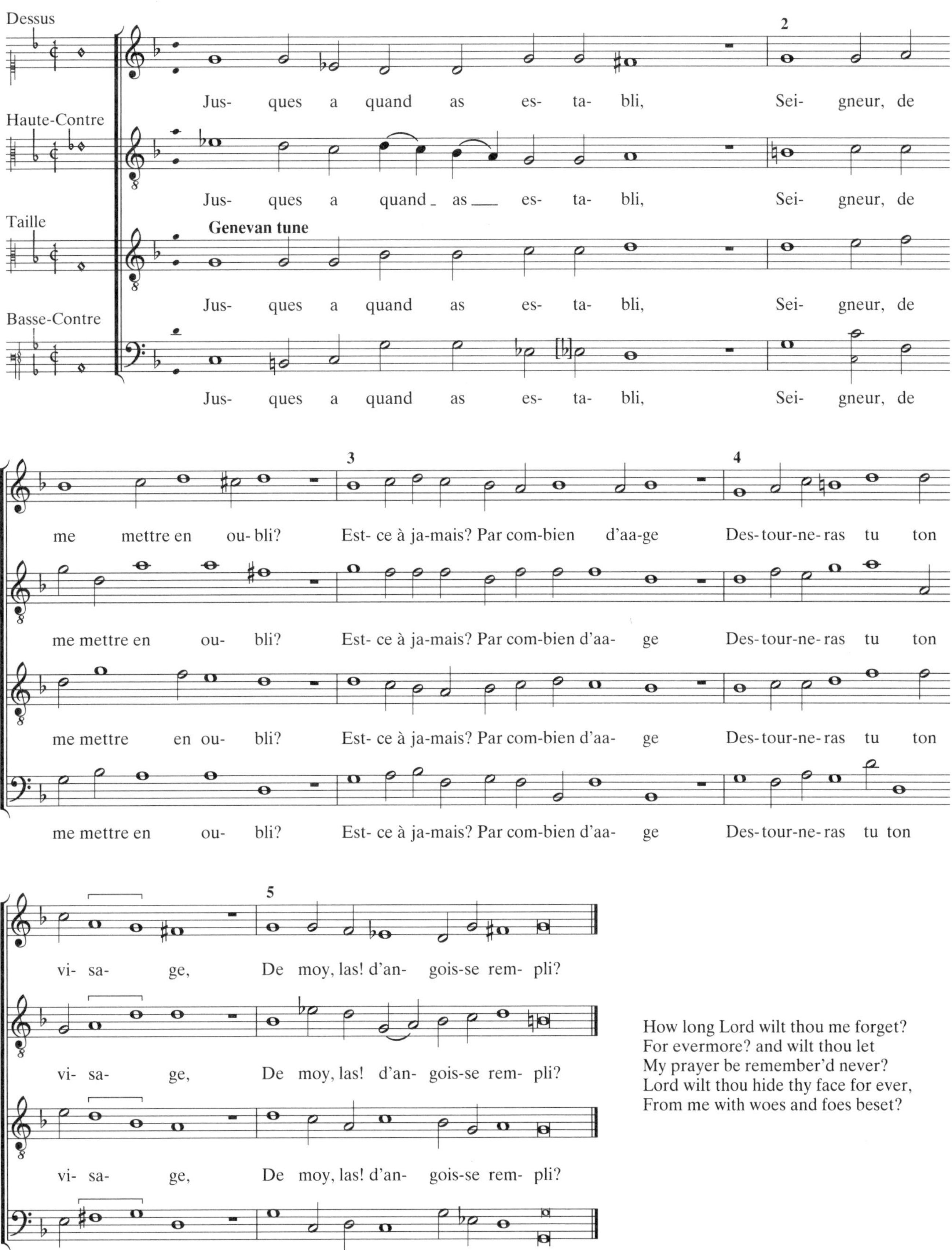

How long Lord wilt thou me forget?
For evermore? and wilt thou let
My prayer be remember'd never?
Lord wilt thou hide thy face for ever,
From me with woes and foes beset?

Psalm 14

The fool in heart, the holy God denyes:
They are corrupt in all their enterprises,
To be abhord in all their exercises:
Good works none do, nor thereunto advise,
All are unwise.

*Also set in Psalm 53

Psalm 15

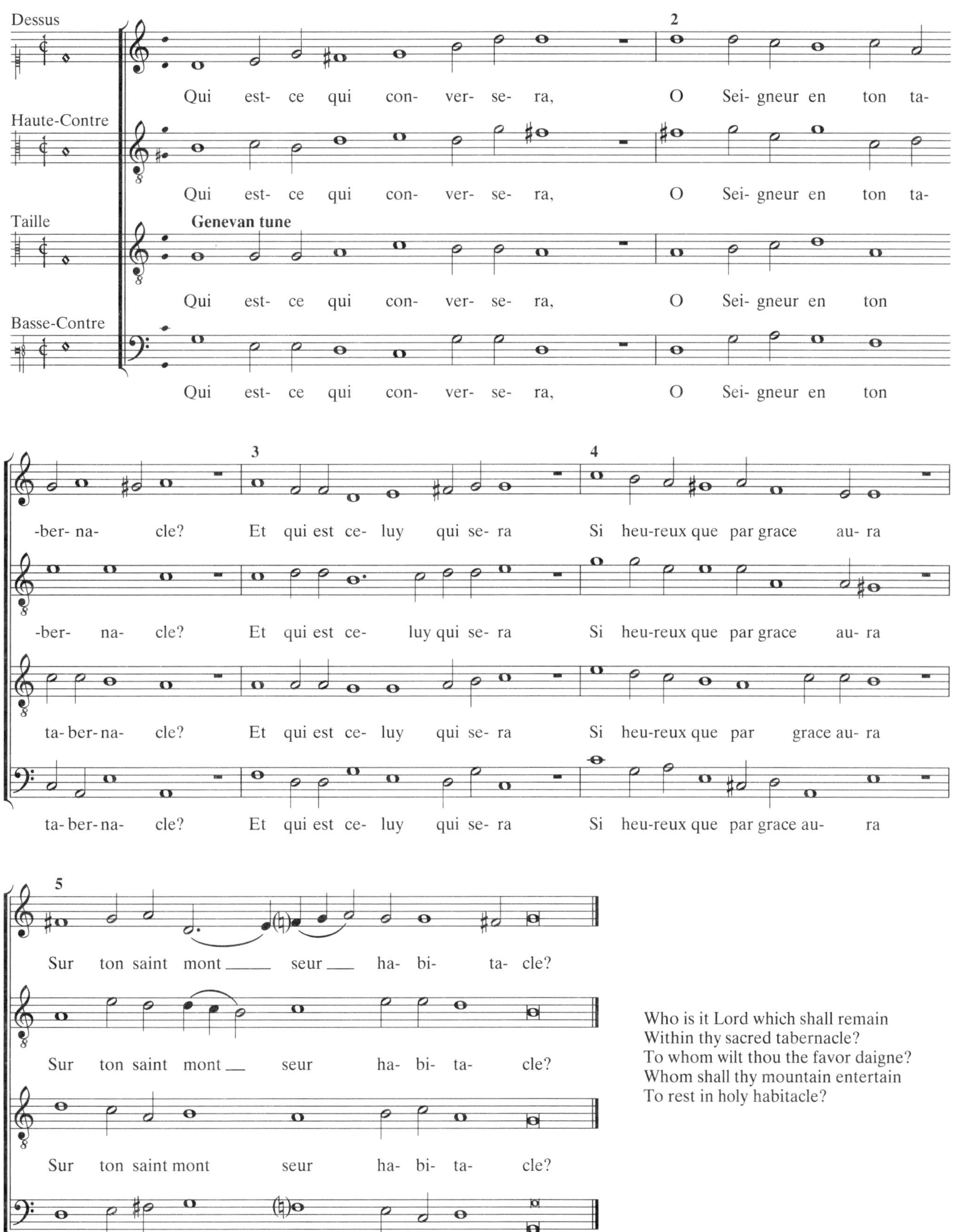

Who is it Lord which shall remain
Within thy sacred tabernacle?
To whom wilt thou the favor daigne?
Whom shall thy mountain entertain
To rest in holy habitacle?

Psalm 16

Dessus
Haute-Contre
Taille
Basse-Contre
Genevan tune
2
Sois moy, Sei-gneur, ma gard' et mon ap- puy: Car en toy gist tou-
Sois moy, Sei- gneur, ma gard' et mon ap- puy: Car en toy gist tou-
Sois moy, Sei- gneur, ma gard' et mon ap- puy: Car en toy gist tou-
Sois moy, Sei- gneur, ma gard' et mon ap- puy: Car en toy gist tou-
3
-te mon es- pe- ran- ce. Sus donc aus- si, ô mon a- me, dy luy
-te mon es- pe- ran- ce. Sus donc aus- si, ô mon a- me, dy luy
-te mon es- pe- ran- ce. Sus donc aus- si, ô mon a- me, dy luy
-te mon es- pe- ran- ce. Sus donc aus- si, ô mon a- me, dy luy
4
5
Sei- gneur, tu as sur moy tou- te puis- san- ce: Et tou- tes fois point n'y a
Sei- gneur, tu as sur moy tou- te puis- san- ce: Et tou- tes fois point n'y a
Sei- gneur, tu as sur moy tou- te puis- san- ce: Et tou- tes fois point n'y a
Sei- gneur, tu as sur moy tou- te puis- san- ce: Et tou- tes fois point n'y a

6
d'oeu-vre mien- ne, Dont jus- qu'à toy quel- que pro- fit re- vien- ne.
d'oeu- vre _ mien- ne, Dont jus- qu'à toy quel- que pro- fit re- vien- ne.
d'oeu-vre mien- ne, Dont jus- qu'à toy quel- que pro- fit re- vien- ne.
d'oeu-vre mien- ne, Dont jus- qu'à toy quel- que pro- fit re- vien- ne.

Preserve me Lord, be thou my help and ayd,
For I do trust in thee my hope reposing.
And thou my soul, this unto God hast said,
Thou art my Lord, I am at thy disposing,
Of all the good thy bounty to me lendeth,
No benefit at all to thee extendeth.

Psalm 17

Dessus
Haute-Contre
Taille
Basse-Contre
Genevan tune*
2
3
4
5
Sei- gneur, en- ten à mon bon droit,
En- ten, he- las!
ce que je cri- e:
Vueil- les ou- ir ce que je pri- e,
Et de bouche et de coeur tout droit.
De toy, qui cognois tou- te

*Also set in Psalms 63 and 70

Lord, hear my right, and entertain
My ernest suit for justice crying,
Thy eare unto my prayer applying.
I plead with lips that do not fain.
Let my doom be by thee awarded,
Let it come forth just Judg from thee.
And in thine eyes which all things see,
Let all the righteous be regarded.

Psalm 18

*Also set in Psalm 144

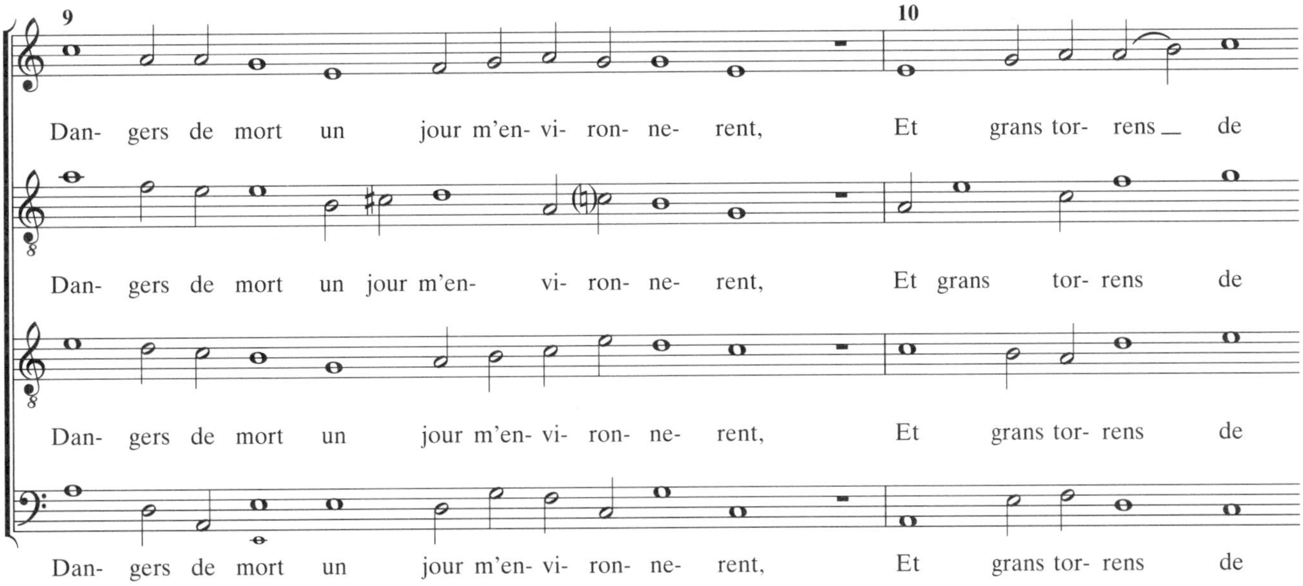

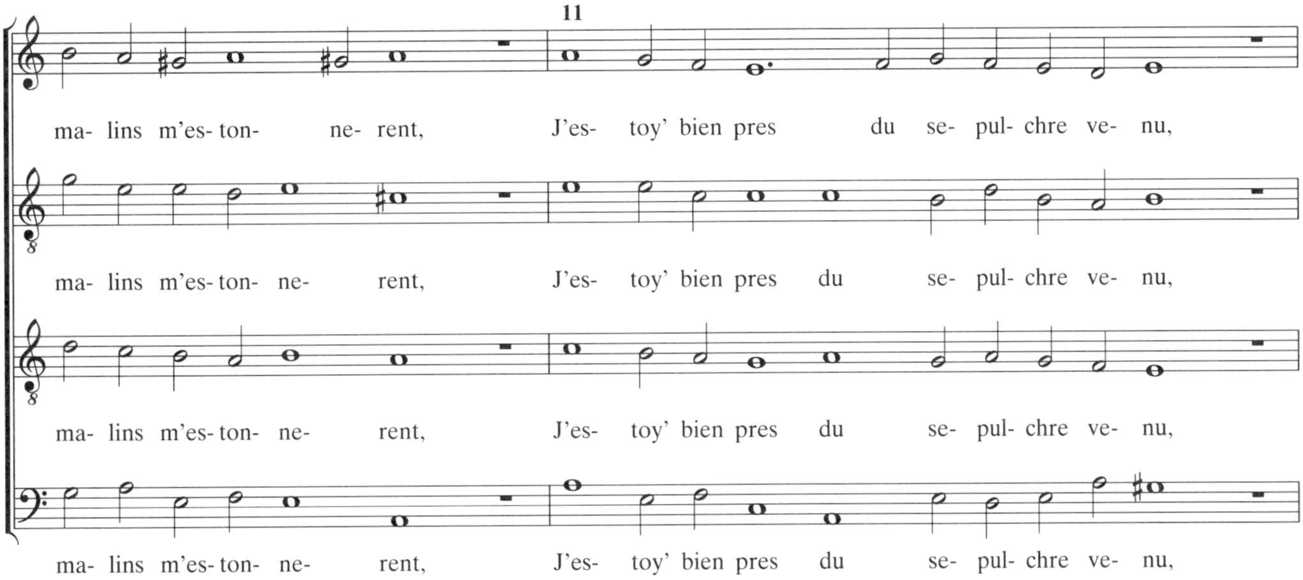

9
10
Dan- gers de mort un jour m'en- vi- ron- ne- rent, Et grans tor- rens de
Dan- gers de mort un jour m'en- vi- ron- ne- rent, Et grans tor- rens de
Dan- gers de mort un jour m'en- vi- ron- ne- rent, Et grans tor- rens de
Dan- gers de mort un jour m'en- vi- ron- ne- rent, Et grans tor- rens de

11
ma- lins m'es- ton- ne- rent, J'es- toy' bien pres du se- pul- chre ve- nu,
ma- lins m'es- ton- ne- rent, J'es- toy' bien pres du se- pul- chre ve- nu,
ma- lins m'es- ton- ne- rent, J'es- toy' bien pres du se- pul- chre ve- nu,
ma- lins m'es- ton- ne- rent, J'es- toy' bien pres du se- pul- chre ve- nu,

12
Et des fi- lets de la mort pre- ve- nu.
Et des fi- lets de la mort pre- ve- nu.
Et des fi- lets de la mort pre- ve- nu.
Et des fi- lets de la mort pre- ve- nu.

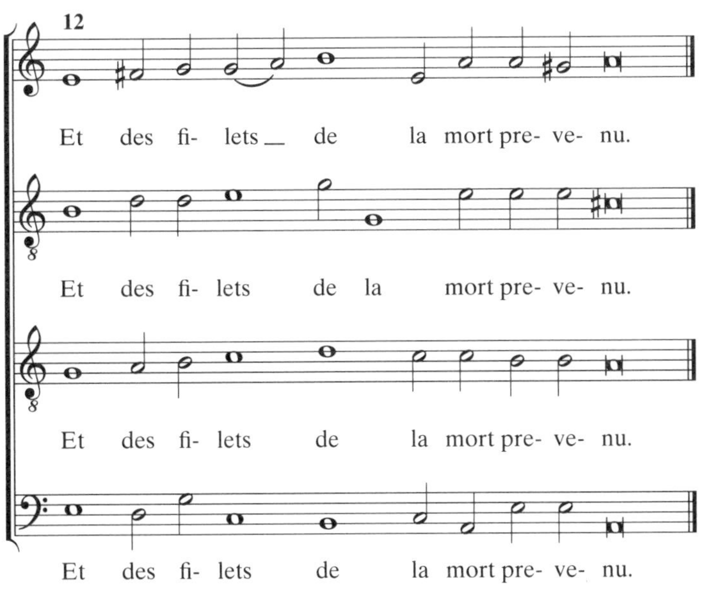

Thee will I love with hearty pure affection,
O Lord my strength, and my most sure protection.
God is my rock, my refuge, my defence,
My Saviour dear, my hope, my confidence.
My God, my strength, the horn of my salvation,
My trust, my shield, my strong fortification.
I on the Lord most worthy praise will call:
And so from all my foes be sav'd I shall.
The pangs of death did round about dismay me,
And torrents strong of wicked men did fray me.
Encompast round with sorrowes of the grave,
The snares of death my life prevented have.

Psalm 19

Dessus
Haute-Contre
Taille
Basse-Contre
Genevan tune
Les cieux en cha- cun lieu, La puis-san- ce de Dieu
Ra- con- tent aux hu- mains. Ce grand en- tour es- pars, Pu- blie
en tou- tes pars L'ou- vra- ge de ses mains. Jour a- pres jour cou-

8
9
-lant, Du Sei- gneur va par- lant, Par longue ex- pe- ri- en- ce.
-lant, Du Sei- gneur va par- lant, Par longue ex- pe- ri- en- ce.
-lant, Du Sei- gneur va par- lant, Par longue ex- pe- ri- en- ce.
-lant, Du Sei- gneur va par- lant, Par longue ex- pe- ri- en- ce.
10
11
La nuict sui- vant la nuict, Nous presche et nous ins- truit
La nuict sui- vant la nuict, Nous presche et nous ins- truit
La nuict sui- vant la nuict, Nous presche et nous ins- truit
La nuict sui- vant la nuict, Nous presche et nous ins- truit
12
De sa grand sa- pi- en- ce.
De sa grand sa- pi- en- ce.
De sa grand sa- pi- en- ce.
De sa grand sa- pi- en- ce.
The heav'ns so framed are
That they to all declare,
God's glory doth excell.
The skyes and firmament,
Bright, clear, and permanent,
His handy work doth tell.
Day unto day doth teach,
And of the Lord do preach,
His wondrous powr relating:
Night unto night doth show,
That every one may know,
His wisdome them creating.

Psalm 20

Dessus
Haute-Contre
Taille
Basse-Contre
Genevan tune
2
3
4
5
6
Le Seigneur ta priere entende En ta necessité,
Le Dieu de Jacob te defende En ton adversité.
De ton lieu sainct en ta complainte
A tes maux il subviene,

7
8
De Si- on sa mon- tai- gne sain- te Il te gard' et sous- tien- ne.
De Si- on sa mon- tai- gne sain- te Il te gard' et sous- tien- ne.
De Si- on sa mon- tai- gne sain- te Il te gard' et sous- tien- ne.
De Si- on sa mon- tai- gne sain- te Il te gard' et sous- tien- ne.

When thou dost pray, the Lord attend thee
In thy necessity.
The name of Jacobs God defend thee
In thy adversity.
He send thee help, thy cause maintaining
Against thine adversary.
He strengthen thee, thy state sustaining,
From Sions Sanctuary.

Psalm 21

Dessus
Haute-Contre
Taille
Basse-Contre
Genevan tune
2
3
4
Sei- gneur, le Roy s'es- jou- i- ra D'a- voir eu
de- li- vran- ce Par ta gran- de puis- san- ce.
O com- bien joy- eux il se- ra,

5
6
D'ain- si sou- dain se voir Re- coux par ton pou- voir.
D'ain- si sou- dain se voir Re- coux par ton pou- voir.
D'ain- si sou- dain se voir Re- coux par ton pou- voir.
D'ain- si sou- dain se voir Re- coux par ton pou- voir.

The King O Lord in thy great might
Doth joy with exultation,
Triumphs in thy salvation.
O what exceeding great delight
In him always remains
That thy grace him maintains.

Psalm 22

Dessus
Mon Dieu, mon Dieu pour- quoy m'as tu lais- sé
Haute-Contre
Mon Dieu, mon Dieu pour- quoy m'as tu lais- sé
Taille
Genevan tune
Mon Dieu, mon Dieu pour- quoy m'as tu lais- sé
Basse-Contre
Mon Dieu, mon Dieu pour- quoy m'as tu lais- sé
2
Loin de se- cours, d'en- nuy tant op- pres- sé,
3
Et loin du cri que
Loin de se- cours, d'en- nuy tant op- pres- sé,
Et loin du cri que
Loin de se- cours, d'en- nuy tant op- pres- sé,
Et loin du cri que
Loin de se- cours, d'en- nuy tant op- pres- sé,
Et loin du cri que
je t'ay ad- dres- sé
4
En ma com-plain- te?
5
De jour mon Dieu, je
je t'ay ad- dres- sé
En ma com-plain- te?
De jour mon Dieu, je t'in-
je t'ay ad- dres- sé
En ma com-plain- te?
De jour mon Dieu, je
je t'ay ad- dres- sé
En ma com-plain- te?
De jour mon Dieu, je

My God my God, why leav'st thou me distrest?
And why hast thou forsaken me, opprest?
Far from my ayd and cryes to thee exprest,
Thy selfe detayning.
All day my God, to thee my voice high straining,
Thou hear'st me not, to me no answer daigning,
All night I call to thee, no time refraining,
I rest no space.

Psalm 23

Dessus
Mon Dieu me pait sous sa puis- san- ce hau- te:
Haute-Contre
Mon Dieu me pait sous sa puis- san- ce hau- te:
Taille
Genevan tune
Mon Dieu me pait sous sa puis- san- ce hau- te:
Basse-Contre
Mon Dieu me pait sous sa puis- san- ce hau- te:
2
C'est mon ber- ger, de rien je n'au- ray fau- te,
3
En tect bien
C'est mon ber- ger, de rien je n'au- ray fau- te, En tect bien
C'est mon ber- ger, de rien je n'au- ray fau- te, En tect bien
C'est mon ber- ger, de rien je n'au- ray fau- te, En tect bien
seur, joi- gnant les beaux her- ba- ges
4
Cou- cher me fait, me mein' aux
seur, joi- gnant les beaux her- ba- ges Cou- cher me fait, me mein' aux
seur, joi- gnant les beaux her- ba- ges Cou- cher me fait, me mein' aux
seur, joi- gnant les beaux her- ba- ges Cou- cher me fait, me mein' aux

The living Lord me ever loving feedeth,
My Pastor true my soul now nothing needeth.
He leads me forth in fields and foulds inclosing,
Of plenteous food by fountains clear reposing.
My soul revives where he me safely leadeth,
For his Names sake in right paths my foot treadeth.

Psalm 24

*Also set in Psalms 62, 95, and 111

6
-vi- ron- na, De main- te ri- vie- re tres- bel- le.
-vi- ron- na, De main- te ri- vie- re tres- bel- le.
-vi- ron- na, De main- te ri- vie- re tres- bel- le.
-vi- ron- na, De main- te ri- vie- re tres- bel- le.

The earth belongs unto the Lord,
With all the store it doth afford,
What in the world hath scituation.
For on the flouds he plac'd the land,
Which on the waters firm doth stand,
Establisht on a sure foundation.

Psalm 25

Dessus
Haute-Contre
Taille
Basse-Contre
Genevan tune
2
A toy mon Dieu, mon coeur mon- te, En toy mon
A toy mon Dieu, mon coeur mon- te, En toy mon
A toy mon Dieu, mon coeur mon- te, En toy mon
A toy mon Dieu, mon coeur mon- te, En toy mon
3
4
es- poir ay mis: Fay que je ne tombe à hon- te, Au gré de
es- poir ay mis: Fay que je ne tombe à hon- te, Au gré de
es- poir ay mis: Fay que je ne tombe à hon- te, Au gré de
es- poir ay mis: Fay que je ne tombe à hon- te, Au gré de
5
6
mes en- ne- mis. Hon- te n'au-ront voi- re- ment Ceux qui des- sus toy
mes en- ne- mis. Hon- te n'au-ront voi- re- ment Ceux qui des- sus toy
mes en- ne- mis. Hon- te n'au-ront voi- re- ment Ceux qui des- sus toy
mes en- ne- mis. Hon- te n'au-ront voi- re- ment Ceux qui des- sus toy

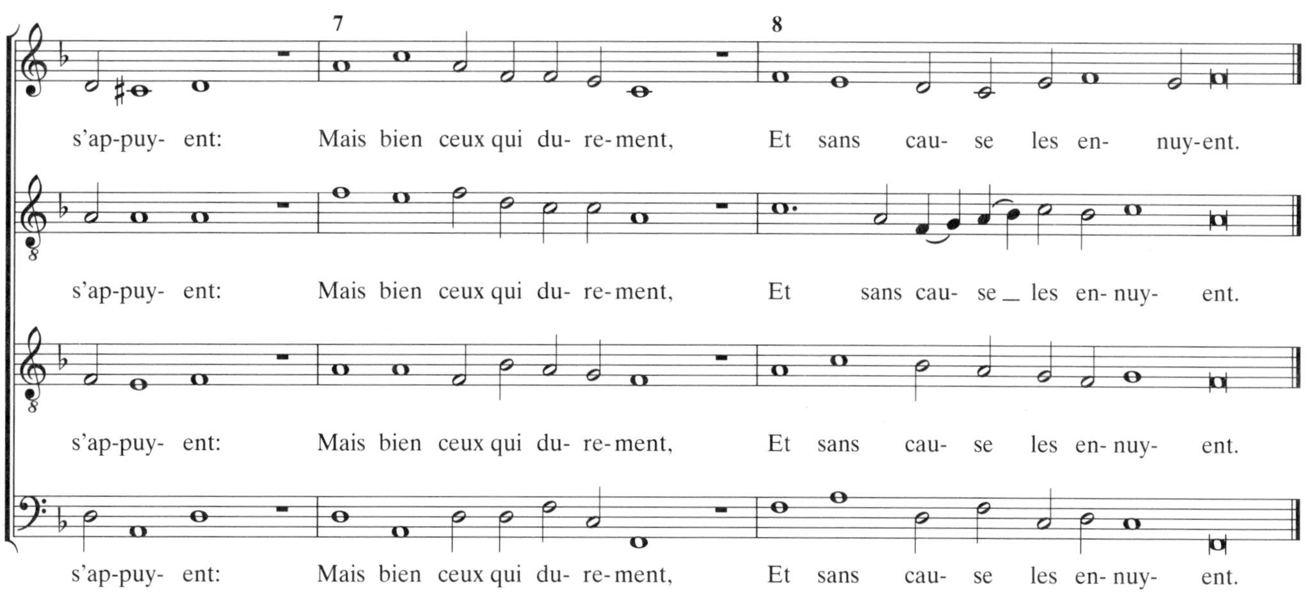
7
8
s'ap-puy- ent: Mais bien ceux qui du- re-ment, Et sans cau- se les en- nuy-ent.
s'ap-puy- ent: Mais bien ceux qui du- re-ment, Et sans cau- se _ les en- nuy- ent.
s'ap-puy- ent: Mais bien ceux qui du- re-ment, Et sans cau- se les en- nuy- ent.
s'ap-puy- ent: Mais bien ceux qui du- re-ment, Et sans cau- se les en- nuy- ent.

All my hearts desire is raised
To thee Lord, I trust in thee.
Let me never be disgraced,
Nor my foes joy over me.
By thy grace, do thou protect
Them from shame, which do attend thee,
But confound, with shame deject
Them that causelessly offend thee.

Psalm 26

O Lord God, judg thou me,
For in integritie,
I walked have, and so abide,
In God I trust assured,
Who hath me safe secured,
Therefore I shall not fall nor slide.

Psalm 27

Dessus
Haute-Contre
Taille
Basse-Contre
Genevan tune
2
3
4
Le Sei- gneur est la clar- té qui m'ad- dres- se, Et mon sa- lut, que doy- je re- dou- ter? Le Sei- gneur est l'ap- puy qui me re- dres- se, Où est ce- luy qui peust m'es- pou- van- ter?
Le Sei- gneur est la clar- té qui m'ad-dres- se, Et mon sa- lut, que doy- je re- dou- ter? Le Sei- gneur est l'ap- puy qui me re- dres- se, Où est ce- luy qui peust m'es-pou- van- ter?
Le Sei- gneur est la clar- té qui m'ad-dres- se, Et mon sa- lut, que doy- je re- dou- ter? Le Sei- gneur est l'ap- puy qui me re- dres- se, Où est ce- luy qui peust m'es-pou- van- ter?
Le Sei- gneur est la clar- té qui m'ad-dres- se, Et mon sa- lut, que doy- je re- dou- ter? Le Sei- gneur est l'ap- puy qui me re- dres- se, Où est ce- luy qui peust m'es-pou- van- ter?

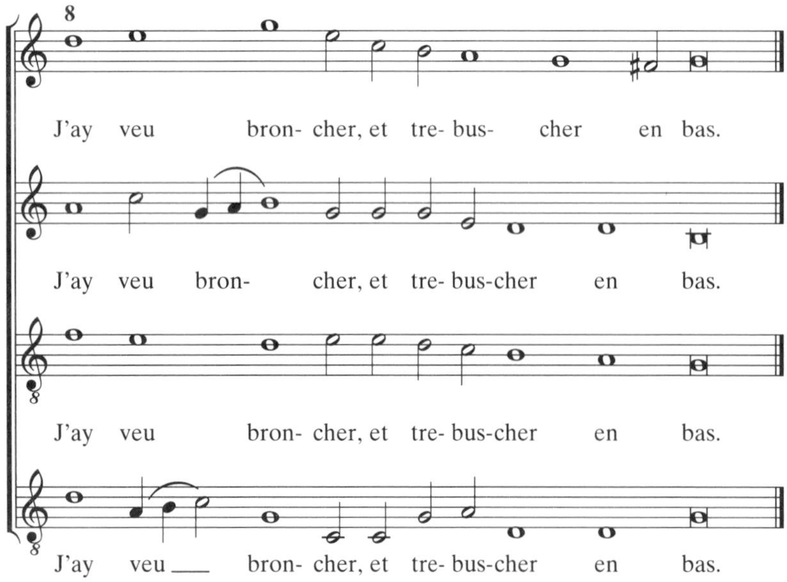

The Lord God is my light and my salvation,
Then who is he that can make me affraid?
The Lord is my lifes strong fortification,
What then is he that can make me dismaid?
When wicked men approached against me
To eat my flesh, my cruell deadly foes,
My enemies, whose hate did me oppose,
They stumbled then, and fell down fearfully.

Psalm 28

*Also set in Psalm 109

Psalm 29

Dessus
2
Vous tous Prin- ces et Sei- gneurs, Rem- plis de gloire et
Haute-Contre
Vous tous Prin- ces et Sei- gneurs, Rem- plis de gloire et
Taille
Genevan tune
Vous tous Prin- ces et Sei- gneurs, Rem- plis de gloire et
Basse-Contre
Vous tous Prin- ces et Sei- gneurs, Rem- plis de gloire et
3
4
d'hon-neurs, Ren- dez, ren- dez au Sei-gneur, Tou- te force et tout hon-neur.
d'hon-neurs, Ren- dez, ren- dez au Sei-gneur, Tou- te force et tout hon-neur.
d'hon-neurs, Ren- dez, ren- dez au Sei-gneur, Tou- te force et tout hon-neur.
d'hon-neurs, Ren- dez, ren- dez au Sei-gneur, Tou- te force et tout hon-neur.
5
6
Fai- tes luy re- co- gnois- san- ce Qui res- ponde à sa puis- san- ce:
Fai- tes luy re- co- gnois-san- ce Qui res- ponde à sa puis- san- ce:
Fai- tes luy re- co- gnois-san- ce Qui res- ponde à sa puis- san- ce:
Fai- tes luy re- co- gnois-san- ce Qui res- ponde à sa puis- san- ce:

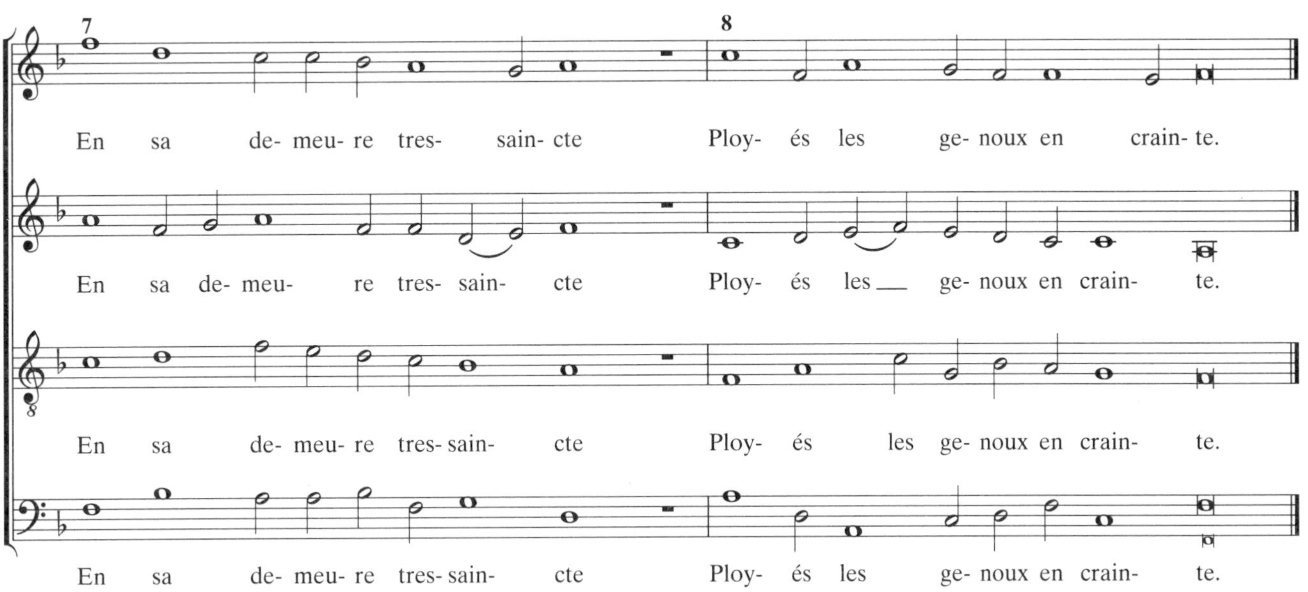

All ye princes, mighty States,
Monarchs, Kings, and Potentates,
Render to the Lord his right:
Glory, Majesty, and might.
To his Name most honorable,
Render praises answerable:
Worship God performe this duty
In his house of sacred beauty.

Psalm 30

I will exalt thee Lord with praise,
For thou from troubles didst me raise,
And hast not suffered them that be
My foes, to triumph over me;
Therefore thou shalt be magnified
And ever highly glorified.

*Also set in Psalms 76 and 139

Psalm 31

In thee alone O Lord my trust is,
My hope is in thy Name.
Let me not suffer shame:
But me deliver in thy justice,
When trouble me assaileth,
For thy word never faileth.

*Also set in Psalm 71

Psalm 32

Dessus
Haute-Contre
Taille
Basse-Contre
Genevan tune
2
O bien heu- reux ce- luy dont les com- mi- ses Trans-gres- si-
O bien heu- reux ce- luy dont les com- mi- ses Trans-gres- si-
O bien heu- reux ce- luy dont les com- mi- ses Trans-gres- si-
O bien heu- reux ce- luy dont les com- mi- ses Trans-gres- si-
3
-ons sont par gra- ce re- mi- ses, Du- quel aus- si les i- ni- ques pe- chés
-ons sont par gra- ce re- mi- ses, Du- quel aus- si les i- ni- ques pe- chés
-ons sont par gra- ce re- mi- ses, Du- quel aus- si les i- ni- ques pe- chés
-ons sont par gra- ce re- mi- ses, Du- quel aus- si les i- ni- ques pe- chés
4
5
De- vant son Dieu sont cou- vers et ca- chez! O com- bien plein
De- vant son Dieu sont cou- vers et ca- chez! O com- bien plein
De- vant son Dieu sont cou- vers et ca- chez! O com- bien plein
De- vant son Dieu sont cou- vers et ca- chez! O com- bien plein

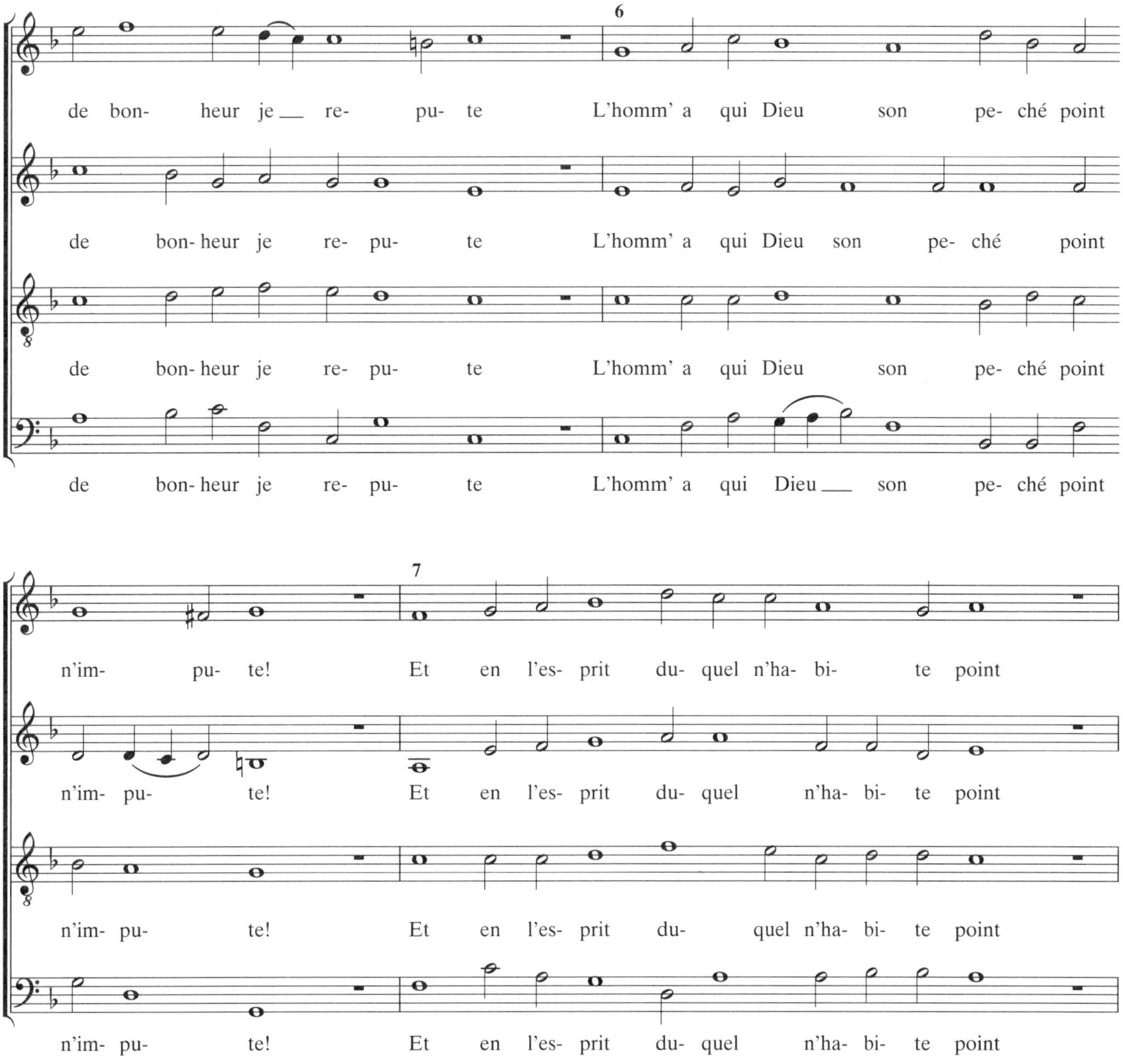

6
de bon- heur je — re- pu- te L'homm' a qui Dieu son pe- ché point
de bon- heur je re- pu- te L'homm' a qui Dieu son pe- ché point
de bon- heur je re- pu- te L'homm' a qui Dieu son pe- ché point
de bon- heur je re- pu- te L'homm' a qui Dieu — son pe- ché point
7
n'im- pu- te! Et en l'es- prit du- quel n'ha- bi- te point
n'im- pu- te! Et en l'es- prit du- quel n'ha- bi- te point
n'im- pu- te! Et en l'es- prit du- quel n'ha- bi- te point
n'im- pu- te! Et en l'es- prit du- quel n'ha- bi- te point

8
D'hy- po- cri- sie et de — fraude un seul poinct!
D'hy- po- cri- sie et de fraude un seul poinct!
D'hy- po- cri- sie et de fraude un seul poinct!
D'hy- po- cri- sie et de fraude un seul poinct!

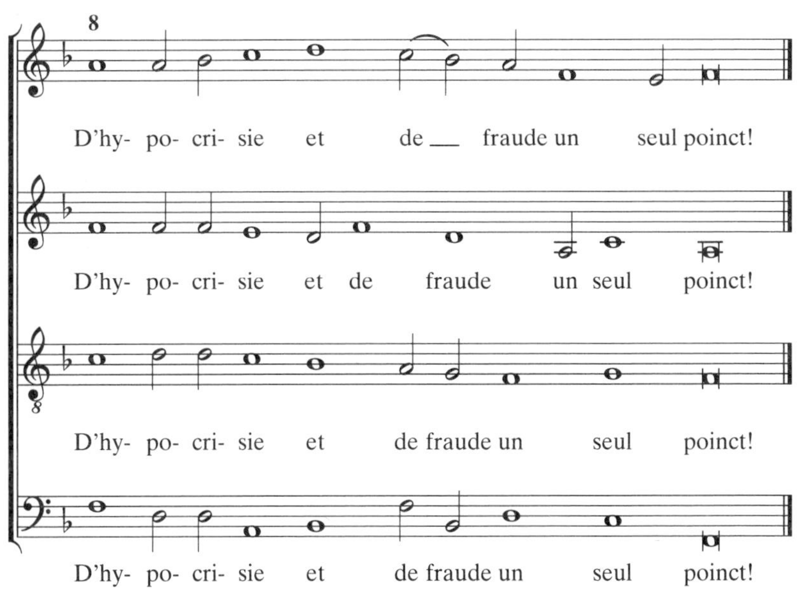

In blessed state he evermore remaineth,
Who of his sins, forgivenesse free obtaineth.
Whose trespasses shall never be revealed,
And whose offence shall ever be concealed.
Thrice happy is that man to be reputed,
To whom his sins the Lord hath not imputed:
Within whose soul doth dwell integrity,
Free from all fraud, guile, and hypocrisie.

Psalm 33

*Also set in Psalm 67

With joyfull shouts, peals gladly ringing,
Ye righteous in the Lord rejoyce:
It well becoms you his praise singing.
Praise ye the Lord with Harp and voice.
Making musick meetest,
Consorts sounding sweetest
On the psalterie,
With ten strings resounding,
Sing Psalms to him sounding,
Praise his Name with glee.

Psalm 34

Dessus
Haute-Contre
Taille
Basse-Contre
Genevan tune
2
Ja- mais ne ces- se- ray De ma- gni- fi- er le Sei- gneur,
Ja- mais ne ces- se- ray De ma- gni- fi- er le Sei- gneur,
Ja- mais ne ces- se- ray De ma- gni- fi- er le Sei- gneur,
Ja- mais ne ces- se- ray De ma- gni- fi- er le Sei- gneur,
3
4
En ma bouche au- ray son hon- neur, Tant que vi- vant se- ray.
En ma bouche au- ray son hon- neur, Tant que vi- vant se- ray.
En ma bouche au- ray son hon- neur, Tant que vi- vant se- ray.
En ma bouche au- ray son hon- neur, Tant que vi- vant se- ray.
5
6
Mon coeur plai- sir n'au- ra Qu'à voir son Dieu glo- ri- fi- é.
Mon coeur plai- sir n'au- ra Qu'à voir son Dieu glo- ri- fi- é.
Mon coeur plai- sir n'au- ra Qu'à voir son Dieu glo- ri- fi- é.
Mon coeur plai- sir n'au- ra Qu'à voir son Dieu glo- ri- fi- é.

At all times I will bles
The Lord my God, his worthy praise,
His glory and renown alwayes
My mouth shall still expres.
Break forth, my souls glad voyce,
Boast in thy glorious Saver deare:
The faithful meeke, thereof shall heare,
And shall with me rejoyce.

Psalm 35

Dessus
Haute-Contre
Taille
Basse-Contre
Genevan tune
2
De- ba con- tre mes de- ba- teurs, Com- ba, Sei-gneur, mes com-
De- ba con- tre mes de- ba- teurs, Com- ba, Sei-gneur, mes com-
De- ba con- tre mes de- ba- teurs, Com- ba, Sei- gneur, _ mes com-
De- ba con- tre mes de- ba- teurs, Com- ba, Sei-gneur, mes com-
3
4
-ba- teurs, Em- poi- gne moy bou- clier et lan- ce, Et pour me se- cou- rir
-ba- teurs, Em- poi- gne moy bou- clier et _ lan- ce, Et pour me se- cou- rir
-ba- teurs, Em- poi- gne moy bou- clier et lan- ce, Et pour me se- cou- rir
-ba- teurs, Em- poi- gne moy bou- clier et lan- ce, Et pour me se- cou- rir
5
6
t'a- van- ce. Char- ge les, et marche au de- vant, Gar- de les d'al- ler
t'a- van- ce. Char- ge les, et marche au de- vant, Gar- de les d'al- ler
t'a- van- ce. Char- ge les, et marche au de- vant, Gar- de les d'al- ler
t'a- van- ce. Char- ge les, et marche au de- vant, Gar- de les d'al- ler

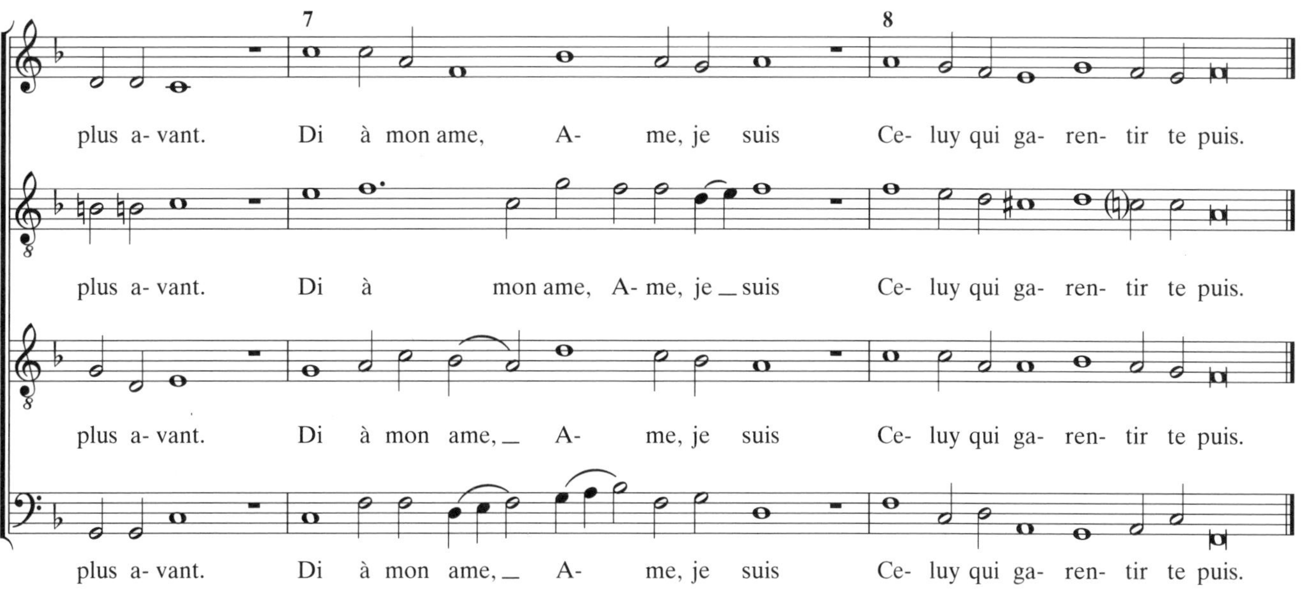
7
8
plus a- vant. Di à mon ame, A- me, je suis Ce- luy qui ga- ren- tir te puis.
plus a- vant. Di à mon ame, A- me, je _ suis Ce- luy qui ga- ren- tir te puis.
plus a- vant. Di à mon ame, _ A- me, je suis Ce- luy qui ga- ren- tir te puis.
plus a- vant. Di à mon ame, _ A- me, je suis Ce- luy qui ga- ren- tir te puis.

Against my foes Lord plead my right,
And smite thou them who me do smite,
With shield and speare compleatly armed,
Stand for my ayd, save me unharmed:
Charge on them, march before my face,
Block up their way who do me chase:
Say to my soul, loe, I am hee
That can and will deliver thee.

Psalm 36

*Also set in Psalm 68

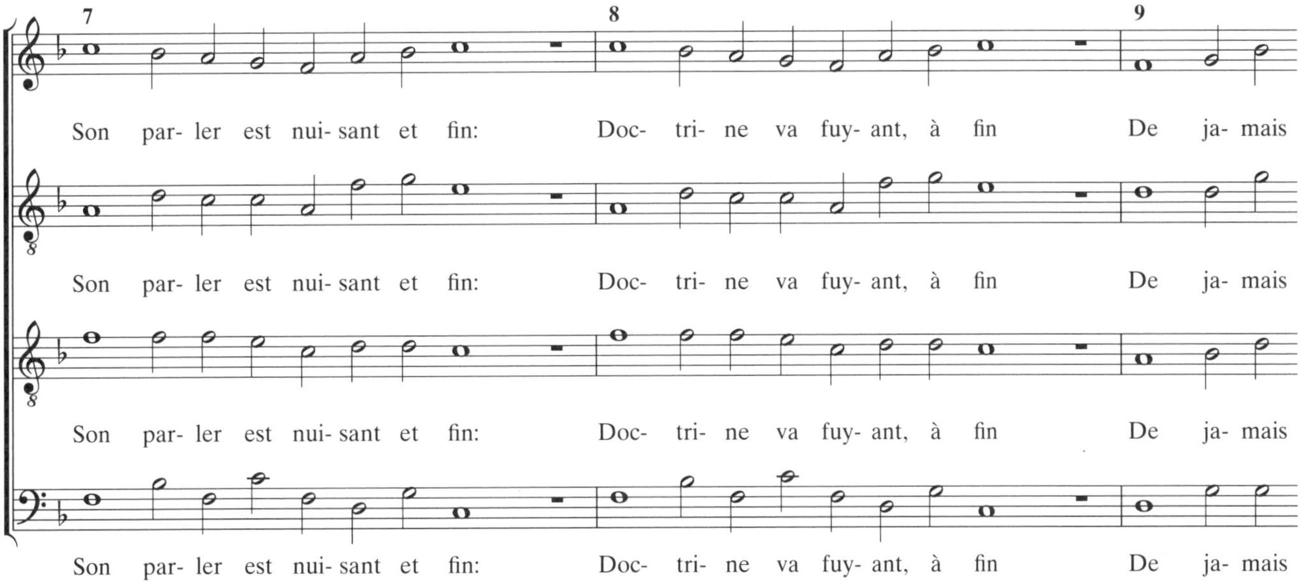

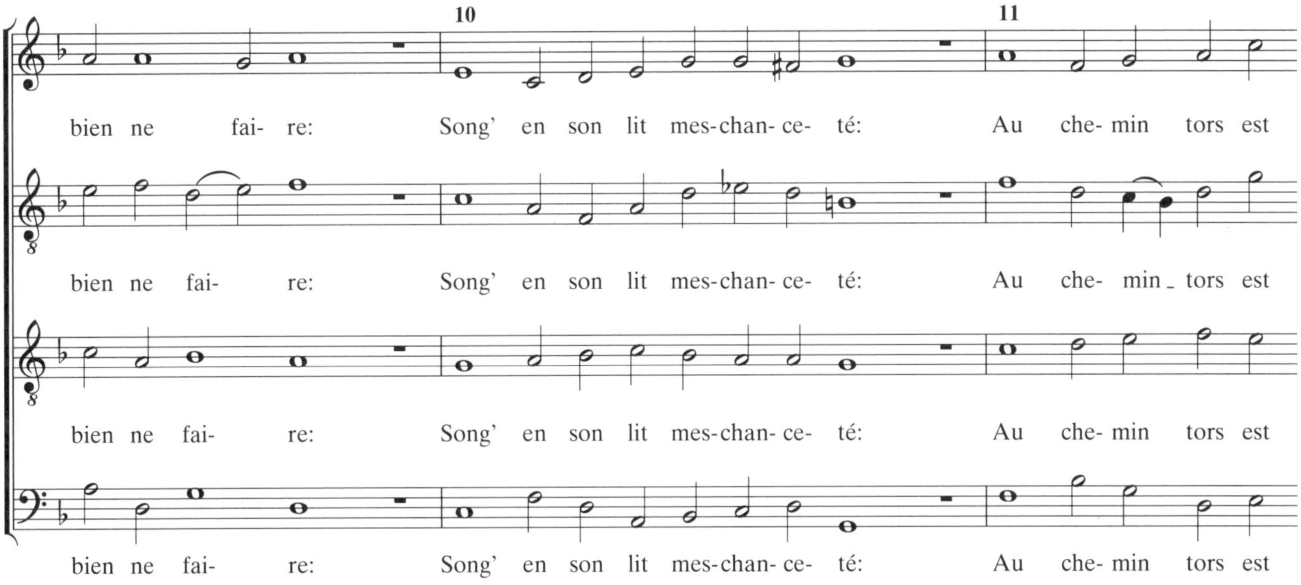

7
8
9
Son par- ler est nui- sant et fin: Doc- tri- ne va fuy- ant, à fin De ja- mais
Son par- ler est nui- sant et fin: Doc- tri- ne va fuy- ant, à fin De ja- mais
Son par- ler est nui- sant et fin: Doc- tri- ne va fuy- ant, à fin De ja- mais
Son par- ler est nui- sant et fin: Doc- tri- ne va fuy- ant, à fin De ja- mais

10
11
bien ne fai- re: Song' en son lit mes-chan- ce- té: Au che- min tors est
bien ne fai- re: Song' en son lit mes-chan- ce- té: Au che- min _ tors est
bien ne fai- re: Song' en son lit mes-chan- ce- té: Au che- min tors est
bien ne fai- re: Song' en son lit mes-chan- ce- té: Au che- min tors est

12
ar- res- té: A nul mal n'est con- trai- re.
ar- res- té: A nul mal n'est con- trai- re.
ar- res- té: A nul mal n'est con- trai- re.
ar- res- té: A nul mal n'est con- trai- re.

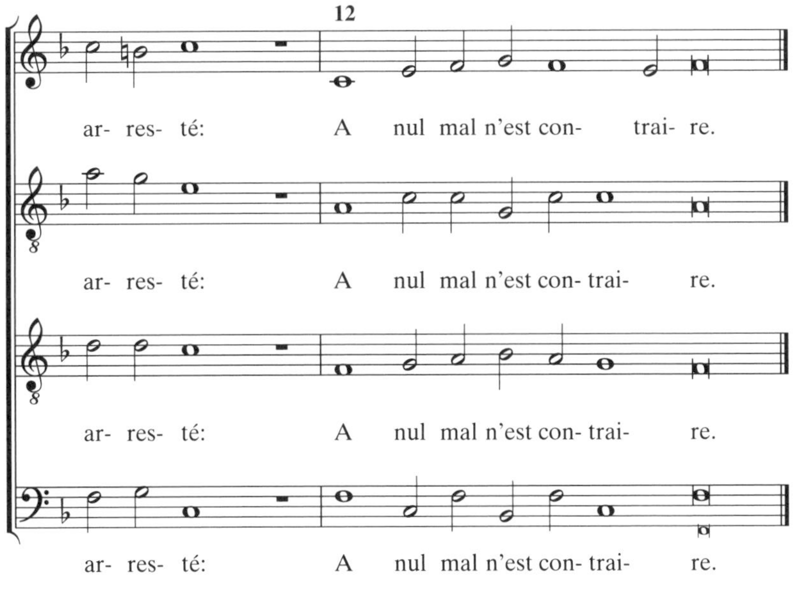

The wicked man hath so transgrest,
That in my heart tis manifest
He hath Gods fear rejected,
For so long himself flattereth he,
In his own eyes, till his sin be
Found hatefull when detected.
His words unjust are fraud and lyes;
He hath surceased to be wise,
No good he exerciseth,
On's bed he mischief doth invent,
In wayes not good to walk he's bent,
No evill he despiseth.

Psalm 37

Dessus
Haute-Contre
Taille
Basse-Contre
Genevan tune
2
3
4
Ne sois fa- ché si du- rant ces- te vi- e, Sou- vent tu
vois pros- pe- rer les mes- chans Et des ma- lins aux biens
ne porte en- vi- e: Car en ru- ine à la fin tre- bu- chans,
biens ne porte en- vi- e: Car en ru- ine à la fin tre- bu- chans,

At wicked men to envy be not moved,
Fret not at them who work iniquitie,
Nor grieve that their designs have prosprous proved,
For they shall fall to ruin suddenly,
Like grasse mow'd down, they perish shall forever,
And as green herbs shall wither finally.

Psalm 38

Lord my God, in thy displeasure,
To the measure
Of my sins, rebuke not me:
Neither in thy furies terrors,
For my errors,
Let me not chastised be.

Psalm 39

Dessus
Haute-Contre
Taille
Basse-Contre
Genevan tune
2
3
4
5
6
J'ay dit en moy, de pres je vi- se- ray A tout ce- la que je fe- ray,
J'ay dit en moy, de pres je vi- se- ray A tout ce- la que je fe- ray,
J'ay dit en moy, de pres je vi- se- ray A tout ce- la que je fe- ray,
J'ay dit en moy, de pres je vi- se- ray A tout ce- la que je fe- ray,
Pour ne par-ler un seul mot de tra-vers, En voy-ant de-bout le per- vers. Voi- re deus-se- je à fin
Pour ne par-ler un seul mot de tra-vers, En voy-ant de- bout le per- vers. Voi- re deus-se- je à fin
Pour ne par-ler un seul mot de tra-vers, En voy-ant de-bout le per-vers. Voi- re deus-se- je à fin de
Pour ne par-ler un seul mot de tra-vers, En voy-ant de- bout le per- vers. Voi- re deus-se- je à fin
de ne par- ler, Ma pro-pre bouche em-mu- se- ler.
de ne par- ler, Ma pro-pre bouche em- mu-se- ler.
ne par- ler, Ma pro-pre bouche em- mu-se- ler.
de ne par- ler, Ma pro-pre bouche em- mu-se- ler.
I said I will to all my wayes take heed,
That I sin not in word or deed:
My tong from speech I strictly will restrain,
While wicked men with me remain:
And lest my mouth my meaning do unfould,
As with a bridle I'le with-hold.

Psalm 40

Dessus
Haute-Contre
Taille
Basse-Contre
Genevan tune
2
3
4
5
A- pres a- voir con- stam-ment at- ten- du De l'E- ter-
-nel la vo- lon- té, Il s'est tour- né de mon cos- té, Et à
mon cri au be- soin en- ten- du. Hors de fange et d'or- du- re,

While I did long with patient constancy,
The pleasure of my God attend,
He unto me his eare did bend
And to my cryes he hearkened graciously.
Me from deep pit bemired,
From dungeon he retired,
Where I in horror lay:
And set my feet upon
A stedfast rocky stone,
And my weak steps did stay.

Psalm 41

Dessus
Haute-Contre
Taille
Basse-Contre
Genevan tune
2
O bien-heu-reux qui ju- ge sa- ge-ment Du pauvre en _ son tour- ment!
O bien-heu-reux qui ju- ge sa- ge-ment Du pauvre en son tour-ment!
O bien-heu-reux qui ju- ge sa- ge- ment Du pauvre en son tour- ment!
O bien-heu-reux qui ju- ge sa- ge- ment Du pauvre en son tour- ment!
3
4
Cer- tai- ne- ment Dieu le sou- la- ge- ra, Quand af- fli- gé se- ra:
Cer- tai- ne- ment Dieu le sou- la- ge- ra, Quand af- fli- gé se- ra:
Cer- tai- ne- ment Dieu le sou- la- ge- ra, Quand af- fli- gé se- ra:
Cer- tai- ne- ment Dieu le sou- la- ge- ra, Quand af- fli- gé se- ra:
5
6
Dieu le ren- dra sain et sauf, et ___ fe- ra Qu'en-core il flo- ri- ra:
Dieu le ren- dra sain et sauf, et fe- ra Qu'en-core il flo- ri- ra:
Dieu le ren- dra sain et sauf, et fe- ra Qu'en-core il flo- ri- ra:
Dieu le ren- dra sain et sauf, et fe- ra Qu'en-core il flo- ri- ra:

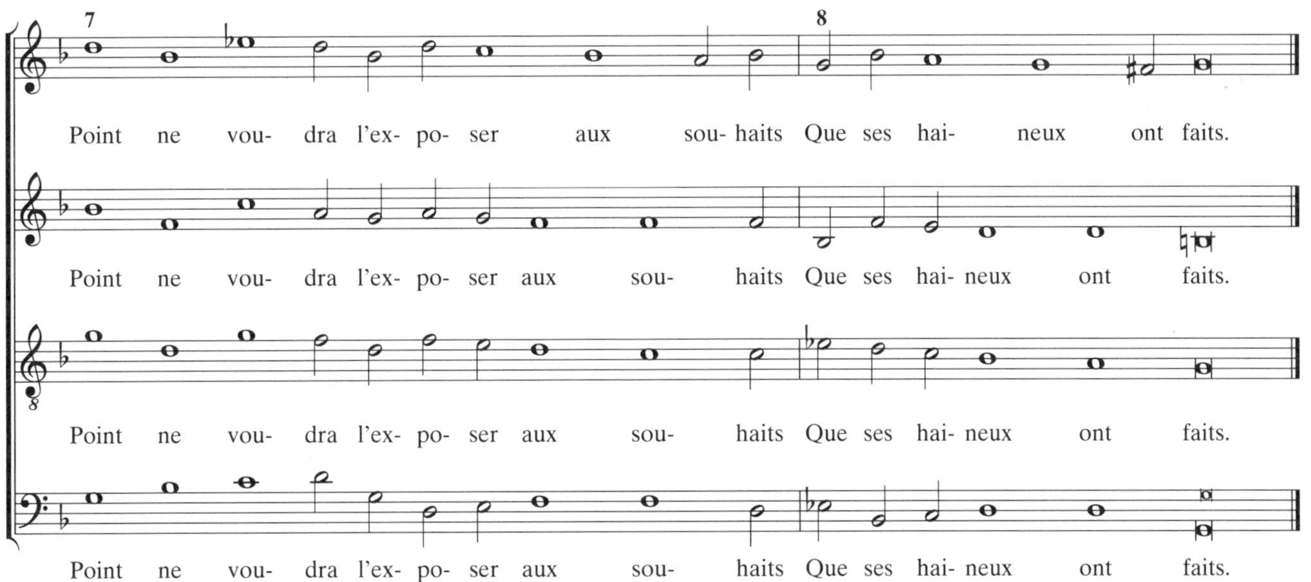

He blessed is that doth compassion show
To them that are brought low:
He from the Lord of comfort shall not mis
When he afflicted is.
The Lord will him preserve alive, that he
On earth shall blessed be.
He will not him deliver, nor expose
Unto his furious foes.

Psalm 42

Dessus
Haute-Contre
Taille
Basse-Contre
Genevan tune
Ain- si qu'on oit le cerf brui-re Pour-chas-sant le frais des eaux,
Ain- si qu'on oit le cerf brui- re Pour-chas-sant le frais des eaux,
Ain- si qu'on oit le cerf brui- re Pour-chas-sant le frais des eaux,
Ain- si qu'on oit le cerf brui- re Pour-chas-sant le frais des eaux,
Ain- si mon coeur qui sou- pi- re, Sei- gneur a- pres tes ruis-seaux,
Ain- si mon coeur qui sou- pi- re, Sei- gneur a- pres tes ruis- seaux,
Ain- si mon coeur qui sou- pi- re, Sei- gneur a- pres tes ruis- seaux,
Ain- si mon coeur qui sou- pi- re, Sei- gneur a- pres tes ruis- seaux,
Va tous- jours cri- ant, suy- vant Le grand, le grand Dieu vi- vant.
Va tous- jours cri- ant, suy- vant Le grand, le grand Dieu vi- vant.
Va tous- jours cri- ant, suy- vant Le grand, le grand Dieu vi- vant.
Va tous- jours cri- ant, suy- vant Le grand, le grand Dieu vi- vant.

7
8
He- las don- ques, quand se- ra- ce, Que ver- ray de Dieu la fa- ce?
He- las don- ques, quand se- ra- ce, Que ver- ray de Dieu la fa- ce?
He- las don- ques, quand se- ra- ce, Que ver- ray de Dieu la fa- ce?
He- las don- ques, quand se- ra- ce, Que ver- ray de Dieu la fa- ce?

As the chased Hart pants braying,
Seeking some refreshing brooke,
So my thirsty soul longs praying,
Zealous on my God to looke.
My soul thirsteth eagerly,
Everliving God for thee:
Lord when shall I come before thee,
In thy presence to adore thee.

Psalm 43

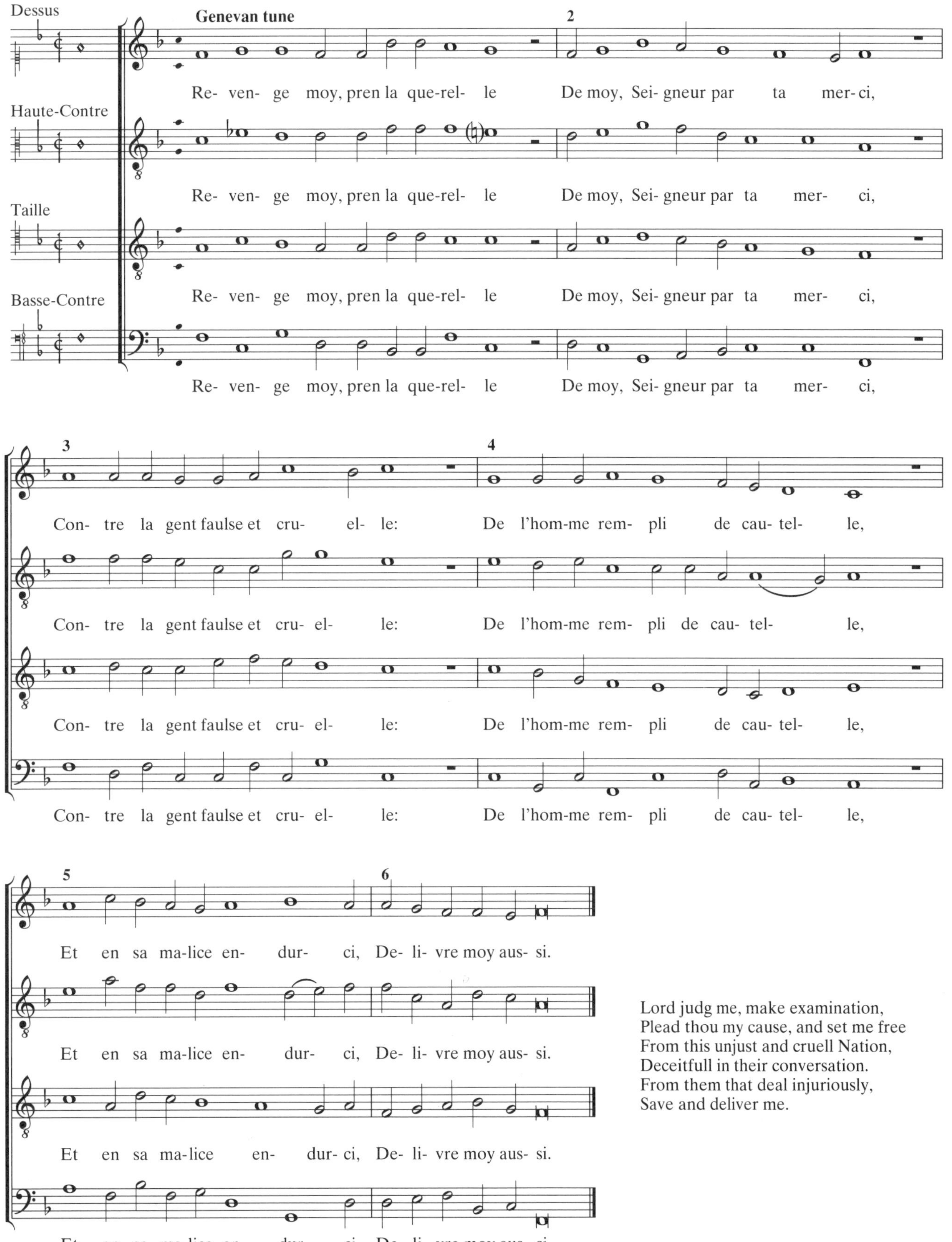

Lord judg me, make examination,
Plead thou my cause, and set me free
From this unjust and cruell Nation,
Deceitfull in their conversation.
From them that deal injuriously,
Save and deliver me.

Psalm 44

Dessus
Haute-Contre
Taille
Genevan tune
Basse-Contre
2
Or a- vons nous de noz au- reil- les, Sei- gneur, en- ten- du
Or a- vons nous de noz au- reil- les, Sei- gneur, en- ten- du
Or a- vons nous de noz au- reil- les, Sei- gneur, en- ten- du
Or a- vons nous de noz au- reil- les, Sei- gneur, en- ten- du
3
4
tes mer- veil- les: Ra- con- ter à noz pe- res vieux, Fai- tes ja-
tes mer- veil- les: Ra- con- ter à noz pe- res vieux, Fai- tes ja-
tes mer- veil- les: Ra- con- ter à noz pe- res vieux, Fai- tes ja-
tes mer- veil- les: Ra- con- ter à noz pe- res vieux, Fai- tes ja-
5
6
-dis et de- vant eux. Ta main à les peu- ples chas- sez, Plan- tant noz pe- res en
-dis et de- vant eux. Ta main à les peu- ples chas- sez, Plan- tant noz pe- res en
-dis et de- vant eux. Ta main à les peu- ples chas- sez, Plan- tant noz pe- res en
-dis et de- vant eux. Ta main à les peu- ples chas- sez, Plan- tant noz pe- res en

7
8
leur pla- ce: Tu as les peu-ples op- pres- sés, Y fai-sant ger- mer nos- tre ra- ce.
leur pla- ce: Tu as les peu- ples _ op- pres- sés, Y fai-sant ger- mer nos-tre ra- ce.
leur pla- ce: Tu as les peu-ples op- pres- sés, Y fai-sant ger- mer nos-tre ra- ce.
leur pla- ce: Tu as les peu-ples op- pres- sés, Y fai-sant ger- mer __ nos-tre ra- ce.

Lord God of high renown and glory,
Our eares have heard the joyous story
Which our forefathers have us told:
Of wondrous workes thou didst of old,
How thou the heathen didst expell,
And in that land our fathers planted,
By thy strong hand therein to dwell,
Their foes were plagued and supplanted.

Psalm 45

Dessus
Haute-Contre
Taille
Basse-Contre
Genevan tune
2
Pro- pos ex- quis faut que de mon coeur sor- te: Car du Roy
Pro- pos ex- quis faut que de mon coeur sor- te: Car du Roy
Pro- pos ex- quis faut que de mon coeur sor- te: Car du Roy
Pro- pos ex- quis faut que de mon coeur sor- te: Car du Roy
3
veux di- re chan- son de sor- te, Qu'à ces- te fois ma lan-gue mieux di- ra,
veux di- re chan-son de sor- te, Qu'à ces- te fois ma lan-gue mieux di- ra,
veux di- re chan-son de sor- te, Qu'à ces- te fois ma lan-gue mieux di- ra,
veux di- re chan-son de sor- te, Qu'à ces- te fois ma lan-gue mieux di- ra,
4
5
Qu'un scri- be prompt de plu- me n'es- cri- ra. Le mieux for- mé
Qu'un scri- be prompt de plu- me n'es- cri- ra. Le mieux for- mé
Qu'un scri- be prompt de plu- me n'es- cri- ra. Le mieux for- mé
Qu'un scri- be prompt de plu- me n'es- cri- ra. Le mieux for- mé

A high designe my fervent heart inflameth,
Of King divine heroycall song it frameth.
Invention quicke to fluent tong indites,
Which faster flows then swiftest penman writes.
Thy beauty rare the sons of men exceedeth,
Past all compare grace from thy lips proceedeth:
Therefore thy God hath thee forever blest,
And thou of blisse eternall art possest.

Psalm 46

*Also set in Psalm 82

When as adversity offendeth,
God is our refuge, us defendeth.
In all distres, and time of need,
His help we finde with present speed.
Therefore we fear no molestation,
Though moved be the earths foundation,
Although the mountains high and steep,
Were thrown i' the middle of the deepe.

Psalm 47

Dessus
Haute-Contre
Taille
Basse-Contre
Genevan tune
2
3
4
5
6
7
Or sus, tous hu- mains, Frap- pez en vos mains: Qu'on oy- e
Or sus, tous hu- mains, Frap- pez en vos mains: Qu'on oy- e
Or sus, tous hu- mains, Frap- pez en vos mains: Qu'on oy- e
Or sus, tous hu- mains, Frap- pez en vos mains: Qu'on oy- e
son- ner, Qu'on oye en- ton- ner Le nom so- len- nel
son- ner, Qu'on oye en- ton- ner Le nom so- len- nel
son- ner, Qu'on oye en- ton- ner Le nom so- len- nel
son- ner, Qu'on oye en- ton- ner Le nom so- len- nel
De Dieu e- ter- nel. C'est le Dieu tres- haut
De Dieu e- ter- nel. C'est le Dieu tres- haut
De Dieu e- ter- nel. C'est le Dieu tres- haut
De Dieu e- ter- nel. C'est le Dieu tres- haut

8
Que craindr' il nous faut.
9
Le grand Roy qui fait
Que craindr' il nous faut.
Le grand Roy qui fait
Que craindr' il nous faut.
Le grand Roy qui fait
Que craindr' il nous faut.
Le grand Roy qui fait
10
Sen- tir en ef- fect
11
Sa force au tra- vers
12
De tout l'u- ni- vers.
Sen- tir en ef- fect
Sa force au tra- vers De tout l'u- ni- vers.
Sen- tir en ef- fect
Sa force au tra- vers De tout l'u- ni- vers.
Sen- tir en ef- fect
Sa force au tra- vers De tout l'u- ni- vers.

People of all Lands,
Joyfull clap your hands
Praising God our King,
Shout, truimphant sing.
With a strong, shrill voyce
Chearfully rejoyce.
For the Lord most high
Far above the sky,
Is of dreadfull might,
Terrible in fight:
Monarch over all
Kings terrestriall.

Psalm 48

Dessus
Haute-Contre
Taille
Basse-Contre
Genevan tune
2
C'est en sa tres- sain- cte ci- té, Lieu choi- si pour
C'est en sa tres- sain- cte ci- té, Lieu choi- si pour
C'est en sa tres- sain- cte ci- té, Lieu choi- si pour
C'est en sa tres- sain- cte ci- té, Lieu choi- si pour
3
4
sa sain- cte- té, Que Dieu des-ploye en ex- cel- len- ce Sa gloire et sa ma-
sa sain- cte- té, Que Dieu des-ploye en ex- cel- len- ce Sa gloire et sa ma-
sa sain- cte- té, Que Dieu des-ploye en ex- cel- len- ce Sa gloire et sa ma-
sa sain- cte- té, Que Dieu des-ploye en ex- cel- len- ce Sa gloire et sa ma-
5
6
-gni- fi- cen- ce. La mon- tai- gne de Si- on, De- vers le Sep- ten- tri- on,
-gni- fi- cen- ce. La mon- tai- gne de Si- on, De- vers le Sep- ten- tri- on,
-gni- fi- cen- ce. La mon- tai- gne de Si- on, De- vers le Sep- ten- tri- on,
-gni- fi- cen- ce. La mon- tai- gne de Si- on, De- vers le Sep- ten- tri- on,

Great is the Lord in this his seat,
His praises are exceeding great:
In our God's city his own dwelling,
His sacred mountain high excelling:
Sion mountain is in place,
Full of beauty, full of grace:
Northward being scituated,
To the great King consecrated:
All the earth therewith delighted,
To rejoyce there are invited.

Psalm 49

Dessus
Haute-Contre
Taille
Basse-Contre
Genevan tune
2
3
4
5
Peu- ples oy- ez, et l'au- reil- le pres- tez, Hom- mes
mor- tels qui le monde ha- bi- tez, Des plus pe- tis jus- ques aux plus
puis-sans, Ri- ches hau- tains, et pau- vres lan- guis- sans, Sa- ges pro- pos

6

ma bouche an- non- ce- ra, Gra- ves di- scours mon coeur en- ta- me- ra.

ma bouche an- non- ce- ra, Gra- ves di- scours mon coeur en- ta- me- ra.

ma bouche an- non- ce- ra, Gra- ves di- scours mon coeur en- ta- me- ra.

ma bouche an- non- ce- ra, Gra- ves di- scours mon coeur en- ta- me- ra.

7 8

A mes beaux mots l'au- reil- le je veux ten- dre, Et sur mon lut

A mes beaux _ mots l'au- reil- le je veux ten- dre, Et sur mon lut

A mes beaux mots l'au- reil- le je veux ten- dre, Et sur mon lut

A mes beaux mots l'au- reil- le je veux ten- dre, Et sur mon lut

grand's cho- ses vous ap- pren- dre.
grand's _ cho- ses vous ap- pren- dre.
grand's cho- ses vous ap- pren- dre.
grand's cho- ses vous ap- pren- dre.

To this my speech all people give good eare,
All dwellers in the earth attentive heare.
The noble and the base, both rich and poore,
All famous and obscure, both high and lore.
My mouth shall speak of wisdom prudent speach,
My hearts discourse shall understanding teach.
I will incline my eare to heare revealed,
With harp exprest, my parable concealed.

Psalm 50

Dessus
Haute-Contre
Taille
Basse-Contre
Genevan tune
2
Le Dieu le fort, l'E- ter- nel par- le- ra, Et hault et clair
3
la terre ap- pel- le- ra: De l'O- ri- ent jus- ques à l'Oc- ci- dent,
4
5
De- vers Si- on, Dieu clair et e- vi- dent Ap- pa- rois- tra, or- né

6
de beau- té tou- te, Nos- tre grand Dieu vien- dra, n'en faic- tes dou- te.
de beau- té tou- te, Nos- tre grand Dieu vien- dra, n'en faic- tes dou- te.
de beau- té tou- te, Nos- tre grand Dieu vien- dra, n'en faic- tes dou- te.
de beau- té tou- te, Nos- tre grand Dieu vien- dra, n'en faic- tes dou- te.

The mighty God, the Lord eternall blest,
Hath spoke, and cald the earth from East to West,
From Sion fair, in perfect beauty bright,
Our God hath shin'd, and showd forth glorious light.
Our God will come, his Majesty revealing,
His sentence just, in silence not concealing.

Psalm 51

*Also set in Psalm 69

Have mercy Lord have mercy most of might
On me, alas, most wicked wretch of wretches;
According to thy mercies boundles riches,
Remit my sins, remove them from thy sight.
Wash me O Lord, and throughly clense my soul,
From th'odious fact my folly hath committed,
And from my crimes so crying, fell, and foul,
By thy free Grace let me be clear'd, and quitted.

Psalm 52

Dessus

Di moy, mal- heu- reux, qui te fi- es En ton au- tho- ri- té,

Haute-Contre

Di moy, mal- heu- reux, qui te fi- es En ton au- tho- ri- té,

Taille

Genevan tune

Di moy, mal- heu- reux, qui te fi- es En ton au- tho- ri- té,

Basse-Contre

Di moy, mal- heu- reux, qui te fi- es En ton au- tho- ri- té,

2

3 4 5

D'ou vient que tu te glo- ri- fi- es De ta mes- chan- ce- té? Quoy que soit, de

D'ou vient que tu te glo- ri- fi- es De ta mes- chan- ce- té? Quoy que soit, de

D'ou vient que tu te glo- ri- fi- es De ta mes- chan- ce- té? Quoy que soit, de

D'ou vient que tu te glo- ri- fi- es De ta mes- chan- ce- té? Quoy que soit, de

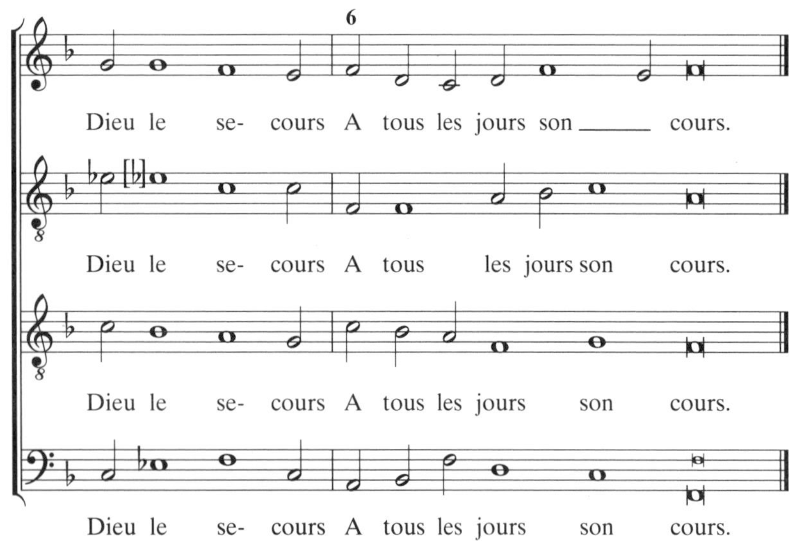
6
Dieu le se- cours A tous les jours son ______ cours.
Dieu le se- cours A tous les jours son cours.
Dieu le se- cours A tous les jours son cours.
Dieu le se- cours A tous les jours son cours.

In mischief which thou multipliest,
In thy iniquity,
Why vantest thou? and magnifiest
Thyself in vanity?
But yet know thou Gods goodnes sure,
Doth evermore endure.

Psalm 53

The foole in heart the holy God denyes,
They are corrupt in all their enterprises,
To be abhord in all their exercises:
Good works none do, nor thereunto advise,
All are unwise.

*Also set in Psalm 14

Psalm 54

Dessus
Haute-Contre
Taille
Basse-Contre
Genevan tune
2
O Dieu tout puis- sant, sau- ve moy Par ton Nom et force im- mor-
O Dieu tout puis- sant, sau- ve moy Par ton Nom et force im- mor-
O Dieu tout puis- sant, sau- ve moy Par ton Nom et force im- mor-
O Dieu tout puis- sant, sau- ve moy Par ton Nom et force im- mor-
3
4
-tel- le, Et pour de- fen- dre ma que- rel- le Fay sor- tir la for- ce
-tel- le, Et pour de- fen- dre ma que- rel- le Fay sor- tir la for- ce
-tel- le, Et pour de- fen- dre ma que- rel- le Fay sor- tir la for- ce
-tel- le, Et pour de- fen- dre ma que- rel- le Fay sor- tir la for- ce
5
6
de toy. Oy l'o- rai- son que je fe- ray, Plai- se toy l'au-reil- le me ten- dre,
de toy. Oy l'o- rai- son que je fe- ray, Plai- se toy l'au-reil- le me ten- dre,
de toy. Oy l'o- rai- son que je fe- ray, Plai- se toy l'au-reil- le me ten- dre,
de toy. Oy l'o- rai- son que je fe- ray, Plai- se toy l'au-reil- le me ten- dre,

Lord God almighty, save thou me,
By thy great Name my soule sustain thou,
And by thy strength my cause maintain thou,
And vouchsafe thou my Judg to be.
O hear me when to thee I pray,
Thy sacred eare to me down bend thou,
And gratiously O Lord attend thou
To all the words that I shall say.

Psalm 55

Dessus
Haute-Contre
Taille
Basse-Contre
Genevan tune
2
3
4
5
Ex- auce, ô mon Dieu, ma pri- e- re, Ne te re-
-cu- le point ar- rie- re De l'o- rai- son que te pre-
-sen- te. En- tens à moy, ex- au- ce moy, Tan- dis qu'en
pre- sen- te.

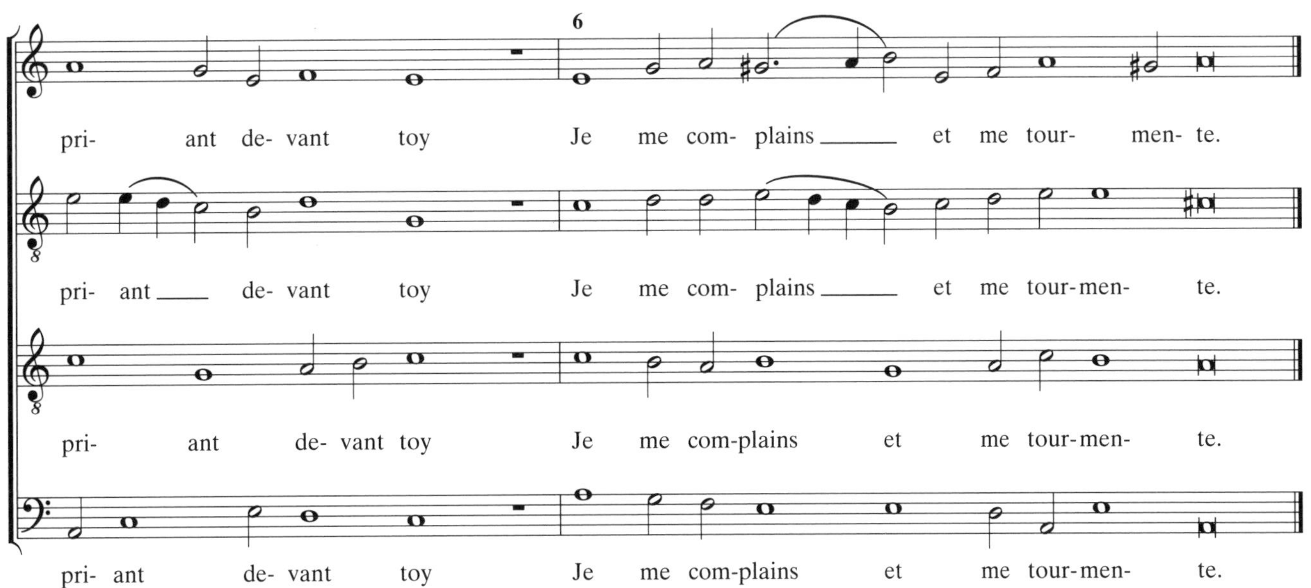

O Lord hearke thou to my poore petition,
Hide not thy eyes at my contrition,
Do not despise my deprecation,
But bend thy gracious eare to me,
My cryes, oh heare, my sorrow see,
Regard my mournfull meditation.

Psalm 56

Dessus
Haute-Contre
Taille
Basse-Contre
Genevan tune
Mi- se- ri- corde à moy pauvre af- fli- gé,
Mi- se- ri- corde à moy pauvre af- fli- gé,
Mi- se- ri- corde à moy pauvre af- fli- gé,
Mi- se- ri- corde à moy pauvre af- fli- gé,
2
3
O Sei-gneur Dieu! car me voy- la man- gé De ce mes-chant qui me
O Sei-gneur Dieu! car me voy- la man- gé De ce mes-chant qui me tient
O Sei-gneur Dieu! car me voy- la man- gé De ce mes-chant qui me
O Sei-gneur Dieu! car me voy- la man- gé De ce mes-chant qui me
4
5
tient as- sie- gé, Et tout les jours m'op- pres- se. Mes en- vi- eux me de- vo- rent
as- sie- gé, Et tout les jours m'op-pres- se. Mes en- vi- eux me de- vo- rent
tient as- sie- gé, Et tout les jours m'op-pres- se. Mes en- vi- eux me de- vo- rent
tient as- sie- gé, Et tout les jours m'op-pres- se. Mes en- vi- eux me de- vo- rent

Have mercy Lord on me, for certainly
The cruell man at once would swallow me:
He fights against me daily furiously,
Oppressing me each houre.
My enemies would daily me devoure,
And many fight gainst me with all their power.
O God most high in thee I trust, my tower,
To thee in feare I fly.

Psalm 57

Dessus
Haute-Contre
Taille
Basse-Contre
Genevan tune
2
Ay- es pi- tié, ay- es pi- tié de moy: Car, ô mon Dieu, mon ame es-pere en toy:
3
4
Et jus-qu'à tant que ces mes-chans re- bel- les Soyent tous pas- sez, es- pe- ran- ce ne foy
5
Ja-mais n'au-ray qu'en l'om- bre de tes ai- les.
Thy mercy shew, some pitty take on me,
For O my God, my soul doth trust in thee:
And till these woes and troubles be past over,
My soul doth hope thou my defence wilt be
And that with thy wings shade thou wilt me cover.

Psalm 58

Ye Rulers all to whom the trust is
Committed to defend the right
Against oppressors wrongfull might,
Are all your judgments truth and justice?
Ye sons of men have you regard
To all just judgments to award?

Psalm 59

Dessus
Haute-Contre
Taille
Basse-Contre
Genevan tune
2
3
4
5
6
Mon Dieu l'en- ne- my m'en- vi- ron- ne, Ta bon- té donc se- cours me don- ne, Gar- de moy des gens ir- ri- tez, Qui des- sus moy se sont jet- tez. De- li- vre moy de l'ad-ver- sai- re Qui ne de-man-de qu'a

My God, my enemies surround me,
Save me from them that would confound me,
Let me my God defended be
From them that rise up against me.
Deliver me from all transgressors,
Save me from them that be oppressors:
From workers of iniquity,
From cruell men, and bloud-thirsty.

Psalm 60

Dessus
Haute-Contre
Taille
Basse-Contre
Genevan tune*
2
O Dieu qui nous as de-bou- tez, Qui nous as de toy es- car- tez,
O Dieu qui nous as de-bou- tez, Qui nous as de toy es- car- tez,
O Dieu qui nous as de- bou-tez, Qui nous as de toy es- car- tez,
O Dieu qui nous as de-bou- tez, Qui nous as de toy es- car- tez,
3
4
Ja- dis con- tre nous ir- ri- té, Tour- ne toy de nos- tre cos- té.
Ja- dis con- tre nous ir- ri- té, Tour- ne toy de nos- tre cos- té.
Ja- dis con- tre nous ir- ri- té, Tour- ne toy de nos- tre cos- té.
Ja- dis con- tre nous ir- ri- té, Tour- ne toy de nos- tre cos- té.
5
6
Tu as nos- tre pa- ïs se- coux, Et cas- sé à for- ce de coups:
Tu as nos- tre pa- ïs se- coux, Et cas- sé à for- ce de coups:
Tu as nos- tre pa- ïs se- coux, Et cas- sé à for- ce de coups:
Tu as nos- tre pa- ïs se- coux, Et cas- sé à for- ce de coups:

*Also set in Psalm 108

O God thou didst us quite reject,
And scattring us thou didst deject.
Thou hast against us bin displeas'd,
Return to us and be appeas'd.
The earth to tremble thou hast made,
Thou hast it broke, and waste it layd.
The breaches and the broken shivers
Heal thou, for now it quakes and quivers.

Psalm 61

Lord my God, hear thou my crying,
To thee flying,
Give eare to my prayr and mone.
From earths end, when griefs oppres me
And distres me,
I will cry to thee alone.

Psalm 62

My soul on God alone attends,
Who me assistance surely sends.
He is my Rock, and my salvation,
In greatest dangers drawing nigh,
He me defendeth from on high,
Unmov'd I stand, on firm foundation.

*Also set in Psalms 24, 95, and 111

Psalm 63

*Also set in Psalms 17 and 70

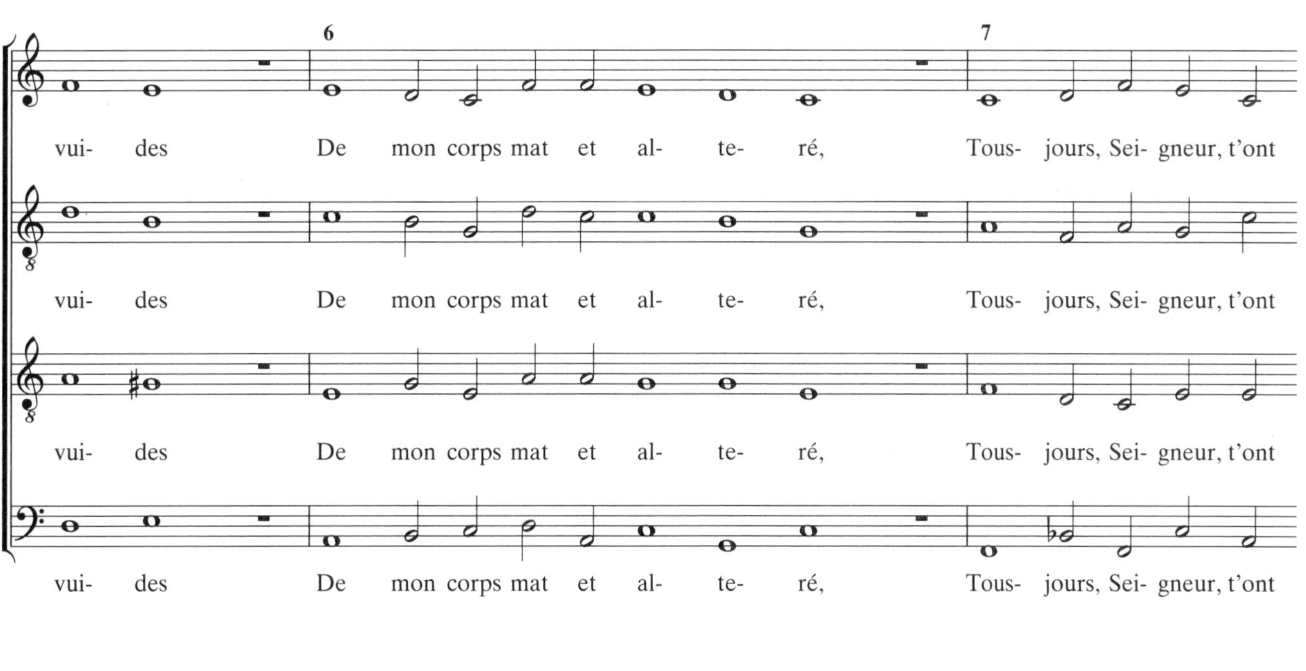
6
7
vui- des De mon corps mat et al- te- ré, Tous- jours, Sei- gneur, t'ont
vui- des De mon corps mat et al- te- ré, Tous- jours, Sei- gneur, t'ont
vui- des De mon corps mat et al- te- ré, Tous- jours, Sei- gneur, t'ont
vui- des De mon corps mat et al- te- ré, Tous- jours, Sei- gneur, t'ont

8
de- si- ré En ces lieux de- serts et a- ri- des.
de- si- ré En ces lieux de- serts et a- ri- des.
de- si- ré En ces lieux de- serts et a- ri- des.
de- si- ré En ces lieux de- serts et a- ri- des.

O Lord I have no God but thee,
I will seek thee betimes, in anguish,
For thee my soul with thirst doth languish,
And oft it faints, and failes in me.
My flesh such pining pain hath tryed,
For want of thee to ease my grief,
Longing to tast of thy relief,
In desart land, unwatred dryed.

Psalm 64

Lord hear my voyce and prayr ascending,
To me vouchsafe thy gracious eare,
Preserve my life safe from the feare
Of enemies, me succour sending,
My soul defending.

*Also set in Psalm 5

Psalm 65

Dessus
Haute-Contre
Taille
Basse-Contre
Genevan tune*
2
O Dieu, la gloi- re qui t'est deu- ë T'at- tends
3
4
de- dans Si- on: En ce lieu te se- ra ren- du- ë De voeus
5
6
ob- la- ti- on: Et d'au-tant que la voix en- ten- dre Des tiens il

*Also set in Psalm 72

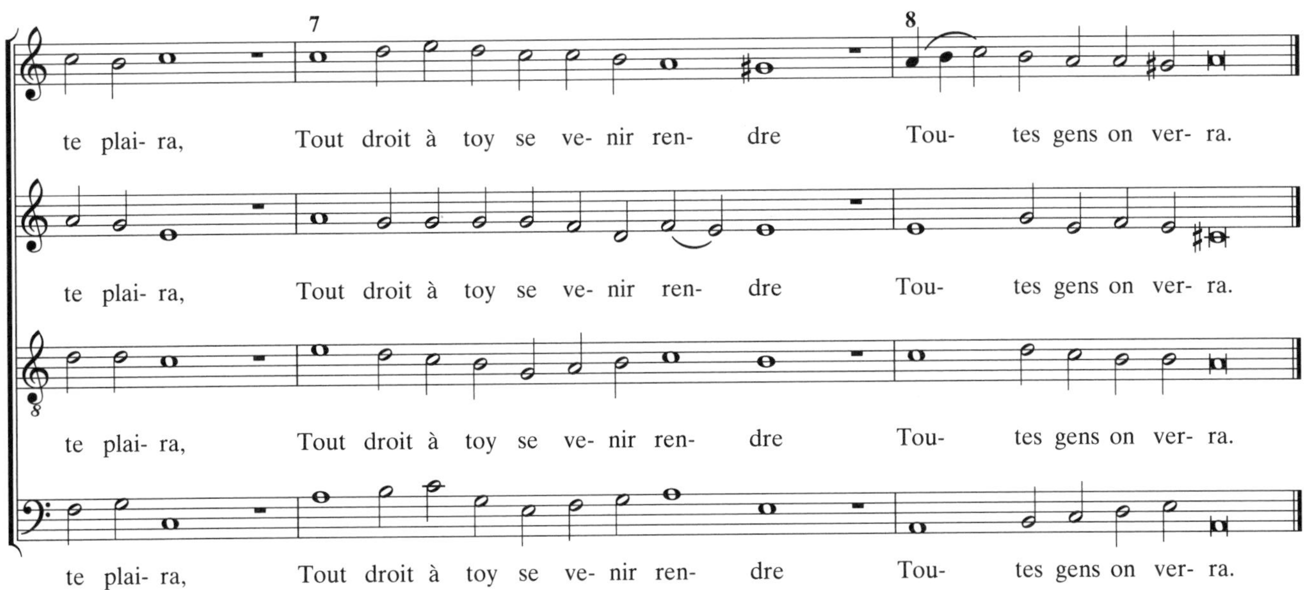
7
8
te plai- ra, Tout droit à toy se ve- nir ren- dre Tou- tes gens on ver- ra.
te plai- ra, Tout droit à toy se ve- nir ren- dre Tou- tes gens on ver- ra.
te plai- ra, Tout droit à toy se ve- nir ren- dre Tou- tes gens on ver- ra.
te plai- ra, Tout droit à toy se ve- nir ren- dre Tou- tes gens on ver- ra.

All praise on thee O God attendeth,
In Sion peacefully,
To thee on whom our trust dependeth,
The vow there paid shall be.
And thou again thy eare applying,
The prayr of thine dost heare,
All flesh unto thy presence flying,
Before thee shall appear.

Psalm 66

Dessus
Haute-Contre
Taille
Basse-Contre
Genevan tune*
2
3
4
5
6
Or sus louëz Dieu tout le monde, Chantez le los de son renom: Chantez si haut que tout redonde De la loüange de son Nom. Dites, ô que tu es terrible, Seigneur, en tout
Or sus louëz Dieu tout le monde, Chantez le los de son renom: Chantez si haut que tout redonde De la loüange de son Nom. Dites, ô que tu es terrible, Seigneur, en tout
Or sus louëz Dieu tout le monde, Chantez le los de son renom: Chantez si haut que tout redonde De la loüange de son Nom. Dites, ô que tu es terrible, Seigneur, en tout
Or sus louëz Dieu tout le monde, Chantez le los de son renom: Chantez si haut que tout redonde De la loüange de son Nom. Dites, ô que tu es terrible, Seigneur, en tout

*Also set in Psalms 98 and 118

7
8
ce que tu fais: Tes hai-neux, tant es in- vin- ci- ble, Te fla-tent pour a- voir la paix.
ce que tu fais: Tes hai-neux, tant es in- vin- ci- ble, Te fla-tent pour a- voir la paix.
ce que tu fais: Tes hai-neux, tant es in- vin- ci- ble, Te fla-tent pour a- voir la paix.
ce que tu fais: Tes hai-neux, tant es in- vin- ci- ble, Te fla-tent pour a- voir la paix.

Triumph and shout with joy abounding
In God, all people on the earth.
His glorious Name with Psalms resounding,
His worthy praise sing ye with mirth.
To God say, in thy works of wonder,
How terrible thou shewst to be,
Thy great powr shall thy foes bring under,
Faining subjection unto thee.

Psalm 67

*Also set in Psalm 33

Lord God to us be favourable,
To us vouchsafe thou blessings thine,
Thy gracious face most amiable,
Upon us make thou bright to shine.
That thy way excelling,
To all on earth dwelling,
May be fully known:
And that thy salvation
Unto every nation
May be plainly shown.

Psalm 68

*Also set in Psalm 36

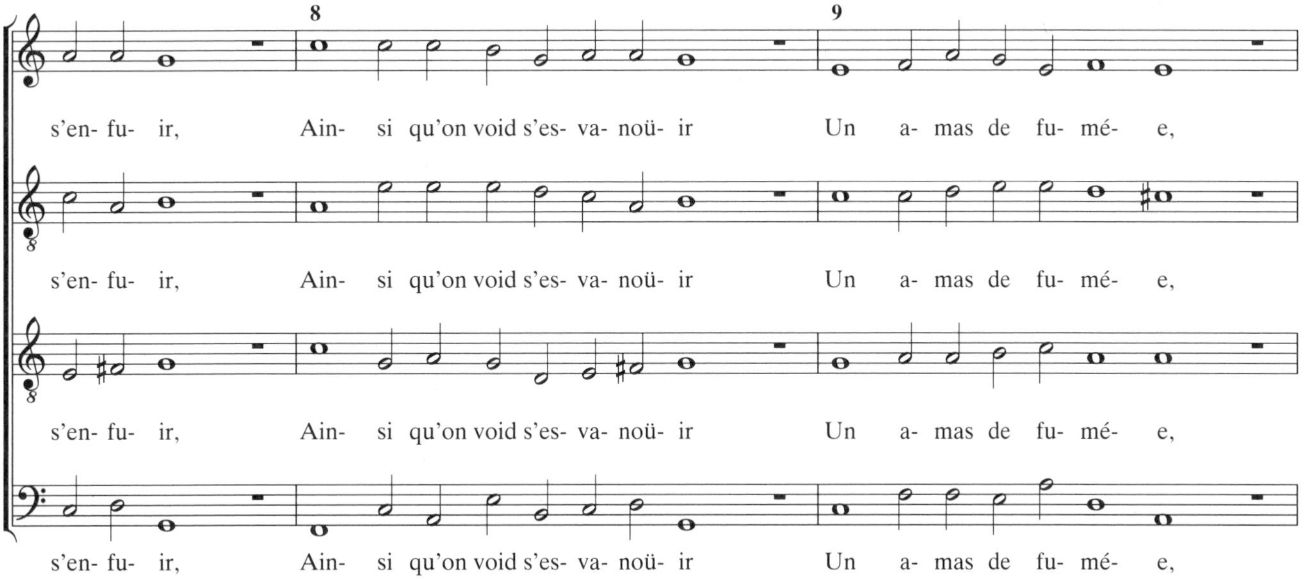

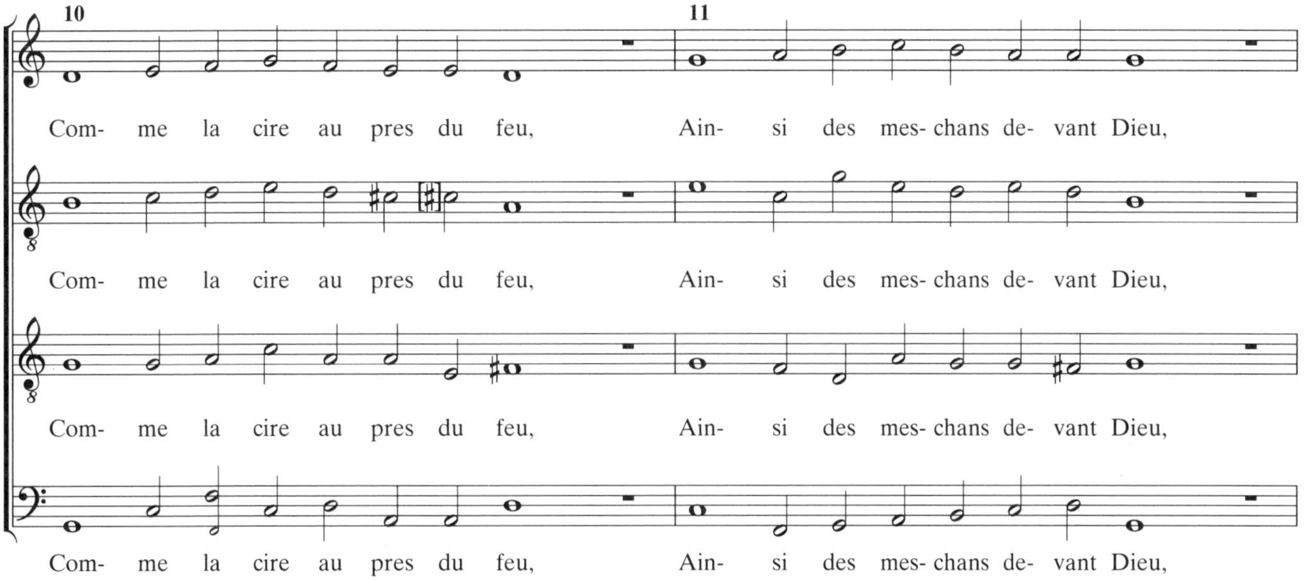

8
9
s'en- fu- ir, Ain- si qu'on void s'es- va- noü- ir Un a- mas de fu- mé- e,
s'en- fu- ir, Ain- si qu'on void s'es- va- noü- ir Un a- mas de fu- mé- e,
s'en- fu- ir, Ain- si qu'on void s'es- va- noü- ir Un a- mas de fu- mé- e,
s'en- fu- ir, Ain- si qu'on void s'es- va- noü- ir Un a- mas de fu- mé- e,

10
11
Com- me la cire au pres du feu, Ain- si des mes- chans de- vant Dieu,
Com- me la cire au pres du feu, Ain- si des mes- chans de- vant Dieu,
Com- me la cire au pres du feu, Ain- si des mes- chans de- vant Dieu,
Com- me la cire au pres du feu, Ain- si des mes- chans de- vant Dieu,

12
La force est con- su- mé- e.
La force est con- su- mé- e.
La force est con- su- mé- e.
La force est con- su- mé- e.

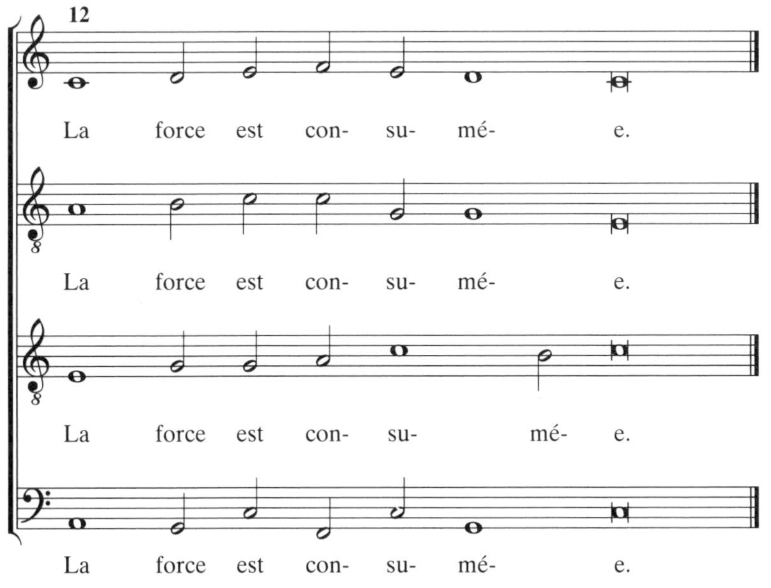

Let God the powrfull Lord arise,
And let his hatefull enemies
With fear and dread confounded,
Be all disperst from place to place,
Fly from the frowning of his face,
With gastly terror wounded.
As smoke by winds is suddenly
Driven quite away, so let them be,
From Gods high presence banisht:
As wax doth melt before the fire,
So be the wicked in his ire,
Consum'd forever, vanisht.

Psalm 69

Dessus
Cinquiesme
"une octave plus haut"
Haute-Contre
Taille
Basse-Contre
Genevan tune*
2
He- las! Sei- gneur je te pri' sau- ve moy Car les eaux
He- las! Sei-gneur je te pri' sau- ve moy Car les eaux
He- las! Sei- gneur je te pri' sau- ve moy Car les eaux
He- las! Sei-gneur je te pri' sau- ve moy Car les eaux
He- las! Sei-gneur je te pri' sau- ve moy Car les eaux

3
m'ont sai- si jus-ques à l'a- me: Et au bour-bier tres- pro-fond et in- fa- me,
m'ont sai- si jus-ques à l'a- me: Et au bour-bier tres- pro-fond et in- fa- me,
m'ont sai- si jus-ques à l'a- me: Et au bour-bier tres- pro-fond et in- fa- me,
m'ont sai- si jus-ques à l'a- me: Et au bour-bier tres- pro-fond et in- fa- me,
m'ont sai- si jus-ques à l'a- me: Et au bour-bier tres- pro-fond et in- fa- me,

*Also set in Psalm 51

4
5
Sans fond ne rive en- fon- dré je me voy. Ain- si plon- gé l'eau m'em-por- te,
Sans fond ne rive en- fon- dré je me voy. Ain- si plon- gé l'eau m'em-por- te,
Sans fond ne rive en- fon- dré je me voy. Ain- si plon- gé l'eau m'em-por- te,
Sans fond ne rive en- fon- dré je me voy. Ain- si plon- gé l'eau m'em- por- te,
Sans fond ne rive en- fon- dré je me voy. Ain- si plon- gé l'eau m'em-por- te,
6
7
tant las De m'es-cri- er, que j'en ay gor-ge sei- che: Et de mon Dieu at- ten-dant
tant las De m'es-cri- er, que j'en ay gor-ge sei- che: Et de mon Dieu at- ten-dant
tant las De m'es-cri- er, que j'en ay gor-ge sei- che: Et de mon Dieu at- ten-dant
tant las De m'es- cri- er, que j'en ay gor-ge sei- che: Et de mon Dieu at-ten-
tant las De m'es-cri- er, que j'en ay gor-ge sei- che: Et de mon Dieu at- ten-dant

8
le sou- las, De mes deux yeux la vi- geur se des- sei- che.
le sou- las, De mes deux yeux la vi- geur se des- sei- che.
le sou- las, De mes deux yeux la vi- geur se des- sei- che.
-dant le sou- las, De mes deux yeux la vi- geur se des- sei- che.
le sou- las, De mes deux yeux la vi- geur se des- sei- che.

Save me O God, the waters do me drown,
To swallow up my soul, the seas are ready.
I sinke in mire, where is no footing steady.
Plung'd in the deep, the flouds have me oreflown.
With cying weak, I weary, weep and wail,
My throat is hoarse with dolefull lamentation,
With showring teares consum'd, my eyes do fail,
While on my God I wait with expectation.

Psalm 70

*Also set in Psalms 17 and 63

O God in whom I trust repose,
Make speedy haste, me to deliver.
Make hast O Lord, of ayd the giver,
To send me help against my foes.
Who have my soul pursewd and chased.
Let them with shame confounded be.
Let them that seek to ruin me
Be turned back, destroyd, defaced.

Psalm 71

*Also set in Psalm 31

Psalm 72

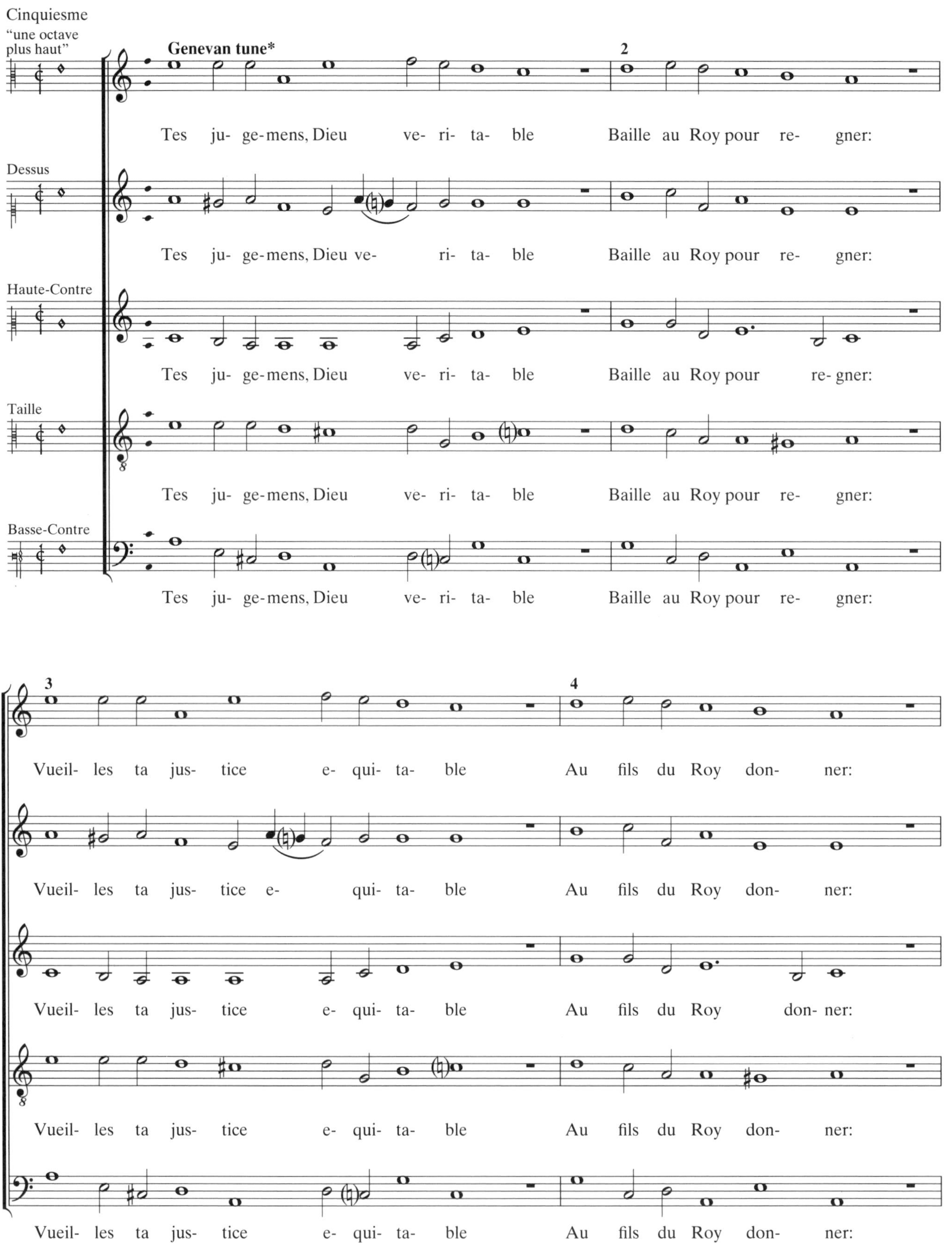

*Also set in Psalm 65

Upon the King by thee elected
Thy judgments Lord bestow.
His princely Son by thee directed,
With justice thine endow.
That he thy chosen people guiding,
His justice may shine bright,
The poore opprest with patience biding,
By him may have their right.

Psalm 73

Dessus
Haute-Contre
Taille
Basse-Contre
Genevan tune
2
Si est- ce que Dieu est tres doux A son Is- ra- ël, voire
Si est- ce que_ Dieu_ est___ tres_ doux A son Is- ra- ël, voire
Si est- ce que Dieu est tres doux A son Is- ra- ël,
Si est- ce que Dieu est tres_ doux A son Is- ra- ël,
3
4
à tous, Qui gar-dent en tou- te droic- tu- re Leur con- sci-ence en- tiere_
à tous, Qui gar-dent en tou- te_ droic-tu- re Leur con- sci-ence en-tiere
voire à tous, Qui gar-dent en tou- te droic- tu- re Leur con- sci-ence en- tiere
voire à tous, Qui gar-dent en tou- te droic- tu- re Leur con- sci-ence en-tiere
5
6
et pu- re. Mais j'ay es- té tout prest à voir Mes pieds le bon che- min lais-ser,
et pu- re. Mais j'ay es- té tout prest___ à voir Mes pieds le bon che- min___lais-ser,
et pu- re. Mais j'ay es- té tout prest à voir Mes pieds le bon che-min lais- ser,
et pu- re. Mais j'ay es- té tout prest à voir Mes pieds le bon che-min lais- ser,

Yet sure is the Lord good and kinde
To Israel, his love they finde,
Who be of righteous conversation,
And serve him with pure adoration.
My steps were like to goe astray,
And neer to misse the rightfull way,
My feet did almost swerve aside
And into error neer did slide.

Psalm 74

Dessus
Haute-Contre
Taille
Basse-Contre
Genevan tune*
2
D'où vient, Sei-gneur, que tu nous as es- pars, Et si long temps ta
3
fu- reur en- fla- mé- e Vo- mit sur nous tant es- pes- se fu- mé- e,
4
Voi- re sur nous les bre- bis de tes parcs?

Why Lord hast thou for ever us off cast?
Why is thy wrath and fury so inflamed
Against thy flock, thy congregation named,
Thy pasture sheep, that thou forgot them hast?

*Also set in Psalm 116

Psalm 75

Dessus
Haute-Contre
Taille
Basse-Contre
Genevan tune
2
O Sei- gneur, lou- é se- ra, Loü- é se- ra ton re- nom.
O Sei- gneur, lou- é se- ra, Loü- é se- ra ton re- nom.
O Sei- gneur, lou- é se- ra, Loü- é se- ra ton re- nom.
O Sei- gneur, lou- é se- ra, Loü- é se- ra ton re- nom.
3
4
5
Car la gloi- re de ton Nom Pres de nous s'ap- pro- che- ra: Et de nous
Car la gloi- re de ton Nom Pres de nous s'ap- pro- che- ra: Et de nous
Car la gloi- re de ton Nom Pres de nous s'ap- pro- che- ra: Et de nous
Car la gloi- re de ton Nom Pres de nous s'ap- pro- che- ra: Et de nous se-
6
se- ront chan- tez Les hauts faits de tes bon- tez.
se- ront chan- tez Les hauts faits de tes bon- tez.
se- ront chan- tez Les hauts faits de tes bon- tez.
-ront chan- tez Les hauts faits de tes bon- tez.
Lord our God, we will praise thee,
We praise thee for thy Name:
And the glory of the same,
Neer and deer appeares to be,
This thy wondrous works declare,
Which for us performed are.

Psalm 76

Dessus
Haute-Contre
Taille
Basse-Contre
Genevan tune*
2
3
4
5
C'est en Ju- dé- e pro- pre- ment, Que Dieu s'est ac- quis un
re- nom: C'est en Is- ra- ël voi- re- ment,
C'est en ___ Is- ra- ël voi- re- ment,
Qu'on void la for- ce de son Nom: En Sa- lem est son

*Also set in Psalms 30 and 139

6
ta- ber- na- cle, En Si- on son sainct ha- bi- ta- cle.
ta- ber- na- cle, En Si- on son sainct ha- bi- ta- cle.
ta- ber- na- cle, En Si- on son sainct ha- bi- ta- cle.
ta- ber- na- cle, En Si- on son sainct ha- bi- ta- cle.

In Juda, God the Lord is known,
He there hath woon eternall fame,
In Israel of great renown,
And glory is his mighty name.
In Salem is his house excelling,
In Sion is his sacred dwelling.

Psalm 77

*Also set in Psalm 86

With my voyce to God I cryed,
To him I my plaints applied.
I to God my voyce did reare,
He to me gave gracious eare.
In the time I was distressed,
To the Lord I me addressed.
Nightly sorrowes did not cease,
Hands erected sought release.

Psalm 78

*Also set in Psalm 90

6
et que par moy soient dits Les grands se- crets des oeu- vres de ja- dis.
et que par moy soient dits Les grands se- crets des oeu- vres de ja- dis.
et que par moy soient dits Les grands se- crets des oeu- vres de ja- dis.
et que par moy soient dits Les grands se- crets des oeu- vres de ja- dis.

Attentive be unto my law declared,
My people all, let your eares be prepared
The words to heare which my mouth now propoundeth,
My voyce to you a parable expoundeth,
Which I will shew and unto you unfold,
Grave secrets hid dark sentences of old.

Psalm 79

Dessus
Les gens en- trez sont en ton he- ri- ta- ge, Ils ont pol- lu, Sei-gneur,
Haute-Contre
Les gens en- trez sont en ton he- ri- ta- ge, Ils ont pol- lu, Sei- gneur,
Taille
Genevan tune
Les gens en- trez sont en ton he- ri- ta- ge, Ils ont pol- lu, Sei- gneur,
Basse-Contre
Les gens en- trez sont en ton he- ri- ta- ge, Ils ont pol- lu, Sei- gneur,
par leur ou- tra- ge, Ton Tem- ple sainct, Je- ru- sa- lem des- trui- te,
par leur ou- tra- ge, Ton Tem- ple sainct, Je- ru- sa- lem des- trui- te,
par leur ou- tra- ge, Ton Tem- ple sainct, Je- ru- sa- lem des- trui- te,
par leur ou- tra- ge, Ton Tem- ple sainct, Je- ru- sa- lem des- trui- te,
Si qu'en mon-ceaux de pier-res l'on re- dui- te. Ils ont bail- lé les corps
Si qu'en mon-ceaux de pier-res l'on re- dui- te. Ils ont bail- lé les corps
Si qu'en mon-ceaux de pier-res l'on re- dui- te. Ils ont bail- lé les corps
Si qu'en mon-ceaux de pier-res l'on re- dui- te. Ils ont bail- lé les corps

The heathen have thy heritage obtained,
Thy holy house O Lord they have profaned;
Jerusalem thy sacred habitation,
On heaps is laid, and brought to desolation.
Thy saints dead bodies they
To fowls of heav'n for prey;
Have cast without the city
Thy servants flesh made food
For wild beasts of the wood,
Inhumane voyd of pitty.

Psalm 80

Hear us, thy Israel who feedest,
Who like a flock thy Joseph leadest:
Vouchsafe to shew to us thy grace,
That we may view thy shining face.
Thou that dost dwell in majesty,
Between the Cherubs gloriously.

Psalm 81

Sing we with loud voyce
To God our salvation.
Make a joyfull noyse,
Jacobs God praise we,
Sing Psalms joyfully,
Sing with exultation.

Psalm 82

Cinquiesme
"une octave plus haut"
Genevan tune*
2
Dieu est as- sis en l'as-sem-blé- e Des Prin-ces qu'il a as- sem- blé- e.
Dessus
Dieu est as- sis en l'as-sem-blé- e Des Prin-ces qu'il a as- sem- blé- e.
Haute-Contre
Dieu est as- sis en l'as-sem- blé- e Des Prin-ces qu'il a as- sem- blé- e.
Taille
Dieu est as- sis en l'as-sem-blé- e Des Prin-ces qu'il a as- sem- blé- e.
Basse-Contre
Dieu est as- sis en l'as-sem-blé- e Des Prin-ces qu'il a as- sem- blé- e.
3
4
Et des plus grands est au mi- lieu, Pour y pre- si- der com- me Dieu.
Et des plus grands est au mi- lieu, Pour y pre- si- der com- me Dieu.
Et des plus grands est au mi- lieu, Pour y pre- si- der com- me Dieu.
Et des plus grands est au mi- lieu, Pour y pre- si- der com- me Dieu.
Et des plus grands est au mi- lieu, Pour y pre- si- der com- me Dieu.

*Also set in Psalm 46

God is amidst the congregation
Where Princes meet in consultation.
As Judg supreme, his place hee takes
Mongst Judges, whom as Gods he makes.
How long will ye in place of justice,
Award such sentence as unjust is?
Far off from equity ye erre,
For ye the wickeds cause prefer.

Psalm 83

In silence Lord hold not your peace,
Delay not thou, nor longer cease:
Defer not Lord, be still no longer,
For lo thy foes in tumults rising,
Exalt themselves, thy powr despising,
Make head against thee, still grow stronger.

Psalm 84

Dessus
Haute-Contre
Taille
Basse-Contre
Genevan tune
O Dieu des ar- mé- es! com- bien Le sa- cré ta- ber- na- cle tien
O Dieu des ar- mé- es! com- bien Le sa- cré ta- ber- na- cle tien
O Dieu des ar- mé- es! com- bien Le sa- cré ta- ber- na- cle tien
O Dieu des ar- mé- es! com- bien Le sa- cré ta- ber- na- cle tien
Est sur tou- tes cho- ses ai- ma- ble! Mon coeur lan- guit, mes sens ra- vis
Est sur tou- tes cho- ses ai- ma- ble! Mon coeur lan- guit, mes sens ra- vis
Est sur tou- tes cho- ses ai- ma- ble! Mon coeur lan- guit, mes sens ra- vis
Est sur tou- tes cho- ses ai- ma- ble! Mon coeur lan- guit, mes sens ra- vis
De- fail- lent a- pres tes par- vis, O Sei- gneur Dieu tres- de- si- ra- ble!
De- fail- lent a- pres tes par- vis, O Sei- gneur Dieu tres- de- si- ra- ble!
De- fail- lent a- pres tes par- vis, O Sei- gneur Dieu tres- de- si- ra- ble!
De- fail- lent a- pres tes par- vis, O Sei- gneur Dieu tres- de- si- ra- ble!

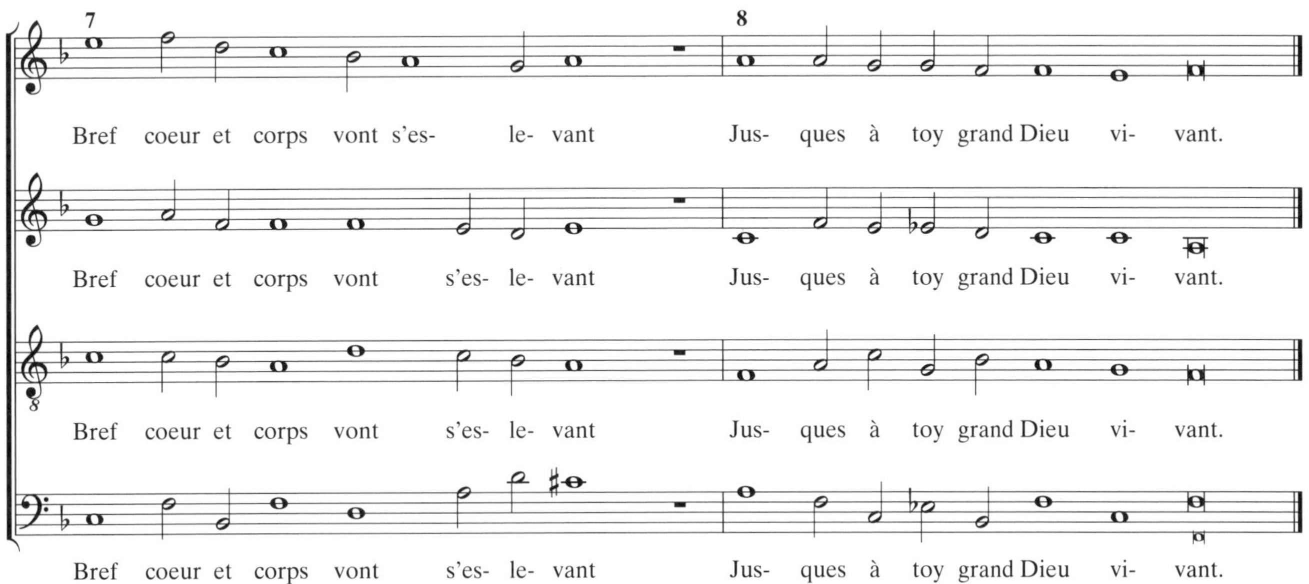
7
8
Bref coeur et corps vont s'es- le- vant Jus- ques à toy grand Dieu vi- vant.
Bref coeur et corps vont s'es- le- vant Jus- ques à toy grand Dieu vi- vant.
Bref coeur et corps vont s'es- le- vant Jus- ques à toy grand Dieu vi- vant.
Bref coeur et corps vont s'es- le- vant Jus- ques à toy grand Dieu vi- vant.

Lord God of hosts, how lovely fair,
How sweet thy dwelling places are:
How pleasing and how amiable
My longing soul faints with desire:
That to thy courts I might aspire,
Whose beauty is so admirable:
My heart, my flesh doth pant and cry,
The living God to come more nigh.

Psalm 85

Dessus
Haute-Contre
Taille
Basse-Contre
Genevan tune
2
A- vec les tiens, Sei-gneur, tu as fait paix,
Et de Ja-cob les pri-son- niers las-chez,
3
4
Tu as quit-té à ta gent ses mes- faits,
Voi- re tu as cou-vert tous ses pe-chez.
5
6
Tu as loin d'eux ton des-pit re- ti- ré,
Et ton cou-roux vi- o- lent mo- de- ré.

7
8
O Dieu! en qui gist le sa- lut de nous, Res- ta- bli-nous, ap- pai-sant ton cour-roux.
O Dieu! en qui gist le sa- lut de nous, Res- ta- bli-nous, ap- pai- sant ton cour- roux.
O Dieu! en qui gist le sa- lut de nous, Res- ta- bli-nous, ap- pai-sant ton cour-roux.
O Dieu! en qui gist le sa- lut de nous, Res- ta- bli-nous, ap- pai-sant ton cour- roux.

Lord to thy land thy grace thou didst declare,
Thou Jacob hast freed from captivity,
Thy peoples sins by thee all cov'red are,
Thou hast forgiven them their iniquity.
Thou tookst away thy anger and thy rage,
The fierceness of thy wrath thou didst assuage,
O God of our salvation, us returne,
Cease thou thy wrath against us, which doth burn.

Psalm 86

*Also set in Psalm 77

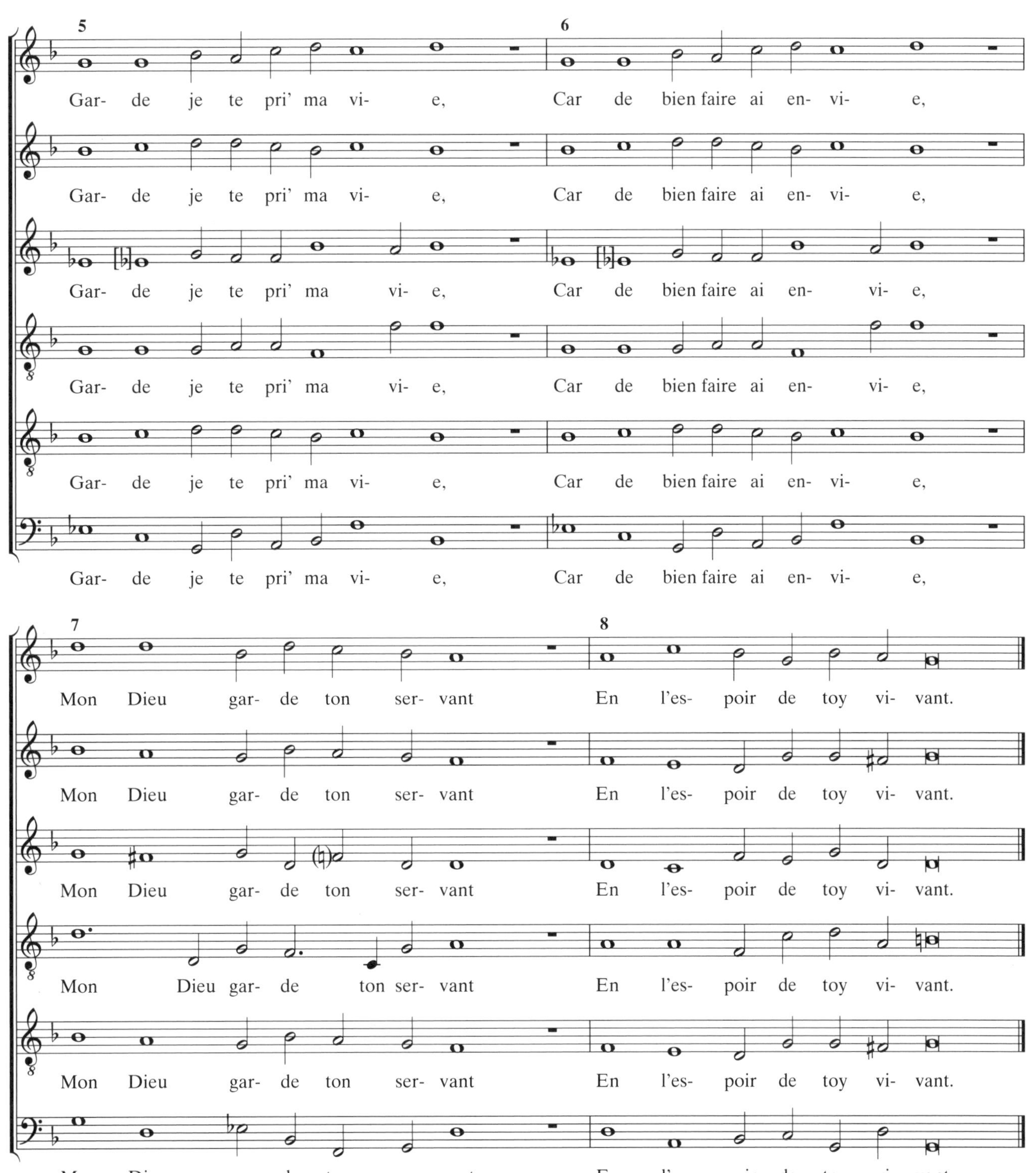

To my humble supplication,
Lord, give eare and acceptation,
Hear me now, so weak, so poor,
That ah I can beare no more.
Save my life O my defender,
For my holy heart is tender,
Save thy servant Lord most just,
For in thee alone I trust.

Psalm 87

Dessus
Haute-Contre
Taille
Basse-Contre
Genevan tune
2
3
4
Dieu pour fon- der son tres-seur ha- bi- ta- cle, Es mons sa- crez a prins af- fec- ti- on,
Et mieux ai- me les por- tes de Si- on, Que de Ja- -cob onc- ques nul ta- ber- na- cle.

On sacred hils and mountains, her foundations
The Lord hath layd, they never shall remove,
Fair Sions gates the most high God doth love
Above the rest of Jacobs habitations.

Psalm 88

Eternall Lord, my Saver dear,
Both day and night my cryes implore thee,
O let my prayer come before thee:
Unto thy presence entring near:
Incline to heare, thy eare applying!
To my sad plaints, and rufull crying.

Psalm 89

Dessus
Haute-Contre
Taille
Basse-Contre
Genevan tune
Du Seigneur les bontez sans fin je chanterai,
Et sa fidelité à jamais prescherai:
Car c'est un point conclu, que sa grace est bastie,
Pour durer à jamais, comme
2
3
4

5
on voit es- ta- bli- e Dans le pour- pris des cieux leur course in- va- ri-
on voit es- ta- bli- e Dans le pour- pris des cieux leur course in- va-
on voit es- ta- bli- e Dans le pour- pris des cieux leur course in- va-
voit es- ta- bli- e Dans le pour- pris des cieux leur course in- va-
6
-a- ble, Si- gne seur et cer- tain de son dire im- mu- a- ble.
-ri- a- ble, Si- gne seur et cer- tain de son dire im- mu- a- ble.
-ri- a- ble, Si- gne seur et cer- tain de son dire im- mu- a- ble.
-ri- a- ble, Si- gne seur et cer- tain de son dire im- mu- a- ble.

The mercies of the Lord Ile sing continually:
To ages all record his truths fidelity.
For this is truth most sure, it cannot be denyed,
His grace doth ay endure, establisht, verified.
As heav'n perpetually, keepes course invariable,
So his fidelity, much more is firm, and stable.

Psalm 90

*Also set in Psalm 78

Lord thou hast bin to us a habitation
From age to age in every generation:
Before the hils or spacious worlds creation,
Long time before thou laidst the earths foundation,
Before all things received form from thee,
Thou Lord art God from all eternitie.

Psalm 91

Dessus
Haute-Contre
Taille
Basse-Contre
Genevan tune
2
3
4
5
Qui en la gar- de du haut Dieu Pour ja- mais se re- ti- re, En om- bre bonne et en fort lieu Re- ti- ré se peut di- re. Con- clu donc en l'en- ten- de- ment,
Qui en la gar- de du haut Dieu Pour ja- mais se re- ti- re, En om- bre bonne et en fort lieu Re- ti- ré se peut di- re. Con- clu donc en l'en- ten- de- ment,
Qui en la gar- de du haut Dieu Pour ja- mais se re- ti- re, En om- bre bonne et en fort lieu Re- ti- ré se peut di- re. Con- clu donc en l'en- ten- de- ment,
Qui en la gar- de du haut Dieu Pour ja- mais se re- ti- re, En om- bre bonne et en fort lieu Re- ti- ré se peut di- re. Con- clu donc en l'en- ten- de- ment,

6
7
8
Dieu est ma gar- de seu- re, Ma hau- te tour et fon- de- ment, Sur le- quel je m'as- seu- re.
Dieu est ma gar- de seu- re, Ma hau- te tour et fon- de- ment, Sur le- quel je m'as- seu- re.
Dieu est ma gar- de seu- re, Ma hau- te tour et fon- de- ment, Sur le- quel je m'as- seu- re.
Dieu est ma gar- de seu- re, Ma hau- te tour et fon- de- ment, Sur le- quel je m'as- seu- re.

Who in the house of God most high,
For his defence resideth,
And to th'Almighties shade doth fly,
In safety sure abideth.
Of God the Lord this say I must,
He is my sure salvation:
In him my God I hope and trust,
My strong fortification.

Psalm 92

Dessus
Haute-Contre
Taille
Basse-Contre
Genevan tune
2
3
4
5
6
O que c'est cho- se bel- le De te lou- er, Sei- gneur,
Et du Tres- haut, l'hon- neur Chan- ter d'un coeur fi- del- le!
Pres- chant à la ve- nu- ë Du ma- tin ta bon- té,

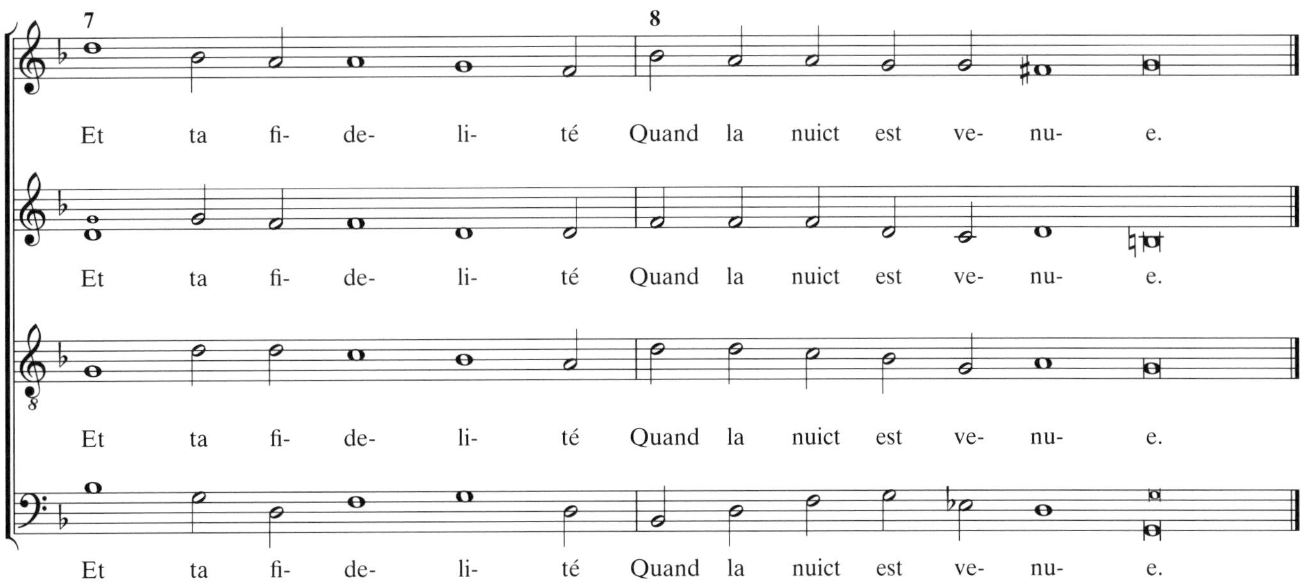

To God give thanks, confessing
It is a gracious thing,
Thy Name most high to sing:
In Psalms thy praise expressing.
I'th morn betimes prepared,
Thy mercies forth to shew,
Thy faithfulnes most trew,
Each night shall be declared.

Psalm 93

The Lord doth raign in soveraign royalty,
Is cloath'd with strength and highest majesty,
With powr hath girt himselfe, supreme hath prov'd,
The world he set so sure, shall not be mov'd.

Psalm 94

O Lord to whom revenge pertaineth,
The God who vengeance just ordaineth:
Of all the earth, thou Judg suprem,
O let thy justice shine forth clear,
Advance thy self, in powr appear,
Cast down the proud, reward thou them.

Psalm 95

*Also set in Psalms 24, 62, and 111

†This flat appears in the 1562 psalter and in the melody parts of both Psalm 24 and Psalm 62 (in transposition) but not here or in Psalm 111.

5
6
De- vant sa face, et de chan- ter Le los de sa ma- gni- fi- cen- ce.
De- vant sa face, et de chan- ter Le los de sa ma- gni- fi- cen- ce.
De- vant sa face, et de chan- ter Le los de sa ma- gni- fi- cen- ce.
De- vant sa face, et de chan- ter Le los de sa ma- gni- fi- cen- ce.
De- vant sa face, et de chan- ter Le los de sa ma- gni- fi- cen- ce.

Come let us sing with pleasant voyce
To God, and make a joyfull noyse
Unto the rock of our salvation.
His presence let us come before,
With thanks and praises him adore,
Sing Psalms to him with exultation.

Psalm 96

Dessus
Haute-Contre
Taille
Basse-Contre
Genevan tune
2
Chan- tez à Dieu chan- son nou- vel- le, Chan- tez, ô terre
Chan- tez à Dieu chan- son nou- vel- le, Chan- tez, ô terre
Chan- tez à Dieu chan- son nou- vel- le, Chan- tez, ô terre
Chan- tez à Dieu chan- son nou- vel- le, Chan- tez, ô terre
3
u- ni- ver- sel- le, Chan- tez, et son nom
u- ni- ver- sel- le, Chan- tez, et son nom
u- ni- ver- sel- le, Chan- tez, et son nom
u- ni- ver- sel- le, Chan- tez, et son nom
4
be- nis- sez, Et de jour en jour an- non- cez
be- nis- sez, Et de jour en jour an- non- cez
be- nis- sez, Et de jour en jour an- non- cez
be- nis- sez, Et de jour en jour an- non- cez

O sing to God new songs composed,
To God Sing all on earth reposed:
Sing to the Lord, his praise expres,
His sacred Name praise we and bles,
Let his grace daily be disclosed.

Psalm 97

Dessus
Haute-Contre
Taille
Basse-Contre
Genevan tune
2
3
4
5
6
L'E- ter- nel est re- gnant, La ter- re main- te- nant
En soit joy- euse et gay- e, Toute is- le s'en es- gay- e:
Es- paisse ob- scu- ri- té Ca- che sa ma- je- sté:

7
8
Jus- tice et ju- ge- ment, Sont le
Jus- tice et ju- ge- ment, Sont le
Jus- tice et ju- ge- ment, Sont le
Jus- tice et ju- ge- ment, Sont le
9
seur fon- de- ment De son throne ar- res- té.
seur fon- de- ment De son throne ar- res- té.
seur fon- de- ment De son throne ar- res- té.
seur fon- de- ment De son throne ar- res- té.

The Lord eternall raignes,
Who righteousnes maintaines:
Let all earth, low and high lands,
Therof rejoyce all Ilands.
Thick clouds obscurity,
Surround his Majesty:
Both justice and judgment,
His thrones establishment,
On him attendant be.

Psalm 98

*Also set in Psalms 66 and 118

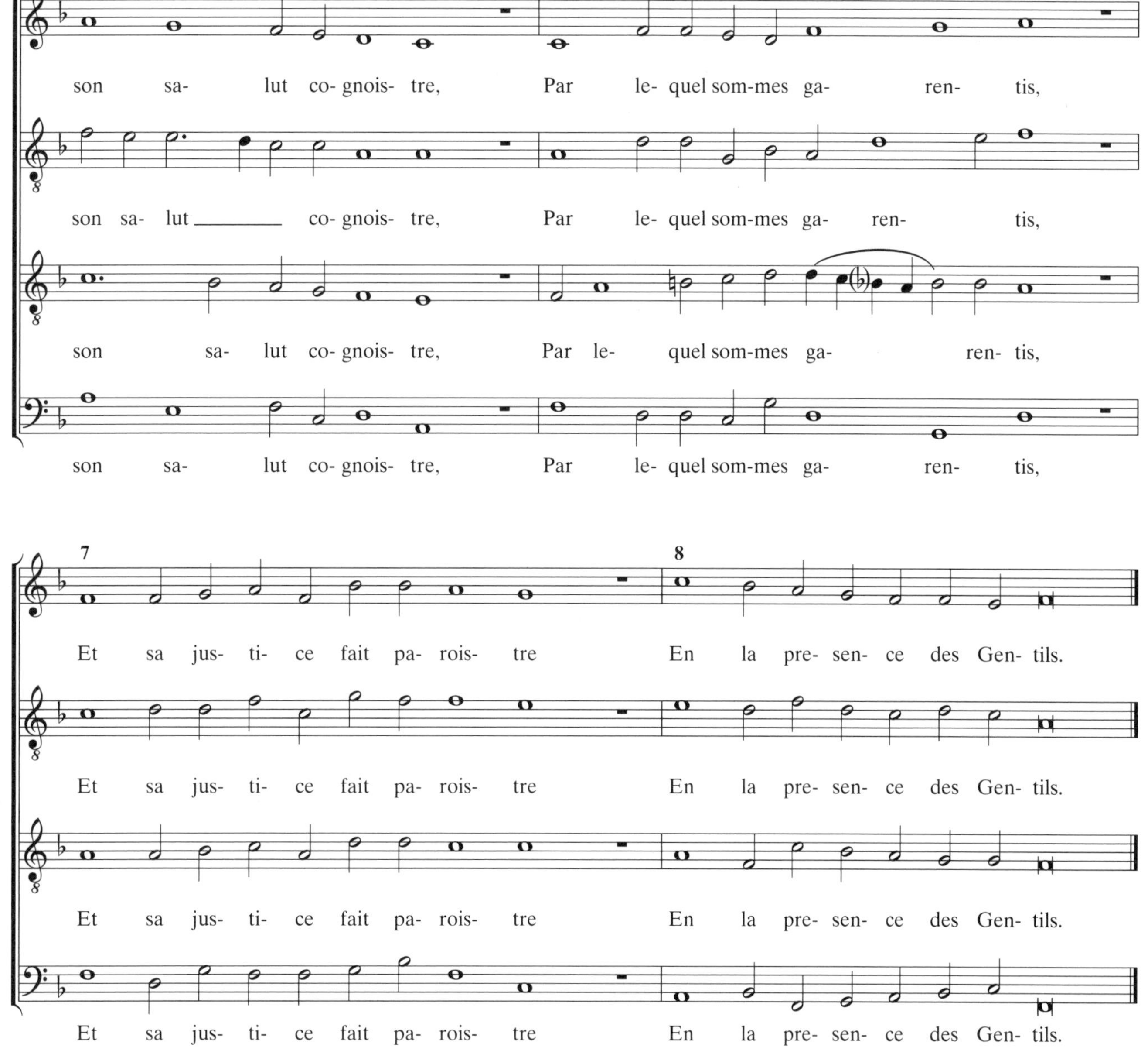

Sing to the Lord new songs delightfull,
For he great wondrous works hath done:
His holy arm of justice rightfull,
His right hand victory hath won.
The Lord our God hath his salvation,
Most gratious to all made known:
And in the sight of every Nation,
His justice openly hath shown.

Psalm 99

ter- re tou- te Trem- blant le re- dou- te.
ter- re tou- te Trem- blant le re- dou- te.
ter- re tou- te Trem- blant le re- dou- te.
ter- re tou- te Trem- blant le re- dou- te.

God the Lord doth raign, suprem doth remain,
People obstinate, quake amaz'd therat:
He doth sit upon Cherubims his throne,
Let the earth be moved, which his powr hath proved.

Psalm 100

All people dwelling on the earth,
Sing to the Lord with joy and mirth:
The Lord adore with thankfull voyce,
Approach his presence, sing, rejoyce.

*Also set in Psalms 131 and 142

Psalm 101

Of mercy milde, with judgment just uniting,
Now will I sing to thee O Lord, inditing:
The Psalm I sing, to thee my God belongs,
Such Psalms, such songs.

Psalm 102

Dessus
Haute-Contre
Taille
Basse-Contre
Genevan tune
2
Sei- gneur, en- ten ma re- ques- te, Rien n'em- pes-che ny n'ar- res- te
Sei- gneur, en- ten ma re- ques- te, Rien n'em- pes-che ny n'ar-res- te
Sei- gneur, en- ten ma re-ques- te, Rien n'em- pes-che ny n'ar-res- te
Sei- gneur, en- ten ma re-ques- te, Rien n'em- pes-che ny n'ar-res- te
3
4
Mon cri d'al- ler ju- squ'à toy, Ne te ca- che point de moy.
Mon cri d'al- ler ju- squ'à toy, Ne te ca- che point de moy.
Mon cri d'al- ler ju- squ'à toy, Ne te ca- che point de moy.
Mon cri d'al- ler ju- squ'à toy, Ne te ca- che point de moy.
5
6
En ma dou- leur nom- pa- reil- le, Tour- ne vers moi ton o- reil- le:
En ma dou- leur nom- pa- reil- le, Tour- ne vers moi ton o- reil- le:
En ma dou-leur nom- pa- reil- le, Tour- ne vers moi ton o- reil- le:
En ma dou- leur nom- pa- reil- le, Tour- ne vers moi ton o- reil- le:

To my prayr O Lord attend thou,
Gracious eare to my suit bend thou:
Let my cry come unto thee,
Do not hide thy face from me.
In the day I am distressed,
When I am with grief oppressed:
When I call, afflicted needy,
Daign to me thy succor speedy.

Psalm 103

Dessus
Haute-Contre
Taille
Basse-Contre
Genevan tune
Sus louez Dieu, mon ame, en toute chose,
Et tout cela qui dedans moy repose,
Louez son nom tres-sainct et accomply.
Presente à Dieu loüanges et services,

My soul praise thou the Lord for ever blessed,
Let all that is within my powr possessed,
His holy Name extoll and magnifie:
Of all his gifts so gratious, great and many,
Which he on thee bestow'd, forget not any,
But bles the Lord my soul, him glorifie.

Psalm 104

Dessus
Haute-Contre
Taille
Basse-Contre
Genevan tune
2
3
4
5
Sus, sus, mon ame, il te faut di- re bien De l'E- ter- nel:
ô mon vray Dieu, com-bien Ta gran-deur est ex- cel-lente et no- toi- re:
Tu es ves- tu de splen- deur et de gloi- re:
Tu es ves- tu de splen- deur

Bles thou the Lord my soul, O Lord my God,
Thy greatnes far exceedeth all abroad:
Thou majesty most glorious daily wearest,
With honor thou most beautifull appearest.
With light most bright, resplendant every morn,
As with a robe, thy self thou dost adorn:
The firmament bedeckt with stars extending,
Like curtains drawn forth by thy powr transcending.

Psalm 105

Dessus
Haute-Contre
Taille
Basse-Contre
Genevan tune
2
Sus, qu'un cha- cun de nous sans ces- se Lou- e du
Sus, qu'un cha- cun ___ de nous sans ces- se Lou- e du
Sus, qu'un cha- cun de nous sans ces- se Lou- e du
Sus, qu'un cha- cun de nous sans ces- se Lou- e du
3
Sei-gneur la hau- tes- se, Que son sainct Nom soit re- cla- mé,
Sei- gneur la hau- tes- se, Que son sainct Nom soit re- cla- mé,
Sei- gneur la hau- tes- se, Que son sainct Nom soit re- cla- mé,
Sei- gneur ______ la hau- tes- se, Que son sainct Nom soit re- cla- mé,
4
5
Soit en- tre les peu- ples se- mé Le re- nom
Soit en- tre les peu- ples se- mé Le re- nom
Soit en- tre les peu- ples se- mé Le re- nom
Soit en- tre les peu- ples se- mé Le re- nom

Let every one of us confessing,
Give thanks to God, his praise expressing:
The glory of his sacred Name,
Among the people all proclaime,
His honor great and precious,
Make known his actions glorious.

Psalm 106

Dessus
Haute-Contre
Taille
Basse-Contre
Genevan tune
2
Lou- ez Dieu car il est be- nin, Et sa bon- té
Lou- ez Dieu car il est be- nin, Et sa bon- té
Lou- ez Dieu car il est be- nin, Et sa bon- té
Lou- ez Dieu car il est be- nin, Et sa bon- té
3
n'a point de fin. Où est ce- luy qui la prou- ës- se
n'a point de fin. Où est ce- luy qui la prou- ës- se
n'a point de fin. Où est ce- luy qui la prou- ës- se
n'a point de fin. Où est ce- luy qui la prou- ës- se
4
5
De l'E- ter- nel re- ci- te- ra Et tous les faicts de sa
De l'E- ter- nel re- ci- te- ra Et tous les faicts de sa
De l'E- ter- nel re- ci- te- ra Et tous les faicts de sa
De l'E- ter- nel re- ci- te- ra Et tous les faicts de sa

6
hau- tes- se En- tie- re- ment nous chan- te- ra?
hau- tes- se En- tie- re- ment nous chan- te- ra?
hau- tes- se En- tie- re- ment nous chan- te- ra?
hau- tes- se En- tie- re- ment nous chan- te- ra?

Praise ye the Lord, to him confes,
Give thanks to God for his goodnes:
For his sweet mercy lasteth ever,
Who can expres Gods powr and might,
Or shew his praise which ceaseth never,
Or worthily his acts recite?

Psalm 107

Dessus
Don- nez au Sei- gneur gloi- re,
Haute-Contre
Don- nez au Sei- gneur gloi- re,
Taille
Genevan tune
Don- nez au Sei- gneur gloi- re,
Basse-Contre
Don- nez au Sei- gneur gloi- re,
2
Il est doux et clé- ment,
Il est doux et clé- ment,
Il est doux et clé- ment,
Il est doux et clé- ment,
3
Et sa bon- té no-
Et sa bon- té no-
Et sa bon- té no-
Et sa bon- té no-
4
-toi- re Dure e- ter- nel- le- ment.
-toi- re Dure e- ter- nel- le- ment.
-toi- re Dure e- ter- nel- le- ment.
-toi- re Dure e- ter- nel- le- ment.
5
Ceux qu'il
Ceux qu'il a
Ceux qu'il a
Ceux qu'il a

Give thanks to God, confessing
His goodnes, give him praise,
Us with his mercies blessing,
Which do endure alwayes:
Let them declare and show,
Whom God to save decreed,
How from their cruell foe,
He them redeem'd and freed.

Psalm 108

*Also set in Psalm 60

O God my heart is firm prepard,
In Psalms thy praise shall be declar'd:
My glory sing his worthy praise,
My Lute, my Harp, yourselves upraise.
Before the day do dawn, awake,
Right early I this taske will take,
With heart and hand, my voyce concenting,
Betimes i'th morning, day preventing.

Psalm 109

*Also set in Psalm 28

Psalm 110

The mighty Lord, unto my Lord declared
His sacred minde, to him these words he spake:
At my right hand take thou thy seat prepared,
Untill thy foes thy footstool I shall make.

Psalm 111

*Also set in Psalms 24, 62, and 95

†This flat appears in the 1562 psalter and in the melody parts of both Psalm 24 and Psalm 62 (in transposition) but not here or in Psalm 95.

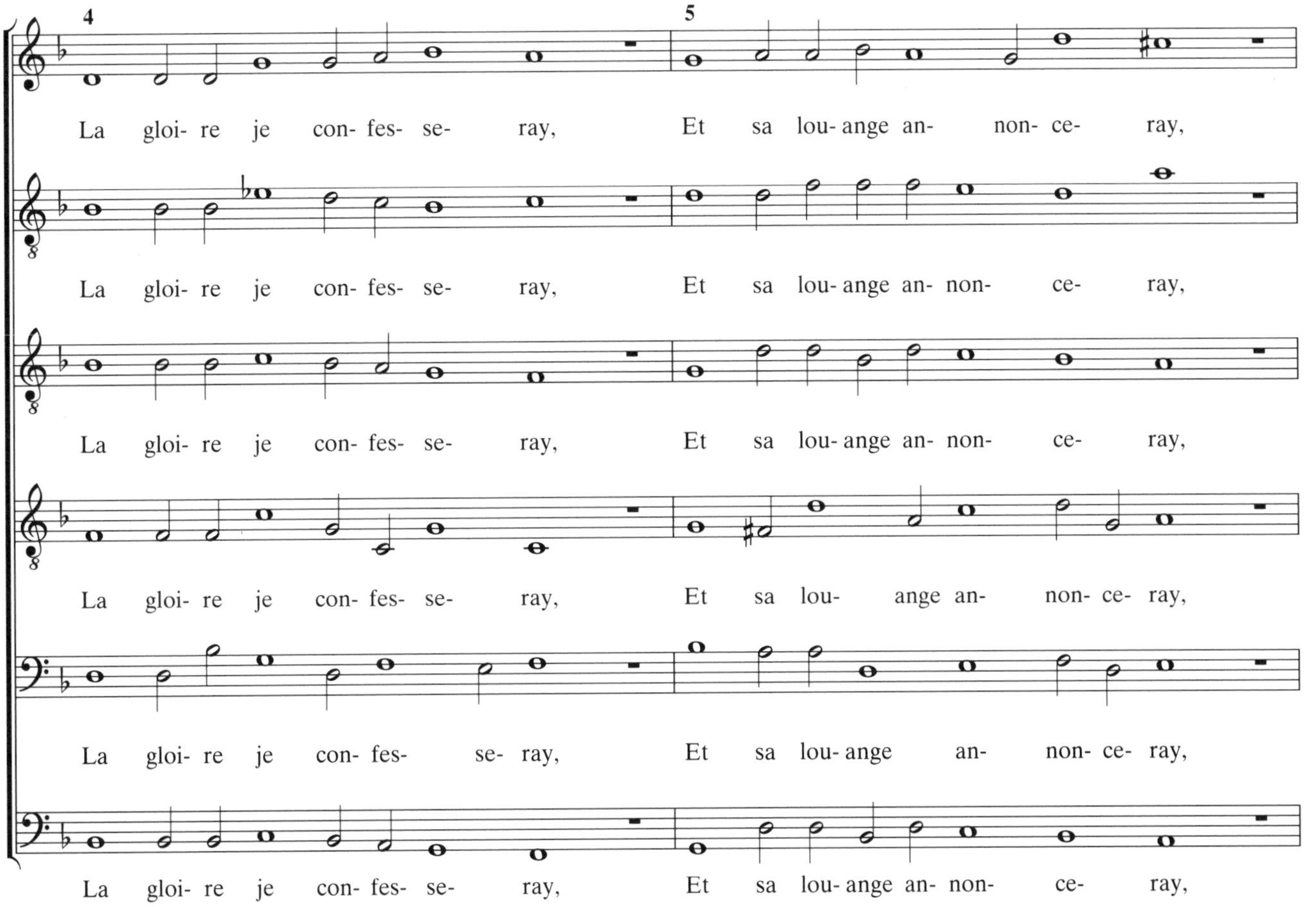

4
5
La gloi- re je con- fes- se- ray, Et sa lou- ange an- non- ce- ray,
La gloi- re je con- fes- se- ray, Et sa lou- ange an- non- ce- ray,
La gloi- re je con- fes- se- ray, Et sa lou- ange an- non- ce- ray,
La gloi- re je con- fes- se- ray, Et sa lou- ange an- non- ce- ray,
La gloi- re je con- fes- se- ray, Et sa lou- ange an- non- ce- ray,
La gloi- re je con- fes- se- ray, Et sa lou- ange an- non- ce- ray,

6
D'une af- fec- ti- on toute en- tie- re.
D'une af- fec- ti- on toute en- tie- re.
D'une af- fec- ti- on toute en- tie- re.
D'une af- fec- ti- on toute en- tie- re.
D'une af- fec- ti- on toute en- tie- re.
D'une af- fec- ti- on toute en- tie- re.

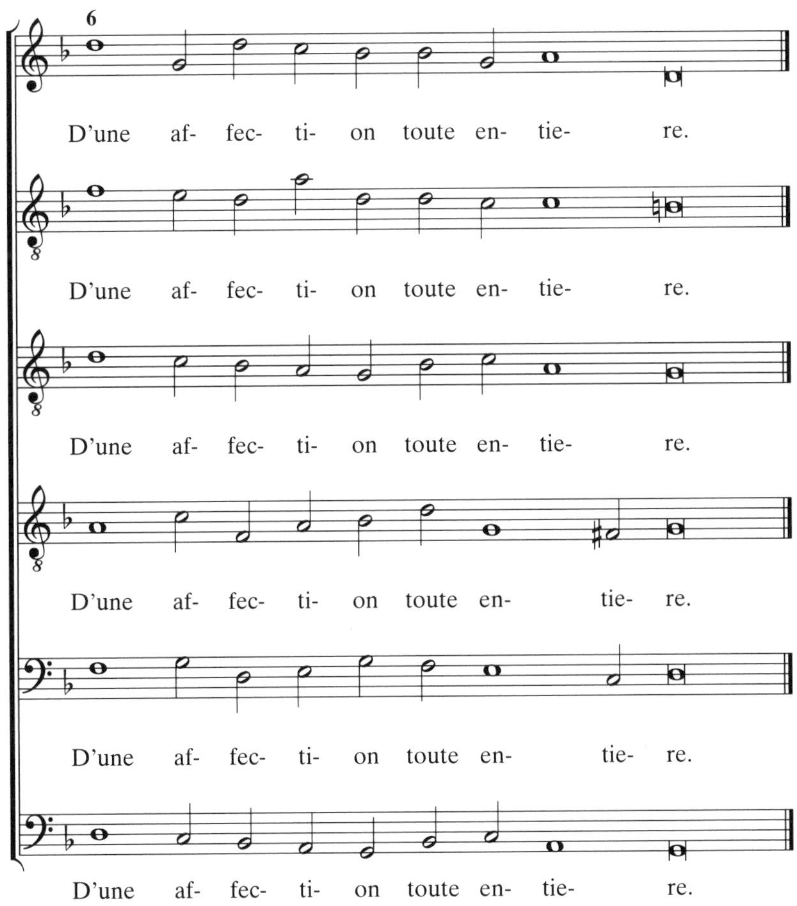

To God the Lord I will confes,
With all my heart him praise and bles,
Among the righteous congregation,
His benefits I will relate,
With thanks his glory celebrate,
And of his praise make declaration.

Psalm 112

Dessus
O bien- heu- reu- se la per- son- ne Qui craint
Haute-Contre
O bien- heu- reu- se la per- son- ne Qui craint
Taille
Genevan tune
O bien- heu- reu- se la per- son- ne Qui craint
Basse-Contre
O bien- heu- reu- se la per- son- ne Qui craint
2
l'E- ter- nel,_ et s'ad- don- ne Du tout à sa Loy tres- en- tie- re:
l'E- ter- nel, et s'ad- don- ne Du tout à sa Loy tres- en- tie- re:
l'E- ter- nel, et s'ad- don- ne Du tout à sa Loy tres- en- tie- re:
l'E- ter- nel, et s'ad- don- ne Du tout à sa Loy tres- en- tie- re:
3
4
Sa race en ter- re se- ra for- te: Car Dieu be- nit en
Sa race en ter- re se- ra for- te: Car Dieu be- nit en
Sa race en ter- re se- ra for- te: Car Dieu be- nit en
Sa race en ter- re se- ra for- te: Car Dieu be- nit en
5

6
tou- te for- te, Des bons la ra- ce droi- tu- rie- re.
tou- te for- te, Des bons la ra- ce droi- tu- rie- re.
tou- te for- te, Des bons la ra- ce droi- tu- rie- re.
tou- te for- te, Des bons la ra- ce droi- tu- rie- re.

The man is blest, the Lord who feareth,
And to his Law affection beareth.
His seed upon the earth remaining,
Shall mighty be, as princes raigning:
The just and righteous generation,
Shall ever be a blessed Nation.

Psalm 113

Dessus
Haute-Contre
Taille
Basse-Contre
Genevan tune
2
En- fans qui le Sei- gneur ser- vez, Lou- ez- le et son
3
Nom es- le- vez, Lou- ez son Nom et sa
4
5
hau- tes- se: Soit pres- ché, soit fait so- len- nel, Le Nom du

Praise ye the Lord his servants all,
The Name of God right blessed call:
His Name to praise, let all endever,
His honor'd Fame let all relate,
His glorious Name to celebrate,
And magnifie both now and ever.

Psalm 114

Dessus
Haute-Contre
Taille
Basse-Contre
Genevan tune
2
3
4
5
Quand Is- ra- ël hors d'E- gip- te sor- tit, Et la
Quand Is- ra- ël hors d'E- gip- te sor- tit, Et la
Quand Is- ra- ël hors d'E- gip- te sor- tit, Et la
Quand Is- ra- ël hors d'E- gip- te sor- tit, Et la
mai- son de Ja- cob se par- tit D'en- tre le peuple es- tran- ge,
mai- son de Ja- cob se par- tit D'en- tre le peuple es- tran- ge,
mai- son de Ja- cob se par- tit D'en- tre le peuple es- tran- ge,
mai- son de Ja- cob se par- tit D'en- tre le peuple es- tran- ge,
Ju- da fut fait la grand' gloi- re de Dieu: Et Dieu se fit
Ju- da fut fait la grand' gloi- re de Dieu: Et Dieu se fit
Ju- da fut fait la grand' gloi- re de Dieu: Et Dieu se fit
Ju- da fut fait la grand' gloi- re de Dieu: Et Dieu se fit

6
Prin- ce du peuple He- brieu, Prin- ce de grand' loü- an- ge.
Prin- ce du peuple He- brieu, Prin- ce de grand' loü- an- ge.
Prin- ce du peuple He- brieu, Prin- ce de grand' loü- an- ge.
Prin- ce du peuple He- brieu, Prin- ce de grand' loü- an- ge.

When Israel from out of Egypt went,
And Jacobs house from people strange were sent,
From cruell thrall secured:
Then Juda was his Sanctuary made,
He Israel for his dominion had,
Unto himself procured.

Psalm 115

Dessus
Non point à nous, non point à nous, Sei- gneur, Mais à ton
Haute-Contre
Non point à nous, non point à nous, Sei- gneur, Mais à ton
Taille
Genevan tune
Non point à nous, non point à nous, Sei- gneur, Mais à ton
Basse-Contre
Non point à nous, non point à nous, Sei- gneur, Mais à ton
2
Nom don- ne gloire et hon- neur, Pour ta grace et foy seu- re:
Nom don- ne gloire et hon- neur, Pour ta grace et foy seu- re:
Nom don- ne gloire et hon- neur, Pour ta grace et foy seu- re:
Nom don- ne gloire et hon- neur, Pour ta grace et foy seu- re:
3
4
Pour- quoy di- royent les gens en se mo- quant, Où est ce Dieu
Pour- quoy di- royent les gens en se mo- quant, Où est ce Dieu
Pour- quoy di- royent les gens en se mo- quant, Où est ce Dieu
Pour- quoy di- royent les gens en se mo- quant, Où est ce Dieu
5

6
qu'ils vont tant in- vo- quant, Où est- il à ceste heu- re?
qu'ils vont tant in- vo- quant, Où est- il à ceste heu- re?
qu'ils vont tant in- vo- quant, Où est- il à ceste heu- re?
qu'ils vont tant in- vo- quant, Où est- il à ceste heu- re?

Not to us Lord, not to us we intreat,
But to thy Name give thou the glory great:
For thy truth and thy faver:
Why should the proud, the heathen, mock and jeer,
Wher's now your God? why doth he not appear,
Wher's now your trust, your Saver?

Psalm 116

I love the Lord, because he eare doth give,
Unto my voyce, and to my supplication,
Since he inclin'd to hear with acceptation,
Therfore will I call on him while I live.

*Also set in Psalm 74

Psalm 117

*Also set in Psalm 127

All nations laud the Lord our God,
Praise him all people all abroad.
For in his mercies bounteous,
Hath he exceeded toward us:
His truth abides eternally,
Him therfore ever magnifie.

Psalm 118

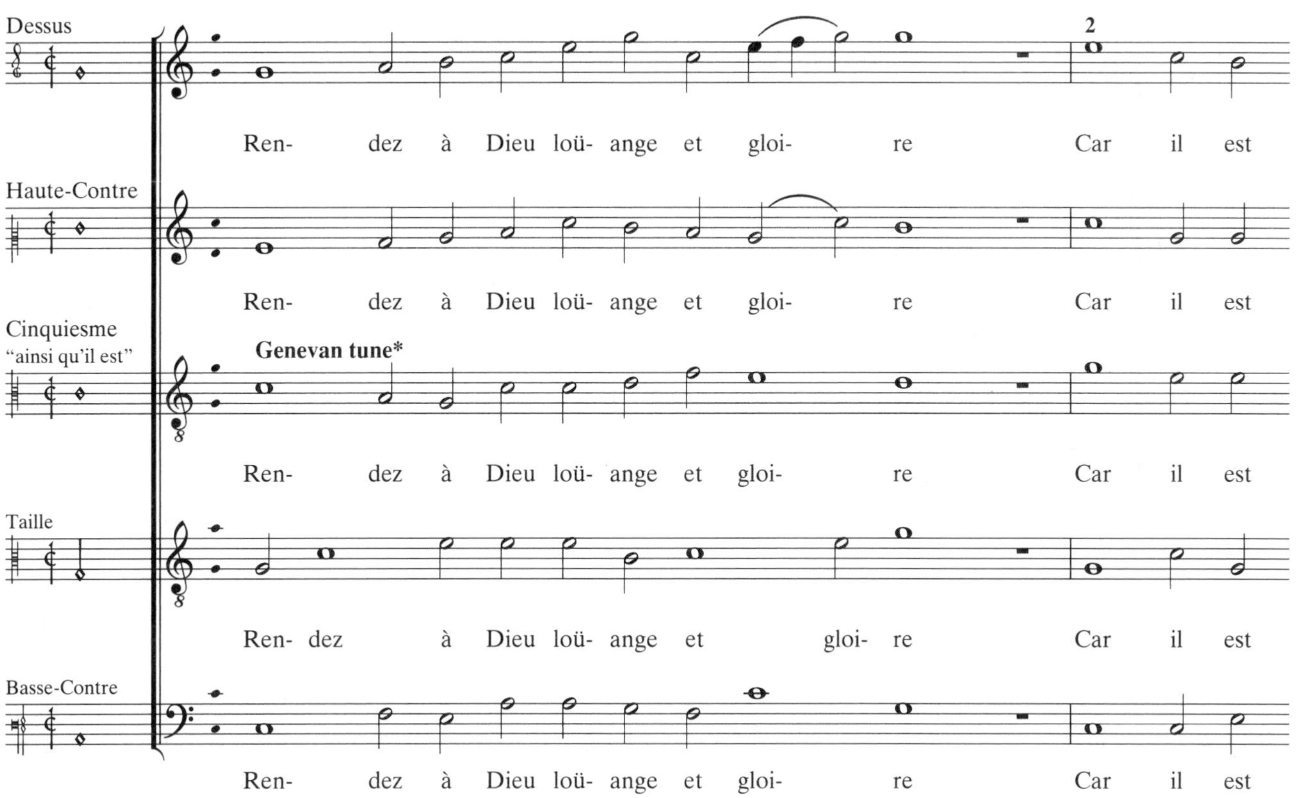
Dessus
Haute-Contre
Cinquiesme
"ainsi qu'il est"
Genevan tune*
Taille
Basse-Contre
2
Ren- dez à Dieu loü- ange et gloi- re Car il est
Ren- dez à Dieu loü- ange et gloi- re Car il est
Ren- dez à Dieu loü- ange et gloi- re Car il est
Ren- dez à Dieu loü- ange et gloi- re Car il est
Ren- dez à Dieu loü- ange et gloi- re Car il est

3
be- nin et cle- ment: Qui plus est sa bon- té no- toi- re
be- nin et cle- ment: Qui plus est sa bon- té no- toi- re
be- nin et cle- ment: Qui plus est sa bon- té no- toi- re
be- nin et cle- ment: Qui plus est sa bon- té no- toi- re
be- nin et cle- ment: Qui plus est sa bon- té no- toi- re

*Also set in Psalms 66 and 98

4 5

Du- re per- pe- tu- el- le- ment. Qu'Is- ra- ël o- res se

Du- re per- pe- tu- el- le- ment. Qu'Is- ra- ël o- res se

Du- re per- pe- tu- el- le- ment. Qu'Is- ra- ël o- res se

Du- re per- pe- tu- el- le- ment. Qu'Is- ra- ël o- res se

Du- re per- pe- tu- el- le- ment. Qu'Is- ra- ël o- res se

6 7

re- cor- de De chan-ter so- len- nel- le- ment, Que sa gran- de

re- cor- de De chan-ter so- len- nel- le- ment, Que sa gran- de

re- cor- de De chan-ter so- len- nel- le- ment, Que sa gran- de

re- cor- de De chan-ter so- len- nel- le- ment, Que sa gran- de

re- cor- de De chan-ter so- len- nel- le- ment, Que sa gran- de

To God give thanks, all praises render,
Because so gracious good is he,
For his compassion, mercy tender,
Endureth sure eternally.
Let Israel make declaration,
And singing publish solumnly,
That his so great commiseration,
Most sure endures perpetually.

Psalm 119

Dessus
Haute-Contre
Taille
Basse-Contre
Genevan tune
2
Bien- heu- reuse est la per- son- ne qui vit A- vec
Bien- heu- reuse est la per- son- ne qui vit A- vec
Bien- heu- reuse est la per- son- ne qui vit A- vec
Bien- heu- reuse est la per- son- ne qui vit A- vec
3
en- tiere et sai- ne con- sci- en- ce, Et qui de Dieu
en- tiere et sai- ne con- sci- en- ce, Et qui de Dieu
en- tiere et sai- ne con- sci- en- ce, Et qui de Dieu
en- tiere et sai- ne con- sci- en- ce, Et qui de Dieu
4
les sain- ctes loix en- suit. Heu- reux qui met tout soin et
les sain- ctes loix en- suit. Heu- reux qui met tout soin et
les sain- ctes loix en- suit. Heu- reux qui met tout soin et
les sain- ctes loix en- suit. Heu- reux qui met tout soin et

All they are blest, who keep the perfect way,
Of upright life, and spotles conversation,
Who in the law of God do walk alway:
O happy they, who with due observation,
Do truly keep his statutes constantly,
And seek him with their whole hearts application.

Psalm 120

Dessus
A- lors qu'af- flic- ti- on me pres- se,
2
Ma cla- meur
Haute-Contre
A- lors qu'af- flic- ti- on me pres- se,
Ma cla- meur
Taille
Genevan tune
A- lors qu'af- flic- ti- on me pres- se,
Ma cla- meur
Basse-Contre
A- lors qu'af- flic- ti- on me pres- se,
Ma cla- meur
au Sei- gneur j'ad- dres- se:
3
Car quand je viens à le se- mon- dre,
au Sei- gneur j'ad- dres- se:
Car quand je viens à le se- mon- dre,
au Sei- gneur j'ad- dres- se:
Car quand je viens à le se- mon- dre,
au Sei- gneur j'ad- dres- se:
Car quand je viens à le se- mon- dre,
4
Ja- mais ne faut à me res- pon- dre.
5
Con- tre ces le- vres tant
Ja- mais ne faut à me res- pon- dre.
Con- tre ces le- vres tant
Ja- mais ne faut à me res- pon- dre.
Con- tre ces le- vres tant
Ja- mais ne faut à me res- pon- dre.
Con- tre ces le- vres tant

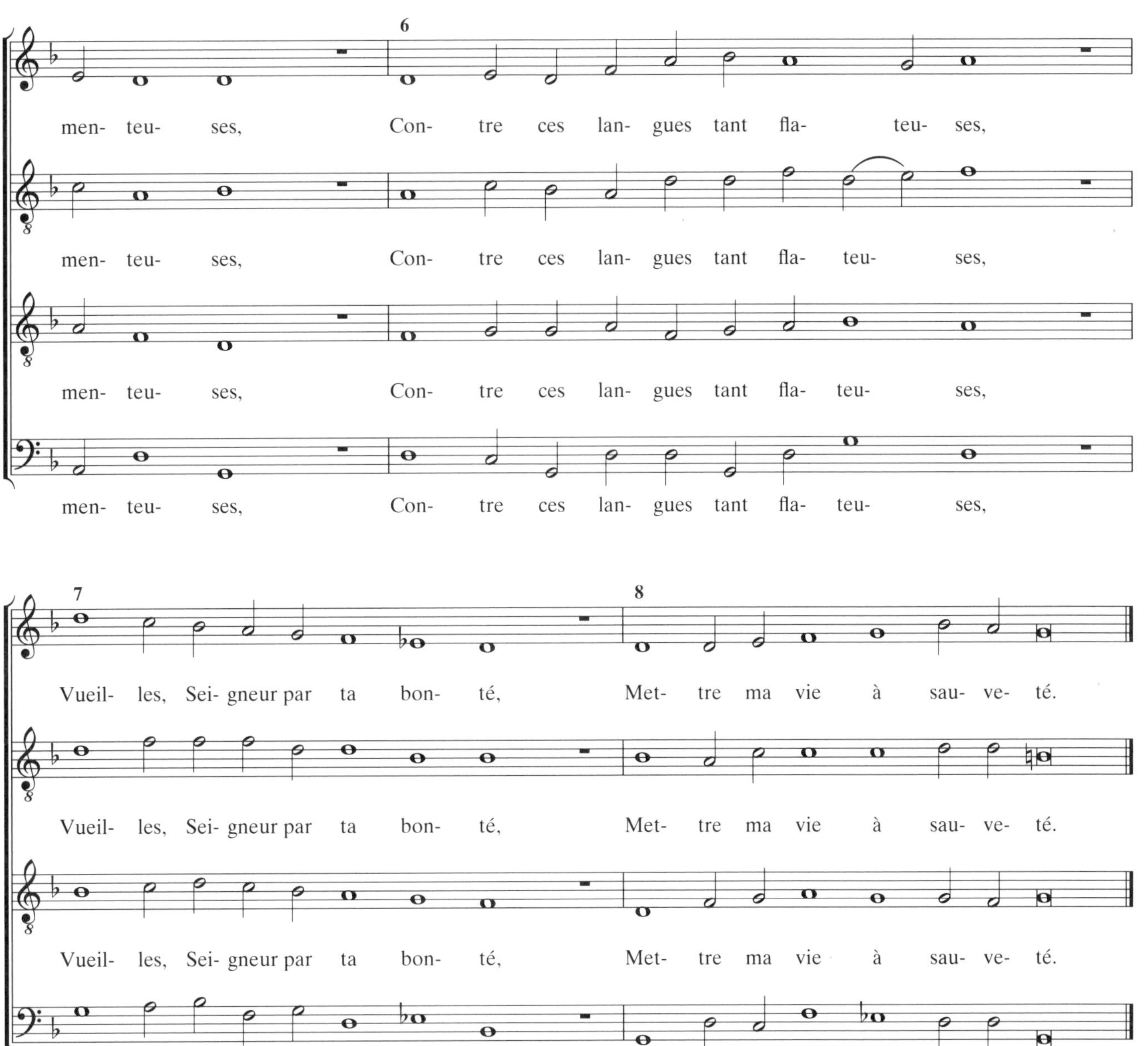
6
men- teu- ses, Con- tre ces lan- gues tant fla- teu- ses,
men- teu- ses, Con- tre ces lan- gues tant fla- teu- ses,
men- teu- ses, Con- tre ces lan- gues tant fla- teu- ses,
men- teu- ses, Con- tre ces lan- gues tant fla- teu- ses,
7
8
Vueil- les, Sei- gneur par ta bon- té, Met- tre ma vie à sau- ve- té.
Vueil- les, Sei- gneur par ta bon- té, Met- tre ma vie à sau- ve- té.
Vueil- les, Sei- gneur par ta bon- té, Met- tre ma vie à sau- ve- té.
Vueil- les, Sei- gneur par ta bon- té, Met- tre ma vie à sau- ve- té.

When sharp afflictions me oppressed,
I to the Lord my prayr addressed:
He heard me when to him I cryed,
And me with timely ayd supplyed.
Now also Lord my soul deliver
From lying lips of the deceiver:
Preserve my life safe from the wrong
And harm of the deceitfull tong.

Psalm 121

Up to the hils I lift mine eyes,
From whence comes help to me.
My help Lord comes from thee,
Whose powr hath made the earth and skyes,
He hath them surely founded,
On him my hope is grounded.

Psalm 122

Dessus
Haute-Contre
Taille
Basse-Contre
Genevan tune
2
In- con- ti- nent que j'eus ou- ï, Sus al-
-lons le lieu vi- si- ter,
3
Où le Sei- gneur veut ha- bi- ter:
4
O que mon coeur s'est res- joü- i!
5
Or en tes por- ches en- tre- ront

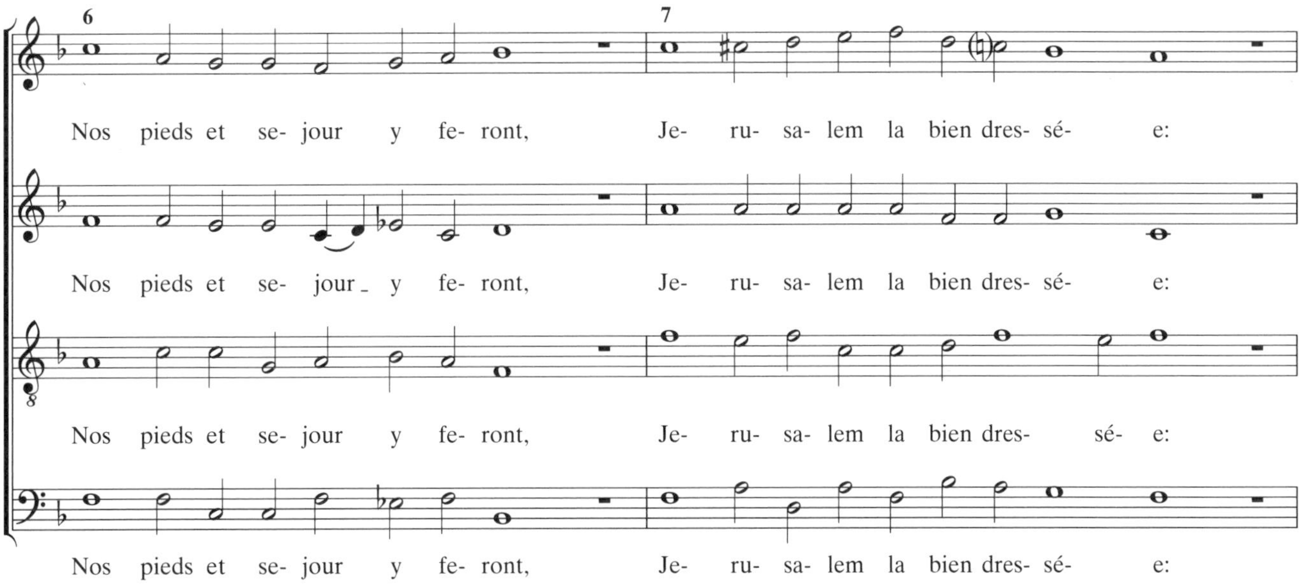

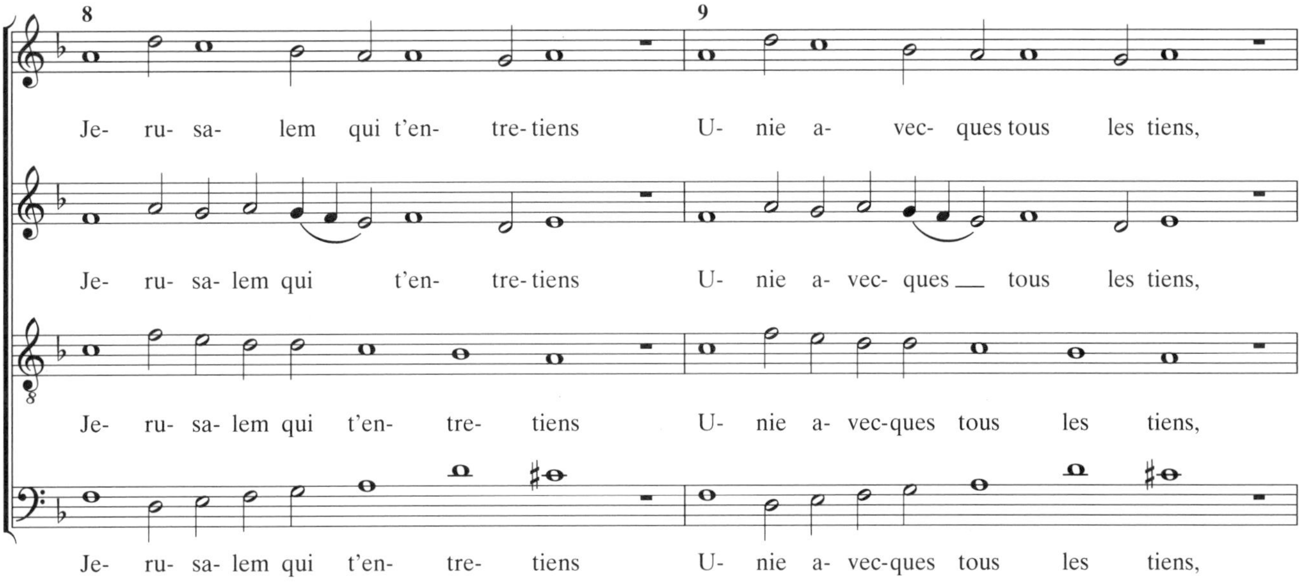

6
7
Nos pieds et se- jour y fe- ront, Je- ru- sa- lem la bien dres- sé- e:
Nos pieds et se- jour y fe- ront, Je- ru- sa- lem la bien dres- sé- e:
Nos pieds et se- jour y fe- ront, Je- ru- sa- lem la bien dres- sé- e:
Nos pieds et se- jour y fe- ront, Je- ru- sa- lem la bien dres- sé- e:

8
9
Je- ru- sa- lem qui t'en- tre- tiens U- nie a- vec- ques tous les tiens,
Je- ru- sa- lem qui t'en- tre- tiens U- nie a- vec- ques tous les tiens,
Je- ru- sa- lem qui t'en- tre- tiens U- nie a- vec-ques tous les tiens,
Je- ru- sa- lem qui t'en- tre- tiens U- nie a- vec-ques tous les tiens,

10
Com- me ci- té bien po- li- cé- e.
Com- me ci- té bien po- li- cé- e.
Com- me ci- té bien po- li- cé- e.
Com- me ci- té bien po- li- cé- e.

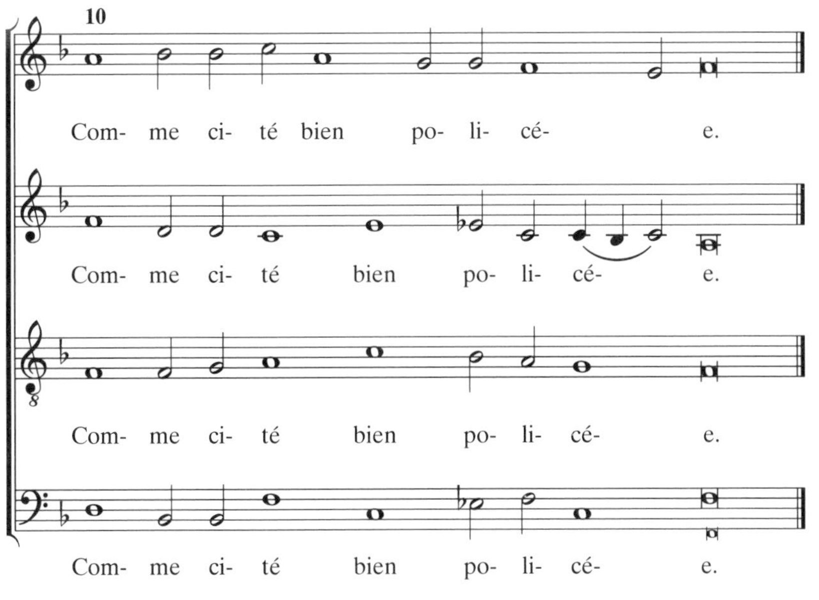

When I did hear the peoples voyce,
Say, let us goe with one accord,
Into the Temple of the Lord,
O how my heart it did rejoyce.
Our willing feet now walk the way,
Within thy gates where we shall stay,
Jerusalem thou city blessed,
Jerusalem now built doth seem
A city of most high esteeme,
Within it self, of peace possessed.

Psalm 123

Dessus
Haute-Contre
Taille
Basse-Contre
Genevan tune
A toy, ô Dieu qui es là haut aux cieux,
Nous es- le- vons nos yeux:
Comm' un ser- vant qui pres- sé
se voit es- tre, N'a re- cours qu'à son mais- tre,
Et la ser- vante a
2
3
4
5

6
l'oeil sur sa mais- tres- se, Aus- si tost qu'on la bles- se:
l'oeil sur sa mais- tres- se, Aus- si tost qu'on la bles- se:
l'oeil sur sa mais- tres- se, Aus- si tost qu'on la bles- se:
l'oeil sur sa mais- tres- se, Aus- si tost qu'on la bles- se:
7
8
Vers nos- tre Dieu nous re- gar- dons ain- si, At- ten- dans sa mer- ci.
Vers nos- tre Dieu nous re- gar- dons ain- si, At- ten- dans sa mer- ci.
Vers nos- tre Dieu nous re- gar- dons ain- si, At- ten- dans sa mer- ci.
Vers nos- tre Dieu nous re- gar- dons ain- si, At- ten- dans sa mer- ci.

To thee O Lord, whose throne is in the skyes,
Do I lift up mine eyes:
As servants lo, distressed by disaster,
Have recourse to their Master,
As handmaids on their Mistres hand attending,
So we on God depending,
Attend the Lord till he most gracious
Have mercy upon us.

Psalm 124

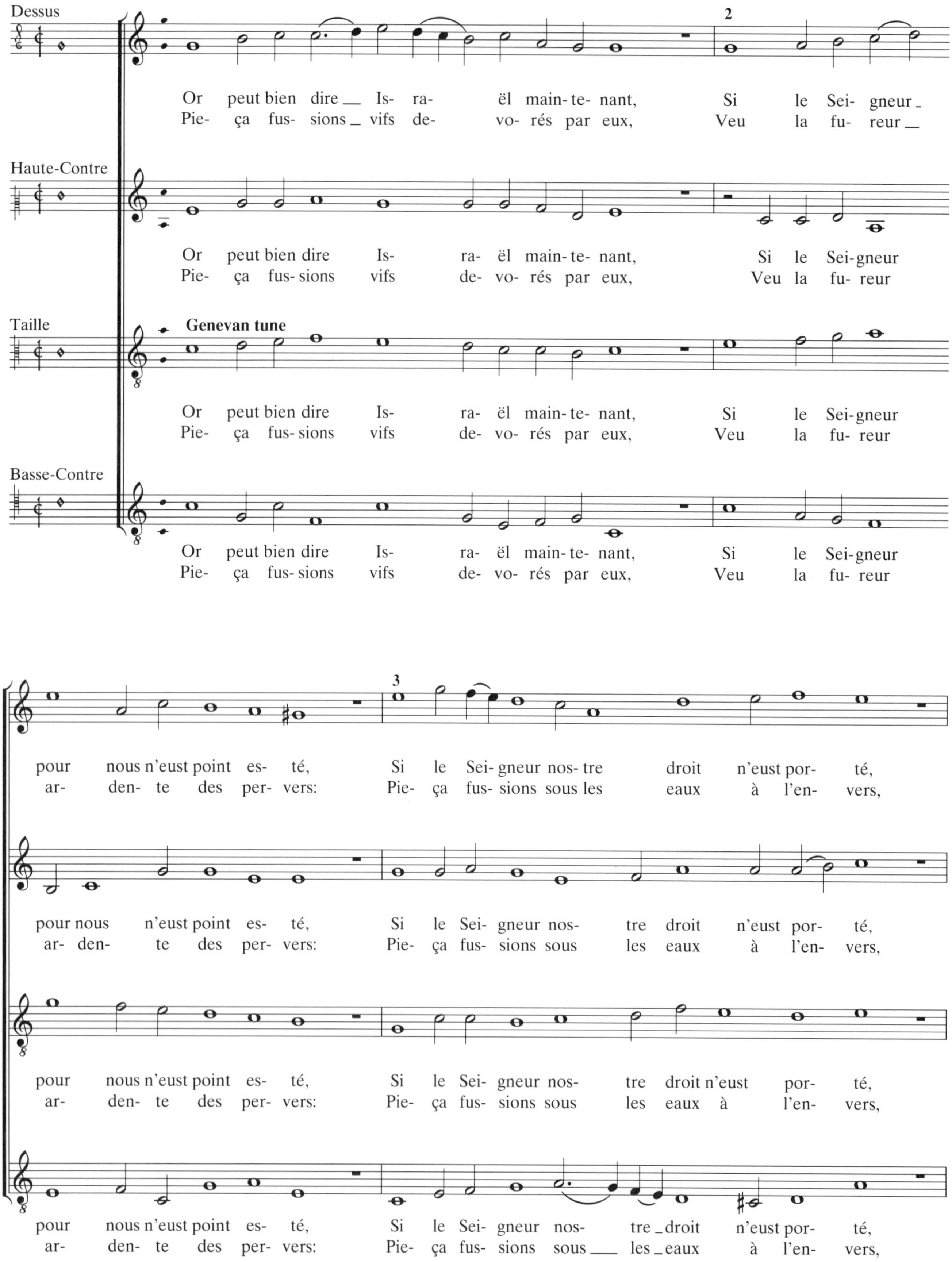

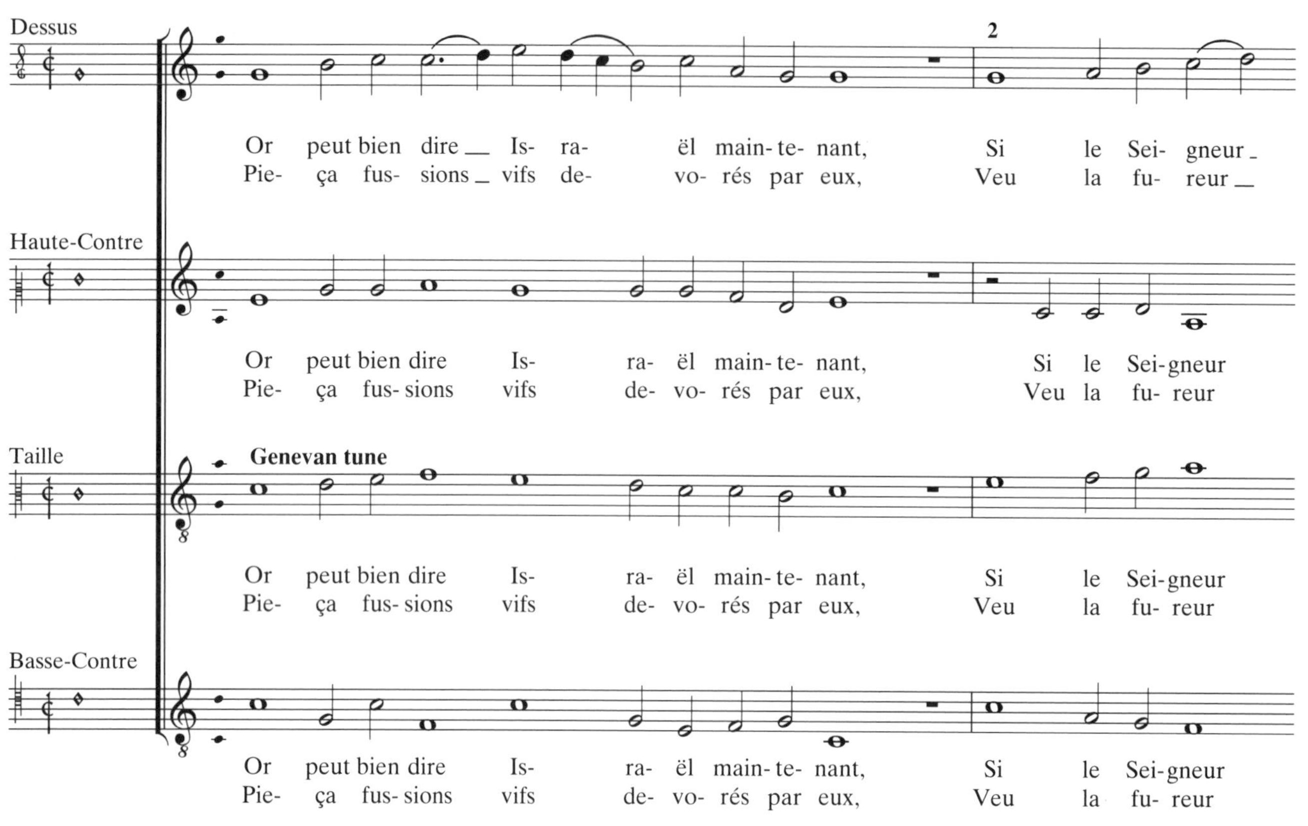

Dessus
2
Or peut bien dire Is- ra- ël main- te- nant, Si le Sei- gneur
Pie- ça fus- sions vifs de- vo- rés par eux, Veu la fu- reur
Haute-Contre
Or peut bien dire Is- ra- ël main- te- nant, Si le Sei-gneur
Pie- ça fus- sions vifs de- vo- rés par eux, Veu la fu- reur
Taille
Genevan tune
Or peut bien dire Is- ra- ël main- te- nant, Si le Sei-gneur
Pie- ça fus- sions vifs de- vo- rés par eux, Veu la fu- reur
Basse-Contre
Or peut bien dire Is- ra- ël main- te- nant, Si le Sei-gneur
Pie- ça fus- sions vifs de- vo- rés par eux, Veu la fu- reur
3
pour nous n'eust point es- té, Si le Sei- gneur nos- tre droit n'eust por- té,
ar- den- te des per- vers: Pie- ça fus- sions sous les eaux à l'en- vers,
pour nous n'eust point es- té, Si le Sei- gneur nos- tre droit n'eust por- té,
ar- den- te des per- vers: Pie- ça fus- sions sous les eaux à l'en- vers,
pour nous n'eust point es- té, Si le Sei- gneur nos- tre droit n'eust por- té,
ar- den- te des per- vers: Pie- ça fus- sions sous les eaux à l'en- vers,
pour nous n'eust point es- té, Si le Sei- gneur nos- tre droit n'eust por- té,
ar- den- te des per- vers: Pie- ça fus- sions sous les eaux à l'en- vers,

Let Israel now say, and make it known,
Unles the Lord of hosts had fought for us,
Unles the Lord his mighty powr had shown,
In our defense, when men most furious,
Their forces joynd us to have overthrown,

They had devourd us quick in gulf profound,
When their fierce wrath inflam'd, thirsting for bloud,
Against us rag'd: even then the boistrous floud
Had us orewhelmd, and sunke us to the ground,
The surging waves and storms our souls had drownd.

Psalm 125

Dessus
Haute-Contre
Taille
Basse-Contre
Genevan tune
Tout hom- me qui son es- pe- ran- ce
En Dieu as- seu- re- ra,
Ja- mais ne ver- se- ra:
Ains au- ra si grande as- seu- ran- ce,
Que Si- on mon- tai- gne
2
3
4
5

6
tres- fer- me, N'est _ point plus fer- me.
tres- fer- me, N'est _ point plus fer- me.
tres- fer- me, N'est point plus fer- me.
tres- fer- me, N'est point plus fer- me.

Who trust in God, and him rely on,
Reposing confidence
Alone in his defence,
They shall stand sure like to mount Sion,
Unmov'd remaining failing never,
But biding ever.

Psalm 126

Dessus
Haute-Contre
Taille
Basse-Contre
Genevan tune
2
A- lors que de cap- ti- vi- té Dieu mit Si- on
A- lors que de cap- ti- vi- té Dieu_ mit Si- on
A- lors que de cap- ti- vi- té Dieu mit Si- on
A- lors que de cap- ti- vi- té Dieu mit Si- on
3
en li- ber- té, Ad- vis nous es- toit pro- pre- ment
en li- ber- té, Ad- vis nous es- toit pro- pre- ment
en li- ber- té, Ad- vis nous es- toit pro- pre- ment
en li- ber- té, Ad- vis nous es- toit pro- pre- ment
4
5
Que nous son- gions tant seu- le- ment, Bou- ches et lan- gues à
Que nous son- gions tant_____ seu- le- ment, Bou- ches et lan- gues_ à
Que nous son- gions tant seu- le- ment, Bou- ches et lan- gues à
Que nous son- gions tant seu- le- ment, Bou- ches et lan- gues à

When Sions sad captivity,
The Lord returnd to liberty,
Amaz'd twixt sudden joy and feare,
Much like to them that dream, we were.
Our tears and grones who long had mourned,
To songs of joy and laughter turned:
The heathen people were afraid,
God wonders wrought for us, they said.

Psalm 127

Dessus
Haute-Contre
Taille
Basse-Contre
Genevan tune*
2
On a beau sa mai- son bas- tir, Si le Sei- gneur
3
n'y met la main, Ce- la n'est que bas- tir en vain.
4
5
Quand on veut vil- les ga- ren- tir, On a beau

*Also set in Psalm 117

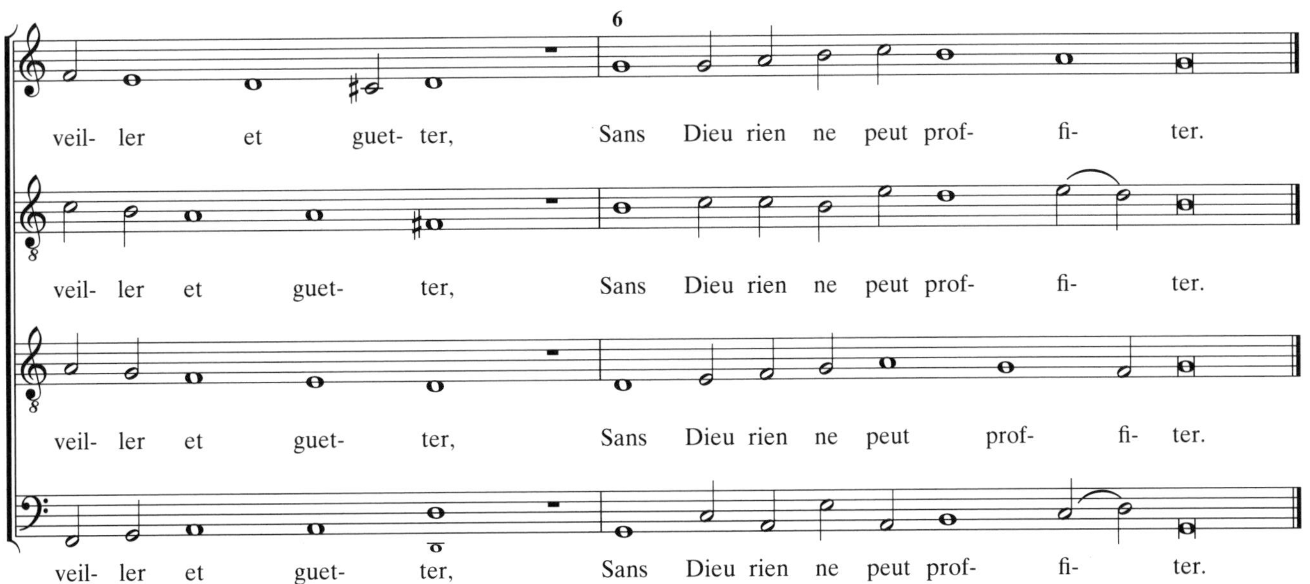
6
veil- ler et guet- ter, Sans Dieu rien ne peut prof- fi- ter.
veil- ler et guet- ter, Sans Dieu rien ne peut prof- fi- ter.
veil- ler et guet- ter, Sans Dieu rien ne peut prof- fi- ter.
veil- ler et guet- ter, Sans Dieu rien ne peut prof- fi- ter.

Unles the Lord the house doth build,
The builders cost and care is vain,
Their charge is lost, and all their pain,
Though stuffe be strong, and men be skilled,
Unles the Lord the city gard,
In vain men watch, in vain they ward.

Psalm 128

Dessus
Haute-Contre
Taille
Basse-Contre
Genevan tune
Bien heu- reux est qui- con- ques Sert à Dieu vo- lon- tiers
Et ne se las- sa on- ques De sui- vre ses sen- tiers.
Du la- beur que sçais fai- re Vi- vras com- mo- de- ment,

Blessed is whosoever doth fear the Lord of might.
And truly doth indever to walk his waies aright.
For thou shalt in thy calling of thy hands labour eat,
And all things fair befalling, thy welfare shall be great.

Psalm 129

Oft from my youth now Israel may say,
They have beset me round, and sore assailed,
Oft from my youth they have sought every way
My overthrow, but never yet prevailed.

Psalm 130

Dessus
Haute-Contre
Taille
Basse-Contre
Genevan tune
Du fonds de ma pen- sé- e, Au fonds de tous en- nuis,
A toy s'est ad- dres- sé- e Ma cla- meur jours et nuicts:
En- ten ma voix plain- ti- ve, Sei- gneur, il est sai- son,

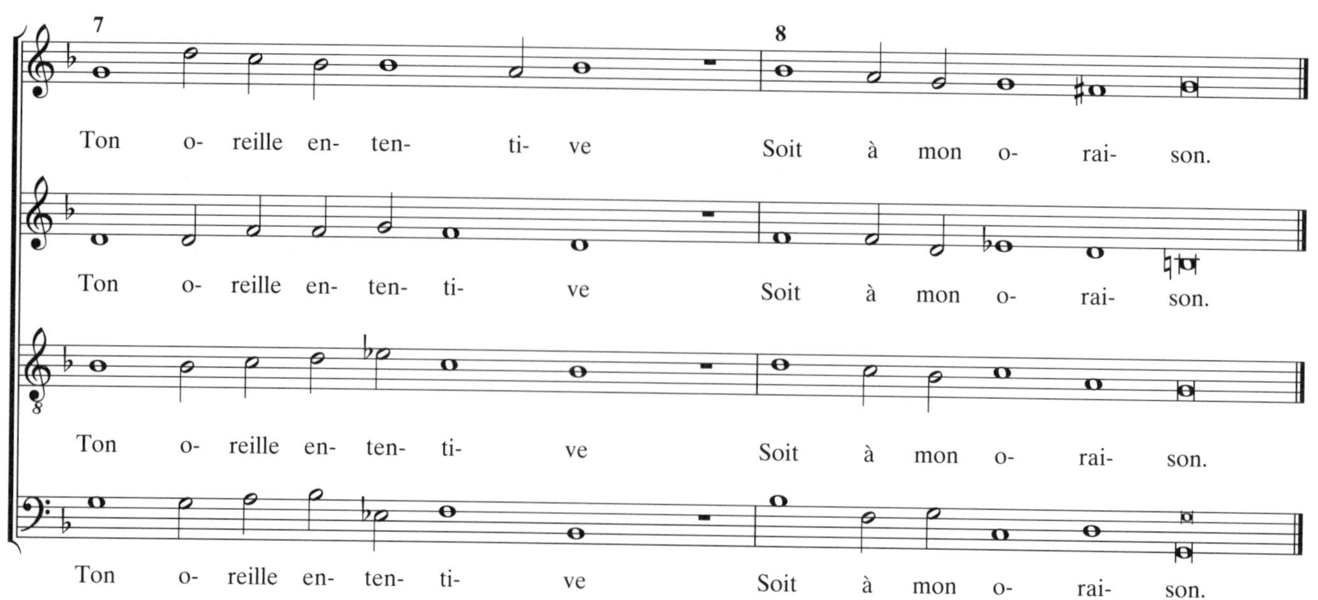
7
8
Ton o- reille en- ten- ti- ve Soit à mon o- rai- son.
Ton o- reille en- ten- ti- ve Soit à mon o- rai- son.
Ton o- reille en- ten- ti- ve Soit à mon o- rai- son.
Ton o- reille en- ten- ti- ve Soit à mon o- rai- son.

From depth profound distressed, in grief and miserie,
My cryes I have addressed, O Lord my God to thee.
Lord heare my lamentation, vouchsafe my voyce to hear,
And to my supplication, bow down attentive eare.

Psalm 131

Dessus
Haute-Contre
Taille
Basse-Contre
Genevan tune*
Sei- gneur, je n'ay point le coeur fier,
Je n'ay point le re- gard trop haut,
Et rien plus grand qu'il ne me faut
Ne vou- lus on- ques ma- ni- er.

O Lord I have no haughty minde,
I have no lofty looking eye,
I have nought dared nor design'd,
Too great for me, too hard, too high.

*Also set in Psalms 100 and 142

Psalm 132

O Lord our God recall to minde
Thy servant Davids misery,
Affliction, and calamity.
How he by oath himself did binde,
To Jacobs God vow'd solemnly.

Psalm 133

Dessus
Haute-Contre
Taille
Basse-Contre
Genevan tune
2
O com- bien est plai-sant et sou- hai- ta- ble De voir en-semble
O com- bien est plai-sant et sou- hai- ta- ble De voir en-semble
O com- bien est plai-sant et sou- hai- ta- ble De voir en-semble
O com- bien est plai-sant et sou- hai- ta- ble De voir en-semble
3
en con-corde a- mi- a- ble Fre- res u- nis s'en- tre- te- nir.
en con-corde a- mi- a- ble Fre- res u- nis s'en- tre- te- nir.
en con-corde a- mi- a- ble Fre- res u- nis s'en- tre- te- nir.
en con-corde a- mi- a- ble Fre- res u- nis s'en- tre- te- nir.
4
5
Ce- la me fait de l'on- guent sou- ve- nir Tant pre- ci- eux dont
Ce- la me fait de l'on- guent sou- ve- nir Tant pre- ci- eux dont
Ce- la me fait de l'on- guent sou- ve- nir Tant pre- ci- eux dont
Ce- la me fait de l'on- guent sou- ve- nir Tant pre- ci- eux dont

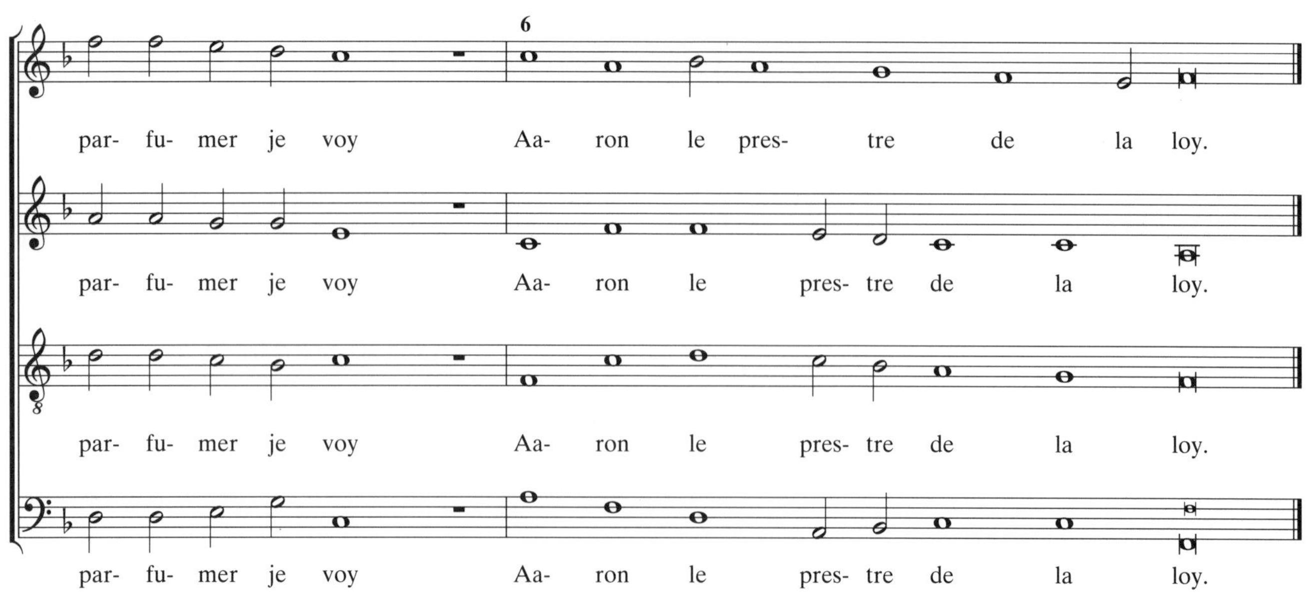
6
par- fu- mer je voy Aa- ron le pres- tre de la loy.
par- fu- mer je voy Aa- ron le pres- tre de la loy.
par- fu- mer je voy Aa- ron le pres- tre de la loy.
par- fu- mer je voy Aa- ron le pres- tre de la loy.

Behold, how good, how pleasant, amiable,
And gracious is the love inviolable,
Of brethren which together dwell.
Resembling right the precious oyntment smell,
The sacred oyl which Gods law did appoint,
The high Priest Aaron to annoint.

Psalm 134

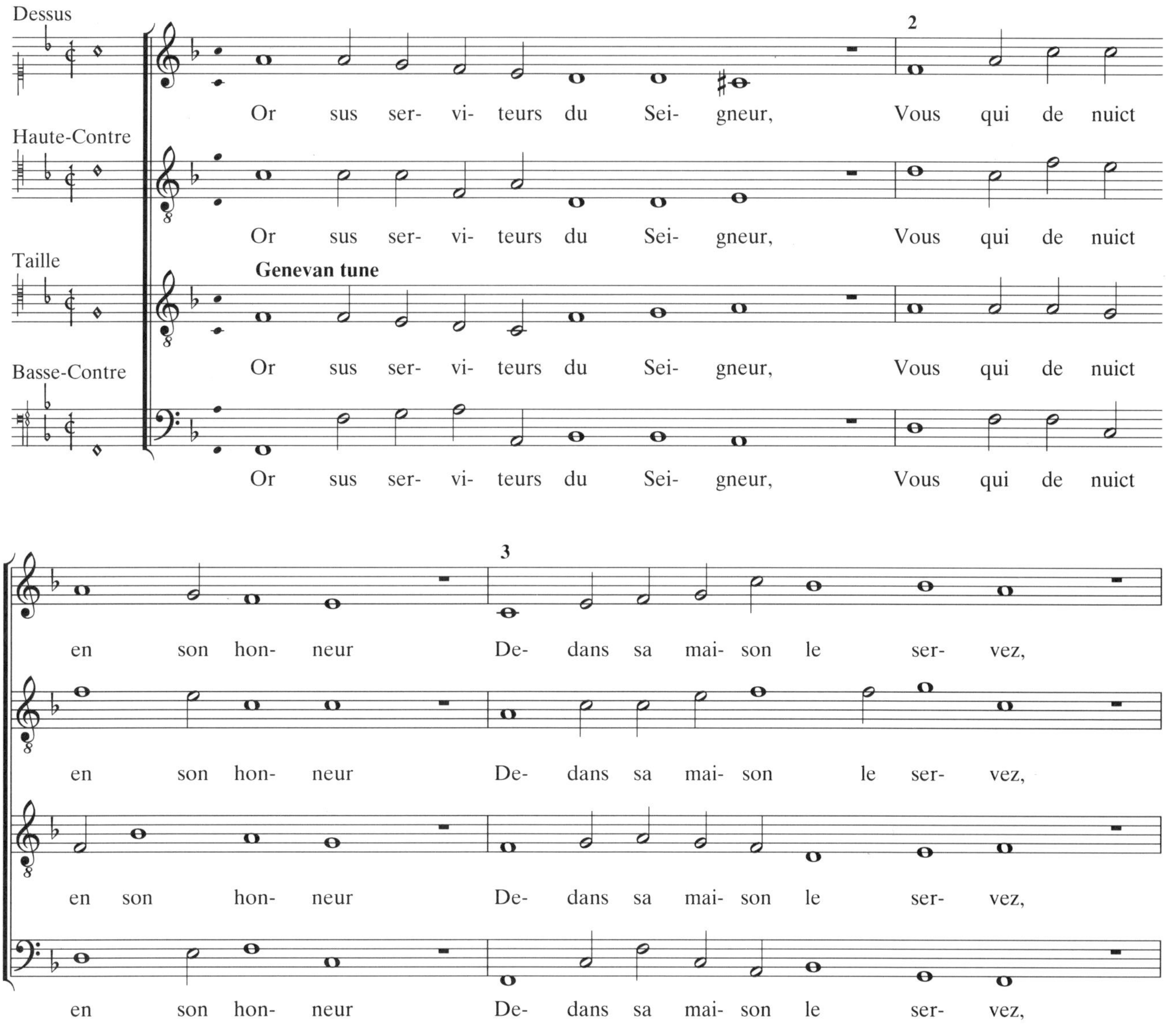

Dessus
2
Or sus ser- vi- teurs du Sei- gneur, Vous qui de nuict

Haute-Contre
Or sus ser- vi- teurs du Sei- gneur, Vous qui de nuict

Taille
Genevan tune
Or sus ser- vi- teurs du Sei- gneur, Vous qui de nuict

Basse-Contre
Or sus ser- vi- teurs du Sei- gneur, Vous qui de nuict

3
en son hon- neur De- dans sa mai- son le ser- vez,

en son hon- neur De- dans sa mai- son le ser- vez,

en son hon- neur De- dans sa mai- son le ser- vez,

en son hon- neur De- dans sa mai- son le ser- vez,

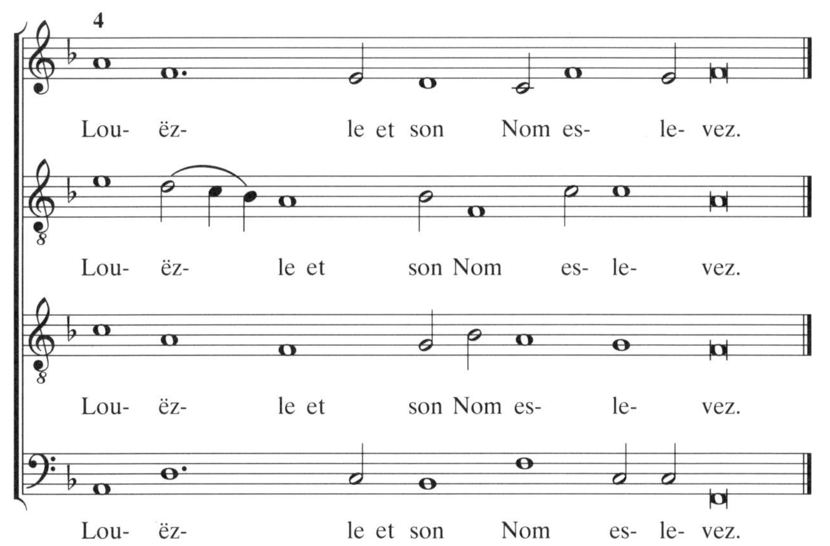

Ye servants of the Lord of might,
Who in his house do watch by night,
Attending there, your selves addres,
The Lord our God to praise and bles.

Psalm 135

All ye servants of the Lord
Praise his name with one accord.
Ye that in Gods house do stand
There performing his command,
Ye that in his courts do dwell
Praise his Name which doth excell.

Psalm 136

Praise the Lord to him confes,
Give him thanks for his goodnes,
For his great benignity,
Dureth to eternity.

Psalm 137

Dessus
Es- tans as- sis aux ri- ves a- qua- ti- ques De Ba- by- lon,
Haute-Contre
Es- tans as- sis aux ri- ves a- qua- ti- ques De Ba- by- lon,
Taille
Genevan tune
Es- tans as- sis aux ri- ves a- qua- ti- ques De Ba- by- lon,
Basse-Contre
Es- tans as- sis aux ri- ves a- qua- ti- ques De Ba- by- lon,
plo- rions me- lan- cho- li- ques, Nous sou- ve- nans du pa- ïs de Si- on,
plo- rions me- lan- cho- li- ques, Nous sou- ve- nans du pa- ïs de Si- on,
plo- rions me- lan- cho- li- ques, Nous sou- ve- nans du pa- ïs de Si- on,
plo- rions me- lan- cho- li- ques, Nous sou- ve- nans du pa- ïs de Si- on,
Et au mi- lieu de l'ha- bi- ta- ti- on, Où de re- gret tant de pleurs
Et au mi- lieu de l'ha- bi- ta- ti- on, Où de re- gret tant de pleurs
Et au mi- lieu de l'ha- bi- ta- ti- on, Où de re- gret tant de pleurs
Et au mi- lieu de l'ha- bi- ta- ti- on, Où de re- gret tant de pleurs

6
es- pan- dis- mes, Aux sau- les verds nos har- pes nous pen- dis- mes.
es- pan- dis- mes, Aux sau- les verds nos har- pes nous pen- dis- mes.
es- pan- dis- mes, Aux sau- les verds nos har- pes nous pen- dis- mes.
es- pan- dis- mes, Aux sau- les verds nos har- pes nous pen- dis- mes.

By Euphrates we captive sat lamenting,
Proud Babels streams with streaming tears augmenting,
O Sion dear when we remembred thee,
In midst of thrall abiding exiles we,
With hearts grief pang'd, with flouds of plaints oreflowing,
Our harps we hang'd on willow plants there growing.

Psalm 138

Dessus
Haute-Contre
Taille
Basse-Contre
Genevan tune
2
3
4
5
6
Il faut que de tous mes es- pris Ton los et pris J'ex- alte et pri- se: De- vant les grands me pre- sen- ter Pour te chan- ter J'ay fait em- pri- se:
Il faut que de tous mes es- pris Ton los et pris J'ex-alte et pri- se: De- vant les grands me pre- sen- ter Pour te chan- ter J'ay fait em- pri- se:
Il faut que de tous mes es- pris Ton los et pris J'ex- - alte et pri- se: De- vant les grands me pre- sen- ter Pour te chan- ter J'ay fait em- pri- se:
Il faut que de tous mes es- pris Ton los et pris J'ex- - alte et pri- se: De- vant les grands me pre- sen- ter Pour te chan- ter J'ay fait em- pri- se:

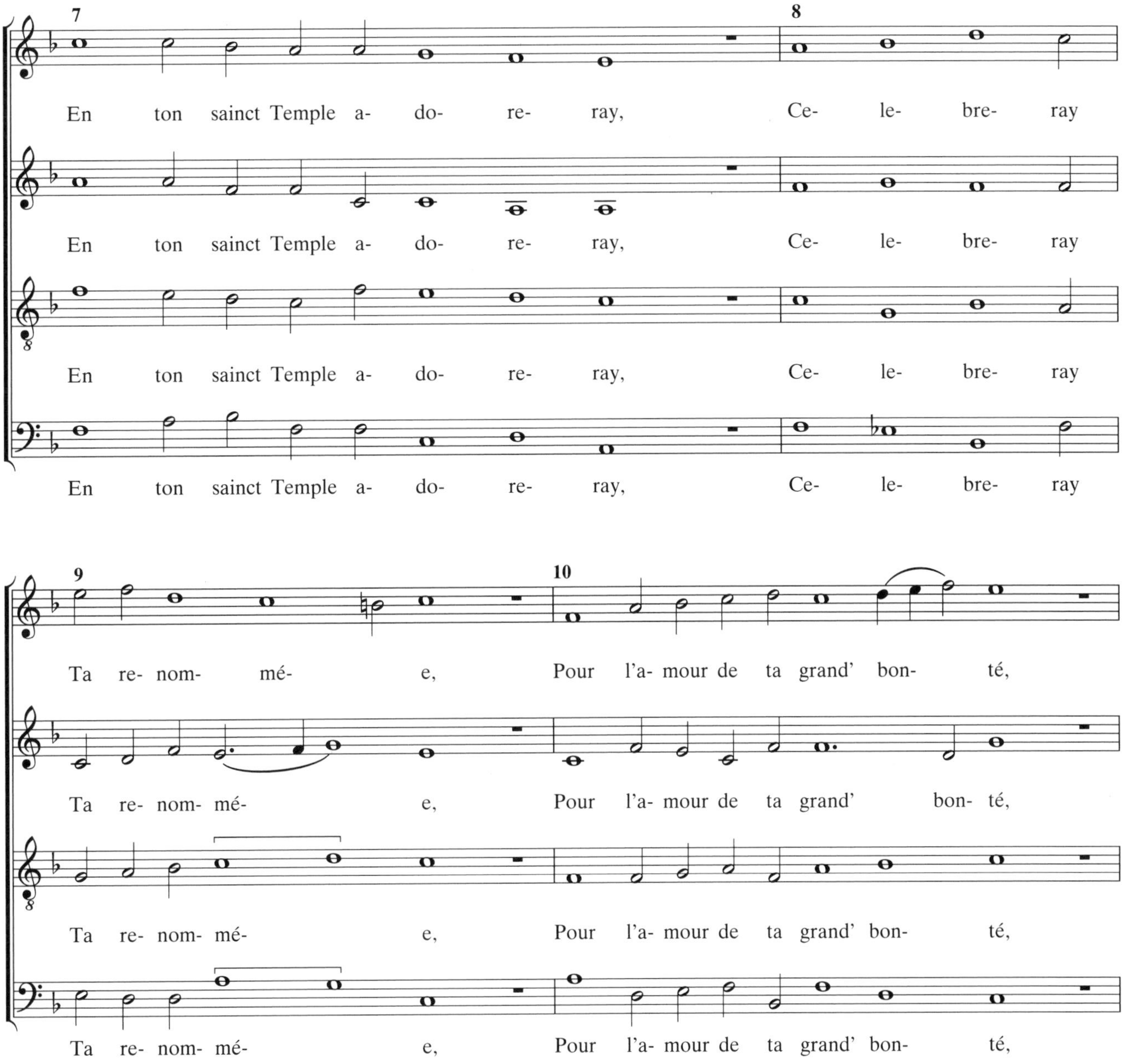

7
En ton sainct Temple a- do- re- ray,
8
Ce- le- bre- ray
En ton sainct Temple a- do- re- ray,
Ce- le- bre- ray
En ton sainct Temple a- do- re- ray,
Ce- le- bre- ray
En ton sainct Temple a- do- re- ray,
Ce- le- bre- ray
9
Ta re- nom- mé- e,
10
Pour l'a- mour de ta grand' bon- té,
Ta re- nom- mé- e,
Pour l'a- mour de ta grand' bon- té,
Ta re- nom- mé- e,
Pour l'a- mour de ta grand' bon- té,
Ta re- nom- mé- e,
Pour l'a- mour de ta grand' bon- té,

11
Et fe- au- té
12
Tant es- ti- mé- e.
Et fe- au- té Tant es- ti- mé- e.
Et fe- au- té Tant es- ti- mé- e.
Et fe- au- té Tant es- ti- mé- e.

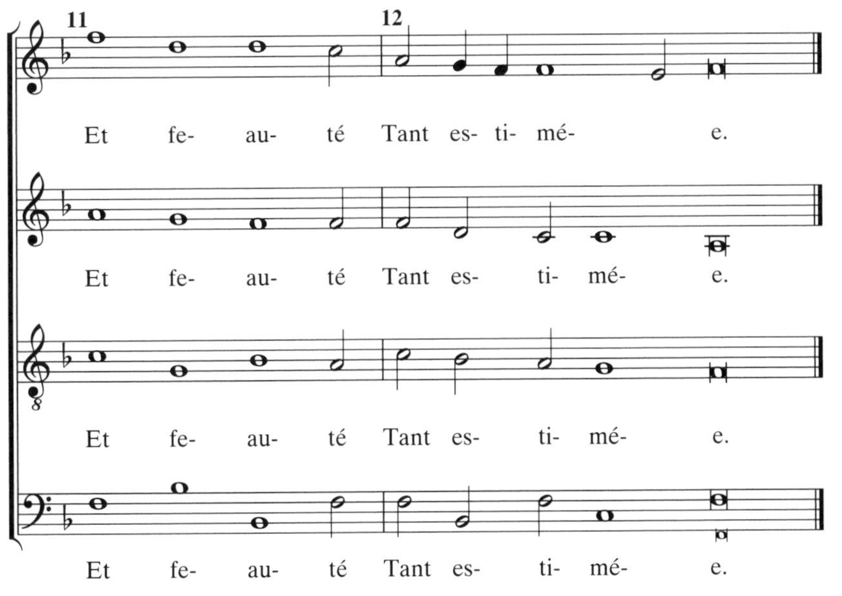

With all my heart I unto thee
Will thankfull be,
Thy goodnes praising,
Where mighty States assembled be,
I'le sing of thee,
Thy Name high raising.
And in thy sacred Temple I
Will magnifie
Thy Name renowned,
Adoring thee for mercy thine,
And truth divine,
With glory crowned.

Psalm 139

Dessus
O Dieu, tu co- gnois qui je suis, Tu sçais tout

Haute-Contre
O Dieu, tu co- gnois qui je suis, Tu sçais tout

Cinquiesme "ainsi qu'il est"
Genevan tune*
O Dieu, tu co- gnois qui je suis, Tu sçais tout

Taille
O Dieu, tu co- gnois qui je suis, Tu sçais tout

Basse-Contre
O Dieu, tu co- gnois qui je suis, Tu sçais tout

*Also set in Psalms 30 and 76

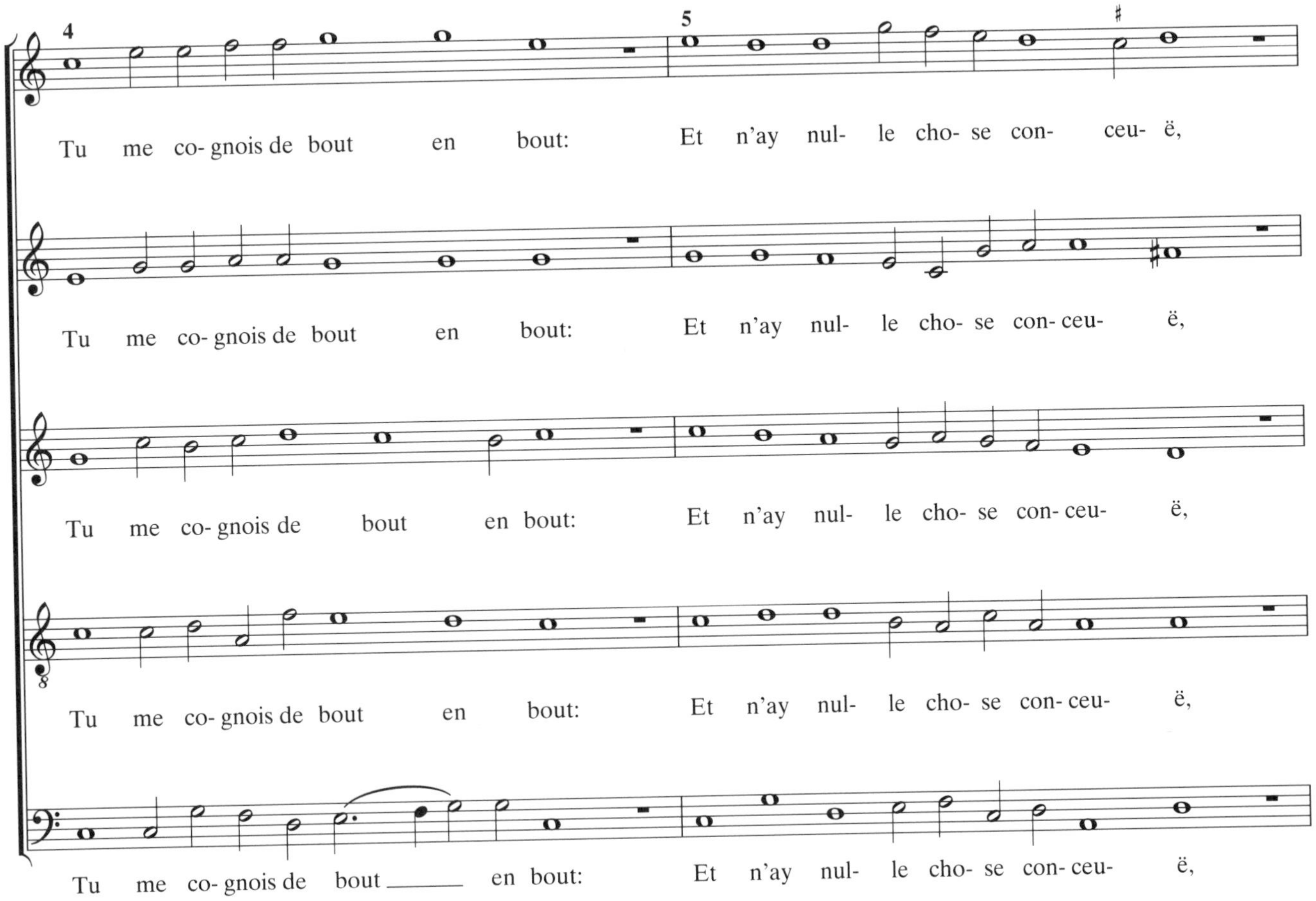

4
5
Tu me co- gnois de bout en bout: Et n'ay nul- le cho- se con- ceu- ë,
Tu me co- gnois de bout en bout: Et n'ay nul- le cho- se con- ceu- ë,
Tu me co- gnois de bout en bout: Et n'ay nul- le cho- se con- ceu- ë,
Tu me co- gnois de bout en bout: Et n'ay nul- le cho- se con- ceu- ë,
Tu me co- gnois de bout en bout: Et n'ay nul- le cho- se con- ceu- ë,

6
Que n'ay- es de loin ap- per- ceu- ë.
Que n'ay- es de loin ap- per- ceu- ë.
Que n'ay- es de loin ap- per- ceu- ë.
Que n'ay- es de loin ap- per- ceu- ë.
Que n'ay- es de loin ap- per- ceu- ë.

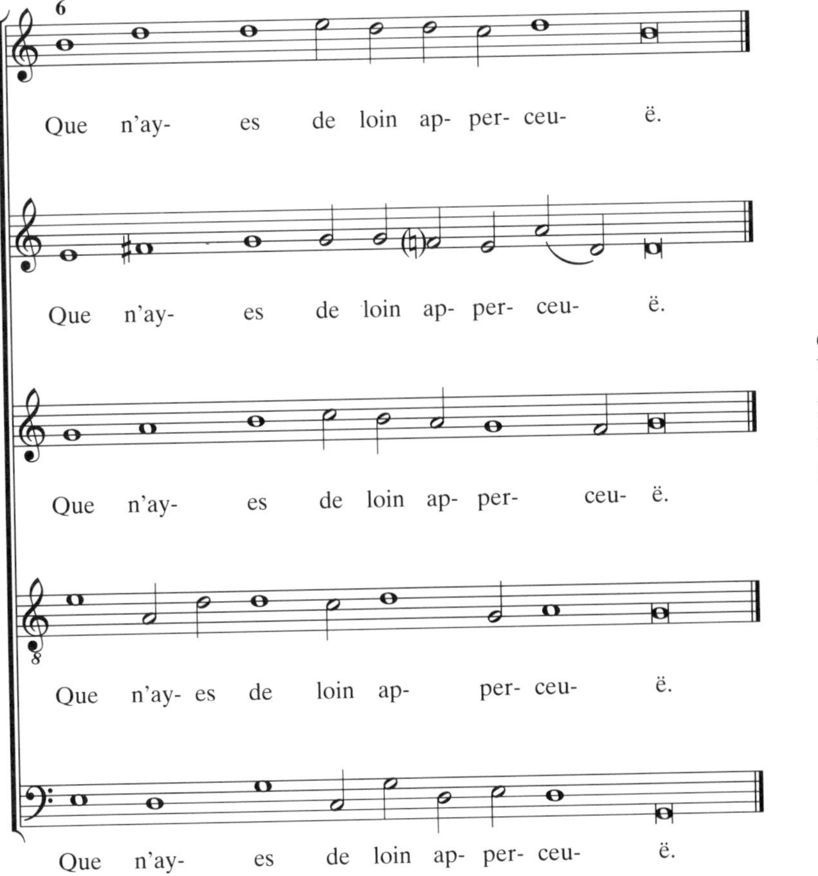

O God thou hast me search'd and try'd,
What is in me thou hast espy'd,
And unto thee is throughly known,
My rising up, and lying down,
What thought so ere my heart conceived,
By thee a far off is perceived.

Psalm 140

Let me O Lord be quite released,
From wicked men be my defence,
Me to preserve, O be thou pleased,
From men of wrongfull violence.

*Also set in Les Commandemens de Dieu

Psalm 141

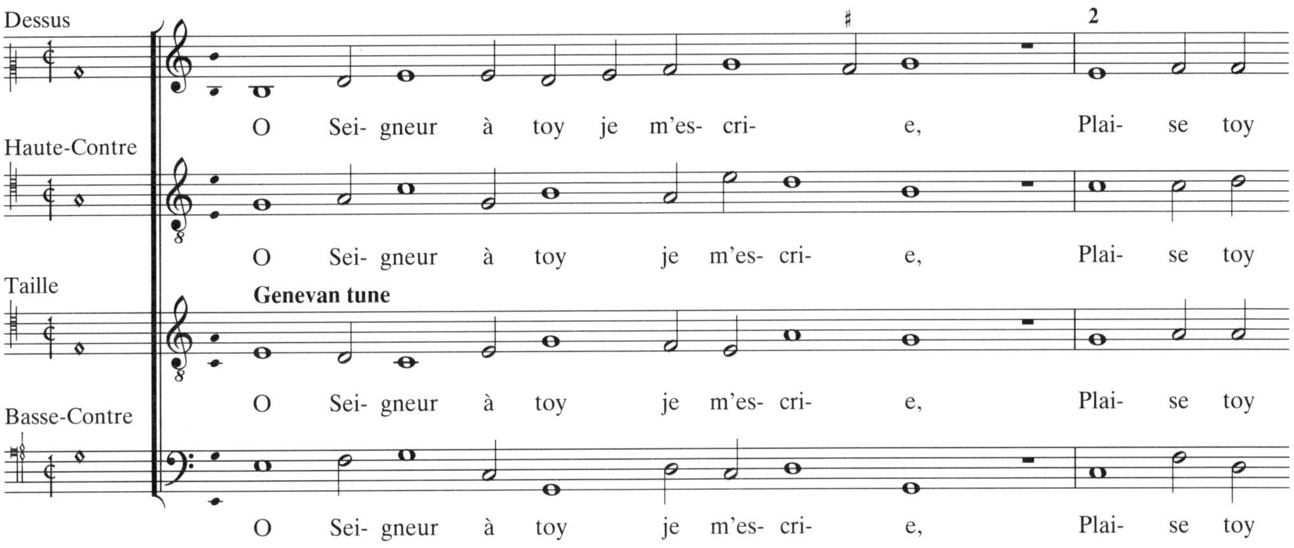

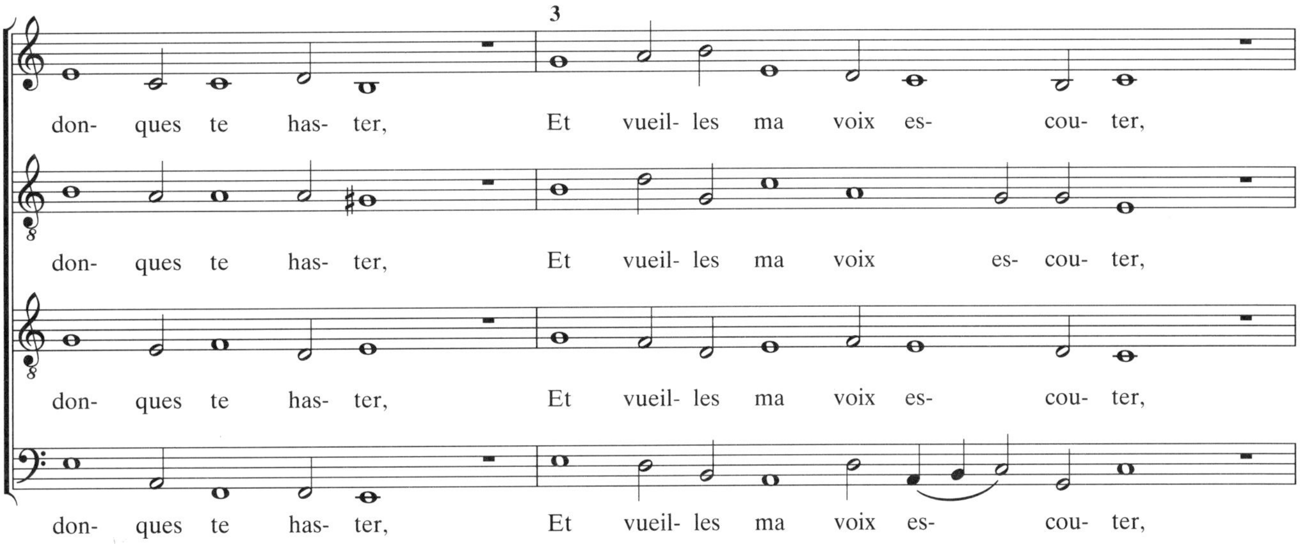

Dessus
Haute-Contre
Taille
Basse-Contre
Genevan tune
2
O Sei- gneur à toy je m'es- cri- e, Plai- se toy
O Sei- gneur à toy je m'es- cri- e, Plai- se toy
O Sei- gneur à toy je m'es- cri- e, Plai- se toy
O Sei- gneur à toy je m'es- cri- e, Plai- se toy

3
don- ques te has- ter, Et vueil- les ma voix es- cou- ter,
don- ques te has- ter, Et vueil- les ma voix es- cou- ter,
don- ques te has- ter, Et vueil- les ma voix es- cou- ter,
don- ques te has- ter, Et vueil- les ma voix es- cou- ter,

4
Car c'est toy qu'en cri- ant je pri- e.
Car c'est toy qu'en cri- ant je pri- e.
Car c'est toy qu'en cri- ant je pri- e.
Car c'est toy qu'en cri- ant je pri- e.

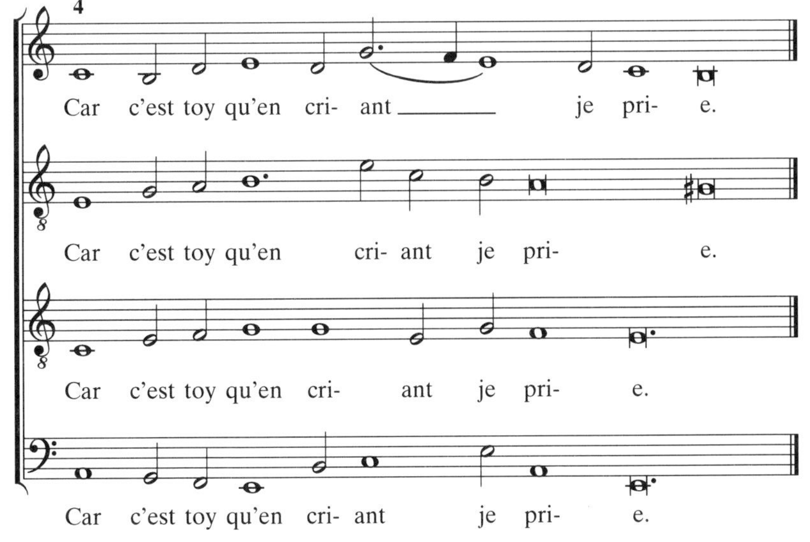

To thee I crie, Lord, heare my crying,
Make haste to me approching neere,
Do thou vouchsafe my voyce to heare,
Heare me, my cryes to thee applying.

Psalm 142

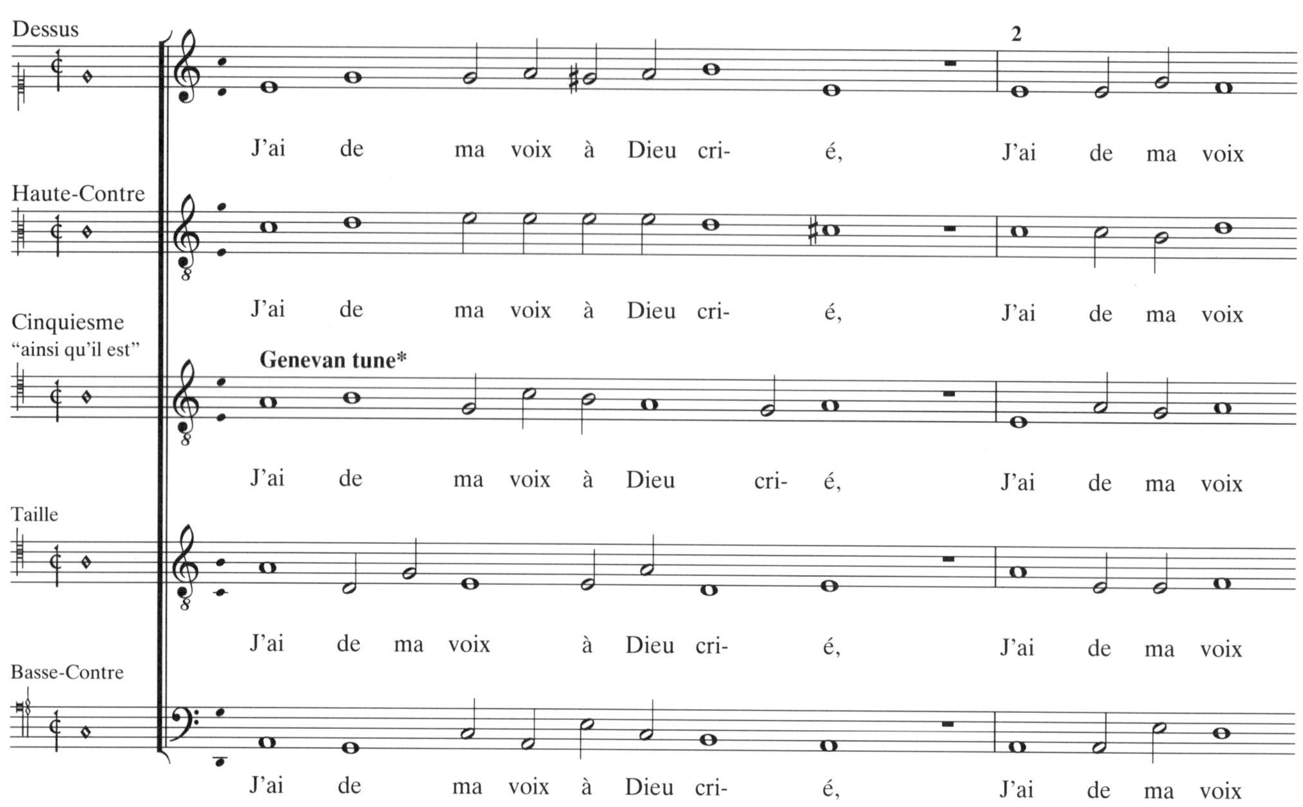

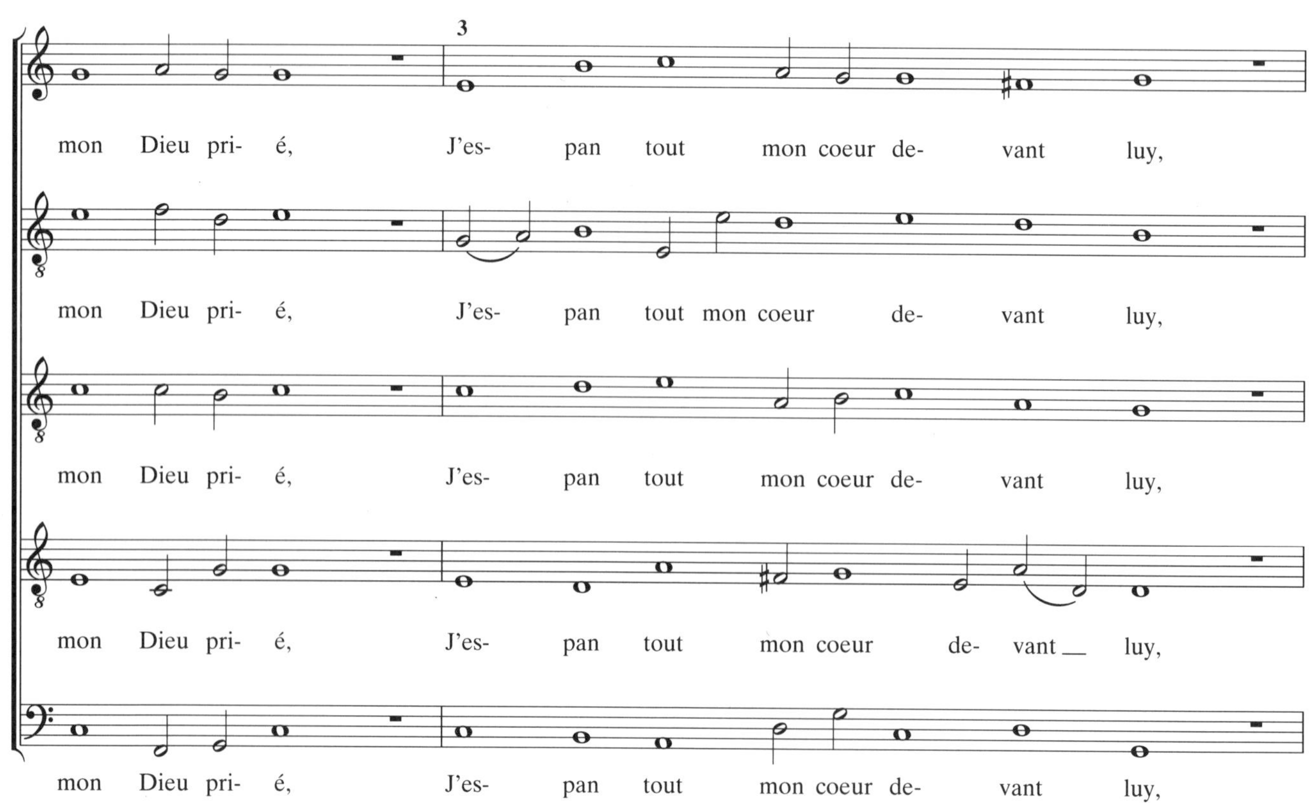

*Also set in Psalms 100 and 131

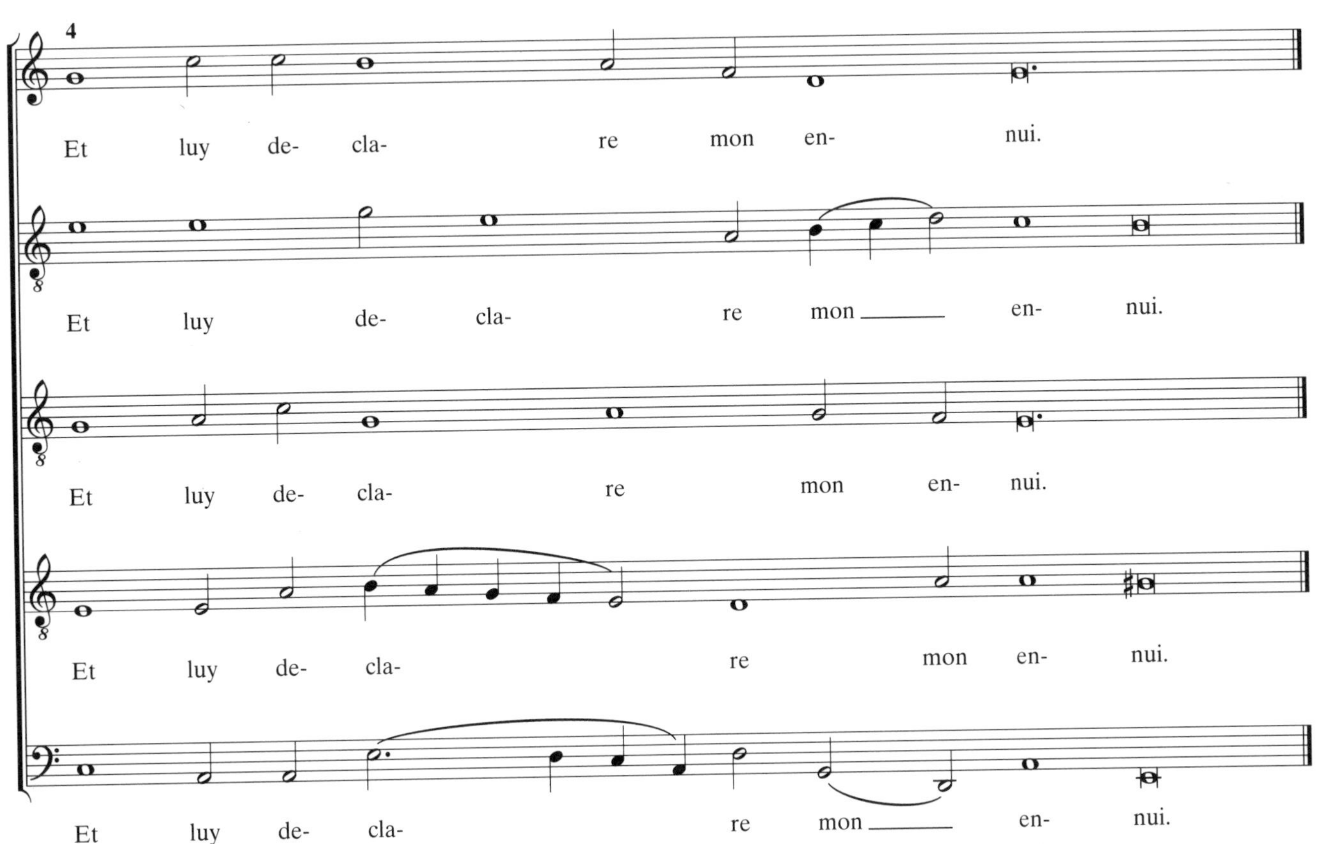

With my voyce to God did cry,
My prayer for grace I did apply.
Before him seeking for reliefe
My plaint I pour'd, showd him my grief.

Psalm 143

Dessus
Haute-Contre
Taille
Basse-Contre
Genevan tune
Sei- gneur Dieu, oy l'o- rai- son mien- ne,
Sei- gneur Dieu, oy l'o- rai- son mien- ne,
Sei- gneur Dieu, oy l'o- rai- son mien- ne,
Sei- gneur Dieu, oy l'o- rai- son mien- ne,
2
3
Jus- qu'à tes o- reil- les par- vien- ne Mon hum- ble
Jus- qu'à tes o- reil- les par- vien- ne Mon hum- ble
Jus- qu'à tes o- reil- les par- vien- ne Mon hum- ble
Jus- qu'à tes o- reil- les par- vien- ne Mon hum- ble
4
sup- pli- ca- ti- on: Se- lon la vray- e
sup- pli- ca- ti- on: Se- lon la vray- e
sup- pli- ca- ti- on: Se- lon la vray- e
sup- pli- ca- ti- on: Se- lon la vray- e

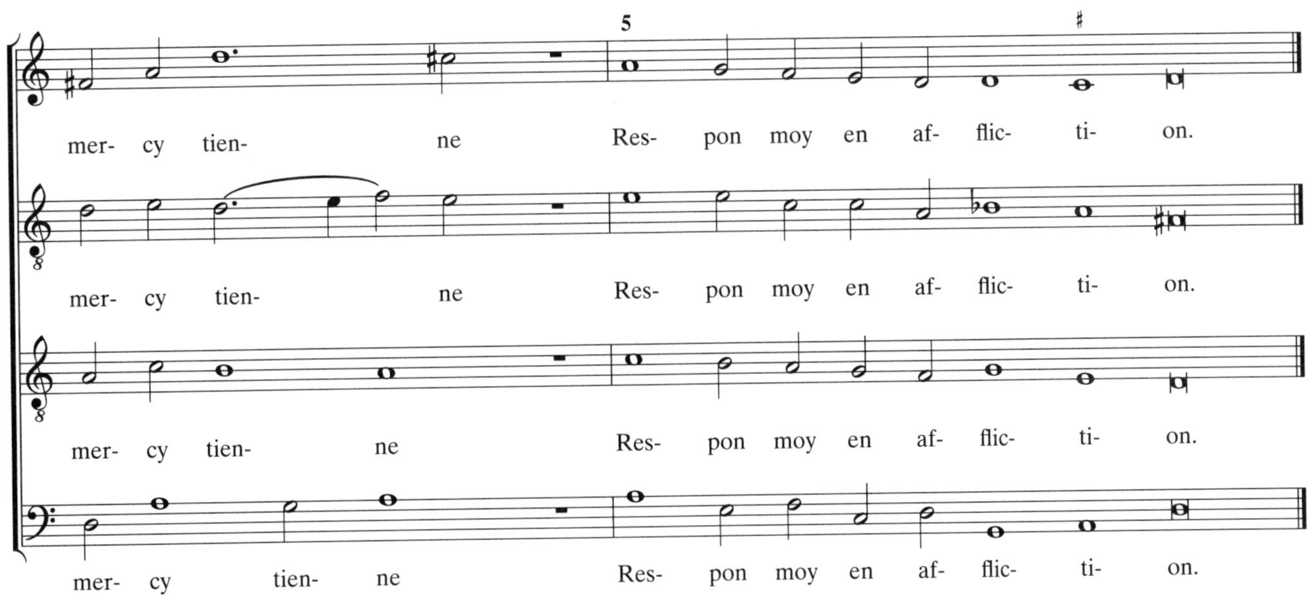
5
mer- cy tien- ne Res- pon moy en af- flic- ti- on.
mer- cy tien- ne Res- pon moy en af- flic- ti- on.
mer- cy tien- ne Res- pon moy en af- flic- ti- on.
mer- cy tien- ne Res- pon moy en af- flic- ti- on.

Lord hear my prayer and invocation,
Give eare unto my supplication,
Me answer in thy faithfulnes,
Relieve me with commiseration,
According to thy righteousnes.

Psalm 144

*Also set in Psalm 18

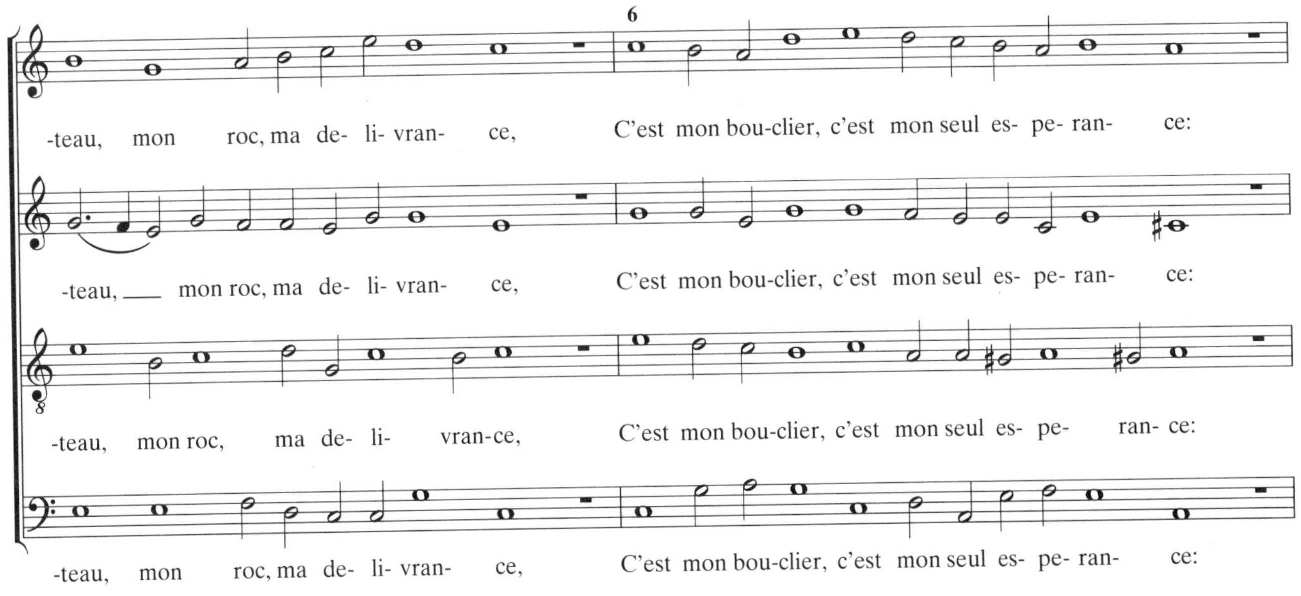

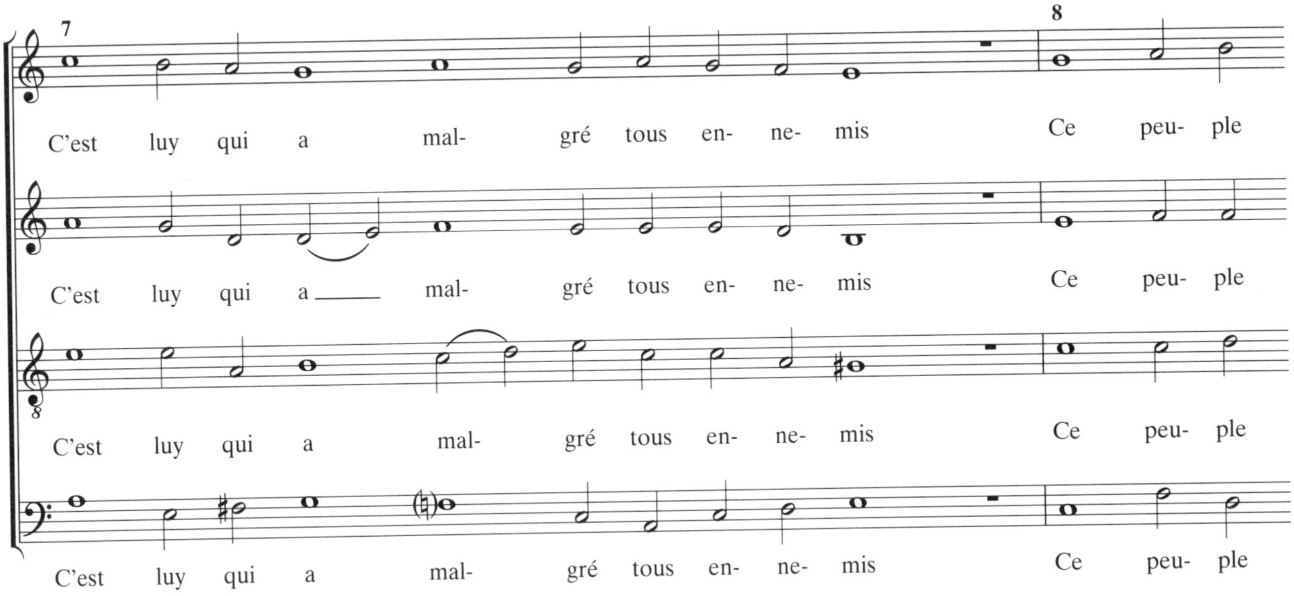

6
-teau, mon roc, ma de- li- vran- ce, C'est mon bou-clier, c'est mon seul es- pe- ran- ce:
-teau, mon roc, ma de- li- vran- ce, C'est mon bou-clier, c'est mon seul es- pe- ran- ce:
-teau, mon roc, ma de- li- vran-ce, C'est mon bou-clier, c'est mon seul es- pe- ran- ce:
-teau, mon roc, ma de- li- vran- ce, C'est mon bou-clier, c'est mon seul es- pe- ran- ce:

7
8
C'est luy qui a mal- gré tous en- ne- mis Ce peu- ple
C'est luy qui a mal- gré tous en- ne- mis Ce peu- ple
C'est luy qui a mal- gré tous en- ne- mis Ce peu- ple
C'est luy qui a mal- gré tous en- ne- mis Ce peu- ple

mien à mon pou- voir sous- mis.
mien à mon pou- voir sous- mis.
mien à mon pou- voir sous- mis.
mien à mon pou- voir sous- mis.

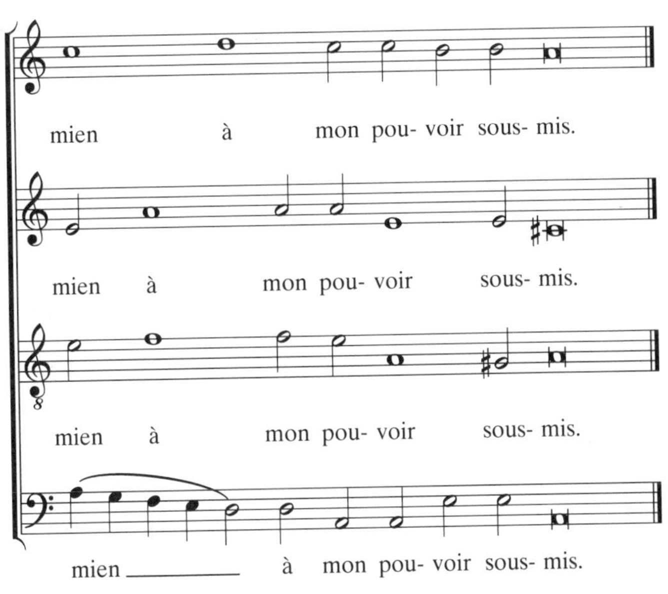

The Lord who is my strength, my God be blessed,
Who hath my hands to manage armes addressed,
With warlike skill my fingers taught to fight,
Victoriously conqu'ring my foes to smite.
His favor is my freedom, my salvation,
My towr of strength, my strong forticiation,
My only hope, my sure defence, my shield,
By him subdewd to me the people yeeld.

Psalm 145

Dessus
Haute-Contre
Taille
Basse-Contre
Genevan tune
2
3
4
5
Mon Dieu, mon Roy, haut je t'é- le- ve- ray, Et ton nom
Mon Dieu, mon Roy, haut je t'é- le- ve- ray, Et ton nom
Mon Dieu, mon Roy, haut je t'é- le- ve- ray, Et ton nom
Mon Dieu, mon Roy, haut je t'é- le- ve- ray, Et ton nom
sainct sans fin je be- ni- ray: Je veux ton los cha- cun jour pu- bli- er,
sainct sans fin je be- ni- ray: Je veux ton los cha- cun jour pu- bli- er,
sainct sans fin je be- ni- ray: Je veux ton los cha- cun jour pu- bli- er,
sainct sans fin je be- ni- ray: Je veux ton los cha- cun jour pu- bli- er,
Et pour ja- mais ton Nom glo- ri- fi- er. Le Sei- gneur est tres- grand
Et pour ja- mais ton Nom glo- ri- fi- er. Le Sei- gneur est tres- grand
Et pour ja- mais ton Nom glo- ri- fi- er. Le Sei- gneur est tres- grand
Et pour ja- mais ton Nom glo- ri- fi- er. Le Sei- gneur est tres-grand

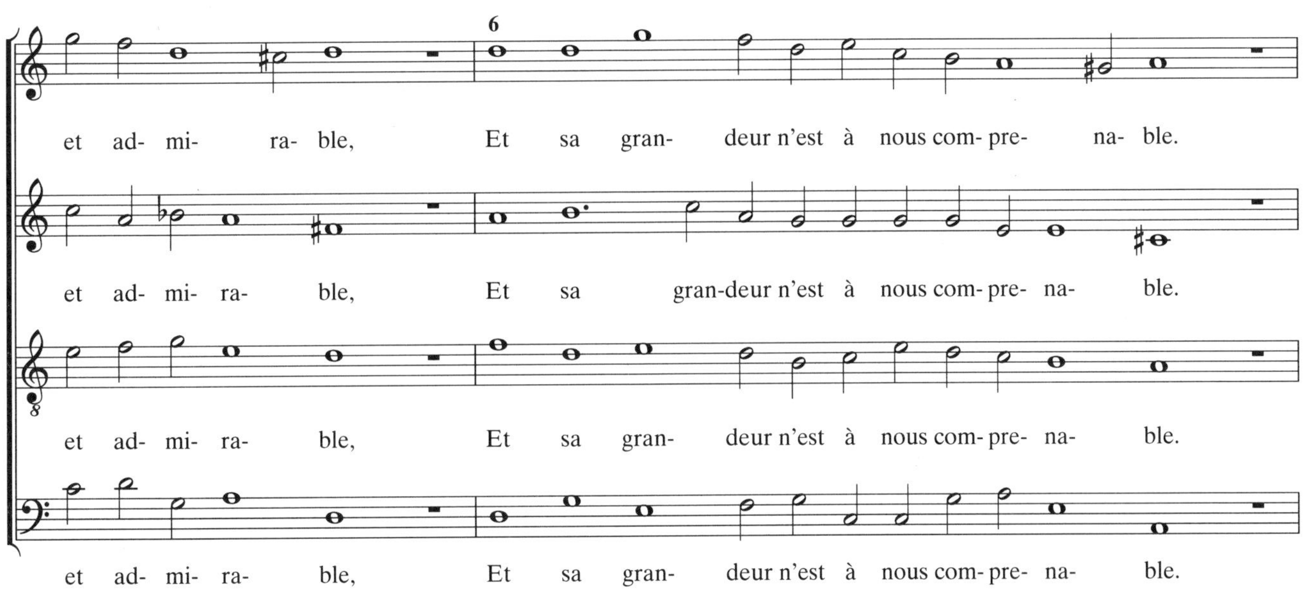
6
et ad- mi- ra- ble, Et sa gran- deur n'est à nous com- pre- na- ble.
et ad- mi- ra- ble, Et sa gran-deur n'est à nous com- pre- na- ble.
et ad- mi- ra- ble, Et sa gran- deur n'est à nous com- pre- na- ble.
et ad- mi- ra- ble, Et sa gran- deur n'est à nous com- pre- na- ble.

7
De pere en fils ses faits on ma- gni- fi- e,
De pere en fils ses faits on ma- gni- fi- e,
De pere en fils ses faits on ma- gni- fi- e,
De pere en fils ses faits on ma- gni- fi- e,

8
Et sa puis-sance entre i- ceux se pu- bli- e.
Et sa puis-sance entre i- ceux se pu- bli- e.
Et sa puis-sance entre i- ceux se pu- bli- e.
Et sa puis-sance entre i- ceux se pu- bli- e.

My God, my King, I will thee magnifie,
And bles thy name for evermore will I.
Bles thee I will and praise thee every day,
And glorifie thy sacred name for ay.
The Lord my God is great and admirable,
To comprehend his greatnes, none is able.
Due praise of all thy works, each generation
Shall give, and of thy powr make declaration.

Psalm 146

Dessus
Haute-Contre
Taille
Basse-Contre
Genevan tune
2
3
4
5
Sus mon a- me, qu'on be- ni- e Le Sou- ve- rain,
Sus mon a- me, qu'on be- ni- e Le Sou- ve- rain,
Sus mon a- me, qu'on be- ni- e Le Sou- ve- rain,
Sus mon a- me, qu'on be- ni- e Le Sou- ve- rain,
car il faut, Tant que du- re- ra ma vi- e,
car il faut, Tant que du- re- ra ma vi- e,
car il faut, Tant que du- re- ra ma vi- e,
car il faut, Tant que du- re- ra ma vi- e,
Que je loü- e le tres- haut, Et tant que
Que je loü- e le tres- haut, Et tant que je
Que je loü- e le tres- haut, Et tant que
Que je loü- e le tres- haut, Et tant que

6
je du- re- ray, Pseau- mes, je luy chan- te- ray.
du- re- ray, Pseau- mes, je luy chan- te- ray.
je du- re- ray, Pseau- mes, je luy chan- te- ray.
je du- re- ray, Pseau- mes, je luy chan- te- ray.

Praise to God my soul be giving,
To the Lord my soul give praise.
His Ile laud while I am living,
To my God Ile sing alwayes,
To the Lord my God, my King,
While I am I Psalms will sing.

Psalm 147

Dessus
Haute-Contre
Taille
Basse-Contre
Genevan tune
2
3
4
5
Lou- ez Dieu, car c'est cho- se bon- ne Qu'à nos- tre
Dieu lou- ange on don- ne, C'est di- je, u- ne cho- se plai- san- te
De le lou- er, et bien se- an- te. Puis que c'est luy

Praise ye the Lord, such praise is meetest,
Sing Psalms to God, such Psalms are sweetest,
The Lord to praise sing, never ceasing,
His praise is gracefull, ever pleasing.
The Lord most gracious, full of pity,
Build up Jerusalem his city,
His Israel disperst, deplored,
He hath assembled and restored.

Psalm 148

Dessus
Haute-Contre
Taille
Basse-Contre
Genevan tune
2
3
4
5
6
Vous tous les ha- bi- tans des cieux,
Lou- ëz hau- te- ment le Sei- gneur,
Vous les ha- bi- tans des hauts lieux,
Chan- tez hau- te- ment son hon-neur.
Chan- tez hau- te- ment son hon- neur.
An- ges chan-tez sa re- nom- mé- e,
Lou- ëz- le tou- te son ar- mé- e:

Praise ye the Lord from heaven on high,
Praise him ye dwellers in the sky,
All ye inhabitants of heav'n
To God all praise by you be giv'n.
All ye his Angels high renown him,
Victorious hosts with glory crown him.
Both Sun and Moon, praise ye his Name,
All stars of light his praise proclaime.

Psalm 149

Dessus
Haute-Contre
Taille
Basse-Contre
Genevan tune
2
3
4
5
6
Chan-tez à Dieu chan- son nou- vel- le, Et sa lou-an- ge so-len- nel- le,
Chan-tez à Dieu chan-son nou-vel- le, Et sa lou-an- ge so-len- nel- le,
Chan-tez à Dieu chan- son nou-vel- le, Et sa lou-an- ge so-len-nel- le,
Chan-tez à Dieu chan- son nou-vel- le, Et sa lou-an- ge so-len- nel- le,
Des bons par- mi la com- pa- gni- e Main- te- nant soit oü- i- e.
Des bons par- mi la com- pa- gni- e Main- te- nant soit oü- i- e.
Des bons par- mi la com- pa- gni- e Main- te- nant soit oü- i- e.
Des bons par- mi la com- pa- gni- e Main- te- nant soit oü- i- e.
Is- ra- ël s'es- gaye en son coeur De l'E- ter- nel son Cre- a- teur:
Is- ra- ël s'es- gaye en son coeur De l'E- ter- nel son Cre- a- teur:
Is- ra- ël s'es- gaye en son coeur De l'E- ter- nel son Cre- a- teur:
Is- ra- ël s'es- gaye en son coeur De l'E- ter- nel son Cre- a- teur:

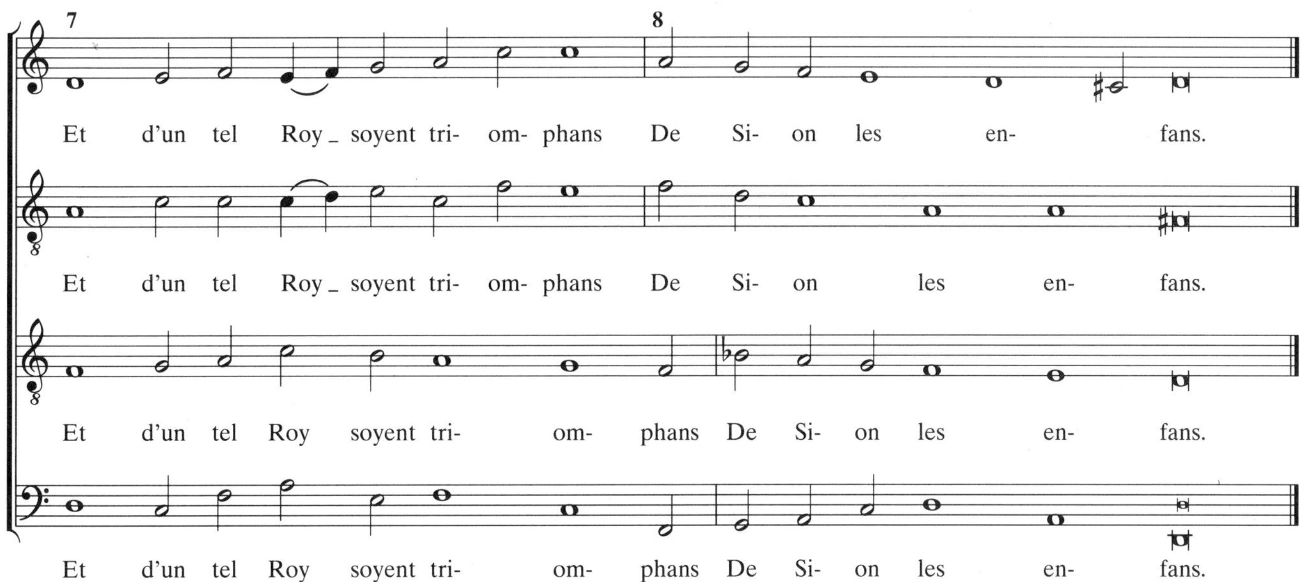

Sing to the Lord new songs excelling,
All in the Church of his Saints dwelling,
Sing praises in your congregation,
To God with adoration.
Let Israel in songs relate
His high praise who did him create,
Let Sions sons rejoyce and sing,
And triumph in their King.

Psalm 150

Dessus
Haute-Contre
Taille
Basse-Contre
Genevan tune
2
3
4
5
6
Or soit loü- é l'E- ter- nel De son sainct lieu su- per- nel:
Soit di- je, tout hau- te- ment Lou- é de ce fir- ma- ment
Plein de sa ma- gni- fi- cen- ce. Loü- ez- le tous ses grands faits:

7
8
Soit loü- é de tant d'ef- fets, Tes- moins de son ex- cel- len- ce.
Soit loü- é de tant d'ef- fets, Tes- moins de son ex- cel- len- ce.
Soit loü- é de tant d'ef- fets, Tes- moins de son ex- cel- len- ce.
Soit loü- é de tant d'ef- fets, Tes- moins de son ex- cel- len- ce.

Let us all Gods praise expres,
Praise him in his holines:
Praise him in the firmament
Of his power permanent,
And his high magnificency.
Praise him in his greatnes shewd,
In his goodnes multitude,
Witnessing his excellency.

Les Commandemens de Dieu, Exode XX

Lift up your hearts to God addressed,
All people hear what he doth say:
Give ear unto his word expressed,
And his commandments all obey.

*Also set in Psalm 140

Le Cantique de Simeon, Luc II

Index of First Lines